THE VOICES BEYOND

THE VOICES BEYOND

Johan Theorin

Translated from the Swedish
by Marlaine Delargy

*For Andrew
— med bästa hälsningar
från

Johan Theorin
Sep 12 2015*

Doubleday
LONDON · TORONTO · SYDNEY · AUCKLAND · JOHANNESBURG

TRANSWORLD PUBLISHERS
61–63 Uxbridge Road, London W5 5SA
www.transworldbooks.co.uk

Transworld is part of the Penguin Random House group of companies
whose addresses can be found at global.penguinrandomhouse.com

First published in Great Britain in 2015 by Doubleday
an imprint of Transworld Publishers

Poem on page 21 from Harry Martinson: *'Midsommardrömmen'*, *Gräsen i Thule*, 1958
Poem on page 197 from Lennart Sjögren: *'Jag säger inte att livet är gott'*, *Sent, tidigt*, 2001
Poem on page 443 from Dan Andersson: *'En gång i min ungdom'*, *Efterlämnade dikter*, 1922
All poetry translations are the translator's own.

Every effort has been made to obtain the necessary permissions with
reference to copyright material, both illustrative and quoted. We apologize
for any omissions in this respect and will be pleased to make the
appropriate acknowledgements in any future edition.

A CIP catalogue record for this book
is available from the British Library.

ISBN 9780857520067

Typeset in 12/15pt Garamond by Kestrel Data, Exeter, Devon
Printed and bound by Clays Ltd, Bungay, Suffolk

Penguin Random House is committed to a sustainable
future for our business, our readers and our planet. This book
is made from Forest Stewardship Council® certified paper.

1 3 5 7 9 10 8 6 4 2

The ghost ship came gliding out of the darkness across the black waters of the Sound, giving way to nothing and no one.

The boy in the rubber dinghy didn't have time to get away when the ship suddenly appeared. His small inflatable craft almost capsized in the collision, but at the very last moment he managed to pull close to the steel hull and throw a line around the gunwale.

The ship loomed above him. It was oily and rusty, as if it had been sailing the seven seas for many years. Nothing was moving on deck, but deep inside he could hear the throbbing of an engine, like the beating of a heart.

The dinghy had been damaged and was letting in water, so the boy had no choice. He reached up to the gunwale and clambered aboard.

Cautiously, he climbed over and down on to the dark deck; there was a powerful stench of rotten fish.

Slowly, he crept forward, along the side of a closed hatch.

After only five or six metres he saw the first dead man. A seaman dressed in filthy dungarees, lying on his back and staring blankly up at the night sky.

Then more seamen came staggering out of the darkness towards him — dying or already dead. Yet still alive. They reached out to him, spoke to him in weak voices, in some foreign language.

The boy screamed and tried to flee.

Thus began the last summer of the twentieth century in the village of Stenvik.

And thus began the story of the ghost that haunted the village.

Or perhaps it all began some seventy years earlier, in a small inland churchyard. With another young man, Gerlof Davidsson, who heard the sound of someone knocking loudly from inside a coffin.

Summer 1930

Gerlof Davidsson left school at the age of fourteen, and went to sea as a boy sailor two years later. In between, he worked on the island of Öland, when he wasn't helping out on the family smallholding. Some of the jobs he did were good, some less so. The only one that ended badly was his stint as a gravedigger in Marnäs churchyard.

As long as he lived, Gerlof would remember his last day there, when Edvard Kloss the farmer had to be buried twice. Even when he was an old man, Gerlof still had no explanation for what had happened.

He liked ghost stories, but he had never believed in them. Nor did he believe in vengeance from beyond the grave. And Gerlof would normally have associated words like 'ghost' or 'phantom' with darkness and unhappiness.

Not with sunshine and a summer's day.

It was a Sunday in the middle of June, and Gerlof had borrowed his father's big bike so that he could cycle up to the church. He could manage it now; he had shot up over the past year and caught up with his tall father.

Gerlof bowed his head and pedalled away from the village on the coast, wearing a thin white shirt with his sleeves rolled up. He was heading east, inland. Blue viper's bugloss and purple alliums bloomed alongside the straight dirt track, with juniper and hazel bushes behind; in the distance on the horizon he could just see the sails of a couple of windmills. Cows were grazing in the meadows, and the sheep were bleating. Twice, he had to jump down to open the wide gates that kept the cattle safely enclosed.

The landscape was vast and open, almost treeless, and when the swallows swept past his bicycle and soared up towards the sun, Gerlof just wanted to leave the track and head off into the wind and freedom.

Then he thought about the task that awaited him, and a little of the joy went out of the day.

Edvard Kloss had been sixty-two years old when he died the previous week, a solid, well-established farmer. Kloss was regarded as well off in northern Öland; he didn't have a great deal in terms of money, but was rich in land along the coast south of Stenvik, Gerlof's village.

'Taken suddenly, sadly missed by everyone,' as Gerlof had read in his death notice. Kloss had died during the construction of a large wooden barn. Late one night, a newly erected wall had fallen on him.

But was he really sadly missed by everyone? There were plenty of stories about Kloss, and the accident that had caused his death had yet to be fully explained. His younger brothers Sigfrid and Gilbert were the only ones who had been there that night, and each blamed the other. Sigfrid insisted that he had been out of sight over by the piles of timber when the wall came down, but claimed that Gilbert had been right by the barn when their brother died. According to Gilbert, it was the other way round. In addition, a neighbour said he had heard loud voices from the construction site that night, voices he didn't recognize.

Gerlof was pleased to see that there was no sign of the brothers when he reached the churchyard and propped his bike against the wall. He suspected this was going to be a grim burial.

It was only half past eight in the morning, but the sun was already blazing down on the grass and the graves. The whitewashed stone church, built like a fortified castle with thick walls, rose up against the blue sky. The muted sound of a bell echoed across the flat landscape from the western tower, tolling for the deceased.

Gerlof opened the wooden gate and made his way among the graves. The hut that served as a mortuary was over on the left.

There was a myling sitting behind it.

At first, Gerlof couldn't believe his eyes: was he really seeing a myling, the restless ghost of an unbaptized child? He blinked, but the child was still there.

It was a boy, a few years younger than Gerlof. He was extremely pale, as if he had spent the entire spring locked in an earth cellar. He was crouching down with his back to the mortuary, barefoot and dressed in a white shirt and light-coloured short trousers. The only thing about him that wasn't pale was a long, dark scratch across his forehead.

'Davidsson! Over here!'

Gerlof turned his head and saw Roland Bengtsson, the grave-digger, waving to him over by the churchyard wall.

Gerlof set off towards him, but glanced back at the boy. He was still there. Gerlof didn't recognize him and was puzzled by his pallor, but at least he wasn't a ghost.

Bengtsson was waiting for Gerlof with a couple of iron spades. He was a tall man with a permanent stoop; he had tanned, sinewy arms and a firm handshake.

'Good morning, Davidsson,' he said cheerfully. 'That's where we're digging.'

Gerlof saw that a broad rectangle of turf had been removed over by the wall. Edvard Kloss's grave. When they reached the plot, Bengtsson asked quietly, 'How about a cold beer before we start?'

He nodded towards the wide wall behind them, where a couple of brown bottles were waiting on the grass. Gerlof knew that Bengtsson's wife was a Good Templar and presumed that the gravedigger drank beer while he was working because he wasn't allowed to do so at home.

Gerlof could see that the bottles were cold and covered in conden-sation but, in spite of the fact that he had cycled all the way from the coast, he shook his head.

'Not for me, thanks.'

He wasn't all that keen on beer and wanted to be in good shape when he started digging.

Bengtsson picked up one of the bottles and looked over towards the mortuary. Gerlof noticed that the pale boy had got to his feet and was standing by one of the graves, as if he were waiting for something.

Bengtsson raised his hand.

'Aron!' he shouted.

The boy looked up.

'Come over here and give us a hand, Aron! You can have twenty-five öre if you help us dig!'

11

The boy nodded.

'Good,' Bengtsson said. 'Go to the toolshed and get yourself a spade.'

The boy loped off.

'Who's he?' Gerlof asked when he was out of earshot. 'He's not from round here, is he?'

'Aron Fredh? No, he's from the south, from Rödtorp . . . But he's a kind of relative.' Bengtsson put down the bottle behind a gravestone and looked wearily at Gerlof. 'He's a *relative incognitus*, if you know what I mean.'

Gerlof hadn't a clue. He'd never heard of Rödtorp and he couldn't speak any foreign languages, but he nodded anyway. He knew that Bengtsson only had a little girl, so perhaps the boy was one of his nephews?

Aron came back from the shed carrying a spade. He didn't say a word, simply positioned himself next to Bengtsson and Gerlof and started digging. The earth was as dry as dust and free of stones, but Gerlof's spade found the first body part after just a few minutes. It was a dark-brown human bone, possibly part of a thigh bone. Having worked as a gravedigger for a month, he was used to such discoveries, and simply placed the bone carefully to one side on the grass and covered it with a small pile of earth. Then he carried on digging.

They worked their way downwards for over an hour.

The sun disappeared and the air grew colder. As Gerlof shovelled away, an old story kept going through his mind:

Once upon a time there was a door-to-door salesman who called at a farm on the island of Öland. A little boy opened the door.

'*Is your daddy at home, son?*'

'*No, sir.*'

'*Is he far away?*'

'*No, sir. He's in the churchyard.*'

'*What on earth is he doing there?*'

'*I don't think he's doing anything. Daddy's dead . . .*'

When it was almost eleven o'clock, they heard the sound of whinnying echoing off the walls of the church. Gerlof looked up and saw two white horses trotting through the gates, surrounded by a cloud of buzzing flies. The horses were pulling a black carriage with

12

a wooden cross on the top – a hearse. Erling Samuelsson, the priest, was sitting next to the coachman. He had conducted the funeral service at the dead man's farm.

By this stage, the grave was deep enough, and Bengtsson helped the two boys out of the hole. Then he brushed the dirt off his clothes and went over to the mortuary.

The hearse had stopped there, some distance away from the church. The shiny, expensive wooden coffin containing the body of Edvard Kloss had been lifted down and placed on the grass. Most of the relatives who had made up the funeral procession turned around and went home once they reached the gate; there was only the interment left now.

Gerlof saw the two brothers standing on either side of the coffin. Sigfrid and Gilbert had nothing to say to one another today; they stood in silence in their black suits, and it seemed as if there were a grey cloud hanging between them.

However, they had no choice but to work together. The brothers were to carry the coffin over to the grave, along with Bengtsson and Gerlof.

'Up we go,' Bengtsson said.

Edvard Kloss had enjoyed his food and the good things in life, and the base of the coffin cut into Gerlof's shoulder. He set off, taking short steps; he thought he could feel the heavy body moving around inside, as if it were shifting back and forth – or was it just his imagination?

Slowly, they moved towards the grave. Gerlof saw that Aron was now standing by some tall headstones over by the churchyard wall, as if he were hiding.

But he wasn't alone. A man in his thirties was on the other side of the wall, talking quietly to Aron. He was simply dressed, a bit like a farmhand, and he seemed on edge. When he took a step to one side, Gerlof noticed that he had a slight limp.

'Davidsson!' Bengtsson said. 'Give me a hand with this!'

He had laid out two ropes on the grass. The coffin was placed upon them, then lifted again and positioned above the black grave.

Slowly, slowly, it was lowered into the hole.

When it reached the bottom, the priest picked up a handful of earth from the pile the gravediggers had made. He threw it on to the lid of the coffin as he spoke over the body of Edvard Kloss:

'Earth to earth, ashes to ashes, dust to dust. In the sure and certain hope of the resurrection to eternal life through Our Lord Jesus Christ . . .'

The priest threw three more handfuls of earth on to the coffin, committing the deceased to his final rest. When he had finished, Bengtsson and Gerlof picked up their spades.

Before Gerlof began to fill in the grave he glanced at the Kloss brothers. The older brother, Gilbert, was standing behind him as steady as a rock, his hands behind his back. Sigfrid was wandering up and down by the wall, looking a lot more anxious.

Gerlof and Bengtsson shovelled the earth back into the hole. When they had finished they would lay their spades on top in the form of a cross, as was the tradition.

After a little while they took a break. They straightened their backs, took a few steps away from the grave and let out a long breath. Gerlof turned his face up to the sun and closed his eyes.

He could hear something in the silence. A faint sound. He listened carefully.

Knocking. Then silence, then three more faint knocks.

The sound seemed to be coming from the ground.

Gerlof blinked and looked down into the grave.

He glanced over at Bengtsson, and could see from the other man's tense expression that he had heard the same thing. And the Kloss brothers, who were standing further away, had gone white. Even further away, young Aron had also turned his head.

Gerlof wasn't going mad – they had all heard the sound.

Time had stopped in the churchyard. There was no more knocking, but everyone seemed to be holding their breath.

Gilbert Kloss walked slowly to the edge of the grave, his mouth hanging open. He stared down at the coffin and said quietly, 'We need to get him out of there.'

The priest stepped forward, rubbing his forehead nervously.

'That's not possible.'

'Yes, it is,' Gilbert said.

'But I've just committed his body to the earth!'

Kloss didn't speak, but his expression was determined. Eventually, another voice from behind said firmly, 'Get him out.'

It was Sigfrid Kloss.

The priest sighed.

'Oh, very well, you'd better bring him up. I'll go and telephone Dr Blom.'

Daniel Blom was one of the two doctors in the parish.

Bengtsson put down his spade, sighed loudly and looked at Gerlof. 'Will you go down, Davidsson? With Aron?'

Gerlof gazed down into the darkness of the grave. Did he want to go down there? No. But what if Edvard Kloss had woken up and was suffocating inside the coffin? If that was the case, they had to hurry.

He scrambled down into the hole and cautiously stepped on top of the lid, which was covered in soil. He remembered what he had read in his confirmation class, about Jesus's encounter with Lazarus:

The man who had died came out, his hands and feet bound with linen strips, and his face wrapped with a cloth. Jesus said to them, 'Unbind him, and let him go.'

Gerlof listened as hard as he could for any sound from inside the coffin, but there was nothing. However, he didn't like being down there; the air was icy cold. At some point in the future he too would end up in a place like this. For all eternity. Unless Jesus came along and raised him from the dead.

A scraping noise behind him made him jump, but it was only the boy clambering down on to the lid of the coffin, clutching a spade. Aron Fredh from Rödtorp. Gerlof nodded to him in the darkness.

'Let's dig,' he said quietly.

Aron was staring down at the coffin. He whispered something – just one word.

'What? What did you say?'

'America,' the boy repeated. 'That's where I'm going.'

'Really?' Gerlof was sceptical. 'How old are you, Aron?'

'Twelve.'

'In that case, you're too young.'

'Sven's going to take me. I'm going to be a sheriff when we get there!'

'Oh yes?'

'I'm a good shot,' Aron said.

Gerlof didn't ask any more questions. He didn't know who Sven was, but he'd heard of America. The promised land. Things weren't going too well in America at the moment, with the Wall Street Crash and high unemployment, but the attraction was still there.

At that moment, standing on top of Edvard Kloss's coffin, Gerlof decided to stop being a gravedigger. He would leave Stenvik and his strict father. He didn't want to go to America; he would go to sea instead. He would take himself off to Borgholm and get a job on some cargo ship travelling between the island and the mainland.

Do something that would give him more freedom. Become a seaman in the sunshine.

'How's it going?' Bengtsson shouted from above his head. Gerlof looked up.

'Fine.'

He and Aron, the future sheriff, began to dig, and they quickly cleared all the earth from the lid of the coffin.

'Done!'

Bengtsson threw down the ropes. Gerlof managed to get them around each end of the coffin, then climbed out of the grave as quickly as he could.

Edvard Kloss was lifted out and carried into the cool sacristy.

'Put it down,' the priest said quietly.

The coffin was placed on the stone floor with a scraping sound.

Then there was silence. Edvard Kloss was dead.

And yet he had knocked.

Dr Blom arrived twenty minutes later, carrying his black medical bag. His shirt was soaked in sweat and his face was bright red with the heat, and he was clearly in need of an explanation. He asked just one question, his voice echoing loudly beneath the vaulted stone ceiling: 'What's going on here?'

The men waiting in the aisle looked at one another.

'We heard something,' the priest said eventually.

'You heard something?'

'Yes.' The priest nodded in the direction of the coffin. 'A knocking noise from down in the ground . . . Just when they started filling in the grave.'

The doctor looked at the lid of the coffin, filthy and covered in scratches from the spades.

'I see. In that case I'd better take a look.'

The Kloss brothers stood in silence as Bengtsson removed the screws and lifted the lid.

Lazarus had spent four days in his grave, Gerlof recalled. 'Lord, by this time he *stinks*,' his sister, Martha, had said to Jesus as they stood before the stone.

The lid was off now. Gerlof didn't move closer, but he could still see the body, washed and arranged for its final rest. The arms were crossed over the big belly, the eyes were closed and there were black bruises on his face, possibly from the wall that had killed him. But Edvard Kloss was smartly dressed; the corpse was wearing a black suit made of thick fabric.

'If you dress the deceased as well as you speak of him, he will have a smile on his face when he is lying in his coffin,' Gerlof's grand-mother used to say.

But Edvard Kloss's mouth was no more than a narrow, straight line, his lips hard and dry.

Dr Blom opened his leather bag and bent over the corpse; Gerlof turned away, but he could hear the doctor muttering to himself. A stethoscope rattled against the stone floor.

'No heartbeat,' the doctor said.

There was silence, then came Gilbert's voice, sounding strained:

'Open a vein so we can be absolutely sure.'

That was enough for Gerlof. He went out into the sunshine and stood in the shade of the church tower.

'Now will you have a beer?'

Bengtsson came over, carrying two fresh bottles.

This time, Gerlof nodded and gratefully accepted a drink. The bottle was ice cold, and he raised it to his lips and drank deeply. The alcohol went straight to his head and slowed down his thought processes. He looked at Bengtsson.

'Has this happened before?'

'What?'

'Have you heard noises before?'

The gravedigger shook his head.

'Not personally, at any rate.' He gave a tight little smile, took a swig of his beer and looked over at the church. 'But of course the Kloss brothers are a bit different . . . I have a problem with that family. They just take whatever they want. All the time, all over the place.'

'But Edvard Kloss . . .' Gerlof said, struggling to find the right words. 'He can't have . . .'

'Calm down,' Bengtsson broke in. 'This isn't your problem.' He had another drink, and added: 'In the old days, they used to tie the hands together. When someone died, I mean, so that they'd lie still down there in the coffin. Did you know that?'

Gerlof shook his head and didn't say another word.

After a few moments the church door opened, and Gerlof and Bengtsson quickly hid the bottles of beer. Dr Blom stuck his head out and waved them over.

'I've finished.'

'And he's . . .'

'He's dead, of course. No sign of life whatsoever. You can put him back where you got him from.'

The interment was repeated. The coffin was carried out of the church, the ropes were slipped underneath and it was lowered into the grave. Gerlof and Bengtsson started shovelling earth into the hole once more, clutching their spades with a certain amount of grim determination; they were feeling a little unsteady after the beer. Gerlof looked around for Aron Fredh, but both the boy and the man with the limp had disappeared.

Everyone gathered around the grave, including Dr Blom, who was holding tightly on to his leather bag.

The earth thudded against the coffin lid.

Then the sound came again: three sharp raps from down in the ground. Quiet but clear.

Gerlof froze in mid-movement, his heart pounding. Suddenly, he was completely sober, and frightened. He looked across at Bengtsson on the other side of the mound of earth; he, too, had stopped dead.

Sigfrid Kloss looked tense, but his brother, Gilbert, seemed to be absolutely terrified. He was staring at the coffin as if mesmerized.

Even Dr Blom had stiffened at the sound. Gerlof realized the scepticism was gone, but the doctor shook his head.

'Fill in the grave,' he said firmly.

The priest was silent for a moment, then he nodded.

'There's nothing more we can do.'

The gravediggers had no option but to comply. Gerlof shivered in spite of the sunshine, but he set to work. His spade felt as heavy as an iron bar in his hands.

The earth began to thud against the coffin lid once more; the rhythmic beat was the only sound.

After twenty shovelfuls the lid had begun to disappear beneath a layer of earth.

There was still no other sound in the churchyard.

But, suddenly, someone sighed next to Gerlof. It was Gilbert Kloss, edging towards the grave. The sigh sounded like a long, heavy exhalation; he lifted his feet and moved slowly across the grass. He stopped by the open grave and tried to take a deep breath, but his lungs managed only a thin whistling.

'Gilbert?' Sigfrid said.

His brother didn't reply; he stood there motionless, his mouth open.

Then he stopped breathing, and his eyes lost focus.

Gerlof watched as Gilbert Kloss fell sideways by the grave. He saw Bengtsson simply standing there staring, along with the doctor and the priest.

Sigfrid called out behind them; Gerlof was the only one who rushed forward, but he was still several steps away when Gilbert's heart stopped beating.

Gilbert's body fell head first on to the grass beside the grave, rolled slowly over the edge and landed on the lid of the coffin like a heavy sack of flour.

Early Summer

When the sun gives the summer its streams
then the nightingale wakes the dreams
we have gathered around death
like midsummer myths in the valley.

Harry Martinson

Gerlof

Could a boat die? And, if so, when was it dead? Gerlof gazed at his old wooden gig and considered the question. She should have been in the water on this sunny June day, but she was still ashore. Cracks all over the place, tipped on her side on the grass. The name of the gig was *Swallow*; it was carved on a little wooden nameplate on the stern, but she no longer flew across the water. A fat green fly was crawling idly around the dry hull.

'What do you think?' asked John Hagman, who was standing on the other side of the boat.

'She's a wreck,' Gerlof replied. 'Old and useless.'

'She's younger than us.'

'Indeed. So that probably means we're wrecks as well.'

Gerlof was eighty-four years old, while John would turn eighty next year. They had sailed across the Baltic on cargo ships together for almost three decades as captain and first mate, carrying limestone and oil and general cargo to and from Stockholm, through stormy weather and calm waters. But that was a long time ago, and now the Öland gig was the only boat they had left.

Swallow had been built in 1925, when Gerlof was just ten. His father had used her to fish for flounder for almost thirty years, then Gerlof had taken over in the fifties and had sailed her every summer for another forty years. But one spring in the early nineties, when the ice had receded out into the Sound and it was time to carry *Swallow* down to the water, Gerlof simply hadn't had the energy.

He was too old. And so was *Swallow*.

Since then she had been lying there next to Gerlof's boathouse as her planks dried out and split in the sunshine.

23

The light on Öland was intense, and on this cloudless day the sun was blazing down on the coast. A fresh, cooling breeze was coming off the sea in gentle gusts. So far, there had been no heatwave on the island; the really hot weather didn't usually arrive until July, and sometimes it didn't arrive at all.

Gerlof poked at the gig's dried-out oak planks with his stick and watched as it penetrated the wood. He shook his head.

'She's a wreck,' he said again. 'She'll sink in seconds if we put her in the water.'

'She can be fixed,' John said.

'Do you think so?'

'Absolutely. We can seal the cracks. I'm sure Anders will help out.'

'Maybe . . . but the work would be down to the two of you, in that case. All I can do is sit and watch.'

Gerlof suffered from Sjögren's Syndrome, a type of rheumatism that came and went. It was unpredictable; in the summer his legs usually felt better with the warmth, but sometimes he needed a wheelchair to get around.

'There's money in this,' John said.

'Really?'

'Oh, yes. The Öland Wooden Boat Association usually supports projects like this.'

They heard a whining noise from the coast road behind them, and both men turned their heads. They saw a shiny black Volvo, an SUV, but it had foreign number plates and tinted side windows.

It was a Monday, the week before Midsummer's Eve. And Stenvik, the fishing village that had turned into a holiday resort, had come back to life.

Nature had come to life in May, of course, turning the meadows and the alvar purple, yellow and white. Butterflies had emerged, the grass was green once more, the scent of herbs and flowers filled the air. But in spite of the early sunshine and the heat, the summer visitors had decided that the season didn't really begin until now. They arrived in force at midsummer to unlock their chalets, dig out the hammocks and live the rural life, close to nature. Until the beginning of August, when they all set off back to the city.

The Volvo whizzed past, heading north. Gerlof caught a glimpse of several people in the car, but didn't recognize them.

'Was that the Norwegian family from Tönsberg?' he said. 'The ones who bought the Brown House a couple of years ago?'

'The Brown House?'

'Yes – well, it's painted red now, but it was brown when the Skogmans owned it.'

'The Skogmans?'

'You remember – they were from Ystad.'

John nodded as he watched the Volvo.

'No, it's not turning in at the Skogmans' place . . . I thought somebody from Holland bought their place?'

'When?' Gerlof asked.

'Two years ago, I think . . . spring '97. But they've hardly spent any time here.'

Gerlof shook his head once more.

'I don't remember. There are too many people around these days.'

In the winter, Stenvik was virtually empty, but at this time of year it was impossible to keep up with all the old and new faces. Gerlof had seen generations of summer visitors pass through the village, and these days he found it difficult to distinguish between fathers and sons, mothers and daughters.

No doubt the visitors didn't know who Gerlof was either. He had lived in the residential home for senior citizens up in Marnäs for several years, and it was only recently that he had started coming down to his childhood home in the spring and summer, steadfastly battling the pain in his joints.

It seemed as if his legs were pretty tired of supporting him, and he was tired of it, too. Lately, he had tried turmeric and horseradish for the pain; it had helped to a certain extent, but he could still walk only short distances.

Take me back, he thought, to a period in my life when there was still time.

Several expensive cars were speeding along the coast road, but Gerlof turned his back on them and looked at the gig again.

'Right,' he said. 'We'll fix her up then, with your son's help.'

'Good,' John said. 'She's a fine boat. Perfect for fishing.'

'Indeed she is,' Gerlof agreed, although he hadn't been fishing for many years. 'But can you fit it in?'

'Definitely. The campsite more or less runs itself.'

John had leased the campsite in Stenvik every summer since he had come ashore at the beginning of the sixties. When his son, Anders, was old enough they had started to share the work between them, but John was still the one who went around the tents and caravans each morning and evening, collecting fees and emptying the bins. He hadn't had a single free summer in thirty-five years, but he seemed to enjoy it.

'That's agreed, then,' Gerlof said. 'Perhaps in August we'll be eating plaice that we've caught ourselves.'

'Perhaps,' John said. 'But she can stay here for a while.'

A while. When it came to John, that could mean anything from three days to three years, but Gerlof assumed that *Swallow* would remain by the boathouse for a few weeks before Anders and John set to work on her.

He sighed and looked around. His village, the best place in the whole world. The wide bay with its deep blue waters. The row of boathouses. The old cottages and the new houses. The lush summer greenery of Öland in the background, so different from the tree-less coastal landscape when Gerlof was a little boy. He had spent his childhood here in the bay before going off to sea as a teenager, even-tually returning as a grown man to build a summer cottage for his family.

The road came to an end on the southern point, and that was where the village also ended. The coast was more dramatic over there, with a steep cliff leading down to flat, wide rocks along the shoreline and a burial cairn, known as a *rör* in the local dialect, up on the ridge above the water.

The finest summer cottages were also at the southern end of the village, lining the coast road. Last of all, completely separate, were the two houses belonging to the Kloss family.

The Kloss family. The three brothers, Edvard, Sigfrid and Gilbert. Edvard and Gilbert had died at almost the same time; only Sigfrid had lived to a decent age. He had inherited his father's land and turned it into a holiday complex, which was now run by his grand-children.

'Have the Kloss gang arrived yet?' Gerlof asked.

'Indeed they have. Their place is already packed with cars, and people are out on the golf course.'

The Kloss family's holiday complex lay a few kilometres south of the village, and was called the Ölandic Resort, but John always referred to it as 'the Kloss place'. He regarded it as competition, in spite of the fact that his shop in Stenvik was no more than a shoebox in comparison. The Ölandic Resort had everything – a golf course, a campsite, a range of shops, a nightclub, a swimming pool and an entire holiday village.

In Gerlof's opinion, the Kloss family owned far too much, but what could he do?

All these rich residents bothered him. He did his best to avoid them. Them and their boats and swimming pools and chainsaws – all those new acquisitions making a racket in the countryside. Frightening the birds.

He looked out across the bay.

'You know, John, sometimes I wonder . . . is there anything that's improved on the island over the past hundred years? Anything at all?'

John gave the matter some thought.

'Nobody goes hungry these days . . . And the roads aren't full of potholes.'

'I suppose so,' Gerlof conceded. 'But are we happier these days?'

'Who knows? But we're alive. That's something to be happy about.'

'Mmm.'

But was it? Was Gerlof really happy to have lived to a ripe old age? These days, he took one day at a time. After some seventy years he could still remember Gilbert Kloss collapsing with a heart attack at his brother's grave.

Everything could come to an end at any moment, but right now the sun was shining. *Sol lucet omnibus* – the sun shines on everyone.

Gerlof decided to enjoy this summer. To look forward to the new millennium. He was due to get a hearing aid, so soon he would be able to sit in his garden listening to the birds.

And he would be more friendly towards visitors in the village. Or at least he would try. He wouldn't just mutter when he came across a tourist, and he would answer the people from Stockholm when they spoke to him.

He nodded to himself and said, 'Let's hope we have nice quiet, well-behaved visitors this year.'

27

The Homecomer

The fisherman's cottage had thick walls, and small dark rooms that smelled of blood and booze. The odours didn't bother the old man standing by the doorway; he was used to both.

The smell of booze came from Einar Wall, the owner of the cottage. Wall was in his sixties, bent and wrinkled, and he had obviously made an early start on his midsummer celebrations; a half-empty bottle stood beside the table where he was sitting working.

The stench of blood came from his most recent booty: three large birds were suspended from hooks on the low ceiling. A partridge and two woodcocks. They were peppered with buckshot but had been plucked and drawn.

'Shot them yesterday, out on the shore,' Wall said. 'Woodcocks are supposed to be protected at the moment because they're breeding, but I couldn't give a damn about that. A man should be able to catch fish and birds whenever he wants.'

The old man was a hunter himself, and said nothing. He looked at the other two people in the cottage, a young man and a girl, both in their early twenties, who had just arrived in their own car and settled down on the shabby sofa.

'What are your names?'

'I'm Rita,' said the skinny girl, who was curled up like a cat, one hand on the boy's denim-clad knee.

'Pecka,' the boy said. He was tall; he leaned back with his shaven head resting against the wall, but his leg was twitching.

The old man didn't say any more. It was Wall who had found these two, not him.

A puppy and a kitten, he thought.

But he had also been young once, and had grown more capable as time went by.

Pecka didn't seem to like the silence. He stared at the old man, his eyes narrowed.

'And what do we call you?'

'Nothing.'

'But who the hell *are* you? You sound a bit foreign.'

'My name is Aron,' said the man. 'I've come home.'

'Home?'

'I've come home to Sweden.'

'From where?' Pecka wanted to know.

'From the New World.'

Pecka continued to stare at him, but Rita nodded.

'He means the States . . . don't you?'

The old man said nothing, so Rita tried again: 'You mean America, don't you?'

The man didn't respond.

'OK, so we'll call you Aron,' Pecka said. 'Or the man who's come home. Whatever, as long as you're in.'

The man said nothing. He went over to the table and picked up one of the guns by its slender barrel.

'A Walther,' he said.

Wall nodded with satisfaction, as if he were manning a market stall.

'It's a fine piece,' he said. 'The police used it as their service weapon for many years. Simple and solid . . . Swedish craftsmanship.'

'It's German,' the old man said.

'Mine are made under licence.' Wall pointed to the rest of his display. 'This is a Sig Sauer, and this one is a Swedish automatic assault rifle. That's what's on offer.'

Pecka got up and came over to the table. The old man recognized the look in his eyes: the same curiosity that every young soldier felt when a new weapon appeared. Every young soldier who had never killed someone, at least.

'So you like guns?' Pecka said.

The old man nodded curtly. 'I've used them.'

'So you're an old squaddie?'

The old man looked at him. 'What?'

29

'An old soldier,' Pecka said. 'Did you fight in a war?'

A war, Aron thought. It was something young men might long for. A new country.

'I know what I'm doing,' he said. 'How about you?'

Pecka shook his head gloomily.

'I haven't been in a war,' he said, but then he lifted his chin proudly. 'But I never back down . . . I was in court for GBH last summer.'

Wall didn't look quite so impressed.

'That's crap,' he said. 'It was just a tourist who got out of hand.'

The old man realized that they were family, and that Wall was concerned about Pecka. He calmly pushed in the Walther's magazine and put it down on the table.

He looked out of the window. The sun was shining over the sea and the shore, but barely reached in through the grubby windows. Wall's cottage was in an isolated spot, on a section of the shore where the grass ran all the way down to the water's edge. There was a small enclosure housing a few geese by the shoreline, with a boathouse made of grey limestone beside it, looking every bit as neglected as the cottage itself.

Wall heaved himself to his feet.

'Here,' he said, handing out the guns. Rita was given a small Sig Sauer, Pecka a Walther, and the old man both a Walther and the automatic.

'Will you be needing plastic explosives as well?' Wall asked.

The old man who had come home looked up.

'Have you got some?'

'I brought some back last winter,' Pecka said proudly. 'From a road construction project in Kalmar. Fuses, detonators, the lot.'

Wall looked equally pleased.

'It's all carefully hidden and locked away,' he said. 'Nobody will find it. The cops were here back in May, but they left empty-handed.'

'We can take a couple of charges,' the old man said. 'What about payment?'

'Afterwards,' Wall said. 'Do your job and take care of the safe, then we'll split everything later.'

'We'll need balaclavas as well, Einar,' Pecka said. 'Did you get them?'

Wall didn't ask any questions. He simply opened a cardboard box underneath the table and took out a packet of rubber gloves and several grey balaclavas with holes cut out for the eyes.

'Burn them when you're done,' he said.

The old man looked at them and said, 'I don't need any protection.'

'You'll be recognized,' Pecka said.

The man shook his head.

'That doesn't matter,' he said, gazing out of the cracked window. 'I'm not here.'

The New Country, May 1931

The journey begins one sunny summer's day, eleven months after the death of Edvard Kloss. Aron has almost stopped thinking about that night. About the wall that fell down, about Sven giving him a shove. *'In you go! Get in there and fetch his money.'*

Sven had been Aron's new father for just a couple of years, but he did as he was told. Otherwise he might face a beating.

They don't talk about that night, just about the trip. It feels as if they have been preparing for today all through the spring, but everything they are taking with them still fits into one suitcase each.

Sven has brought the old snuffbox made of apple wood. Aron wants to bring something as well, something precious.

'Can I take my gun to America?'

Aron has his very own single-barrel shotgun, which he fills with pellets so that he can shoot partridge and seabirds.

'Of course you can't,' Sven says. 'They wouldn't let you on board the ship.'

So Aron has to leave his shotgun behind. It was given to him by his grandfather, who is a huntsman himself; he told his daughter, Astrid, that the boy is a pretty decent shot. That sounds good, 'a decent shot'.

And indeed he is; he was only ten years old when he shot his first seal. It was lying on an ice floe that came drifting towards the island one cold, sunny spring day. The seal raised its head, Aron raised his gun and when he fired the seal's body jerked, then lay still. He had hit the back of its neck and broken its spine. It was over a metre long and provided over twenty kilos of blubber.

'But I need a gun,' Aron says. 'How am I supposed to be a sheriff without a gun?'

Sven laughs; it sounds like a dry cough.

'We'll find you a new one when we get there.'

'Do they have shotguns in the new country?'

'Lots of them. They have everything there.'

Aron knows one thing they don't have in the new country: a waiting family. His mother, Astrid, and his sister, Greta, are staying behind in Sweden, and saying goodbye to them is hard. Greta is only nine, and gazes at her brother in silence. His mother clamps her lips together.

'Stay out of trouble,' she says. 'Look after yourself.'

Aron nods, then he picks up his bag and goes with Sven, taking long strides to stop him from turning back.

The day of their departure is dry and sunny.

They walk side by side along the dirt track. Sven has longer legs, but he limps with his right foot, so Aron is able to keep up with him.

'You're off to the new country in the west,' his mother had said, 'the country they call America. You're going to work hard over there for a couple of years, then you'll come home with money.'

And Sven says the same thing, but more concisely.

'The new country. That's where we're going. Away from all this.'

They head north, across the Kloss family's extensive land, almost all the way up to the cairn. It's on top of the ridge in the west and it looks like a harmless pile of stones, but Sven spits anyway, just to be on the safe side.

'I hope it falls into the sea!'

Then they turn to the east, moving inland past several tall windmills, standing on their thick wooden feet with their sails in the air, ready to catch the wind from all directions. Sven glares at the windmills, too.

'We won't have to look at those damned things where we're going either!'

He lopes along, addressing the horizon as if he is giving a speech: 'Free at last – free from all those filthy jobs! As white as a ghost every time I come out of the mill – never again!' He looks at Aron. 'Where we're going, they have machines that take care of everything. They have huge agricultural factories, where the grain goes in at one end and sacks of flour come out at the other. They just press a button, and hey presto!'

Aron listens, but he has just one question: 'When are we coming home?'

Sven slows down, then he turns around and wallops Aron across the back of the head.

'Don't ask me that question! We're not going to think that way! We're going to the new country – forget about home!'

It's not the hardest blow Aron has ever received, it's just making a point, so he feels brave enough to carry on: 'But *when* are we coming home?'

'Impossible to say,' Sven replies.

'Why?'

'Because not everyone comes home.'

The summer air feels colder when Aron hears those words. He doesn't say any more – he doesn't want to provoke any further blows, but even before they reach the train he makes his mind up that he will do what his mother told him to do, and that he will come back home.

Home to the island.

Home to the croft.

Jonas

'What's going on, Officer?' asked Uncle Kent. 'Has there been an accident?'

'No,' replied the policeman, who had just got off his motorbike. 'It's just you.'

'Me? What have I done?'

'You were driving too fast.'

'*Me?*'

Uncle Kent had lowered the window with the press of a button so that he could speak to the police officer, and the faint smell of flowers drifted into the car from the ditches along the roadside, reaching Jonas in the back seat. He could see a profusion of yellow and purple flowers swaying in the breeze. Their scent mingled with the aroma of his uncle's aftershave and a hint of perspiration from his father, who had arrived late and had to run to catch the train. Mum had told him off on the platform, and Mats and Jonas had just looked at one another.

His father sat in silence next to Kent; he seemed tense in the presence of the police officer. But Jonas had a clear view of his uncle's profile and could see a slight smile playing around the corner of his mouth.

'Driving too *fast*?'

'Much too fast.'

The Öland sunshine was bright, dazzling Jonas when he looked out of his own window. The traffic cop was no more than a dark shape next to the car, dressed in a blue uniform.

'Could you tell me how fast?' Uncle Kent said.

'Twenty-two kilometres over the speed limit.'

Kent sighed and leaned back in his seat.

'It's all down to this bloody car. A Corvette only runs really smoothly when you take her up above a hundred.'

Jonas had encountered the police on only one occasion previously, when two officers came to talk to his class in Huskvarna about traffic awareness for cyclists. They had been really nice, but he still felt a bit nervous.

Uncle Kent's car was red with black stripes, and it looked a bit like a spaceship. It felt like a rocket inside, too, low and narrow, particularly in the back seat. Jonas still had some growing to do, but he still had to bend his legs to one side to fit in. His older brother, Mats, had a bit more room because he was sitting behind Niklas, their father, who had shorter legs.

'Are you going to fine me?' Uncle Kent said.

'Indeed I am.'

'Typical, on the sunniest day of the summer so far.' He smiled at the police officer. 'But I hold my hands up . . . I broke the law.'

Jonas looked at his father, who still hadn't said a word. Nor had he so much as looked at the policeman.

Uncle Kent had picked up Jonas and Mats and their father from the station in Kalmar in his red Corvette. He owned a big Volvo as well, but in the summer he preferred to drive his sports car. And it was fast.

They had left the Öland bridge half an hour earlier, whizzing northwards as his father and Uncle Kent chatted in the front, but when the motorcycle came up alongside them and waved the car over to the side of the road, his father had immediately fallen silent. He had stopped speaking and shuffled down in his seat.

Uncle Kent was doing all the talking. He sat there with his hands resting on the wheel, seeming totally relaxed, as if this was merely a minor hiccup on the road to Villa Kloss.

'Do I pay the fine directly to you?' he said.

The police officer shook his head.

'I'll write you a ticket.'

'How much?'

'Eight hundred kronor.'

Uncle Kent looked away and sighed. He gazed out across the sunlit cornfields to the right of the road, then glanced back at the police officer.

'What's your name?'

No reply was forthcoming.

'Is it a secret?' Uncle Kent persisted. 'What's your first name?'

The police officer shook his head. He took a pad and a pen out of his inside pocket.

'My name is Sören,' he said eventually.

'Thank you, Sören. I'm Kent Kloss.' He nodded to his right. 'This is my younger brother, Niklas, and his two boys. We're all going to spend the summer together.'

The officer nodded impassively, but Uncle Kent kept on talking.

'Just one thing, Sören . . . Here we are on a dry, flat road, two days before midsummer. The sun is shining, it's a beautiful day. A fantastic summer's day, the kind of day when you feel most alive . . . What would you have done, if you were me? Would you have stayed behind that caravan all the way to Borgholm?'

Sören didn't bother to answer; he finished filling in the penalty notice and passed it through the window. Kent took it, but refused to give up: 'Couldn't you at least admit it, Sören?'

'Admit what?'

'That you would have done the same thing? If you'd been the one stuck behind that caravan, in the summer sun on your way to the sea? Wouldn't you have put your foot down . . . well, maybe not put your foot down, but gone just a little bit over the speed limit? Won't you admit that?'

Kent wasn't smiling now, he was deadly serious.

The traffic policeman sighed. 'OK, Kent. If it makes you feel better.'

'A little better,' said Kent, smiling once more.

'Good. Drive carefully now.'

He went back to his motorbike and started it up, then did a U-turn and headed south.

'You see that? Look at the speed he's going, the bastard!' Uncle Kent nodded to Jonas and Mats. 'Never let them get the upper hand, boys. Just you remember that!'

With that, the engine kicked into life with a dull roar and Uncle Kent pulled out on to the road, right in front of yet another caravan. He quickly increased his speed.

The sun was shining, the road was flat and straight. Jonas had a warm breeze on his face and the scent of wild flowers in his nostrils. Uncle Kent still had his window down, his left elbow sticking out as he steered the car with one hand, fingers resting lightly on the wheel. Nothing more.

His mobile rang. He answered using his free hand, listened for twelve or fourteen seconds then interrupted loudly: '*No.* A supporting wall, I said. What for? Support, of course! I want it to look old, kind of medieval, but *modern* at the same time. Made of stone, or railway sleepers. And I want the pipework *under* the wall, not next to it. Good . . . Has the digger arrived?' He listened again. 'Fantastic! In that case, we can . . . Hello?' He lowered the mobile. 'Lost the connection – typical.'

Uncle Kent had certain favourite words, like 'typical' and 'fantastic'. He imbued them with an energy and self-confidence that Jonas could never manage, whatever he said.

Kent slipped his mobile into his pocket and said, 'Shall we take the boat out when we arrive?'

'Sure,' Jonas's dad agreed at once. 'As long as it's not too rough out there.'

Uncle Kent laughed.

'Motorboats like waves, they just jump over them! We'll take a little trip, then we can have a Cosmo on the decking.'

Niklas nodded, but he didn't look particularly happy.

'OK.'

Jonas had no idea what a Cosmo was, but he didn't ask. The trick when it came to looking grown up was to listen and to *look* as if you knew exactly what was going on. And to laugh along with everyone else.

Kent glanced in the rear-view mirror.

'We're going to get you up on those skis this summer, JK. All right? Things didn't go too well a couple of years ago, as I recall . . .'

He always called Jonas by his initials, JK.

'I'll give it a go,' Jonas said.

He didn't really want to think about water-skiing. He didn't want to think about that summer either, when his father had just started serving his sentence and Jonas and Mats had come to Öland on their own.

He could see the expanse of the Sound now; they had reached the village and were passing the kiosk and the restaurant. They turned left on to the coast road, with the ridge on one side of the car and houses on the other.

Jonas hadn't managed to get up on his skis once that summer. Uncle Kent must have tried to pull him up with the line from the motorboat at least fifteen times; Jonas had coughed up water and clung to the handle so tightly that his knuckles turned white, but he always ended up pitching forward after just a few metres. In the evenings, his legs had felt like spaghetti.

'You're not going to give it a go, JK, you're going to *do it*! You're much tougher this year. How old are you now?'

'Twelve,' Jonas said, although his birthday wasn't until August. He glanced at his brother, afraid of a scornful correction, but Mats was gazing out at the water and didn't appear to be listening.

They had arrived. The summer place was known as Villa Kloss, even though it consisted of two houses side by side, with huge panoramic windows overlooking the sea. Aunt Veronica and the cousins lived in the north house, Uncle Kent in the south.

Jonas's father no longer had a house of his own. They would be staying in the guest chalets.

'Twelve years old, that's the best time of your life,' Kent said as the Corvette swung into his drive. 'You're totally free. You're going to have a *fantastic* summer here, JK!'

'Mmm,' said Jonas.

But he didn't feel free. Just small.

Gerlof

Gerlof met the Swedish-American on the way to the dance.

He was late, leaning on his chestnut walking stick and making his way along the coast road as quickly as he could. He wouldn't be dancing around the maypole himself, of course, but he enjoyed listening to the music. Midsummer came along only once a year, after all.

The problem was that he had forgotten something – two things, in fact – which was why he was late. His daughters and grandchildren were waiting for him, but when he got to the bottom of the steps and was standing in the garden, he couldn't hear any birds singing in the treetops.

The device. He wasn't used to it yet.

'I'll go and get it,' his daughter, Julia, said.

She was carrying a small folding chair for Gerlof, but she put it down and went back indoors. A minute later she reappeared and handed over the small plastic ear buds.

'Do you mind if we go on ahead? The boys really want to be there from the start.'

Gerlof inserted the hearing aids and waved her away.

'I'll follow you.'

He had only his stick and the birdsong for company as he set off towards the maypole down at the far end of the inlet.

He was pleased to be able to hear the birds, even if he needed some help to do so.

In the spring and summer, Gerlof left his room at the residential home for senior citizens in Marnäs and spent as much time as possible in the cottage on the coast, where he had the sea and the wind and all the birds – the migrants who came back from Africa in the spring. Back home to Gerlof's garden.

Sparrows and bullfinches gathered on the edge of the little limestone bird bath in the corner of the lawn. Gerlof would watch them dip down for a drink of water, then they would open their beaks to chirrup and sing.

The problem was that he could no longer hear their song.

His hearing problem was nothing new; it had been creeping up on him for a long time. Gerlof had stopped hearing the crickets when he was about sixty-five years old, the year after he retired. He had stood on the veranda listening in the evenings, but there was only silence out there in the darkness. At first he had thought that pollution had killed them off, but then a doctor had explained that the sound the crickets made was on such a high frequency that his old ears couldn't pick it up.

Old ears? His ears were the same age as the rest of him. But he could cope with not being able to hear the crickets; they were fairly irritating, and he didn't really miss them. And, in any case, it wasn't the crickets that chirped all day long, it was the grasshoppers.

But Gerlof did want to hear the birdsong. Last spring it had seemed a little more muted than before, as if they were singing through an invisible blanket. And this year the garden had been silent. At that point Gerlof had realized that something was seriously wrong, and had contacted Dr Wahlberg, who had sent him to Kalmar for a hearing test.

Gerlof had been expecting a neatly dressed technician in a white coat, with a pen tucked behind one ear, but the man who greeted him was wearing jeans and had a ponytail.

'Hi, I'm Ulrik. I'm an audiologist.'

'An archaeologist?'

'Audiologist. I'll be producing an audiogram showing the level of your hearing.'

All these new words made Gerlof feel dizzy. He had had to sit in a little booth wearing headphones, and had been told to press a button when he heard a range of sounds. For long periods, things had been worryingly silent.

'How does it look?' he asked when Ulrik released him.

41

'Not too good,' came the reply. 'I think it's probably time for a little technical assistance.'

Technical assistance? Was Gerlof going to have something stuck in his ears? He remembered that his old grandfather – a notoriously mean man – had developed hearing problems in his nineties, and had made himself a metal ear trumpet out of an old snuff tin. Simple and completely free.

Today everything was made of plastic. Ulrik took a cast of Gerlof's ear canal so that a suitable model could be made.

In the middle of May, Gerlof was able to try out the hearing aid in his own garden, when Ulrik came over to Öland with a small computer.

'We don't normally do home visits,' he said, 'but I love this island '. . . The sun and the scenery . . .'

Gerlof was delighted and took him out on to the veranda to see the birds. An olive-green bird was sitting in the bath washing its wings.

'A greenfinch,' he said. 'It sounds like a canary when it sings . . . if you can hear it.'

'When we've finished, you'll be able to hear it perfectly,' Ulrik said, placing his computer on the table.

After a few minutes, Gerlof was sitting motionless on a chair on the veranda, with wires running from the computer to the buds in his ears, which fitted perfectly.

Ulrik gazed at the screen.

'How's that? Can you hear any whistling?'

Gerlof shook his head – very carefully, so that the wires wouldn't come out. Then he closed his eyes and concentrated.

He listened. No, there was no whistling, but there was a faint sighing that he hadn't heard for many years. It seemed to be coming from outside, and he realized that it was the breeze, blowing around the cottage.

And, through the breeze, he suddenly heard the pure, clear sound of birdsong. The greenfinch, warbling in the birdbath. And, somewhere over in the bushes, a whitethroat answered him.

Gerlof opened his eyes and blinked in surprise.

'I can hear them,' he said. 'The birds.'

'Good,' Ulrik said. 'In that case, we're on the right track.'

Gerlof could hear the birds around him, but he couldn't see them. It made him think about a mystery from his childhood, and he decided to ask the question while he had an expert on the spot.

'Can a person hear noises even though they don't exist?'

Ulrik looked confused.

'What do you mean?'

'If someone heard mysterious sounds, coming out of the ground, for example . . . could that be some kind of hallucination? Like an optical illusion, but to do with hearing instead?'

'That's a tricky question. I mean, sometimes we hear sounds that exist only in our heads, if someone has tinnitus, for example.'

'This was nothing like that,' Gerlof said. 'It was knocking. Loud knocking from inside a coffin that had been lowered into the ground. I heard it when I was young, and so did several other people . . . Everyone who was there heard it.'

He looked at Ulrik, but the young man just shook his head.

'I'm afraid I'm no expert on ghosts.'

As he approached the celebrations he could hear the buzz of a large crowd, like the sound of a rushing waterfall in the distance. There was an expectant hum; the dancing hadn't started yet.

Gerlof knew there were a lot of people in the village at the moment, because the water pressure in his taps had dropped over the past few days. Water was less than plentiful on the island in hot weather, and in the summer many people had to share it.

His muscles ached as he hurried along the coast road, past the track leading down to the jetty. He could see a group of young people standing there, dressed in tiny trunks and bikinis. He thought back to the old days, when bathing suits were knitted and smelled of wool.

When Gerlof reached the long row of mailboxes and was about to turn inland towards the crowd surrounding the maypole, he noticed a man of about his own age standing there. He was tall, with white, wavy hair, and he was wearing a dark-brown jacket. He had an old Kodak camera around his neck.

Gerlof looked at the man, with a vague recollection of having seen him before.

The man returned his gaze, then held up the camera in front of him, almost like a shield, and snapped away in the direction of the mailboxes.

Gerlof remembered that he had resolved not to pre-judge strangers, so he went over to the man.

'Good afternoon,' he said. 'We know one another, don't we?'

The man hesitated, then stepped away from the mailboxes and looked Gerlof in the eye once more.

'We've met,' he said. 'But it was a long time ago.'

He spoke with an Öland accent, but there was a hint of something else there. Gerlof held out his hand.

'My name is Davidsson, Gerlof Davidsson.'

The man shook his hand.

'OK, now I remember,' he said. 'Gerlof . . . we went out fishing one evening in your beautiful boat.'

'She's not so beautiful these days.' Gerlof suddenly found the memory he was searching for. 'And you're a Swedish-American, aren't you?'

The man nodded.

'More American than Swedish, though. My name is Bill Carlson, and I'm from Lansing in Michigan. My cousin is Arne Carlson in Långvik . . . I'm visiting his kids this summer.'

He fell silent and glanced over at the mailboxes again. Gerlof realized that not all Americans were talkative.

'I used to know Arne well,' he said. 'Welcome home, Bill.'

'I've never lived here,' the American said, looking almost embarrassed. 'My father emigrated from Öland when he was young. But we spoke Swedish at home, and I usually come over to see the family every five years or so. But there aren't many of them left. I was just looking at the names on these mailboxes, but I hardly recognize any . . .'

'You're not the only one,' Gerlof reassured him. 'So many new people come to the island in the summer these days . . . And you never see hide nor hair of them for the rest of the year.' He nodded in the direction of the maypole. 'Are you coming to listen to the music?'

'Absolutely,' said the American. 'The song about the little frogs is my favourite!'

They set off together, with Bill taking long strides and Gerlof following as best he could. He struggled to keep up so that they could continue the conversation.

'How old are you, Bill – if you don't mind my asking?'

'Almost eighty-six. But I don't feel a day over seventy.'

Gerlof envied the ease with which Bill made his way over the grass. He found sprightly folk who were older than him a little difficult. Some people just never seemed to get *old*.

Lisa

Lisa slept badly the night before the trip, because Silas had gone out during the evening and hadn't come back until dawn. In the summer he stayed out longer, and lived rough. When Lisa got out of bed at seven o'clock in the morning, it looked as if a pile of rags was lying on the sofa.

She tiptoed past without saying anything. There was no point. She packed quietly, locked the door behind her without a sound. No goodbyes. Silas would ring her soon in any case. Silas always rang her.

The old Passat was parked on the street. The lock was as useless as the rest of the car, so she kept her guitar and her records in the apartment. She stowed them in the boot and set off, heading south.

She had played almost every weekend over the past year, and had got used to driving, so she put her foot down once she hit the main road. However, only an hour or so after leaving Stockholm, she became aware of an acrid smell, like burnt rubber or something equally alarming.

Shit. But she was late for the midsummer gig, and she just had to hope the car would make it. She kept on going, blinking and yawning.

Lisa could never get to sleep when she was waiting for Silas. And the nights were too light as well. The summer heat was lovely, but she didn't like it when the line between day and night became blurred.

The southbound traffic was heavy and slow; the midsummer revellers who were on the road now were seriously late. There were a lot of them, and they didn't have much patience.

On the coast road down to Kalmar, Lisa glimpsed the island out in the Baltic several times, like a long, black strip on the horizon, and it was frustrating that the Öland bridge went over to the southern end of the island when she wanted to be in the north. She would have to drive down, then back up again.

Eventually, she reached the long, high bridge across the Sound. She had been here on a school trip fifteen years ago when she was only ten; it was cool to be back.

There was a solid line of cars on the bridge, like a shimmering ribbon, and as Lisa pulled up, the smell from the engine quickly got worse.

The bridge was one of the longest in Europe, and it certainly felt like it today as the traffic edged along. The waves glittered far below as the sun blazed down on the tarmac. She hoped her vinyl records wouldn't melt in the heat. Surely things couldn't get any worse.

She was wrong. As the car began the climb to the highest point of the bridge, the engine started smoking.

She clutched the wheel and took her foot off the accelerator. The car stopped dead, right in the middle of the traffic. There was nowhere to pull off the road, and soon the cars behind her were sounding their horns. It was midsummer, and ten thousand people had decided to go over to the island at the same time. Every single one of them just wanted to get there.

The sun burned in through the windows, the inside of the car grew hotter and hotter, and Lisa hadn't thought to bring any water or soft drinks. All she had was chewing gum.

What should she do? Turn around and forget about Öland?

A traffic cop on a motorbike rode up between the cars and pulled into the gap that had appeared when Lisa stopped halfway up the hill.

Fuck. She lowered her head and hoped he would keep on going.

He didn't, of course. He got off his bike and knocked on the window. She wound it down.

'You can't stop here,' he said.

'I don't want to stop here,' she said, nodding towards the bonnet. 'Something's wrong under there.'

'With the engine?' He sniffed the air. 'I can smell burning.'

'Me too . . .'

'It's probably the clutch. You've been overdoing it on the way up the hill.' He pointed to the other side of the bridge. 'It's OK to drive, but pull off at the first car park and let the engine cool down. You'll find some of my colleagues over there – they'll help you out.'

Lisa nodded. She had held a driving licence for five years, but felt like a complete novice as she put the car in gear and gently pressed the accelerator to rejoin the queue of traffic.

She felt much better once she had passed the highest point and was on her way downhill. The acrid, burning smell was still powerful inside the car, but when she opened the window the stench of exhaust fumes came pouring in instead. The queue of vehicles and caravans stretched the entire length of the bridge, and was moving at roughly the same speed as a rowing boat. It was almost twelve thirty. The gig in Stenvik started at two – under normal circumstances, she would have had plenty of time.

It took twenty-five minutes to cover the seven kilometres over the bridge and to reach the island, but the traffic jam continued on the other side. Lisa spotted a large car park on the right and turned off the road.

There wasn't much room – the police were there, just as the traffic cop had said, and had stopped several cars. Most were small and battered, with very young drivers and passengers who had been asked to get out and open the boot.

Lisa got out and opened the bonnet. God, it stank. The engine was red-hot and ticking angrily, but at least there wasn't any smoke now. She would wait for a little while before setting off again; that would give her an hour before the gig.

After a while, a police officer came over to the car. She was younger than the cop on the bridge, probably around thirty; she was tanned and wearing a short-sleeved shirt.

'Problems?'

Lisa nodded.

'But I think it's just temporary . . . Apparently, the clutch needs to cool down.'

'Good – we need all the space we can get. We're pulling in a lot of cars.'

'Is it a speed check?'

'No. Booze.'

'Booze?'

The officer nodded over towards an old red Volvo estate. Three lads a few years younger than Lisa were unloading box after box of bottles of wine from the boot, under the watchful eye of two policemen. None of them looked particularly happy.

'People bring too much alcohol with them at midsummer,' the officer said. 'If they're under age, or seem to be bootleggers, we confiscate it.'

'Do they get it back?'

'No, I'm afraid we pour it all away.' She looked at Lisa's car. 'How does it seem now?'

Lisa sniffed, but she couldn't smell burning any more. Just exhaust fumes.

'I think I can probably risk it . . . Do you know if the traffic eases off as you head north?'

'Not so you'd notice. It is midsummer, after all.'

'I know,' Lisa said.

She rejoined the queue; a friendly caravan driver braked to let her in. The traffic was moving a little faster, but still at only fifty kilometres an hour. She wouldn't gain much time if she tried overtaking; all she could do was relax and try to enjoy the summer weather.

Try to forget about Silas for a while.

It took her almost forty minutes to reach Borgholm, where a lot of cars turned off. After that, Lisa was able to increase her speed, but by then she had only fifteen minutes to go before she was due on stage.

She consoled herself with the thought that she was only the accompanist. Of course, she would have preferred not to play her guitar at the dance at all – she had given up children's parties and corporate events several years ago – but she needed the money.

At four minutes to two, she turned off the main road and drove down towards the village. The festival site was right by the road, almost at the water's edge, and it was easy to find: the maypole had been raised on the grass, and the audience had gathered.

Lisa jumped out of the car, took a deep breath of sea air, grabbed her guitar – which was no doubt out of tune by now, thanks to the heat, but would have to do – and ran towards the maypole. It must have been set up that morning, because the birch leaves were still bright green in the sunshine. The two flower garlands beneath the crossbar were dancing in the wind, high above the heads of well-dressed children and adults.

Everyone looked horribly cheerful. A load of rich people in the country. Lisa quickly made her way through the crowd.

'Excuse me . . . excuse me . . .'

She held the guitar by the neck in front of her, almost like a cudgel, and people jumped and moved out of the way when she gave them a shove.

Two older men were waiting on the far side of the pole, one holding a microphone, the other with an enormous accordion resting on his belly. They both nodded to her as she arrived.

'Aha, here's our accompanist . . . Are you Lisa Turesson?'

She nodded, looped the guitar around her neck and took a plectrum out of her pocket. She ran it over the strings and quickly tuned up. That would have to do.

'We start at two o'clock,' the accordionist said. 'You knew that, I presume?'

Lisa stared at him from beneath her fringe.

'There was a traffic jam on the bridge.'

'You should have set off in plenty of time,' the singer said. He looked at her guitar. 'Ready?'

'Absolutely.'

He raised the microphone, every trace of irritation gone.

'Good afternoon, everybody! Can you hear me? Excellent, in that case let me welcome both young and old to Stenvik's midsummer celebrations. I'm Sune, and Gunnar and Lisa will be accompanying me today. We're going to sing and play so that you can all dance before you go home and eat your herring and potatoes. Does that sound good?'

A few voices answered, 'Yeesss . . .'

'Good, then take one another by the hand. Don't be shy now!'

People did as they were told, linking together like a living chain.

'We're starting off with "The Priest's Little Crow" . . .' He looked at Lisa. '. . . the song about the poor bird who went out for a drive but ended up in the ditch. Is everyone ready?'

50

Sune counted them in, and Gunnar and Lisa began to play. People started dancing around the maypole, slowly at first, then faster and faster.

Summer had arrived, and Lisa was earning money.

Gerlof

Everyone was dancing around the maypole. The cult of the sun had begun. Gerlof was sitting on his chair on the grass, wondering if all this wasn't in fact too late. The summer solstice had fallen four days ago so, technically, the autumn was closer than the spring at this stage, and the darkness closer than the light.

But the sun and the summer were being celebrated anyway, and Gerlof saw many smiling faces beneath the garlands. Several hundred people of all ages were moving in wide circles around the maypole.

Gerlof couldn't dance; he sat on his chair with stiff legs, thinking longingly of the smorgasbord to come, the herring and potatoes and schnapps. But there was a good atmosphere; he enjoyed listening to the music and watching the people.

He was particularly pleased to see Julia dancing. She had stayed away from Öland for a long time, after her young son disappeared without a trace. Gerlof had brooded about the tragedy for many years and, eventually, he had solved the mystery. One man had ended up in prison and, at long last, Julia had been able to move on, together with a new husband and his children.

Many of the dancers were strangers to him, but Gerlof did recognize the Kloss family, the owners of the Ölandic Resort. They were standing slightly apart, on the edge of the festival site, and they weren't dancing. Kent Kloss often appeared in the newspaper, pontificating about the importance of tourism to the island. His younger brother, Niklas, was next to him, wearing jeans and a T-shirt.

Their sister Veronica was there too, in a white dress, her chestnut locks flowing. Gerlof hadn't seen her since last year, when she gave a talk about the Kloss family history in the common room up at the home in Marnäs. She had made the men in the audience – Gerlof included – smile, their eyes sparkling, even though some of them were over ninety. Veronica Kloss was tall and imposing. She could easily have stood on a palace balcony, waving to the masses.

The children were there too today, all boys, just as suntanned as their parents.

Bill Carlson reappeared, wandering around and clicking away in all directions with his camera. Finally, he came over to Gerlof, grinning from ear to ear.

'Could anything be more Swedish than this?'

'Swedish?' Gerlof said with a little smile. 'Don't tell Anders Zorn or Carl Larsson, but this is a German festival.'

'Really?'

'Originally, yes. German bowmen used a maypole for target practice, before it was adorned with spring flowers. Then the German merchants brought the idea of a flower-clad pole over to Sweden . . . But most of our flowers don't come out until June, so the celebration was moved back a month.'

'Well, there you go,' Bill said. 'From warfare to flower power.'

'That's what happens sometimes.'

'So you read a lot of history, Gerlof? It's something that interests you?'

'Yes. My own history and that of others.'

Gerlof glanced over at the Kloss family again. They looked relaxed but, for them and the rest of the tourist industry, this was the weekend when everything got under way, for six weeks from midsummer onwards. Tourism on Öland was like a Bengal fire that burned only in the summer, brief but intense.

The dancing went on for half an hour and ended with an exploding 'rocket'. Everyone gathered around the pole, clapping their hands, stamping their feet and whooping up into the sky and jumping as high as they could to simulate a rocket. They did this three times, and then the party was over.

The circles broke up and people started heading home. Gerlof had no responsibilities, as his daughters were taking care of everything, but he remembered his vow to be polite to strangers, and looked up at his new acquaintance, Bill from America.

'Are you cycling back up to Långvik, Bill?'

'Yes. Home for the smorgasbord.'

'Would you care for a little something before you set off? A glass of wormwood schnapps, maybe?'

'Can I take a raincheck on that?' Bill said. 'Strong drink goes straight to my head these days, and that road is full of potholes . . .'

Gerlof nodded.

'Another time, then.'

They kept each other company part of the way along the coast, together with lots of other villagers who were on their way home. Gerlof saw girls picking daisies and speedwell by the roadside, in spite of the fact that, according to tradition, they should be picked after sunset to bring the best possible luck.

Midsummer's Eve was the long day when everything was supposed to happen but very little actually did. There was love in the air, the youngsters' love for one another and the older people's love for nature, but it was often swept away overnight.

Bill and Gerlof parted company at the northern end of the road leading to the village.

'Give me your phone number,' Gerlof said. 'We're fixing up the boat, so we might manage a fishing trip towards the end of the summer.'

'Great. And there are more old Americans here on the island who would love to come along, if there's room.'

'Possibly,' Gerlof said. 'But when it comes to groups, Bill . . . I think I prefer birds.'

Lisa

After half an hour, the celebrations were over. They finished off with the song about the three old ladies from Nora, then all the children had to scream as loudly as they could, pretending to be rockets shooting off into the sky.

Then everybody let out a long breath and set off home. The only trace of the dance was wide circles of trampled-down grass around the maypole. Lisa took off her guitar and relaxed.

'Well done,' Sune said.

'Thanks.'

He nodded in the direction of the village bar and restaurant.

'I hear you're playing there this summer?'

'A few times, yes, but mostly down at the Ölandic Resort.'

That reminded her of something important. 'What about the money?'

'Money?'

'Who do I talk to about getting paid?'

'Not us,' Sune said quickly. 'Talk to Kloss.'

Lisa recognized the name; someone called Kloss had booked her through the agency.

'Veronica or Kent,' Sune went on. 'They're over there.'

Lisa saw a group of four adults and four teenage boys on the far side of the maypole. They looked just as happy as all the other families who had been there.

She went to put the guitar back in her car. She had calmed down now, after racing against the clock to get here. She was free now; no more music today.

Just the money, Silas whispered in her head.

The Kloss family were waiting. She went over to them, directing her biggest smile at the woman nearest to her.

'Veronica Kloss? I'm Lisa Turesson – you called me last week . . .'

The woman looked anxious and held up a defensive hand.

'Not me,' she said. 'I am not fru Kloss. I am Paulina.'

Her Swedish was hesitant; she sounded Eastern European. Foreign cleaner, Lisa thought, then wished she hadn't.

The other woman in the group stepped forward. She was in her forties, but her face was unlined. She had attractive dimples.

'Hi, Lisa,' she said. 'I'm Veronica. Well done – thank you!'

'You're welcome,' Lisa said, taking a deep breath. 'I was just wondering about the money?'

'We'll sort that out. You're going to play some more, aren't you? In our restaurant and the nightclub?'

Lisa nodded quickly.

'I'm here until the end of July, but I could do with some cash to be going on with . . .'

'Of course,' Veronica said. She took out her purse and handed over two notes, without asking for a receipt.

Meanwhile, one of the men had come over to Lisa.

'Kent Kloss – welcome to the village,' he said. 'Would you like to join us at the house for a Cosmo?'

'Sorry?'

'A Cosmopolitan on our patio?'

Kent Kloss was wearing shorts and a T-shirt, just like the teenagers, and Lisa thought it was hard to make a guess at his age. His face was that of a middle-aged man, but he was smiling like a boy.

'No, thanks,' Lisa said. 'Best not. I'm driving.'

'So?' Kloss said. 'It's a holiday!'

Lisa put on her best professional smile.

'Thanks, anyway.'

Veronica Kloss took a key out of her pocket and pointed in the direction of the water.

'You're staying down there, on the campsite. We have a number of static caravans for our staff, right by the water. It's a little primitive, but there's no charge . . . and the view is fantastic. Is that OK?'

'Brilliant,' Lisa said.

But as she walked back to the car she was overcome with tiredness.

A static caravan. She had been hoping for a little red chalet by the sea, pretty and cosy.

But, of course, the campsite in Stenvik was just metres from the shore, and the views were stunning.

As she drove in she saw tents and caravans, but there was also a kind of wildness about the place. Campsites were usually neat and well planned, with large, rectangular grass plots, but this was stony and uneven, with lots of bushes and undergrowth. There were no straight roads; the tents and caravans were all over the shop, standing on their own or in groups. Many were old and faded by the sun; a few were new, protected by wooden fences.

She found her way easily following Veronica's directions and arrived at an old-style caravan, white and rounded, with no fence. It was far from new, but at least it appeared to be clean and rust-free.

She unlocked the door and looked inside. It wasn't very big: one room with a kitchen area, with a small bedroom beyond, but it had definitely been cleaned. She sniffed and picked up the smell of disinfectant. No mould.

Good. She sat down on the narrow bed and took out her mobile. Time to call Silas, tell him she'd arrived and see how he was feeling.

The Homecomer

An impressive fence. Not the highest fence the Homecomer had ever seen, but very robust.

Steel posts supported a green wire mesh. The steel sparkled in the sun, and between each pair of posts was a yellow sign: No Unauthorized Entry.

The Homecomer took out his wooden box and slowly picked up a pinch of snuff. The warning was absurd, but the fence was worth examining. It was almost three metres high. It wasn't an electric fence but was topped with four strands of barbed wire. To the left it ran down towards the water, to the right was a dense deciduous forest.

'They haven't enclosed the whole area,' he said.

Pecka was standing beside him, just in front of his girlfriend, Rita.

'No,' Pecka said. 'Kloss has only fenced off the things he wants to protect . . . The central electricity supply and the dock.'

The Homecomer nodded.

'And what about Rödtorp?'

'What's that?'

'A little croft, south of the dock.'

'Never heard of it.' Pecka didn't sound remotely interested. 'But the fence stops just south of the dock, by the bathing area.'

'Can we get in?'

Pecka nodded.

'There's a gate down by the water, but it has a CCTV camera.'

The Homecomer looked up at the fence.

'It's too high for me.'

'We're not climbing it,' Pecka said. 'There are other openings . . . Come with me.'

He set off among the trees and headed east. It was difficult to get through the undergrowth, but Rita and the Homecomer followed him.

The Homecomer had his gun with him, tucked into the waistband of his trousers.

After perhaps sixty paces they reached a small glade; there was a steel gate in the fence. It was locked, but Pecka pulled a key out of his pocket. He smiled.

'I "forgot" to hand this in last year when they kicked me out.'

He unlocked the gate, and all they had to do was walk through.

Pecka raised a hand; it was time to be quiet. It was obvious that he knew the area; he walked straight through the trees and led them to a path. He chose the right-hand fork.

The further they got into the forest, the more cautious Pecka became. He moved slowly, and seemed to be listening all the time. He kept on going, and after a few minutes the Homecomer heard a faint rushing sound. He glimpsed the water through the trees.

The sea, and an open area covered in tarmac.

'This is the dock,' Pecka whispered.

He and Rita stopped, but the Homecomer kept on going, past the tarmac and on through the forest. The path led through trees and dense undergrowth, and he was astonished – he recognized this place from his childhood, and yet he didn't.

The trees were new, but the earth and the water and the smells were the same.

Suddenly, he heard the sound of breaking glass beneath his boot.

A piece of an old windowpane.

He looked up and saw the space just twenty metres away. Everything had been cleared.

This was the spot. This was where the croft had stood. But a giant appeared to have stamped all over it, brushed the bits and pieces to one side, then moved on.

The Homecomer looked at what was left for a little while, then backed away. That was enough.

He turned around and increased his speed – and almost bumped into the other two. Pecka and Rita were crouching down in the undergrowth; Pecka was holding a pair of binoculars and looking in the direction of the dock.

The Homecomer saw that there was a small cargo boat moored by the quayside; it looked rusty, possibly abandoned. But then he noticed movement on deck. People were moving around by the hatches leading to the hold, and on the bridge.

'We know their schedule,' Rita said. 'They've brought goods ashore for the past two days, and she sails straight after midsummer.'

The Homecomer didn't say anything, but Pecka nodded.

'That's when we'll do it.'

They carried on watching the boat in the middle of a cloud of buzzing flies, but the Homecomer couldn't forget the remnants of his childhood, deep in the forest.

The New Country, June 1931

The flies are buzzing inside the carriage, the wind is strong as they speed along, and the train whistle blows. Aron has watched the trains crossing the alvar all his life, but he has never been on one. It's a real adventure, chugging across the island just a few carriages behind the engine, straight through the flat landscape. A journey through emptiness, through the grassy plain that is the alvar, but it's still exciting. Aron sticks his head out of the window, feeling the wind in his hair. The steam train is moving faster than the odd cars and buses he sees on the road.

Sometimes they travel past a barn, which brings back memories of last summer, when the barn wall collapsed and everything went quiet in the darkness.

The wall had fallen to reveal a black gap underneath, like the opening of an underground crypt. Aron had stood stock still, staring at it. Then Sven had placed a hand on his back and given him a shove.

'*In you go,*' Sven had growled, sweaty and stressed. '*Get in there and fetch his money.*'

Aron had done as he was told. He had lain down on the grass and wriggled under the wall.

Into the darkness. He had crawled in over the cold ground, in under the hard, wooden wall. A nail had scratched his forehead, but he had ducked and kept on going.

Towards the body.

Edvard Kloss, lying there under the wall.

Trapped. Motionless.

Aron shudders in the cold wind as he gazes out of the train window. He doesn't want to remember that night.

But the farms alongside the railway line don't seem to bother Sven. When he sees the farmhands working by the barns, he raises a hand and waves.

'Do you know them?' Aron asks.

'No, but all workers are my brothers. They, too, will be liberated from their back-breaking toil one day!'

After Kalleguta, the railway turns sharply to the west, towards the station in Borgholm. Outside the town the sea appears once again, like a blue ribbon in the west. Aron has never travelled on the ferry to the mainland either; he has never crossed the Sound.

When they arrive they alight from the train at the big stone building, then wander through the straight streets. The black-suited residents of the town glance at Aron and Sven's simple clothes as they pass by. Aron can hear them speaking quietly behind them.

'They were gossiping about me,' Sven says. 'They know who I am.'

'Do they?'

Sven nods, his lips compressed into a thin line.

'They haven't forgotten my quarrels with those who were out to exploit the poor.'

They carry on down towards the harbour, where a dozen or so small cargo boats and a couple of ferries are moored, with a large yacht in solitary splendour slightly further away.

In the restaurant they each have an omelette, which costs two kronor and fifty öre. Sven has a glass of beer, Aron a soft drink.

After the meal Sven takes a pinch of snuff from his wooden box, the one Aron gave him, and stares gloomily at the bill for lunch. He shakes his head, but pays.

'In the new country you can eat for free,' he says when they are back on the street.

'Really?'

'Absolutely. You pay only if you have money.'

In the afternoon they leave the island, crossing the Sound on a steamship. Sven keeps his eyes firmly fixed on the mainland, but Aron turns around and watches as the island slowly shrinks to a greyish-brown strip on the horizon. He feels as if it is sinking into the sea, as if his whole world is disappearing behind him.

Jonas

Over the past two years Jonas had forgotten how brilliant it was to wake up by the sea. It was a bit like being an astronaut, waking up on a strange planet where the sounds and the air were different.

On Midsummer's Day, he opened his eyes to the sound of the wind and the cries of the gulls, bumble bees buzzing around the house and bikes rattling by out on the coast road – and, beyond that, the faint rushing of the waves out in the Sound.

Villa Kloss, he thought.

The sounds were strange, yet familiar. Jonas was back in a summer world where his father had brought him ever since he was a little boy. But now he was grown up. Almost. He was nearly twelve years old and no longer slept in Uncle Kent's big house with his dad but in a little chalet of his own twenty metres away. A guest chalet, consisting of nothing more than a narrow room with white walls and a white wooden floor. His older brother, Mats, and cousin Casper were staying in the other two chalets, but he had this one all to himself for the next four weeks.

Aunt Veronica, his father's sister, had helped him make up the bed, bringing a faint hint of perfume with her along with the sheets.

Veronica had been wearing a white dress, and had the same bright-blue eyes as his father. Jonas was fond of his aunt, but he hadn't seen her for almost two years. He hadn't come over last year, and Veronica hadn't had time to come and visit them in Huskvarna. Jonas had a feeling that Veronica and his mother didn't particularly like each other.

'This is your very own space,' Veronica had said when they had finished making the bed. 'Nobody to disturb you – that will be nice, won't it?'

It was lovely. Jonas had slept, and nobody had disturbed him.

He sat up in bed and looked out of the window. He could see water – the pale-blue swimming pool was only ten metres away.

On the other side of the coast road, the dark-blue Sound sparkled at the bottom of the steep cliffs.

And up there on top of the cliffs, almost at the very end of the plateau, lay the old cairn. The big, rounded grave made of stones, which was haunted. But not now, not when the sun was shining.

Jonas jumped out of bed.

All he could hear were the faint sounds of summer. No voices. When he fell asleep last night, the rest of the family had still been awake, celebrating the shortest night of the year in various ways: Mats and his cousins had gone down to the jetty to see if there were any girls around, Jonas's father had been working as a chef in the village restaurant, which was also owned by the Kloss family, and Aunt Veronica and Uncle Kent had been sitting on the decking together with Veronica's husband, who was on a flying visit from Stockholm, and Kent's new girlfriend, whose name Jonas didn't know. Uncle Kent had had a new girlfriend every summer, ever since Jonas could remember. They didn't say much, and they didn't usually stay around for long.

Jonas had been too tired to stay up. He had gone to bed at about ten, and fallen asleep to distant music, quiet voices and loud laughter.

This morning he pulled on his shorts and a thin T-shirt, opened the glass door and went out into the sunshine. It was only eight o'clock, but it was already hot.

The two plots that made up this part of Villa Kloss extended around him, covered in stones, the odd juniper bush and viper's bugloss. His father used to own the third plot at the southern end, but that was several years ago, before he got involved in some business that didn't go too well. His summer cottage had been sold, and Jonas noticed that the new owners had put up a fence to separate the place from Villa Kloss.

He was hungry, and hoped there would be something to eat in Uncle Kent's kitchen.

A wide, gravelled path led past the pool to the main house. The water looked warm and clear, but hardly anyone ever swam in it. The adults never seemed to have time, and Jonas thought it was more fun to go down to the shore. It was somehow wilder down there, with flat rocks and seaweed and tiny shrimps swimming around your legs.

He went up the steps to the wooden decking at the front of the house. This would be Jonas's workplace for the next few weeks, along with Veronica's decking. His job was to sand down all the planks, then oil them. His wages would be thirty-five kronor an hour. That was a lot of money – Jonas had said yes straight away.

Uncle Kent's house was long and wide, with huge panoramic windows at the front. There was also a sliding glass door; Jonas pushed it to one side and went in. He had always thought that walking into this cool room felt like stepping into the command module in a huge spaceship. Not that he had ever done such a thing, but this was what it ought to look like: a rectangular room with enormous windows and electronic gadgets everywhere. There were rows of tiny lights on the ceiling and an impressive stereo next to an even bigger TV, both connected to black speakers built into the wall.

Kent's golf bag was on the right, next to a treadmill, and beyond that lay the entrance to the kitchen, which was every bit as shiny and metallic as the living room. Various things were humming and flashing in there.

Uncle Kent had employed a young housekeeper from Russia or Poland this summer; she was standing by the worktop, where she had laid out an array of breakfast food: bread, butter, juice, eggs, fruit and four kinds of cereal.

Jonas stared. He was glad he was alone right now, because back home in Huskvarna he always had to wait until Mats had finished helping himself. Now he could just dive right in. He picked up a blue bowl, filled it with cornflakes and milk and sat down on the biggest of Uncle Kent's black leather sofas. He had a fantastic view of the coast from here: the stony garden, the coast road, the sea and the burial cairn up on the edge of the cliff.

After about fifteen minutes the sliding door opened and Aunt Veronica came in.

'Good morning, Jonas. Did you sleep well?'

She was already dressed, in a black business suit and red shoes.

Jonas chewed, swallowed and nodded.

'Mmm.'

'Are Kent and Niklas here?'

'I haven't seen anyone,' Jonas replied.

'I expect they're out jogging,' Veronica said with a smile.

In the winter Veronica lived in Stockholm with Urban, who was eighteen, and Casper, who was fifteen, and their father, but in the summer she lived here at Villa Kloss; she was the managing director of the Ölandic Resort. She never took any time off during the period when the complex was open, from the end of May to the beginning of September.

'So what are you going to do today, Jonas? Do you have any plans for the summer?'

He looked out at the wooden decking and nodded.

'I'm going to make a start on rubbing down the decking.'

'Not today. It's Midsummer's Day, and almost everyone is off work. You, too, Jonas. You're on holiday.'

That sounded good.

Holiday, Jonas thought. Not a break from school. He hadn't even started work yet, but he was already on *holiday*, like a grown-up.

Lisa

The Ölandic Resort was a couple of kilometres south of Stenvik and was owned by the Kloss family. Lisa was also working at the resort this summer, and she drove down there at lunchtime to get things ready.

At the entrance there was a reception booth and a barrier, and a CCTV camera. She could feel the cold lens staring at her as she wound down the window and gave her name to the security guard, but everything was fine. The barrier was raised and she drove on to a tarmac road, past rows of tents and caravans, down towards the sea and the gleaming white Ölandic Hotel.

It was Midsummer's Day, the day after the big party. But of course every night was party night at the Ölandic – at least it was in the nightclub in the hotel basement. Two DJs and two cover bands would be working there in shifts right through July, from early evening until late into the night.

This evening was Lady Summertime's debut, and Lisa wanted to make sure everything went well.

The Ölandic Resort was a custom-built holiday complex with straight roads and huge lawns. The contrast with the little campsite in Stenvik was striking. The Ölandic was a place for thousands of summer visitors to gather in the sun, on the beach, on the golf course, in the hotel and in the nightclub. But as Lisa drove down towards the water she didn't see many people, and those she did see looked as if they were sleepwalking. People were probably having a lie-in, or sunbathing down on the shore, beyond the dense deciduous forest.

She parked in front of the hotel. It was four storeys high, built on the slope above the beach. The hotel had the best view in the resort, the summer cottages the next best, and the campsite lay furthest away from the sea.

Lisa picked up her CDs and LPs and went inside; the reception area was cool, with goldfish swimming around in a large aquarium on the limestone floor. Two blonde receptionists, both in their twenties and wearing pale-blue blouses, were on duty behind the desk.

The one nearest to Lisa smiled, and Lisa introduced herself.

'Oh, so you're Lady Summertime. The club's downstairs.'

She led the way, but didn't offer to carry any of Lisa's records.

A red neon sign above the door read 'MAY LAI BAR'. The club beyond the cloakroom was large, with tables on the right and a bar made of dark wood running the entire length of the left-hand wall. There wasn't a soul in sight, but there was a good variety of drinks on the shelves, and green champagne bottles ready and waiting in a glass fridge.

'The calm before the storm,' the receptionist said.

'So does this place get stormy in the evenings?' Lisa asked.

'Well, people do like to let rip . . . It's full every night in July. Quite a few kids with rich parents come here, with a sports car of their own and Daddy's credit card.'

Lisa nodded; she knew the type.

The DJ booth was near the door, next to a wide glass door leading out on to the seafront. The dance floor looked freshly mopped, black and shining, but a faint smell of perspiration and alcohol still lingered.

'Have you got "Summer Is Short"?' the receptionist asked.

Lisa looked blank.

'Tomas Ledin,' the girl said. '"Summer Is Short". Do you play that one?'

'Sometimes.'

Lisa much preferred Daft Punk's "Around The World", but she knew that the old classics brought people in.

The booth was locked, but the receptionist had a bunch of keys. She handed one of them over to Lisa.

'Just say the word if you need anything.'

'Thanks.'

Lisa unlocked the door, went inside and checked out the equipment. The turntables were Technics SL 1200; they looked as if they'd been through some tough times, but the Pioneer mixer desk looked brand new. There was an effects panel which would allow her to control a small light show over the dance floor, complete with glitter ball, and even a cordless microphone for shout-outs.

'We've got a smoke machine, too,' the receptionist said, pointing to a button close to the floor.

'Excellent,' Lisa said. She loved special effects.

The booth was raised above the dance floor, a bit like a pulpit, but it was just as cramped as all the others she had worked in. A sheet of Plexiglas at the front protected her from the public and any alcohol that might be splashing around.

'What about security?' she asked.

'We've got guards here 24/7 in the summer,' the receptionist said. 'In the evenings they move between the hotel and the club. There's an alarm button over by the bar if things kick off.'

'Great.'

'Make yourself at home,' the receptionist said, and headed back up the stairs.

Lisa placed her records and CDs on the floor behind the Plexiglas, then locked the booth and went over to the glass door to have a look outside.

The door was like a wide fire exit or an escape route – which was good. She slid it open and stepped out into the summer heat. The sea air rushed towards her from the sparkling Sound, carrying with it the faint smell of seaweed.

On the large wooden deck there were more tables and metal chairs arranged around a large barbecue made of metal and stone; there was also a bar decorated with bamboo. There was no one in sight, but many of the tables already had a RESERVED notice on them.

Immediately below the hotel she saw a sandy beach in an inlet extending south. To the north there was a verdant deciduous forest, with a low stone wall in front of it. The wall was topped with tightly stretched barbed wire.

A flight of stone steps led down to the lawn in front of the hotel, where croquet hoops had been set up. Lisa walked down past the croquet lawn, and went over to the forest and the wall.

Fences and walls always made her curious. She could see nothing but a dense wall of low trees and tangled bushes, so why the need for barbed wire?

Cautiously, she grabbed hold of the wire and pulled it up so that she could wriggle underneath. First her legs, then the rest of her body. The wire seemed keen to shred the back of her head, but she managed to squeeze through and jump down on the other side of the wall.

Now she was in the forbidden forest. It looked old, with lichen-covered ash trees and gnarled oaks among younger birch and elder. An enchanted forest waiting for a princess, for Lady Summertime.

She was only intending to go a short distance. There was a narrow track leading away from the wall – possibly made by hares or deer – and Lisa took a few tentative steps along it. Then she stopped and took a deep breath.

It was so quiet here. Dark and peaceful, with the muted sound of birdsong and the hum of various insects. She carried on down the track, and when she looked back she could no longer see the hotel. The wall she had climbed over was barely visible through the foliage. Forests on the island weren't tall or extensive but dense and thick with undergrowth; they could hide just about anything.

She heard a twig snap up ahead. It was very distinct, definitely not the product of her imagination, but she couldn't see any movement. Everything around her was green and brown, leaves and branches trembling in the gentle breeze.

The narrow track gradually widened, and after perhaps fifty metres it ended in a glade with tall, overgrown grass. Lisa stepped out into the light and screwed up her eyes as she turned her face up to the sun. It was almost at its zenith now. She could hear splashing and cheerful shouts from the beach to the south.

The Swedish summer. Tomas Ledin was right, it was short, but that made it all the more intense. Lisa was a city girl; she had grown up in Farsta in a family that didn't own a summer cottage, but a vague, almost atavistic longing for a rural community had attracted her to the job on Öland for this summer season.

And the money, of course.

When she looked down at the grass she noticed wide grooves – deep tyre tracks. A large, heavy machine had driven through this ancient forest, straight across the glade and over to the trees on the far side.

70

A small building had once stood there, but the machine must have driven right into it, because now there was nothing left but the foundations and a few grey planks of wood.

Beyond the ruin she saw more trees, and further away the sun glinted on the sea; there was a small beach and a few boulders protruding into the water to form a narrow jetty.

A lost idyll. The family that had lived here once upon a time would have been able to go down for a swim every day . . .

'What are you doing here?' said a voice behind her.

Lisa turned around. A young man was standing in the middle of the glade, staring at her.

He was wearing a black peaked cap, and a shirt and trousers in the same shade of blue as the receptionists' uniform up at the hotel. He was tall and thin; his forehead was covered in sweat as he strode towards her. Lisa noticed a black two-way radio clipped to his belt, and realized that he was one of the guards. Young and determined.

Lisa had nothing against security guards, but Lady Summertime, the rebel within her, didn't like them. *Uniforms* – sooooo boring.

'What am I doing?' she said, staring right back at him. 'I work here.'

'Where?'

'At the Ölandic Resort.'

'Do you?'

'I'm a DJ at the May Lai Bar.'

The guard stopped a metre away from her.

'Oh? I haven't seen you before.'

'It's my first day,' Lisa said. 'I start tonight – Lady Summertime. Do you want to see my ID?'

He stared at her for a little while longer, then shook his head. 'I just wanted to . . .'

Then he glanced over her shoulder and froze. 'Shit, there's somebody else . . .'

He fell silent, and Lisa turned around. At first she couldn't see anything apart from leaves and shimmering water, but then she saw a shadow against the dazzling sunlight. Someone was standing motionless on the jetty, his back to the beach. An old man in a fisherman's jumper, straight-backed and sturdy.

Lisa looked at the guard. 'Can I go?'

71

He glanced at her, then nodded reluctantly. 'OK. Go back to the hotel. You shouldn't be here.'

'This is part of the resort, isn't it?'

'It's private property – it belongs to the Kloss family.'

'I see,' Lisa said.

She had nothing more to say to him, and left the glade without another word. When she looked back for the last time she saw that he was on his way down to the sea and the old man, striding out as before.

Fascist, she thought.

She returned to the track, squeezed carefully under the barbed wire and over the wall, and was back at the hotel.

The glass door was still ajar. She decided to go in and make sure she'd locked the booth before she went back to the caravan to call Silas and grab a few hours' rest before tonight's debut as Lady Summertime.

Just as she was about to step inside, she thought she heard something behind her, a short, sharp noise from the forest. An old oak tree coming down? A firework? Lisa stopped in the doorway for a moment, but she didn't hear anything else.

She went in and closed the glass door behind her.

The Homecomer

The Homecomer was standing out on the makeshift jetty when the guard turned up. The boulders from his childhood, arranged in a row stretching out from the shore – but of course it was a mistake to walk out on to them. It made him too visible, too vulnerable.

He had longed to stand here by this narrow sandy shore almost every day while he was overseas, had dreamed of coming back and walking right to the very end of the jetty. His croft up in the forest was gone, but Kloss couldn't erase these rocks.

He had sat among the trees for a while, watching the Ölandic dock with Pecka, his young recruit, but the flies had been a nuisance and his leg had gone to sleep. Eventually, he had left the protection of the forest and gone down to the sea, with the Walther still tucked into the waistband of his trousers at the back. He had made sure the safety catch was on.

Tentatively, he made his way along the boulders, and for a few moments he had allowed himself to be drawn back to his childhood, although he didn't leap from rock to rock like a boy; he took the slow steps of an old man.

Twelve steps, and the Homecomer was standing on the very last boulder. He straightened his back and gazed out across the empty Sound.

The sun was shining, but the water around him was dark and full of shadows; the bright light barely reached the sandy seabed. However, when he looked north he could clearly see the black ship that Pecka had been watching. It was still moored in the dock, and the crew were working flat out. They seemed to be carrying plastic boxes of fish from the ship to a delivery van on the quayside.

In the other direction, to the south, he could hear the sound of the Ölandic's summer residents enjoying the sunshine, but the bathing area was hidden behind a spit of land. The Homecomer couldn't see them, and no one could see him.

There was an air of calm about the island. No doubt the visitors who weren't down on the shore were fast asleep in their tents and chalets, and many of those who had celebrated the shortest night of the year would wake up with gaps in their memory and trembling hands, feeling ten years older on this bright summer's day.

But the Homecomer was wide awake, and he felt good.

After a while, the van drove away from the quayside. The seamen went back on board, and the Homecomer decided it was time to leave.

'Hey! You there!'

The voice came from behind him, and he slowly turned around.

'Yes, you! This is private property!'

A young man was standing on the shore, but it wasn't Pecka. He was wearing blue trousers and a black peaked cap, and he looked like a park keeper.

'Private?' the Homecomer said, standing his ground.

The security guard nodded. 'Were you looking for someone?'

No doubt this was a question he usually asked unauthorized persons, but out here it sounded rather odd.

The Homecomer shook his head and stayed exactly where he was. He wondered whether Pecka had seen the guard.

'I used to live here when I was a boy,' he said. 'I used to stand here on the rocks catching pike with a wooden spear . . . We had a croft in the forest.'

'Right,' the guard said. 'Well, there's no croft there now.'

'No, it's been knocked down.'

The guard wasn't listening; he seemed to be pondering something.

'How did you get in here?'

'I walked.'

'Didn't you see the notices?'

'No.'

'But what about the fence? You *must* have seen the fence!'

The Homecomer shook his head – and at the same time he felt

for the pistol with his right hand. His fingers touched the butt of the Walther he had bought from Einar Wall.

'This place used to be called Rödtorp,' the Homecomer said, holding the security guard's gaze. He kept the pistol hidden behind his back as he carried on talking. 'Our cottage was small but cosy . . . my grandfather built it. I lived there with my mother, Astrid, and my sister, Greta, and my stepfather, Sven. But Sven wanted to travel to the new country, so that was what we did. We sailed from Borgholm and—'

'I'm sure you did,' the guard interrupted him, his voice hardening, 'but you need to come ashore!'

The Homecomer nodded. He set off along the rocks, but he wasn't quite so steady on his feet now.

He stopped and shook his head. 'My legs have seized up.'

'Hang on,' the guard said wearily. 'I'll give you a hand.'

He stepped on to the first rock.

The Homecomer waited for him, holding the pistol behind his back. He could hear the excited screams and joyful shouts of the holidaymakers in the distance.

The guard took five strides and reached the Homecomer.

'Put your hand on my shoulder and we'll get you back,' he said, turning away. Perhaps he was pleased at the thought of being able to help an old man.

'You're very kind,' the Homecomer said, his eyes fixed on the back of the young man's neck.

He raised the gun, slipped off the safety catch and took aim.

The guard grabbed his radio and began to turn as he heard the sound, but it was too late.

The back of his neck was unusually slender. The line where the skull ended and the vertebrae began was clearly visible.

The Homecomer fired.

The shot echoed out across the water; the guard's body convulsed and he fell sideways. Down into the water, away from the light, with a cascade of white foam all around him.

The Homecomer watched as the waters closed over the young man and the body disappeared into the darkness.

He looked around, listened. The shot had been a sharp report in the wind, short and hard, with no echo. Trees muffled the sound of a bullet being fired, as he knew very well, and there were plenty of trees around the shore.

Pecka had heard the shot. He had got to his feet among the trees and was staring open-mouthed towards the sea. Slowly, he began to move.

After ten seconds, the guard's body floated back to the surface, face up. A stream of bubbles was coming out of his mouth, and his arms were moving feebly.

Pecka appeared. He stared at the guard in the water.

'He's still alive,' he said.

The Homecomer crouched down with his arm outstretched, put the Walther under the water and fired into the guard's head, with hardly a sound.

The bubbles stopped.

Everything went quiet.

'Let's get him out,' the Homecomer said.

Pecka looked at him blankly. 'What?'

The Homecomer didn't reply. He looked around; there was no one in sight, which meant that no one had heard the shot. And if there was one thing he knew about, it was taking care of dead bodies.

He bent down and grabbed hold of the man's belt, then started hauling the body towards the shore.

'Give me a hand,' he ordered.

Pecka moved like a sleepwalker, but stepped down into the water and seized the guard's arms.

They dragged the body to the shore, then pulled it ashore and in among the trees.

'Shit,' Pecka said. 'Shit . . .'

The Homecomer wasted no time on him. He quickly ripped open the guard's shirt and removed the wet clothes.

There was an old ditch under the tangle of dog roses, just a few metres away. He got Pecka to roll away all the big stones in order to make it deeper, then they tipped the naked body into the hollow. He covered it with a thick layer of rotting bladder wrack from the shore to contain the smell of the corpse, then topped the seaweed with several layers of stones.

The Homecomer stepped back to admire their handiwork. They

had built a little burial cairn in the forest. It wasn't old like the one in Stenvik; this one was brand new.

'Have you . . . Have you done this before?' Pecka asked.

'Not here,' the Homecomer said. But he knew what would happen in the grave from now on; that was nothing new.

The birds wouldn't be able to detect the stench of the corpse, so they wouldn't start pecking at it, which was good – but the insects would soon find it. The bluebottles would buzz in among the stones in just a few hours and, since the guard wasn't wearing any clothes, they would start laying their eggs immediately. When the maggots hatched, they would be hungry. They would break down the body, work their way in until they reached the skeleton, until it no longer stank. In a few weeks all the soft parts would have dried out or disappeared, and in two months only the bones would remain.

And by that time the Homecomer would be gone.

He looked to the north through the trees, away from the grave. The ship was still at the quayside. 'Have you been keeping an eye on the ship?'

Pecka had been staring at the stones, but he gave a start and answered mechanically, 'Yes. They've all gone ashore. To the restaurant.'

'Good,' the Homecomer said. 'Let's go.'

With a final glance at the grave, he led the way into the forest, heading back towards the fence. His footsteps were light as he walked along, in spite of his age and what he had just done. He was still *capable*.

Jonas

It was morning, a lazy Sunday when nothing much seemed to be happening along the coast. Jonas was gazing out from the decking in front of Uncle Kent's house. The sun was spreading its warmth, and summer was all around him. Boats in the Sound, holidaymakers relaxing on the shore, the odd car passing by. The stony ground above the water was coloured red and blue by the petals of poppies and viper's bugloss, which were shooting up everywhere.

But something had happened. The door behind him was wide open, and he could hear Uncle Kent's voice in the middle of a phone call. His uncle usually sounded quite pleased, but today his tone was harsh and angry.

'Gone?' Kent said. 'What do you mean, gone? Was he there in the morning, or did he not turn up at all?' Pause. 'He was? So he just cleared off at some point during the day? He's done it again . . .'

Pause.

'I know. We had some trouble with him last season, but Veronica decided to give him a second chance this year. She believed in him. He promised to pull himself together, work harder. And now this . . .'

Jonas didn't want to eavesdrop, so he left the garden and went out on to the coast road. He could see the campsite just a few hundred metres to the north, and the jetty where almost everyone in the village gathered to swim and sunbathe when the weather was good. Summer visitors.

The summer visitors were lying there in the sun; the hotter it got, the more of them there were. The shore was covered with a mosaic of red, white and blue beach towels, with thermos flasks, balls, bottles and bicycle baskets scattered all around. The summer visitors had lots of stuff, but they hardly ever bothered with any of it. They went for a swim and played Frisbee, but mostly they lay motionless in the sunshine.

Jonas waved away a fly and looked in the other direction. Villa Kloss was the last house in the village, then the coast road narrowed to a dirt track. The Ölandic was a few kilometres away, with its huge campsite and luxury hotel, but the resort was hidden by a series of headlands jutting out into the sea.

Jonas crossed the road and walked out on to the plateau known as the ridge. It was covered in gravel and dropped down into a little hollow above the shore.

And right on the edge of the plateau, straight in front of Uncle Kent's house, was the rounded burial cairn. It must have been there for a thousand years.

Jonas slowed down as he reached the cairn. He had never dared to come this close when he was little – not on his own. The cairn looked like a hillock, but at close quarters you could see that it was made up of hundreds of big stones, all piled on top of one another. It had been built during the Bronze Age.

Jonas knew that there was a coffin under all those stones – but not a wooden one. One day when they were standing there studying the cairn, his father had told him that it was a sarcophagus made up of solid blocks. The stones and boulders had been piled up on top of the coffin, to protect it from grave robbers.

Suddenly, he heard a rattling sound; he stopped and turned around a few metres from the cairn and saw his cousin Casper on a dark-blue Yamaha, approaching from the south.

Casper was fifteen now – of course he had bought a moped. Or perhaps Aunt Veronica had given it to him.

The summer before last, they had both had bikes and used to race each other on the gravel tracks in the quarry, but Jonas knew there was no chance of that now.

Casper turned on to the plateau and nodded to Jonas. He didn't get off, but sat there revving the engine impatiently until Jonas went over to him.

'Cool!' he shouted.

Casper nodded. 'Got it back in the spring. What are you doing?'

79

Jonas wasn't doing anything; he was just standing here by the cairn. But he had to say something.

'I'm counting stones.'

Casper revved the engine again. Jonas considered asking if he wanted to play, but suspected that his cousin probably no longer used that word.

'Stones?' Casper said.

'Every year some of the stones fall down from the cairn. I'm keeping a check on them.'

That was in fact true; since he was last here at least three big stones had come tumbling down and were lying on the grass, along with others that had been there for several years. Jonas counted them and looked at his cousin.

'Nine,' he said, and continued in a confident voice: 'When thirteen stones have fallen, the ghost will be free.'

'What ghost?'

'The one that lives in the cairn.'

The idea had only just come to him, but it sounded really good.

'What will he do then?' Casper wanted to know.

He didn't sound all that interested, but Jonas had to keep going.

'He'll go to the houses on the other side of the road and . . .' Jonas tried to think of something terrible that could happen. Something really bad. 'He'll go into every room and raise his sword, then chop off everyone's arms while they're fast asleep. The pain will wake them up, and they'll see the blood pumping out, and their arms lying on the floor. Most of them will survive, but they'll never be able to swim again.'

Casper was listening, but didn't look impressed.

'Wrong. He'll take over their bodies while they're asleep. And when they wake up, they're *possessed*.'

'Possessed?'

'Possessed by the ghost.'

'Right.'

'I saw a film about that kind of thing last winter,' Casper said. '*Fallen*. It was about a demon who came up from hell and took over people's souls. He could move from one person to another, and when someone was possessed they had to do whatever he wanted. He turned them all into serial killers, but when the police arrested the murderer, the demon simply transferred into another body. So nobody could catch him.'

Jonas nodded. He hadn't seen the film, but being possessed by a demon sounded worse than having your arms chopped off. He tried to think of something even more terrifying, but he'd run out of ideas.

He looked down at the cairn. 'More stones have started to come loose – can you see?'

'Maybe the ghost is on his way out,' Casper said. 'But you could always roll them back.'

'OK.'

But Jonas was just saying that; he didn't even want to touch the fallen stones. Anything could happen if he did that.

Casper revved his moped one last time and gazed out across the water. He didn't even look at Jonas; it was as if he was talking to himself.

'I was thinking of going up to Marnäs, to meet some mates by the harbour . . . See what's happening there.'

He didn't ask if Jonas wanted to go with him, and Jonas didn't ask if he could come along, but now Casper looked at him and said, 'You can use my rubber dinghy if you want. If you're going swimming. It's in the boathouse.'

'OK,' Jonas said.

Casper swung the moped around and set off along the coast road, increasing his speed so that the rattling got louder and louder until he turned on to the track leading past the maypole and the mini-golf course, heading up towards the main road.

Slowly, Jonas walked away from the cairn.

He remembered that Uncle Kent had promised him a great summer. He had said it was going to be fantastic.

But now he was all by himself on the coast, completely alone. As Jonas watched his cousin disappear, he knew that the next month was going to be *terrible*.

Lisa

The sun had gone down, and the party was under way.

Lady Summertime gazed out across the room at the crowded dance floor, the bubbling cauldron down below her throne. Hands flew up in the air, hair was tossed around, upper bodies swayed to the beat, forming dark, billowing waves.

'Summer of love!' she yelled into the microphone. 'It's going to be a long, fantastic summer!'

It was one thirty in the morning, the club was packed and Lady Summertime was running the show with flashing lights and a thumping backbeat. She was *completely* in charge, in her purple wig, oversized yellow T-shirt, black nail varnish and black leather jacket. Lisa would never wear such clothes, but this was Lady Summertime's uniform.

She had arrived at seven thirty, and the cooks in the kitchen had provided her with a late dinner. Then she had put on her make-up and her wig. At half past eight, Lisa (Lady Summertime!) had gone into the club and put on a CD with fairly gentle tracks as background music.

People had been a little slow on this Sunday after midsummer, but at about ten o'clock they had started making their way down from the hotel and the campsite, red in the face from too much sunshine and front loading. They had gathered at the bars, both indoor and outdoor, ordering beer and glancing over towards the DJ booth.

At half past ten she suddenly turned up the volume, and everyone jumped.

'OK, everybody on the dance floor! Right now!' Summertime shouted, and people did as they were told.

When they had had enough to drink they became more adventurous, raising their hands in the air – they were ready to party.

By eleven the bar was jam-packed and the tables were covered with ice buckets. Lisa stuck to water all evening, but she was probably the only one.

At quarter past eleven the first glass smashed on the dance floor. The shards went everywhere, but the dancing continued.

At half past eleven the first bottle of champagne was emptied on to the floor, sprayed all over the place by the guy who had paid fourteen hundred kronor for it. He was rich – that was obvious from his early suntan. People screamed with laughter in the shower of bubbles, and several credit cards were waved at the bar staff. 'More champagne!'

By midnight the place stank of booze and sweat. People were dancing with few inhibitions, in sleeveless tops and sweat-drenched shirts. A couple of the boys were wearing nothing but swimming trunks. The girls' hair was plastered to their faces with perspiration; their make-up had slid off long ago. Lady Summertime had acquired her own little group of cheerleaders, standing immediately below her booth. A forest of fists rose in the air, in time with the music.

'Summertime! Summertime!'

And she shouted back: 'Love ya! Love ya!'

After twelve, she put on the Cowley remix of Donna Summer's 'I Feel Love', pressed the button for a strobe effect on the lighting desk and set the smoke machine going – then Summertime jumped down from the booth and set off on tour among the dancers, right into the middle of the chaos.

It was sweaty, it was smoky, the darkness split by flashing lights.

Summertime became a jumping body among all the others, moving to the beat, raising her fists in the air, allowing a hug here and there, and rejecting a proposition whispered in her ear by some guy in a white shirt. She shook her head, smiling – Summertime was always in control – and after a few minutes she was back in her booth. She turned off the smoke and switched to 'Situation' by Yazoo.

'Summertime! Summertime!'

Her little group was growing. Deafening shouts, hands in the air, stumbling feet, drinks spilling everywhere.

Summertime flicked through her vinyl collection and smiled at the chaos, but suddenly she spotted three guys at the far end of the dance floor. They looked like Greeks or Italians, and were standing very close together, about a metre from the bar. They were whispering and glancing around them, almost furtively.

She mixed in 'Firestarter' by Prodigy, and the next time she looked up they had gone.

Booze was knocked back by the bottle, more champagne was ordered. Lisa watched as one guy who was clearly the worse for wear counted out seven thousand-kronor notes to pay his tab; he passed them over to the bartender with a wave of his hand. 'Keep the change!'

It was crazy; it was the height of summer.

A security guard appeared at the side of the DJ booth. He signalled to Lisa, and she took off her headphones and leaned forward.

'We've had some trouble!' he shouted to her. 'Can you say something? Ask people to be a bit more careful?'

'What kind of trouble?'

'Thieving!' the guard yelled. 'Some people have lost their wallets!'

Lisa picked up the microphone, but thought for a second, then shouted back to the guard, 'I saw three guys just now . . . They looked a bit dodgy!'

The guard had started to move away, but he stopped. 'What did they look like?'

'How can I put it? . . . Kind of greasy. Mafia types, if you know what I mean. Slicked-back hair and white shirts.'

The guard nodded, his expression grim.

'OK, we'll see if we can track them down.'

He made his way through the crowd as Lisa turned down the music and warned people to keep an eye on their possessions and their money. Nobody took any notice; they just carried on dancing.

The club closed at two thirty, and it was all over. Lisa finished with a slow number to calm things down.

'Thanks, everyone! I love you all – see you tomorrow!'

The security staff took over and started ushering people out. However, the partying continued as everyone dispersed towards the campsite, chalets or the hotel, dancing their way home. Some would catch the night bus, others might decide to sleep under the full moon, or go for a swim.

The place was almost empty, but a guy who was far too young

for Lisa hung around the booth, helping her pack away. He was wearing a black jacket and was just as tanned as the kids with rich daddies.

'Do you recognize me?' he said.

'Vaguely. From Stockholm?'

He shook his head.

'I was there when you picked up the keys. My name is Urban Kloss. I'm the one who owns all this . . . the Ölandic Resort.'

'Oh, really?' Lisa said; she could see that he was twenty at the most. 'And when did you buy it?'

He stopped smiling, not quite sure what to say. Eventually he said, 'It's in the family.'

'In that case, your family owns the place,' Lisa said. 'Not you, Urban. You just work here.'

'I'm the manager,' he said.

'Oh?'

'I am, I'm the acting catering manager.'

'Whatever,' Lisa said.

Urban smiled at her. He seemed to be enjoying the banter.

'Do you fancy playing golf sometime? It's the Ölandic Open next week.'

Summertime smiled back, anything but sweetly. Guys often chatted her up, and she was much better at dealing with them than Lisa was. She shook her head.

'Balls are delicate; hitting them isn't such a good idea,' she said with a yawn. 'And now I'm heading back to Stenvik with my records and I'm going to bed.'

'I'll help you.'

'It's fine, Urban, I can—'

'Let me help you, for fuck's sake.'

He picked up the bag of LPs and headed off. Lisa locked the booth and followed him, carrying her CDs. The car park was full of people hanging around. Among the Swedish cars there was a Porsche, a BMW, even a Lamborghini. And her Passat.

'There you go,' Urban said, turning to face her.

She gave him a brief hug, an ironic hug, and quickly got into the car.

'Sleep well, Urban.'

If you were wearing a purple wig, giving a guy the brush-off was no problem.

She had split herself into two different people over the last couple of years: one was Lisa Turesson, who played melodic tunes on the guitar and was afraid of most things (like seagulls, wasps and snakes at this time of year), and the other was Lady Summertime, the feisty DJ in the purple wig who yelled into the microphone and got everyone on their feet. Lisa liked Lady Summertime.

She was back at the campsite in Stenvik in fifteen minutes. Everyone seemed to be asleep; there wasn't a sound, but Lisa's ears were still ringing from the music.

It was ten to three. The sun rose at about half past four, but the night sky was still dark grey. She could see a few faint lights along the coast in cottages and boathouses, but nobody saw Lisa carry her bag into the caravan and lock the door. She drew the curtains, too.

Then she opened the bag and started flicking through her records. The stolen wallets were hidden at the bottom. There were five altogether and, in spite of the fact that she was super-sleepy, she couldn't help opening them and counting her spoils.

Mostly credit cards, but a reasonable amount of cash as well. She tipped them out on top of the fridge and counted three thousand-kronor notes and several five hundreds.

Early in the morning, Lisa would go through the wallets looking for scraps of paper with PIN numbers written on them. If she found any, she would drive down to the ATM in Marnäs and take out some money.

But now it was time to go to bed.

By twenty past three she was in a deep sleep. No dreams, no guilty conscience.

It wasn't Lisa who had taken the wallets, it was Lady Summertime. And it wasn't Lisa who needed the money, it was Silas.

Gerlof

Midsummer was over, and many people on the island of Öland could now relax; above all, security staff and those who owned campsites or bars.

Gerlof also relaxed. Stenvik was still standing.

His young relative Tilda Davidsson belonged to the group who perhaps felt the greatest sense of relief; she was a detective inspector with the county police in Kalmar but lived with her husband and children by a lighthouse on eastern Öland and seemed to feel that she was personally responsible for keeping an eye on things on the island.

'So it was a good midsummer as far as the police were concerned?' Gerlof asked when he spoke to her on Monday.

'It was no worse than a normal weekend,' Tilda replied.

'How did you manage that?'

'We ran a checkpoint at this end of the bridge. We pulled over as many cars as we could and confiscated all the alcohol.'

'But surely people will always find booze, if they really want to?'

'Yes, but we locked up those who'd already had too much, so we avoided any major disturbances.'

'So everything was quiet?'

'Well, no, there's always something,' Tilda said. 'We had a couple of cases of GBH, quite a lot of petty thefts, some outboard motors went missing, there was a certain amount of vandalism and five or six drink-driving cases . . . but it was quieter than it's been for a long time.'

'Sounds good,' Gerlof said.

'We've got a missing person too,' Tilda went on. 'A security guard at the Ölandic Resort. But they think he's probably gone off to the mainland.'

'He's disappeared?'

'We're looking for him,' Tilda said.

Gerlof knew that she wouldn't give him any more information. He could get her to talk about her work, but only up to a point.

'Perhaps he'd had enough of Kent Kloss,' Gerlof said. 'Anyway, you'll be finishing work soon, won't you?'

'I've got less than two weeks to go,' Tilda said. 'My holiday starts on the sixteenth.'

'Let's hope things stay nice and quiet, then.'

'Absolutely. I hope you have some peace and quiet, too.'

But Gerlof knew that things were never really quiet when there were teenagers around. He was going to be alone with them for the next five days, until Julia returned from Gothenburg.

Ulrik the audiologist came back to Stenvik the day after the midsummer weekend to make the final adjustments to Gerlof's new hearing aid.

He seemed pleased.

'Don't forget to take it off when you go to bed,' he said. 'And turn it off at night to save the batteries.'

He switched on the device, looked up at the trees and the blue sky, and added, 'I wouldn't mind working in the country all the time.'

Ulrik was talking to himself, but to Gerlof it sounded as if someone was shouting in his ear. It was almost *too* loud. He could hear lots of other things, too: a chainsaw in a garden somewhere inland, a moped rattling along the coast road and the faint buzz of a light aircraft.

All at once the outside world was very close. It was as if a volume control in his ears had been slowly turned down over the course of several years and had suddenly been turned back to full strength.

'I can hear *everything*,' he said, blinking at Ulrik in astonishment. 'Is that normal?'

'How does your own voice sound? Is it echoing inside your head?'

'A little bit.'

The audiologist clicked on his computer and the echo diminished.

'I'm putting on four different programs,' he explained. 'That means you can adjust the hearing aid to suit you, depending on the context – whether you're listening to the birds, chatting to someone, listening to the radio, or you just want to hear more distant sounds.'

'You mean if I want to eavesdrop?'

Ulrik smiled. 'In that case, you need to choose the setting for gossip.'

When Ulrik had gone, Gerlof remained sitting in the garden, amazed at all the sounds he could hear. He had regained a lost world.

An ear-splitting screech from the east almost made him jump, but it was only a lovesick cock pheasant wandering around the freshly mown meadow calling for hens.

Suddenly, Gerlof heard two voices from another direction, somewhere to the south. He turned his head but could see only trees behind him. The voices were coming through the forest, possibly from the coast road. Or from the shore? They sounded so close, but Gerlof had experienced this phenomenon before on Öland. Because the island was so flat, voices could sometimes be heard over a distance of several kilometres, if the wind was in the right direction.

He adjusted the hearing aid.

The eavesdropper's setting, he thought, feeling slightly ashamed of himself.

The voices were much clearer now. A man and a woman were talking; Gerlof couldn't hear what they were actually saying, but the man sounded calm, the woman more agitated. She was speaking much faster and louder; his responses were slow. It seemed like an intimate conversation between close friends. Friends, or lovers?

Gerlof tried to adjust the sound in his ear, improve his ability to eavesdrop, but he still couldn't make out what they were saying. Were they speaking Swedish, or a different language?

Then the catch on the gate rattled and Gerlof saw that his grandchildren were back from the jetty. He sat up straight and quickly turned down the volume; their cheerful shouts were a little too much.

Jonas

Mats looked around as if to make sure that no adults were listening, then leaned closer to Jonas and lowered his voice.

'You can't come to Kalmar with us. You do understand that?'

Jonas was sitting next to him on Uncle Kent's leather sofa. He wanted to protest, have the courage to stand up to his older brother, but he said nothing.

'No,' he said eventually. 'I don't understand it at all.'

'Because you're too young for the film,' Mats said. 'You have to be over fifteen to see *Armageddon*.'

Jonas looked at him. He knew that the battle over the cinema trip was already lost, but he went on anyway: 'I've seen films like that in Marnäs. The two of us have . . . All we had to do was walk in.'

Mats waved a fly away from his ear. 'Yes, but this is different. They check on everybody in Kalmar. They've got security, they ask for ID. You don't have any, which means you wouldn't get in and you'd have to sit on a park bench waiting for the film to end. You'd be hanging around Kalmar on your own all evening . . . Is that what you want?'

Jonas shook his head. Mats was eighteen, Urban nineteen, and he knew they'd got together behind his back and chosen an American action movie with a 15+ certificate so that Casper could go with them but Jonas couldn't.

'You'll get the money for the ticket anyway, that's no problem,' Mats said. 'But Dad and Kent and Veronica will think you're with us in Kalmar, so try and stay out of the way until we get back.' He smiled. 'Go and play with one of your little friends.'

Play? Jonas didn't have any real friends in the village. All the boys were either older than him, or much younger. He wasn't allowed to hang out with the older boys, and the younger ones were boring.

Hiding away inside Villa Kloss wasn't an option, because the adults were having a party. If he could have disappeared without a trace for the evening, he would have done just that.

'Hi there, you two!'

Their father came into the big room. Jonas thought he was looking at his two sons as if they were no more than recent acquaintances, in spite of the fact that they had seen him several times over the past few years.

'So you're off to the cinema in the big city tonight?'

Jonas didn't say a word.

'Are you catching the bus to Kalmar, Mats?'

'Urban's driving.'

'OK. Stay off the beer, in that case.'

Mats looked up at the ceiling, then down at his father.

'But I expect you'll be having a few drinks at the party tonight, Dad? Knocking them back?'

'No,' Niklas said, but he couldn't look his son in the eye. 'Have you ever seen me drunk, Mats?'

'Mum has. She says you were often drunk when you were married.'

Jonas stared at the floor, wondering where everyone else was. Please let Veronica come in . . .

Niklas looked at Mats.

'That was a long time ago. Before you were born. In our first apartment. We had a few parties that got a bit out of hand. And Anita . . . Anita wasn't always sober back then either. I could tell you a few tales about her.'

'Don't start badmouthing Mum.'

'I'm just telling it like it was, Mats.'

Jonas got up, slowly and silently. If he moved very carefully, perhaps no one would notice him. Like a ghost, he drifted towards the glass door leading to the veranda; he was almost there when the call came.

'Jonas?'

He stopped, turned around – and saw that Dad had found a smile somewhere and plastered it on.

'Fancy a swim?'

*

91

The sky was blue and the air dry and warm outside, but Jonas still felt chilled to the bone. And alone, in spite of the fact that he was walking next to his father. There was no trip to the cinema in Kalmar to look forward to tonight, just loneliness.

They walked across the baking-hot coast road and out on to the ridge. Niklas didn't speak until they were passing the burial cairn. He pointed to the stones and said, 'People think there's treasure buried beneath the cairn. You know it's an ancient grave, don't you?'

Jonas nodded. 'We learned about the Bronze Age in school. It came between the Stone Age and the Iron Age.'

'Exactly. So there's a Bronze Age chieftain buried here, just like King Mysing in his burial mound in the south of the island. But you're not scared, are you?'

'Not me,' Jonas said.

Not at the moment, anyway, he thought; not when the sun was shining and his dad was here. The cairn was completely harmless right now. But he didn't like being out here in the evening, when it became a portal to another world, and the ghost came out and turned people into killer zombies.

His dad had said something, asked a question as they started down the stone steps leading to the water.

'What?' Jonas said.

'Is Mum OK?'

'Yes . . . I suppose so. She spends a lot of time working.'

'Good,' his dad said. 'It's good that she's got a job.'

He looked as if he wanted to ask more questions about Mum, so Jonas hurried down the steps.

They could hear cheerful cries from the jetty further north, but the shore down below Villa Kloss was empty and red-hot. The waves lapped gently against the flat, greyish-white rocks. Niklas pointed to a row of thick poles extending a couple of hundred metres straight out into the water, just to the south of the bathing area.

'I see the fishermen have laid their gill nets this year, too. There must be some eels left in the Sound . . .'

A limestone boathouse near the bottom of the steps housed the sun loungers and swimming gear belonging to the Kloss family. It was padlocked, but Casper had given Jonas the combination.

Casper's rubber dinghy was in there, along with a couple of plastic oars, but the air had gone out of it over the winter, and it looked deflated and a bit pathetic. Casper hadn't used it for several years. Jonas must have grown seven or eight centimetres since he last sat in it, and he was definitely heavier. He probably wouldn't be able to use it after this summer, but he dragged it out into the sun anyway.

'Are you going out in that?' his father asked.

Jonas nodded.

'Well, don't go too far . . . I'll help you blow it up.'

While his father was pumping more air into the dinghy, Jonas quickly pulled on his trunks. He just wanted to get out on to the water, follow the nets and see if any eels were moving around down there in the darkness.

He didn't want to spend any more time talking to his father. If he did, then sooner or later he would ask him what he had done to end up in prison; all Jonas knew was that it was something bad. Something to do with money and the customs office. Something Dad didn't want to talk about.

'Dad fucked things up for the whole family,' Mats had once said when they were alone. As if the fault lay not in what their father had done, but in the fact that he had got caught.

The Homecomer

The summer evening seemed to be ageing, turning as grey as the Homecomer as the light vanished on the west coast of the island. The sun began to go down, and the day's short shadows quickly grew longer. The horizon disappeared, and sea and sky became a darkening curtain in the west. The figures moving beneath the trees were almost invisible.

It was time.

Pecka and the Homecomer had entered the Ölandic's private area through the north fence then made their way south through the forest. They had kept out of sight of the shore until they reached the dock. The car park in front of them was empty now; all the cars had left.

'How are you feeling?' the Homecomer asked.

'Fine,' Pecka said, but his eyes were darting all over the place, and he hadn't said much all evening. Pecka had grown a lot quieter since the murder of the security guard, but he still obeyed orders.

They had remained hidden among the trees until the sun went down, but now they stepped out and moved towards the water. Towards the L-shaped quay and the ship on the outer side of the dock.

The Homecomer had spent so much time watching the ship over the past few days that he almost felt like a member of the crew. There were four men on board, all foreigners. Today there had been no loading or unloading, and all the indications were that the ship would set sail tomorrow morning. Tonight the crew were probably up at the hotel, celebrating. Happy and unsuspecting.

Time to get on board.

They made their way quickly towards the quayside, the Home-comer in front, with Pecka a few steps behind him.

Both were armed. Pecka didn't want to carry a gun any more, but he was carrying a freshly sharpened axe. The Homecomer had the Walther hidden behind his back.

'Here we go, then,' he said.

'OK,' Pecka replied, pulling the balaclava over his head.

The Homecomer could feel his age in his legs but increased his speed.

Once they reached the quayside and everything was quiet, Pecka pressed a key on his mobile and allowed it to ring out twice, which was the signal to Rita to start up the launch, come around the point and board the ship from the other side. When they had finished, all three of them would make their escape in Rita's boat. That was the plan.

But suddenly they heard a rumbling noise, disturbing the peaceful evening.

The Homecomer slowed down. At first he couldn't work out what was going on, but then he realized that someone had just started up the ship's engines. He heard Pecka behind him: 'Fuck! We'll have to forget the whole thing!'

The Homecomer shook his head and kept on going.

'There are too many of them!' Pecka yelled. 'They're all on board . . . they're leaving tonight!'

But the Homecomer just kept on walking towards the ship, the gun hidden behind his back. He headed straight for the gangplank, knowing that Pecka was following him, in spite of his protests.

Yes, there were lights on the bridge – the crew were on board. The Homecomer spotted one man in the stern, a seaman who must have just come up on deck. He was in his fifties, dressed in blue overalls, and had started repairing a broken air vent with a piece of corrugated cardboard. He looked extremely bored.

The Homecomer was so close to the ship that he could read the name on the prow: *Elia*. The hull was dark, a mixture of rust and black paint.

He heard an angry buzzing through the throbbing of the engines. Rita had rounded the point in the little launch.

The seaman looked up and saw the two visitors. He stared at them with no trace of suspicion, merely surprise.

The Homecomer walked to the edge of the quay and said, 'Good evening,' in a calm, steady voice.

The seaman opened his mouth and his expression changed from quizzical to uneasy – but by that time the Homecomer had produced his gun.

Pecka had also reached the ship, while at the same time Rita swung the launch around sharply, heading for the stern.

The ship was moored with three hawsers. Pecka positioned himself next to the first one, and raised the axe. Five sharp blows, and the hawser was severed. He quickly moved on to the next one.

The Homecomer was on the deck now, still pointing the Walther at the seaman and speaking quietly but firmly as he issued a series of instructions.

He glanced back and saw that Pecka had lowered the axe. All three hawsers had been cut, and the ship slowly began to drift away from the quayside and out into the dark waters of the Sound.

He looked around. The quayside was still deserted.

The seaman looked confused; he raised his hands and began to back away.

The hijacking had begun.

The New Country, June 1931

Sixty-eight years earlier, the ship that is to take Aron and Sven to the new country is made of metal, and is bigger than any vessel Aron has ever seen.

They have travelled by train from Kalmar, journeying northwards through Sweden. The train has chugged its way through vast coniferous forests, past mountains and lakes, then out into the sun and straight into the heart of a big city.

The station is enormous, packed with travellers and all their luggage. Outside the city awaits, with its long, straight cobbled streets, people strolling along the pavements, and more vehicles than Aron has seen in his whole life. Plenty of carts and horse-drawn carriages clatter by, but there are also big, black motor cars, rumbling along with uniformed chauffeurs behind the wheel and smartly dressed men in the back seat.

'Stockholm,' Sven says.

Aron recognizes the name from school.

'The capital city of Sweden.'

They eat a plate of steaming-hot stew in a smoky café not far from the central station, then buy provisions and the last bits and pieces for their journey. In an ironmonger's, Sven equips himself with a hammer and a decent spade.

'It's easier to get a job if you bring your own tools to the new country,' he explains.

Then they wander across the city's bridges, past the tall buildings and the splendour of the Royal Palace, then down through narrow alleyways, to a long quayside with rows of derricks and crowds of people.

'There she is!'

Both large and small ships are moored alongside, but Sven is pointing to a long, white vessel. A thin curl of smoke is emerging from a big funnel, which has three yellow crowns painted on a blue background. Pennants along the railing flutter in the wind, and a large Swedish flag hangs down from the stern.

The name on the prow reads SS *Kastelholm*.

'That's our bridge,' Sven says. 'The bridge that will take us across the water!'

He quickly takes a pinch of snuff from the wooden box, and seems to have left all his anger, all his troubles, behind.

Aron sees that they will not be crossing the sea alone. There are at least twenty fellow travellers standing on deck, with suitcases and rucksacks and tools in their hands. They are all straight-backed, heads up, as if something great is waiting for them.

'Let's go on board,' Sven says. 'We're off to the new country!'

Aron feels a shiver run down his spine. It might be the cold wind blowing off the water, or a sudden fear of the unknown.

He has no idea what is going to happen in the new country, but he follows Sven up the gangplank and turns his back on Sweden.

Gerlof

The sun disappeared into a huge bank of cloud behind Gerlof's cottage on Monday evening. A dark-grey wall rose up on the horizon, as if there were a forest fire on the mainland – but, as an old seaman, Gerlof knew that more overcast weather was on the way. He must remember not to whistle, because whistling brought gales and thunderstorms.

There was no need to whistle; things were already noisy enough in the cottage. He was the only adult at the dinner table; his daughters had gone back to the mainland after midsummer, back to their jobs. But their children were still here.

Julia and her husband were coming over for a holiday at the beginning of July, and until then Gerlof was in charge. He often missed his wife, particularly at a time like this, because she would have been much better at looking after the three boys. Vincent was nineteen, and old enough to keep an eye on the two younger ones, who were sixteen and eleven, but all three had an energy and speed that Gerlof had lost a long time ago. They and their friends raced around the cottage with enormous water pistols, and played video games – Nintendo and *Super Mario Bros*, or whatever they were called.

Or they watched TV, which was something Gerlof rarely did. He remembered what an old Pentecostalist acquaintance had said to him when he put up his first television aerial towards the end of the sixties: 'That's the Devil himself, sitting on your roof!'

He had suffered in silence so far, but he had formulated an escape plan.

'I'm going to sleep in the boathouse tonight,' he said over dinner.

He would get away from the cottage for the night. Seek sanctuary down there, as the old fishermen had done in days gone by.

'But why, Granddad?' Vincent said.

Gerlof combined a lie with the truth. 'It's . . . darker down there. And a bit quieter.'

Vincent nodded; he was grown up enough to understand.

So, after dinner, Gerlof picked up his pyjamas and a bottle of water and left the cottage. This evening, his legs felt strong enough for him to manage without the wheelchair, but he used his walking stick and linked arms with his grandson as they made their way to the ridge. They strolled along at a leisurely pace, and the smell of meat and oil reached Gerlof's nostrils. Someone was having a barbecue.

On the grass next to the road he noticed an empty beer can, and poked at it with his stick. 'Tourists from Stockholm . . . Terrible.'

'Someone from Småland might have dropped it there,' Vincent said.

Gerlof bent down with some difficulty and picked it up. 'Put this in our bin, would you?'

'No problem,' Vincent replied.

Gerlof made it his business to pick up litter – at least there was something he could still do.

As they passed his old gig, he saw that someone had used a plane to remove all the rotten wood. John, presumably, or his son, Anders. Gerlof wasn't surprised; they always kept their promises.

Vincent unlocked the door of the boathouse up above the shore. The ceiling light was broken and it was dark inside, but Gerlof could see that both camp beds were made up. Had he done that? He couldn't remember.

'You'll have a nice quiet night here, Granddad,' Vincent said, lighting a paraffin lamp in the window.

'Let's hope so,' Gerlof said.

When Vincent had gone, he left the door open. He looked around at the beds, the fishing nets and the little table. He and John had spent many a night in here, when they had laid their nets out in the Sound and were waiting for them to fill up. Back in those days, Gerlof had often woken at sunrise, but tomorrow morning he intended to lie in, at least until seven o'clock.

He stepped outside for a little while to enjoy the cool evening air. He took a deep breath, then let it out slowly, listening to the summer silence.

Peace at last.

It was so quiet, with just the faintest breeze.

But he could hear a distant noise to the south. A dull rumbling; he could only just make it out. Gerlof stood very still and realized that it was a powerful engine idling away, further down the coast.

A big ship? If so, it was hidden by one of the points, because there wasn't a single vessel in sight out in the Sound.

He went back inside and locked the door. There was an old radio in the boathouse, and the last thing he did before going to bed was to switch it on and listen to the weather forecast for Öland and Gotland. Cloudy with virtually no wind overnight, but with the risk of localized showers early in the morning. Tuesday would be sunny once more.

Gerlof put on his pyjamas and removed his hearing aid. Another little gadget to think about, but he'd actually started to like it.

Before he pulled down the blind he looked out across the darkening Sound and saw a strip of deep red below the curtain of cloud on the horizon.

As dark as blood, he thought, but without any misgivings. He had seen that same strip many times before; it was nothing more than the last glow of the sun, lingering on the horizon like a glowing ember.

He left a couple of tea lights burning on the windowsill. They were in glass holders, and would go out during the night; it was perfectly safe.

Slowly, Gerlof lay down on the camp bed and closed his eyes, feeling contented. This was a bit like settling down in his cabin after dropping anchor in some natural harbour on a still summer's evening. The same narrow bed, the same proximity to creation, the same sense of peace. If the wind got up it would no doubt wake him; that was a relic from all those years at sea.

Darkness fell over the shore, and there wasn't a sound.

Gerlof was soon fast asleep, dreaming that he had gone down to the sea and pushed a brand-new wooden gig, smelling of oil, into the water, straight out into the stillness.

Right in the middle of the dream, he woke up with a start. But it wasn't the weather that had disturbed him; someone was hammering on the door of the boathouse.

Jonas

Floating across the depths, drifting along in the sunset.

Jonas was lying on his back in the rubber dinghy, which felt like a water bed. No, it *was* a water bed, because he was floating out by the gill nets, his feet dangling over the side as he gazed up at the sky above the Sound. The vault of the heavens was slowly darkening, and stars had begun to glimmer on the horizon.

Out here, he was free of everything. Alone on the sea, just like someone who had been shipwrecked.

His brother's secret plan for the evening had worked. Just after six o'clock, Jonas had got into the car with Mats and their cousins. The adults had assumed that all four boys were on their way to the cinema in Kalmar, but as soon as they reached the campsite at Stenvik – out of sight of Villa Kloss – Mats had handed Jonas the money from Dad for his cinema ticket, then turfed him out of the car.

'Have fun, bro! We certainly will!'

The cousins smiled and nodded at him, and the car headed off towards the main road.

Jonas had watched the car until it disappeared, then he had gone down to the jetty. It was busy with people taking an evening dip, and he had sat down on a rock to watch them for a while, particularly a girl of his own age, with long, almost pure-white hair. She was sitting on a blanket with two girlfriends, chatting and laughing, and she never even glanced at him. Not once. He might as well have been invisible.

So he had got up and made his way south across the banks of pebbles on the shore until he reached the point below Villa Kloss. The area was deserted at this time of the evening, and it was a good hiding place. He just had to find a way of keeping busy, getting through the evening.

First of all, he had gone for a long swim, then he had dried himself in the sun. He had done a bit of beachcombing, but had found nothing but a few empty German milk cartons.

Then he had had another swim. By this time the sun was low on the horizon and the shallow water had cooled.

When he was dry, he pulled on his shorts before dragging Casper's rubber dinghy out of the boathouse. He slipped on a lifejacket and waded out into the water for an evening outing. Once the sun had set he would creep back up to his little chalet in the darkness and go to bed. In the morning he would tell the adults he had enjoyed the film.

A good plan.

Jonas stepped on to a rock, the dinghy in front of him, and looked around. The surface of the water was calm and shining. The Sound looked perfectly safe, but he knew that the seabed dropped away sharply just ahead of him, and that you could go under and drown just metres from the shore.

The water turned pitch black when the sun disappeared, as if the Sound had suddenly become bottomless. A bit scary, but exciting.

He stepped carefully into the dinghy and started to row along the shoreline; when he reached the gill nets he turned and headed away from the land, following the nets and feeling the pull of the black depths below him. The algae and the fish, the seaweed and the rocks. Another world . . .

Eventually, he reached the middle of the nets and tied the little boat to one of the thick poles.

The water out here was as deep and dark as a grave, but there wasn't a breath of wind.

Jonas settled down in the bottom of the dinghy and watched as the sky above him grew darker and darker. There were gaps in the cloud cover, and small pinpricks of light glimmered through.

They'll be in the cinema in Kalmar by now, he thought.

While Mats and their cousins were watching the film, all Jonas could do was gaze at the stars above the island. But gradually the all-consuming envy faded away, leaving a kind of peace, a sense of floating weightlessly between sea and sky. There were no insects to disturb him this far out in the Sound, not even the mosquitoes.

He closed his eyes. Everything was dark and quiet.

But a faint sound made him open his eyes and raise his head. A dull throbbing that could be felt through the water as well as heard.

It was the sound of a ship. A big ship that had started up its pounding diesel engines, somewhere in the darkness. The throbbing grew louder, then diminished.

He blinked slowly, feeling drowsy. Had he fallen asleep? Jonas didn't have a watch, but the sun had gone down and clouds covered the night sky. The stars had vanished.

He looked to the south, but saw nothing. There were no lights approaching.

The island was even darker than the sea. The two spits of land jutting out into the Sound on either side of the bay were pitch black, apart from the odd light in the windows of the summer cottages closest to the shore.

He could hear the faint sound of voices and laughter; it was probably the party up at Villa Kloss. Dad and Aunt Veronica and Uncle Kent and their guests would be sitting on the veranda, eating and drinking.

Jonas considered spending the whole night in the dinghy. Soon the summer night would be completely black, and perhaps then they would all stop drinking and laughing up at Villa Kloss, and when the car from Kalmar came back without him they would wonder where he was. They would be worried. *Where's Jonas? Has anyone seen Jonas?* For once, he would be important to them.

He would stay down here and row a bit further – out to the very end of the gill nets, further than he had ever been before.

He rowed with even strokes, and through the thin rubber bottom of the dinghy he could feel the water quickly growing colder. He couldn't see any rocks now, only blackness. If the boat got a puncture, he wasn't sure he would be able to swim ashore, even with his lifejacket.

The depth of the water made him feel dizzy.

Finally, he reached the very last pole, tall and slender. He could see that it was held in place by long ropes and chains.

Jonas stopped rowing. The dinghy drifted on and he reached out and grabbed the pole, clinging to the rough wood with both hands. The pole proved that at least there were other people in the world, people who had come out here at the beginning of summer and laid their nets, hoping to catch eels.

He looked over the side but couldn't make out the nets. Were there eels down there right now, trapped in the darkness? The Kloss family ate smoked eel occasionally, but Jonas didn't really like the taste. It was too oily.

Suddenly, he heard the throbbing again. Was it a motor boat? It should have had its lights on if it was out at sea at night, but there was no sign of anything.

Silence.

He let go of the wooden pole and drifted away as the current drew the dinghy out into the sound. *Bye bye, pole.*

He picked up the oars but didn't start rowing, allowing the boat to drift instead.

Out into the blackness. But only for a little longer. It was OK, because he was wearing his lifejacket, but he would turn back soon. He just wanted to see if he could catch a glimpse of the other vessel.

He peered around. A faint haze had begun to rise from the water, a night mist that made it even more difficult to see.

All at once, Jonas had the feeling that something huge and silent had appeared by the spit of land to the south – a grey shadow on the water, long and slender like a sea monster. A sea serpent, or a giant octopus lurking in the Sound . . .

Was the shadow moving? He blinked, but it was gone.

He started rowing. He wanted to get home now, but it was so dark and misty that he was no longer sure exactly where he was, or even how far he was from the shore. There was nothing to give him his bearings. Were those dots of light coming from the houses on the coast, or were they faint stars glimmering in the distance?

He stopped rowing and let out a long breath. He listened.

He could hear splashing. Small ripples lapped against the side of the dinghy, but this was louder. It sounded like rushing waves.

Jonas looked up – and suddenly he could see. The full moon emerged through a gap in the clouds, and the Sound was bathed in light. The water around him turned into a glittering expanse of silver.

And, in the middle of it all, he saw something large and black – a ship.

It was gliding straight towards him, at speed. Making no attempt to slow down. In the moonlight, he could just make out a name in white letters on the prow: *Elia*.

Jonas smelled the diesel and heard the throbbing of the engines.

There was no collision; his dinghy was too small. It was simply sucked towards the bow by the swell and carried along with the ship.

Jonas got on his knees, a cold feeling in his belly; the bow wave was beginning to compress his little boat. It was starting to sink.

He was frightened now, and tried to stand up. His hands fumbled, but he managed to get hold of the end of a rope swinging from side to side. He looked up; it was the end of a nylon rope, dangling from the ship's gunwale like a liana in the jungle.

He clung on as tightly as he could and pulled himself up out of the dinghy, which suddenly freed itself from the swell and spun around like a yellow lifebuoy. Then it slipped away towards the stern, whirled around several times in the glittering waves and disappeared under water.

Casper's dinghy. Gone.

Jonas wanted to save it, but if he let go of the rope he would be sucked down beneath the keel. He held on.

But not for much longer.

He gritted his teeth, swung his legs and managed to get his right foot on a rusty little ledge part way up the hull. Using the ledge for support, he hauled himself up towards the black steel rods that made up the gunwale, then clambered up as if they were the wall bars in a school gym.

He couldn't hear any sound of human activity from the vessel above him. No voices, no footsteps. The engines seemed to have died away, too; there was only the gentle lapping of the waves as the ship drifted on through the night under its own steam.

Jonas gathered his strength, heaved himself over the gunwale and landed on a cold metal deck in his bare feet. He was frozen and shaking, but he was safe.

He breathed out and looked around. Where was he?

On board a large fishing boat, apparently. He couldn't see any nets, but the stench of fish and diesel filled the air.

He was standing next to a closed hatch with a small white structure on either side – a smaller one in the prow and a larger one towards the stern. There was a faint light in one of the windows of the latter; the rest of the ship was in darkness.

Jonas blinked. Where had it come from? He had seen big ships out in the Sound in the summer, but never this close to the shore.

He stood by the hatch, wondering what to do. Should he head for the prow, or the stern? Or just stand here and let the ship decide?

Slowly, he began to make his way along the edge of the hatch, moving towards the stern. He felt it was better to go towards the light, however faint it might be.

Nothing was moving.

He kept on going, taking very small steps. The hatch came to an end, and beyond it he saw something round and dark. At first, he thought it was a ball.

Then he realized it was a head. And a neck, and a pair of shoulders.

There was a man lying on the deck.

Jonas stopped dead.

The man was wearing dark overalls. His face was turned towards Jonas, and the lower half of his body was stuck in a square hole in the deck; it looked as if he had been trying to climb out of the hold.

But he wasn't moving now; he didn't even appear to be breathing. He was just lying there.

Jonas stared at him. He was just thinking about giving the man a little push with his foot when he heard the sound of moaning from down in the hold.

There were more people in there, but their voices didn't sound normal. They sounded muffled, and in terrible pain.

He listened, frozen to the spot.

The voices fell silent.

Jonas heard a rattling noise on deck, right behind him. He turned around and saw a figure stumbling out of the darkness, from the prow. A tall, thin man with black hair. He was young, dressed in jeans and a white sweater – but he looked ill, with staring eyes, his head drooping. He staggered forward as if he were in a trance; he almost tripped over the hatch but slowly straightened up, his expression blank.

The living dead. A zombie.

He spotted Jonas; he raised his arms and made a kind of noise. It sounded like a foreign language, a hoarse wheezing.

108

The zombie reached out; he was only two metres away now.

One metre.

Jonas backed away, turned around and fled along the gunwale. His feet jumped past the man lying on the deck as his eyes searched for a safe place.

The sea was as black as ink. Öland was far away. Jonas ran blindly towards the stern and the wheelhouse, which had a narrow steel door.

But the door was closed. Locked. And there was no handle. He pushed his fingers between the edge of the door and the frame, but it wouldn't budge.

Trapped.

He could hear the wheezing behind him, coming closer and closer. He turned around, saw the outstretched hands. Moving towards him.

Jonas closed his eyes and felt his pants fill with warmth. He had wet himself. At the same time, the steel door shook against his back. Someone on the other side was trying to open it.

Another monster? Jonas shrank in his wet pants as he heard the door squeak.

It was thrust open with such force that he was pushed aside. Someone emerged – first of all a foot in a leather boot, then a denim-clad leg, then a pair of raised arms. Holding an axe.

The man who stepped out on to the deck was also tall and thin; he had a shaven head, and he didn't seem to have noticed Jonas. He took two steps past him and swung the axe.

It had a long handle; the blade flashed and went straight into the zombie's chest. The blow sent the body reeling backwards and it landed on the deck next to Jonas.

The zombie kept on moving, waving its hands and trying to get up. The man with the axe shouted something and hit it again, twice, three times, four times – then the zombie fell back and lay still.

Silence. The ship drifted on through the night.

The man with the axe took a long breath; he sounded as if he was shivering. He turned and saw Jonas.

Their eyes met in the moonlight. Jonas realized that he recognized this man, those blinking eyes, that tense expression. He had definitely seen him before.

But the man's eyes were cold. Cold and afraid. He bent over Jonas and gasped a question: 'Who are *you*?' He gripped Jonas by the shoulder. 'Where's Aron, the Swedish-American?'

Jonas opened his mouth, but nothing came out. Every single word had disappeared from his brain, but the man kept on asking questions.

'The old man – where's he gone?'

He raised the axe, which was dripping with blood.

Jonas managed to make his body move, and rolled to the side. He had to get away, anywhere. He reached out, felt the cold metal of the gunwale and quickly got to his feet. He saw a white lifebelt; his hands grabbed it in passing and tossed it overboard as he clambered to the top of the gunwale.

'Wait!' the man shouted.

But Jonas swung his leg over and glanced behind him one last time. He saw a new figure, someone standing at the window of the wheelhouse. An old man, with grey hair, a pale face . . .

He had seen enough; he threw himself off the ship, straight out into the darkness of the sea.

The water was bitterly cold; it took hold of him, dragged him down. He sank into a world of bubbles. The currents around the hull of the ship pulled at him as a dull rushing sound filled his ears, but his flailing hands carried him back up to the surface.

He gulped in the night air, saw the horror ship looming above him. But it was moving away, its engines still throbbing faintly.

Jonas was floating –his lifejacket was doing its job. The lifebelt was just a metre or so away; he managed to get hold of it and slipped it over his head and under his arms.

The jacket and the lifebelt carried his body, and when he turned his head he saw lights. They were a long way off, but they were glittering. The lights of Öland. His only option was to start swimming towards them.

He kicked his legs ten times, then rested for a while, using the belt to support him, then kicked out ten times more. Slowly, he made his way towards the shore. The lights were getting closer; he could see little houses now.

The dark coast came into focus, and at last Jonas felt the rocks beneath his feet. He had reached the shore.

He could hear a splashing sound; was someone following him? He looked around, but saw only black water. The Sound was in complete darkness; there was no sign of the lights of a ship out there.

But perhaps the dead had jumped in the water after him, perhaps they were slowly swimming towards the shore right now . . .

He crawled out of the sea, water pouring from his shorts and top; he wriggled out of the lifebelt and lay there on the pebbles. He was utterly exhausted, but terror at the thought of the dead made him get to his feet.

Where could he hide?

Whereabouts on the island was he?

The shore was less steep here, and he realized he was further north. He saw a row of boathouses up on the ridge, all in darkness apart from one small wooden hut with a faint light in one window.

Jonas stumbled towards it as quickly as he could and finally he made it. He tugged at the handle, but the door was locked. He started hammering and shouting for help, and at last the door was opened.

Not by a zombie, not by a madman wielding an axe, but by an old man who looked as if he had just woken up. He stepped aside, welcoming Jonas into the warmth and the light.

Jonas almost fell in. The water from his clothes dripped on to a soft rug beneath his feet, but he could do no more. He collapsed.

The man was still staring at him, the door still open to the night.

'Shut the door,' Jonas whispered. 'Lock it! They're after me!'

'Who's after you?'

'The dead. From the ship.'

111

Gerlof

Gerlof had been woken by strange vibrations, a racket that made him think he was lying in his bunk on board a ship. Then he opened his eyes and remembered that he had decided to spend the night in the boathouse in order to get some peace and quiet. But the walls were actually shaking.

Could it be an earthquake? Slowly, he got out of the camp bed, but it was only when he put in his hearing aid that he realized what was going on. Someone was hammering on the door, and a high voice, somewhat muted by the wood, was shouting, begging to be let in.

'I'm coming,' Gerlof muttered.

He pulled on his trousers and his guernsey so that he would be warm and presentable, then opened the door.

Out of the darkness a boy came hurtling in; he almost fell over the doorstep. He was wearing a lifejacket and soaking-wet clothes; Gerlof had never seen him before.

'Dear me,' Gerlof said. He couldn't think of anything else to say.

The boy was kneeling on the rag rug, shaking like a leaf. He looked over at the doorway with terror in his eyes.

'Shut the door,' he whispered. 'Lock it! They're after me!'

'Who's after you?'

'The dead. From the ship.'

Gerlof closed the door and turned the key.

'Someone's after you? What are you talking about?'

The boy crawled further into the boathouse. He stopped when he reached Gerlof's narrow bed, and clung to it, still staring at the door. He didn't look at Gerlof; his expression was blank, trapped in fear. He was holding his breath, and appeared to be listening. Gerlof listened, too, but nobody tried the handle or knocked on the door.

He made an effort to stay calm. Should he be afraid? He was still half asleep.

Slowly, he lit several candles on the table, to chase away the shadows. Then he took a couple of steps towards the boy. 'What's your name?'

'Jonas.'

'And what exactly has happened, Jonas? Can you tell me?'

Finally, the boy met Gerlof's gaze. 'There's a ship out in the Sound,' he said. 'A big ship . . . It came straight at me. I climbed aboard.' Pause. 'From my rubber dinghy.' Pause. 'But they were all dead.' Pause. 'All except one. He had an axe.'

'And he's the one who was chasing you?'

'The ghost,' the boy said, raising his voice. 'The ghost was on the ship. He was fighting with the dead!'

The boy took a deep breath, and a single tear rolled down his cheek. Gerlof waited until he had taken a few more deep breaths before reaching out and gently unfastening the lifejacket. Then he said firmly, 'That was no ghost.'

'Wasn't it?'

'No. Shall I tell you why?'

The boy nodded.

'Because ghosts can't cope with water.' Gerlof slipped off the lifejacket and carried on: 'My grandfather always used to say that you should make your escape by boat if you saw a spirit of some kind. So, whatever you saw tonight, it was no ghost, Jonas. I promise you that.'

The boy looked doubtful, but seemed to calm down, even though he was still glancing anxiously at the door.

Eventually, Gerlof went over and opened it again. He heard a sharp intake of breath behind him, and said reassuringly, 'I'm just going to have a look. And see if I can hear anything.'

There was probably nothing to worry about but, just to be on the safe side, he picked up a weapon. It was a long orthoceras which he kept as an ornament. He had found it on the shore; it was the shell of an extinct cephalopod that had become fossilized after several million years under extreme pressure on the seabed.

The stone felt pleasingly heavy, like a cudgel, as Gerlof stepped out into the darkness, into the mild night. The shore around the boathouse was dark grey, the water like a black abyss down below. He moved silently, listening hard, but he could hear only the lapping waves.

He walked away from the patch of light by the door and gazed out across the Sound. A few white pinpricks of light glimmered over on the mainland but, otherwise, there was nothing to see.

He switched his hearing aid to the setting for background noise, then straightened up and listened again.

Now he could hear something in the night, a distant rumbling sound out at sea. He recognized the dull throbbing – he had heard it just before he went to bed. But now it was coming from the north, and it was heading away. He fiddled with the hearing aid, trying to turn up the volume, but the rumbling slowly died away.

He waited for another minute or two, then he heard the waves splashing on the shore, rattling the pebbles as the swell of a vessel passing through the Sound reached the land.

He went back inside and locked the door.

'There's no one out there,' he said. 'No ghosts.'

Jonas didn't say anything, so Gerlof went on, 'My name is Gerlof.'

'I know,' the boy said. 'You're Kristoffer's granddad.'

A friend of Kristoffer, Gerlof's youngest grandchild. Now he recognized the boy. He had seen him just a few days ago, at the midsummer dance. He was a member of the Kloss family.

'Are you Jonas Kloss?'

The boy nodded, staring at the door again. 'He hit the dead people on the ship with an axe.' Pause. He thought for a second, then continued, 'And he asked about an old American. He said, "Where's Aron, the Swedish-American?"'

A Swedish-American? Gerlof thought.

'And the man who was holding the axe, Jonas . . . Did you recognize him?'

The boy shook his head. 'I don't know . . . I don't know his name.'

Gerlof considered this response. 'But you did recognize him?'

Jonas thought hard. 'I think so.'

'Where had you seen him before?'

'I don't know.'

The boy had lowered his gaze, and Gerlof didn't want to press

114

him, so he simply said quietly, 'Just try to remember . . . What was the first thing that came into your mind when you saw the man on the ship?'

Jonas looked up at Gerlof and frowned, then said, 'Africa.'

The Homecomer

The engines had fallen silent. The ship was drifting in the middle of the Sound now, almost motionless in the calm conditions, but it was still difficult for an old man with weary arms and stiff legs to disembark.

The Homecomer threw the bag containing his booty into the bottom of the launch. Then he tied the end of a long plastic cable around his wrist, climbed over the gunwale and managed to get his feet on the front seat. For a few seconds he was sure the two vessels were going to drift apart, but Rita was in control, revving the outboard motor and keeping them side by side.

The Homecomer slid down into the launch, the plastic cable still around his wrist; it was now the only connection between the ship and the launch.

Rita didn't say anything. She seemed calm and collected, unlike her boyfriend. Pecka was sitting in the middle of the launch with his head down, mumbling to himself. As soon as he got in he had hurled his bloodstained axe into the water, far out into the darkness.

'Fuck . . . fuck . . .'

The Homecomer slumped down in the prow and touched his knee. 'Pecka. Look at me.'

Pecka raised his head. 'Fuck,' he said again. 'They're dead.'

The Homecomer nodded. 'Yes, and now we need to remove all traces.' He held up the cable in the darkness. 'We've got one thing left to do.'

Pecka stared blankly at him. 'We killed them,' he said. 'The whole crew.'

The Homecomer took his hand, which was ice cold. He knew

what was wrong with Pecka. He was in shock, just like many soldiers when they have killed for the first time. The important thing was to get Pecka to focus on details now, to forget the wider picture. When he himself had started killing as a young man, he had thought only about his gun, about handling it correctly – nothing else. Then it had been quite easy.

'They were sick, weren't they?' Pecka went on. 'Because of something in the hold?'

The Homecomer shook his head. He had no answer to that.

'They had only themselves to blame,' he said eventually, passing the end of the cable to Pecka. 'Let's finish this. You can do it.'

Pecka looked at the cable, which ran up over the gunwale of the ship and disappeared into one of the hatches. He grabbed the end in his trembling right hand, clutched the small detonator and pressed hard.

They heard a dull thud from inside the ship. The darkness seemed to shudder, and there was a gurgling noise from beneath the waterline. They had blown a hole in the hull.

The Homecomer had been holding his breath, and now he let it out. 'OK, let's go.'

Rita turned the wheel, and the launch moved away from the ship, which had already begun to list. The Homecomer had placed the explosives in the bow, which went down first. The stern began to tip up, slowly to start with, then faster and faster.

The ship sank majestically but almost silently, with only the odd hiss of air forced out of the vents.

After less than fifteen minutes the surface of the water was empty, and Rita set off at speed, heading home through the night.

The black shape of the island quickly grew larger as they approached. From a distance the shoreline was made up of gentle curves, but as they came closer the Homecomer could see how rocky and jagged it really was.

They had reached the inlets and the headlands between the Ölandic and Stenvik, where they had parked the car. The shore was still dark and deserted; everything was going to be OK.

Just before they landed, the Homecomer reached into the bag and took out two rolls of banknotes. He gave one each to Pecka and Rita.

'That's to keep you going until we meet again.'

Pecka didn't say thank you, but he seemed more composed now. He raised his voice above the sound of the outboard motor. 'That kid who came aboard the ship . . . What was he doing there?'

The Homecomer stared at him. 'A kid?'

'Yes, when were were on our way out into the Sound . . . He just appeared by the hatch, all of a sudden. I was looking for you, but you'd gone, and then this boy turned up with the living dead behind him – one of the crew members, I mean – so I used the axe and—'

'Calm down,' the Homecomer interrupted. He looked at Pecka as the bottom of the boat scraped against the rocks in the shallows. 'This boy – did he see you?'

'Well, yes, he was only a metre away. Right in front of me on the deck. God knows where he came from; I tried to grab hold of him but he disappeared over the gunwale . . .'

Rita turned off the engine. 'But you were wearing your balaclava, weren't you?' she said into the silence. 'He couldn't see your face?'

Pecka shook his head, looking distinctly uncomfortable.

'I wasn't wearing it at the time,' he said after a while. 'I got so fucking hot and sweaty.'

The Homecomer got to his feet and gazed out at the dark shore. 'Do you know who he was?'

'No.'

The Homecomer stepped ashore, but turned back to face Pecka. 'Go straight home,' he said. 'And stay there. Don't go out.'

Pecka seemed to understand the seriousness of the situation. He nodded. 'What about you?' he said. 'Will you be going home soon?'

'Home?'

'Yes . . . Back to America?'

The Homecomer didn't answer. He merely stared out at the black waters of the Sound. He was thinking about his voyage across the sea when he was a boy, when he still believed in the future.

The New Country, July 1931

Aron has left Sven in the cabin. There is nothing he can do. Sven's skinny body is lying in his bunk, but his head is hanging over the edge of the bed as he vomits into an enamel chamber pot on the floor. The smell is indescribable. Aron can't breathe in there.

Between the bouts of vomiting Sven mumbles to himself. He talks about the Kloss family, about the burial cairn and rocks rolling down and falling walls.

'You always have to have the last word . . . He was like a pillar of stone, solid and erect . . . I should have gone home . . . should never have raised my fist to him . . .'

Sometimes, Sven seems to think he is back on the island, that he is lying on the shore at Rödtorp, but that is not the case. He is lying on board the long white ship SS *Kastelholm*, as she steams across a vast, choppy sea.

He and Aron are sharing a bunk, but Aron is rarely in the cabin. He doesn't want to lie next to Sven in the middle of that stench; he spends most of his time on deck. Or on the bridge, where the captain has allowed him to come and watch how they sail the ship.

At the beginning of the voyage, Sven also wandered around SS *Kastelholm*. He would often stand on the foredeck, his hands resting on the gunwale as he gazed out to sea. But on the third day the waves began to get bigger and he took himself back to the cabin. And the chamber pot.

Aron is standing by the gunwale, watching the rushing water.

The sun is hidden behind a bank of cloud, the horizon has disappeared, and there is no sign of land or any other vessels. All he can see are the never-ending waves, racing towards the ship in long lines and breaking against the bow in a burst of spume.

Aron has lost all concept of time at sea, and he longs for them to arrive. To step on to dry land, any land at all. He can almost smell it.

Cold air, a stiff breeze. Aron can hear the sound of the steam engine out here, but he stays away from the machinery. He is happier with the wind and the sun, which reminds him of the shore by the croft.

He waits, and longs for the journey to end.

After a while, he hears someone limping up behind him; Sven has made it. He inhales the sea air and positions himself in front of the short mast, his legs firmly planted on the deck and his gaze fixed on some distant point. On the unknown.

Aron looks at him. 'Are we nearly there?'

Sven sighs. 'The same question, over and over again . . .' He swallows, belches quietly and keeps his eyes fixed on that distant point. 'Can you see any sign of land?'

Aron screws up his eyes and peers into the wind. He shakes his head.

'You will, before too long,' Sven goes on. 'We'll soon arrive in the new country.'

Aron has a question. 'Then can we write to Mum?'

'Of course. When we get there. If you can find what you need . . . a pen and paper and a stamp.'

'I'll do my best.'

'And if it's not too expensive.'

Aron decides that he will find pens and paper and stamps when they go ashore, whatever they cost.

'How long are we going to be there?'

'Be there?' Sven says. 'We're not just going to "be there". We're going to work, make a decent living. We're staying for at least a year.'

'And then we can come home?'

Sven sighs again. 'We'll come home when we come home,' he says. 'Don't ask so many questions.'

Then he turns and heads back to the cabin and the chamber pot.

Aron stays where he is. He stares out to sea, waiting for the coastline to appear, the beginning of the new country, another world.

Gerlof

The sun rose over the island at half past four, but Gerlof didn't wake until after seven. He blinked in the grey light of the boathouse and glanced over at the old nets hanging on the far wall. He remembered the hammering on the door and a frightened, soaking-wet boy tumbling in from the darkness. Was it all a dream?

No, there were some items of clothing hanging up to dry below the ceiling, and he was not alone. A small figure was fast asleep under several blankets on the other camp bed. The boy – Jonas Kloss.

When Gerlof blew out the candles, his breathing had slowly calmed down and, at last, all was quiet.

Gerlof had been too agitated and taken aback to settle down properly. He had nodded off after a while, in a half-sitting position on his bed, the ridiculous stone cudgel by his side, determined to keep a vigil in case of unknown dangers. Dead seamen and hungry monsters. But they had failed to materialize.

Now he placed his feet on the cold floor and opened the blind to look at the world outside.

The shore was just as grey as the water; the sun had yet to reach its summer strength. There wasn't a soul in sight along the coastline, and no sign of a shipwreck out in the Sound. The sea was as calm as a mirror – but, suddenly, he saw something moving down there, a little coal-black head swimming along by the shore.

Behind him, Jonas stirred.

'Good morning,' Gerlof said.

'Is he there?' The boy's voice was full of anxiety.

'No, there's no one out there at all,' Gerlof said quietly. 'All I can see is a mink; he's probably searching for birds' eggs.'

A few gulls were circling above the shore, uttering shrill warning cries. They had also spotted the mink, and soon the first bird came swooping down towards the water, using its sharp beak as a weapon. The mink quickly disappeared beneath the waves as the gull attacked, but popped up again a short distance away and headed towards the shore, where the rocks provided some protection. It emerged from the water, shook itself with a certain elegance, then slunk away like a wriggling black eel.

Gerlof smiled at the boy. 'How are you feeling this morning? Better?'

Jonas nodded, but his expression was strained and frightened. 'Can you see anybody?'

'No,' Gerlof said again. 'And there's no ship either.'

He noticed an old drawing pad on the little bookcase. One of the grandchildren must have left their paper and crayons. The pad gave him an idea.

'Shall we try to work out what the boat looked like?' he said. 'You can describe it to me, and I'll draw it.'

'OK,' Jonas said.

Gerlof picked up a black crayon and drew the outline of an Öland fishing boat. He added a small wheelhouse and a short mast in the prow. 'Was it a fishing boat? One like this?'

'No. I could smell fish on the deck, but it was longer.'

Gerlof drew a tugboat, with a reinforced prow and stern. 'Like this?'

'No . . . even longer than that,' the boy said.

Gerlof screwed up the piece of paper and made a third attempt. This time he drew a bigger ship, with several cargo hatches. 'How about this?'

Jonas nodded silently, and Gerlof felt quite pleased with himself.

'And what was it made of? Wood or metal? Did you notice any rivets in the hull when you climbed aboard?'

Jonas thought for a moment, then nodded again.

'Good, so it was metal . . . What could you see on deck? Any kind of structure?'

Jonas pointed. 'There was a little kind of hut here at the front . . . and a bigger one at the back.'

Gerlof started drawing and asked another question. 'Did you notice any Plimsoll lines on the freeboard?'

The boy looked at him blankly, so Gerlof went on: 'It doesn't matter . . . Were there any masts on the ship?'

Jonas closed his eyes. 'I can't remember. There might have been a little one right at the front. And there was a big hatch in the middle.'

Gerlof drew a thick line to mark the position of the hatch, then asked, 'And where were these men who were dying?'

'They were lying there. And there. And there.'

'And the others?'

'The man with the axe was standing here.' Jonas pointed. 'And there was an old man with white hair up in the wheelhouse . . . there.'

Gerlof marked each spot with a black cross.

'Did the ship have a name? Did you notice a name on the bow?'

Jonas nodded. 'It said "*Elia*".'

'*Elia?* As in the man who raised the dead in Zarephath?'

The boy stared at him, and Gerlof realized that Jonas had yet to be confirmed. Then again, children probably didn't read the Bible when they were preparing for their confirmation these days; they probably gave each other massages and sang happy songs.

He wrote the name *Elia* on the bow of the ship. Good. Then he rolled up the drawing and nodded. 'Well done, Jonas. Shall we go and have some breakfast? It's on me.'

He didn't get a smile in return, but the boy nodded and got to his feet.

Lisa

The day after her second stint as a DJ, Lisa was woken by a noise outside the caravan. Someone was hammering metal. She sat up in bed and looked at the clock. Ten past ten. Her grandmother had always slept until at least ten o'clock in her old age. If I get up any earlier, the day is much too long, she used to say, making it clear how tedious she found life after the death of Lisa's grandfather.

Lisa's life was far from tedious.

The night before, Lady Summertime had almost got caught. Almost. A rich kid who had had far too much to drink and had been throwing his money around all night had placed his sweaty hand on hers just as she was about to remove his wallet from his jacket pocket.

Fuck! she had thought.

But a second later she had let go of the wallet (which was very fat, unfortunately) and allowed it to slip back into his pocket. The boy had stuck his tongue in her ear, then turned back to the bar, as drunk as a skunk. He hadn't noticed a thing.

Lisa got up and peered through the window at the glorious morning. The sky was bright blue and she could hear the rushing of the waves. The only slightly depressing note was struck by the maypole, abandoned over on the festival site and adorned with flowers that had wilted in the sunshine.

She noticed an old man with white hair over by a caravan that was listing to one side. He was bent over a jack, trying to right it. That explained the noise. She turned away from the window and decided it was time for breakfast.

When she had eaten, she picked up her mobile and called the

apartment in Huddinge. It rang out twelve times before a hoarse, weary voice replied, 'Hello?'

Silas. It was quarter to eleven – early in the morning for him.

'Hi, it's me.'

Silas sighed. Lisa could tell from his breathing that he was clean today. Tired, but clean.

'Hi.'

Then there was silence, apart from the sound of breathing.

'How are you?' Lisa asked.

'OK. Thirsty.'

'Well, have a drink then.'

'There's nothing in.'

'Drink tap water.'

'I don't want to . . . There's arsenic in tap water.'

Silence.

'I've sent you a letter,' Lisa said.

'With papers?'

'Yes. Lots of papers.'

'Good . . . Will you be sending more letters this summer?'

'I think so,' Lisa replied. 'It looks that way.'

'Great.'

Silas didn't say thank you, but he sounded pleased.

The conversation didn't last much longer, because Silas was on his way out. He didn't say where he was going. As usual.

Lisa switched off her mobile and sat motionless in the caravan for a little while. Eventually, she picked up an empty plastic container and went out into the sunshine to fetch some water. As she was standing by the taps, the door of one of the neighbouring caravans among the dog roses opened. Lisa recognized the young woman who stepped out; she was the girl who had been at the midsummer dance with the Kloss family.

Paulina, wasn't that her name? They nodded at one another.

'Morning,' Lisa said. 'So you live here, too?'

Paulina nodded again.

'Have you been here long?'

'Two weeks . . . Summer job.'

'Same as me,' Lisa said. 'I'm working here through July. Will you be going back to Poland after that?'

Paulina shook her head. 'Not Poland. I come from Lietuva.'

'Lietuva?' Lisa thought for a moment. 'That's Lithuania, isn't it?'

'Yes . . . Lithuania.'

Paulina didn't say anything else. Lisa gazed at Paulina's caravan; it was smaller and even older than hers, and much shabbier. It resembled a cracked egg more than anything. She suddenly felt privileged, and slightly embarrassed.

'Right,' she said, picking up the container, 'I'd better go and get ready for work . . . Are you working today?'

Another nod.

'For the Kloss family?'

'Not family. I only work for *him*.'

'Him?'

'Yes,' Paulina said, her expression serious. 'Only for Kent Kloss.' She looked away and didn't say any more. But Lisa got the feeling that Paulina didn't much like what she had to do for Kent Kloss.

Gerlof

Jonas was recognized when they walked into the cottage; apparently, eleven-year-old Kristoffer, Julia's bonus child following the loss of her son, Jens, had attended swimming classes with him. They said a slightly shy 'hi' to one another.

Good. An established friendship would make everything easier, Gerlof thought. He led Jonas over to the telephone.

'Ring your parents. They must be worried – tell them you're fine.'

The boy seemed hesitant. 'There's only my dad here . . . We're staying with Auntie Veronica and Uncle Kent.'

Gerlof nodded; he knew about the owners of the Ölandic Resort.

'Well, call the house then. Tell them you're over at the Davidssons'. Do you want them to come and pick you up?'

Jonas shook his head, then slowly picked up the phone. His expression was so troubled Gerlof thought it best to leave the room. He heard the boy talking quietly to someone.

Afterwards, they had breakfast. Gerlof was expecting his three grandsons to ask where he had found Jonas, but they didn't, and after a little while Jonas started to join in with the conversation, smiling when the other boys smiled.

Gerlof wasn't smiling. He glanced over at the coffee table, where he had left the drawing of the ship. *Elia*. He looked at the black crosses by the cargo hatch, and pondered.

After breakfast, he picked up the drawing and his straw hat and asked Jonas to come outside with him for a little while. They sat side by side on deckchairs on the lawn, with the sun starting to burn down on Gerlof's shoulders and legs. Jonas kept his eyes fixed on the grass.

'Are you thinking about what happened yesterday?' Gerlof asked.

The boy looked at him and nodded, and Gerlof knew that the fear had come back.

'Everything you told me about the ship . . . Are you still saying it's all true?'

'Yes.'

'You saw dead seamen on the ship, and two people who were still alive. An older man up in the wheelhouse, and a younger man with an axe . . . and you think he comes from Africa. Is that right?'

'Well, yes,' Jonas said quietly. 'But I didn't say he was *from* Africa. You asked me what came into my mind when I saw him – I thought about African animals and jungle drums.'

Gerlof was puzzled. 'Have you ever been to Africa?'

Jonas shook his head.

Gerlof didn't think he was going to get any further with this; he picked up his stick and slowly got to his feet. 'I think we'd better call the police,' he said.

Jonas looked frightened, but Gerlof held up his hand.

'It'll be fine . . . We're family.'

Tilda Davidsson was the only serving police officer Gerlof knew, and she was also the granddaughter of his late older brother. Gerlof managed to get hold of her at home on the eastern side of the island and briefly explained what had happened.

'So I was wondering whether the coastguard had seen any ships adrift in the Sound last night?'

'I've no idea,' Tilda replied. 'I'm not with the coastguard. And it's my day off.'

Gerlof could hear children laughing in the background, but went on anyway. 'Could you ask them to check?'

'No, that will be up to the central communications office, if we decide the boy's story is credible.'

Gerlof sighed; so much hassle. 'Well, could you come over and see what you think?'

And she did, without any of her colleagues, and out of uniform. She was wearing a loose-fitting denim dress, and Gerlof wondered if she might be pregnant. However, he didn't dare ask.

Tilda said hello to Gerlof and the grandchildren, then shook hands with Jonas Kloss, who was playing a video game.

128

'Tilda is a police officer from Kalmar,' Gerlof explained. 'I think it would be a good idea if you two had a little chat.'

Jonas got up slowly, looking far from thrilled at the prospect. Tilda spoke quietly to Gerlof. 'You can sit in.'

'Can I?'

'You can be a witness; the police sometimes bring in an independent observer to make sure an interview is carried out correctly.'

Gerlof agreed, and followed Jonas and Tilda out into the shimmering heat.

'Do you come here every summer, Jonas?' Tilda asked when they were settled under the parasol.

'No. Last summer we stayed at home with Mum. Because Dad . . .' He fell silent and looked at Gerlof.

'And where does your mum live?' Tilda went on.

'Huskvarna.'

Gerlof sat quietly and let Tilda do the talking. First of all, they chatted about video games and football stickers, which it seemed Tilda knew quite a lot about. After a few moments, she leaned forward. 'I believe you saw something terrible last night . . .'

Jonas nodded.

'Would you like to tell me about it?'

'OK.'

They sat there listening for twenty minutes. Gerlof heard the same story from Jonas Kloss all over again – the same dark ship in the Sound, the same dead seamen, the same man with the axe and the elderly man called Aron – and because it matched his first account so perfectly, Gerlof became more and more convinced that it was true.

Afterwards, Tilda and Gerlof stayed in the garden and let Jonas go back indoors.

'Your interrogation produced the same result as mine,' Gerlof said.

'That wasn't an interrogation,' Tilda quickly corrected him. 'You have to be very careful when you question minors – we have specially trained officers for that. We were just having a chat.'

'So are you going to look into this?'

'Look into what, Gerlof? If the county police are going to send out officers to start knocking on doors and questioning witnesses, there has to be a crime scene. And as far as we know, there isn't one.'

Gerlof unfolded the drawing he had brought from the boathouse.

'There's this. I drew it this morning, with Jonas's help. He says this is the ship he was on. It's not from Öland.'

Tilda looked at the sketch.

'How do you know?'

'It's too big. It looks like a smallish cargo ship, probably around ninety feet, from the period between the wars. It could be an old cement ship from Degerhamn, but none of them is called *Elia*.'

'OK, but in that case, where is it? I drove a little way along the coast road before I came here, and there were no ships in the Sound.'

'It's moved on. The boy said it had engines . . . I heard a ship last night, heading north, and I saw the backwash. It could have left the Sound and carried on into the Baltic.' Gerlof paused for a moment, then added, 'Unless it's sunk. Or been scuttled.'

'All right, you win.' Tilda gave him back the drawing. 'I can ask the coastguard to keep an eye open, but if no ship turns up we don't have much to work on. Just a little boy.'

'A *frightened* boy. His whole body was shaking when he stumbled into my boathouse. He'd seen something truly horrific.'

'Ghosts on a ghost ship,' Tilda said.

'*Seeing* ghosts isn't the same as saying they *exist*,' Gerlof insisted. 'But I could tell you a story . . .'

Tilda smiled wearily. 'One of your ghost stories?'

Gerlof wagged a finger at her. 'Just you listen to me. This is *true*. It's something that happened to me back in the fifties, when we were carrying stone to Stockholm. We sailed along the coast virtually every week – it was pure routine. But one hot summer's day we stopped in Oskarshamn to unload a cargo of machine oil. There was a fishing boat moored beside us at the quayside; she looked completely sea-worthy but seemed to be deserted. There was no sign of anyone on board. But at sea it's a tradition to call on your neighbours, so when we'd finished unloading I went over to see where the crew were, thinking they might be asleep or something.'

He glanced over to the west, where the water was just visible through the trees.

'So I knocked on the wheelhouse door, but there was no response. No one was there. I could have gone back to my own ship, but I had a strange feeling. So I walked around the deck and saw that the cargo hatch was partly open. I looked down into the darkness, and they were just lying there. Two fishermen side by side in the hold.'

'Murdered?'

'That's what I thought at first, so I climbed down. They were dead, but there wasn't a mark on them – just a kind of blue tinge to their faces. That was when I guessed what had happened, and I tried to turn around to climb back up out of the hold. That's the last thing I remember before I woke up on deck, with John yelling at me. Somehow I had managed to crawl up the ladder before I passed out. I felt terrible . . . you could say I was one of the living dead by that stage.'

'So there was poison gas in the hold of this fishing boat?'

Gerlof shook his head. 'No, just fish . . . but it was the fish that had killed them. The fishermen had been cleaning their catch below deck, and the guts had started to rot in the summer heat, producing hydrogen sulphide. It had consumed all the oxygen, suffocating them.'

'Does it happen very often?'

'Not on modern fishing boats. They have refrigeration equipment and ice to keep the fish fresh. But it used to happen sometimes in the past, in the summer. And on an old ship with fish in the hold, the kind of ship Jonas might have been on last night . . . it could happen. He said the deck stank of fish, so the men he saw could have been poisoned by hydrogen sulphide.'

Tilda thought about what he had said. 'So we're talking about a fatal accident?' she said.

'It could have been an accident,' Gerlof conceded. 'But I wonder . . . You have to be in an enclosed space in order to suffocate. And why would they all be below at the same time, on a ship so near to the coast? It's as if someone forced the crew below deck, then locked them in.'

Tilda didn't say anything for a moment, then she took out her mobile and moved a short distance away. Gerlof heard her speaking quietly to someone. After a few minutes she was back.

'I've spoken to the coastguard; they had no reports of ships off Öland last night.'

'What did you say to them?'

'I just said that a member of the public had seen a ship that appeared to be adrift off the coast near Stenvik. They're not going to launch a major search, but they did promise to keep an eye open.'

Gerlof picked up his stick and accompanied Tilda to her car.

'Is this important to you?' she asked.

'Not really,' Gerlof said, then he thought for a second and went on, 'But someone has to listen to young people. When I was a boy I heard the sound of knocking from inside a coffin up in the churchyard, but my father just laughed when I came home and told him about it. And that's why I never laugh, whatever strange tales I might hear.' He looked at Tilda. 'How are you getting on with your ghosts up at the lighthouses, by the way?'

'They're on holiday,' she said tersely. 'Just like I shall be, very soon.' She got in the car and drove off.

There's nothing more I can do, Gerlof thought as he went back to sit in the garden. The birds were singing, the sun was blazing down. But he couldn't stop going over what Jonas had told him.

A ghost ship in the Sound, with an elderly American on board.

And a younger man from Africa?

The Homecomer

On sunny summer days Öland's beaches were crowded; there were more tourists than the Homecomer had ever seen, which was a good thing. He could simply walk around like one of them, an old man in shorts and a red T-shirt and sunglasses.

He could also visit the burial cairn in Stenvik without anyone asking what he was doing there. It was an ancient monument, after all, open to everyone. So he parked the Ford he had bought in Stockholm among all the other cars down by the mailboxes in Stenvik, then headed south.

When he looked out over the Sound he could see a number of vessels: small motorboats close to the shore, and a few larger yachts further out, but not one single ship.

In the warm sunshine, with a good night's sleep behind him, it was difficult to recall exactly what had happened yesterday: boarding the ship, forcing the crew below, blowing a hole in the hull. There was no sign of the ship today.

The Homecomer passed the small campsite down by the water, then headed up towards the ridge. He could stay out of sight of the summer cottages along the coast road, because there was a narrow dip above the shore. It was man-made; it had been hacked out by stonemasons in days gone by as they worked their way down the rock. They had left behind a V-shaped cleft with gravel and broken stones at the bottom. The Homecomer moved cautiously so that he wouldn't trip.

After a while, he saw the cairn above him; it looked like a large pile of stones up on the ridge. It was closer to the edge than he remembered; the cliff face must have suffered from erosion over the past seventy years.

Time smashed everything to pieces.

A few metres below the cairn there was a metal door set in a concrete frame; it seemed to lead right into the rock almost directly below the cairn. It looked like the entrance to a bunker – perhaps it was a defence post left over from the war?

The Homecomer glanced around, but he was still alone.

The metal door was secured with a heavy padlock and chain. He tugged at it, but to no avail. He would need a pair of bolt cutters.

After a minute or so, he walked away from the bunker and found a narrow flight of stone steps that took him up the hill and on to the ridge. He stood by the cairn for a while, silent and still, thinking of Sven.

Then he turned and looked inland, towards the houses on the other side of the coast road. Two rectangular bungalows with enormous windows and an expanse of wooden decking. Between them he could see a huge blue swimming pool.

He was close to the Kloss family now, just a few hundred metres away, but he could move around out of sight in the dip. And they didn't know him. No one knew who he was.

Which made everything so much easier.

The New Country, July 1931

Aron and Sven are standing on deck with their luggage. They have arrived. The steamer SS *Kastelholm* is sliding into a large, unfamiliar harbour full of other ships; she slowly heaves to beside a broad stone quay. Aron watches as the city with its tall buildings and wide streets grows before his very eyes. Vast buildings with long rows of narrow windows.

Stockholm was nothing compared to this. Aron doesn't recognize the name of the city; he just knows they have arrived in America.

The United States. The new country.

Sven carries their bags and tools down the gangplank; they are led through a dark stone doorway where everyone has to stand in line. Eventually, two broad-shouldered men in uniform arrive to interview them, with the help of an interpreter. Aron says nothing; Sven does all the talking. He shows their passports, holds up the spade, smiles at the interpreter and the grim-faced officials.

'We've come here voluntarily.'

'Of course,' says the interpreter. 'But what is it you intend to do here?'

'We want to work, both of us. We want to build the new country.'

The interpreter confers with the guards, then he says, 'What is your profession?'

'We're agricultural workers. I've worked in flour mills, but I've spent most of my time growing crops and tending cattle. And my stepson has attended school and helped me in his spare time.'

The interpreter checks Aron's passport. 'He's only thirteen years old . . .'

'Yes, but he's big and strong and hardworking.'

One of the guards shows Sven a picture, a portrait of a man with sharp eyes, his chin raised. 'Do you know who this is?'

'Your leader,' Sven replies.

'What's his name?'

Aron hears Sven say an unfamiliar name without the slightest hesitation, and the guards nod with satisfaction.

Finally, Sven gives the men some of their dollar bills. That does the trick. Their passports are stamped, travel documents are issued and they are allowed into the new country.

Sven and Aron remain in the city for three days; they stay in a small hotel near a big railway station and wander the wide, crowded streets. Aron hears lots of foreign languages but doesn't understand a single word. Everyone around them appears to know where they are going, but Sven seems somehow lost. In the cramped room, his mood deteriorates, and he hits Aron several times.

In the evenings he goes out, and is gone for hours. Aron can only wait by the window.

On the second evening, Sven is much more cheerful when he returns. Everything is arranged; he has met someone who speaks Swedish.

'We're moving on,' he tells Aron. 'There are lots of Scandinavians in the forests in the north. They've got work for us up there.'

Aron would like to spend longer in the city, but he has no say in the matter.

They leave by train the following day. The concrete buildings disappear, the countryside takes over and they travel north through a green and brown landscape of vast plains, virgin coniferous forests, wide rivers and immense lakes.

The train is packed with optimistic workers, all equipped with their own tools – saws, pickaxes and spades.

Sven and Aron are with them in the third-class carriage. The dollar bills are almost gone. They have hardly any food, but at one end of the carriage you can buy steaming-hot tea. Everything else on the train is freezing cold.

But Sven keeps his eyes firmly fixed on the route ahead, one hand resting on his spade.

Jonas

It was almost twelve o'clock by the time Jonas got back to Villa Kloss. He had only pretended to call home from the Davidssons' house, just to appease Gerlof. No one in his family knew where he had spent the night. If he gave the game away, Mats and their cousins would probably chuck him off the rocks.

On the way home he had gazed out across the bay, but there was no sign of any ships and no dead seamen had floated ashore. The sun was shining and the breeze was warm. People were swimming and sunbathing by the jetty as if it were an ordinary summer's day, but Jonas's heart was pounding.

He had reached Villa Kloss. Might as well go straight in.

He slid open the glass door of Uncle Kent's house, expecting to see everyone gathered around the long dining table: Uncle Kent, Dad, Mats and the cousins, all worried and with lots of questions, but no one seemed to have noticed his absence. They weren't even there.

Only Paulina was around, standing in the kitchen, stacking dishes after the party. Everyone else was probably still in bed, or else they'd gone off to the Ölandic. Jonas had a drink of water and went over to his chalet. On the way he met Mats and Urban, both wearing green shorts and sunglasses. They were carrying two racing bikes.

'Hi, bro.'

'How's things?' Urban said.

'Fine,' Jonas replied.

Mats stopped and spoke quietly. 'We told Dad you stayed over with a friend last night. That's what you did, isn't it?'

'Well, yes, kind of . . . I slept in a boathouse.'

'Good . . . I should think that was a lot more fun than Kalmar. The film was crap.'

Jonas nodded and thought about dead men on the deck of a ship. And then about Africa. He could hear jungle drums pounding in his head, and he just wanted to ring his mum in Huskvarna. Ask her to come and pick him up, take him home.

But he didn't. He had to stay here; he had work to do.

So when Mats and Urban had cycled off down the coast, he went out on to Uncle Kent's warm, sunlit decking. The planks were waiting. First of all he had to sand them down, then he would apply Chinese wood oil, which had been ordered specially.

Suddenly, he heard the sound of an engine behind him. Uncle Kent drove in and parked over by the garage. He was holding his mobile phone and seemed to be doing a lot of listening, with occasional monosyllabic responses. He was red-faced and sweaty, and when the call was over he sat in the car, looking out towards the Sound.

Then he shook his head and made another call.

Something seemed to have upset Uncle Kent, but Jonas didn't want to know what it was. Kent didn't appear to have noticed him, anyway, he was too stressed – after only a minute or so, he reversed on to the coast road and drove off again.

Jonas looked down at the decking. He was no longer on holiday. The previous evening, his father had shown him what to do. 'Steady, even strokes, Jonas, and make them as long as possible. Keep your hand moving all the time so that you don't chip the wood.'

Jonas picked up the sander, switched it on and ran it over each plank. It was hard work. The dirt was ingrained in every piece of wood, and he had to go over each one several times in order to bring it back to its original pale colour.

But it was good to be working; it stopped him thinking. About the man with the axe, and the dying seamen.

After perhaps twenty minutes the glass door slid open.

'Afternoon, Jonas!'

His father emerged, wearing sandals, shorts and a shirt. He blinked up at the sun and waved to Jonas. 'Everything OK?'

Jonas nodded. His father went and sat on a sun lounger by the pool and closed his eyes.

Did he have a hangover from the party? Jonas couldn't tell.

He carried on working, but when he had sanded down two more planks and the sweat was pouring down his back, he took a break. He went over to join his father and sat down on the edge of the pool, dangling his feet in the cool water. Niklas smiled at him, and Jonas asked, 'Did you see the ship?'

Niklas stared at him, then looked out across the Sound. 'What ship?'

'A big ship. Last night.'

'Not last night,' his father said. 'But I have seen a few cargo ships passing through the Sound since we arrived.'

Jonas didn't say any more about the ship. He sat there for a few minutes longer with his feet in the water, until he had stopped sweating, then he stood up. 'I'd better get on.'

It was easier now; he had learned how to hold the sander.

After a while he got up and stretched, and saw that he was being watched from the other side of the coast road. A grey-haired man with a white beard and sunglasses was standing on the ridge above the shore, staring at Villa Kloss. He was wearing a red T-shirt, but Jonas couldn't make out his face. Too far away.

He was standing in the middle of the rocks that had rolled down from the cairn, and when Jonas realized that he went cold all over.

He turned to see whether his father had noticed the man as well, but Niklas was lying back on the sun lounger with his mouth open. He had fallen asleep.

Jonas slowly bent down and resumed his sanding, but when he had finished the plank he looked over at the cairn once more.

The man had disappeared.

Gerlof

The birds were singing at the tops of their voices. Gerlof was sitting in the garden with his hearing aid turned up to full volume, and the song in the bushes rose and fell like a summer concert.

Who needed a gramophone when there were blackbirds? Not Gerlof.

It was early evening, but still warm and calm. The entire day had gone, June would soon be over, and he had done very little apart from doze in the sunshine.

He had had a headache, probably due to lack of sleep, so he turned down the opportunity to play mini-golf with his grandchildren and listened to the birds with his eyes closed instead – until he heard the gate opening.

A boy was standing there. Jonas Kloss, his overnight guest, was back.

Gerlof waved and the boy slowly came over to say hello.

'Is Kristoffer home?'

'Not at the moment.'

'We were going to play *FIFA* on his Nintendo,' Jonas said.

Gerlof had no idea what he was talking about, but nodded anyway.

'The boys have gone over to the restaurant, but they'll be back soon. How are you this evening, Jonas?'

'Fine.'

Just one word. Then silence, until Gerlof asked, 'Have you thought much about what happened . . . about the ship?'

Jonas nodded. He was rigid and tense, as if the dead had him in their clutches. And that was probably true; after seventy years, Gerlof still remembered Gilbert Kloss collapsing in the churchyard. He had been a few years older than Jonas at the time, but that day still haunted him. He didn't want Jonas to be affected the same way, so he leaned forward. 'Jonas,' he said slowly. 'I think I know what had happened to those men you saw on the ship. They weren't monsters or zombies. They'd been poisoned by gas.'

Jonas stared at him. 'Gas?'

'From the fish in the hold. You said you could smell fish on board, but I think the fish had gone rotten in the heat.'

He told Jonas the same story he had told Tilda. Jonas listened in silence and seemed to relax slightly when Gerlof stopped speaking. He started to move away, but Gerlof hadn't finished.

'And the man with the axe, Jonas . . . Have you remembered where you'd seen him before?'

The boy shook his head.

'I can try to help you if you like. Would that be all right?'

'OK.'

With some difficulty, Gerlof pulled up another garden chair. 'Sit down.' Now they were sitting face to face, and Gerlof picked up his notebook and a pen. He smiled at Jonas. 'Ready?'

'Ready.'

'Good. In that case, let's try to travel back in time . . . Can you conjure up the man from the ship so that you can see his face?'

Jonas nodded, but kept his eyes lowered.

'Try to think back to where you'd seen him before,' Gerlof said, speaking more slowly. 'Imagine you're going back in time, to the moment just before you saw him.'

'OK,' Jonas said again, his head drooping even more.

The garden was suddenly quiet, apart from a lone bumble bee buzzing past their chairs.

Gerlof waited for a few seconds, then asked, 'What can you see now, Jonas?'

'A building.'

'And what time is it?'

'I don't know . . . but it's summer. Evening.'

'And you're standing outside a building. Is it here on the island?'

'Don't know. I think so.'

'What does this building look like?'

'It's big.'

141

'Is it made of stone, like a castle? Or brick?'

'Wood. Big planks of wood.'

Jonas was staring at the grass. He wasn't in a hypnotic trance, he was just concentrating hard.

A wooden building. Gerlof quickly made a note of that.

'You have to be very careful when you question minors,' Tilda had said. Gerlof would be careful. And this wasn't a real interview, he told himself, it was just a *chat*. He went on, 'What colour is the building?'

'Red.'

Most wooden buildings on Öland were red, of course. The whole of Sweden was full of red buildings. Gerlof tried again. 'So he's inside a big red building?'

'Yes.'

'Are you inside, too?'

'No, but I'm going in.'

'On your own?'

'With Mats.'

'Who's Mats?'

'My older brother.'

'And how do you and Mats get into this building?'

'We go up a big stone staircase.'

'And in through a door?'

'Yes.'

'And the man from the ship is waiting for you in there?'

'Yes . . . He's sitting there, and he's, like, waiting.'

'Does he say anything to you?'

'No. I think he nods.'

'Does he do anything else?'

'He holds out his hand.'

Gerlof thought about this, then asked, 'Does he want something from you?'

'Yes, our money.'

'Your money? How much money?'

'All of it. From Mats. Mats gives him the money.'

'Does the man give . . .'

 . . . *you anything in return?* he was going to ask, but at that moment he heard the gate and the boys came running up the path. They were back from mini-golf.

'Hi, Jonas!' Kristoffer shouted.

Jonas opened his eyes, his concentration broken. He waved to his friend, then quickly got to his feet as if he were embarrassed, and mumbled to Gerlof, 'Got to go.'

'I know, but thanks for the chat.'

Jonas nodded and hurried over to join Kristoffer.

The memory of a man in a big red building. And Africa. Gerlof sat there puzzling over the mystery all evening, but he couldn't solve it.

In the end, he went indoors.

Jonas had gone home but, as usual, his grandchildren were sitting there watching a film with lots of car chases and explosions. They put on a film most evenings, but turned down the volume when Gerlof was around. That was one thing they had learned.

He went to the bathroom, then into his bedroom.

'Goodnight, boys,' he said, closing the door.

He would sleep in the cottage tonight. It seemed like the quieter option, in spite of everything.

Two hours later, the cottage was quiet; the boys had switched off the television and gone to bed. Gerlof's head sank deeper and deeper into the pillow; he was almost asleep.

But suddenly he opened his eyes; he was wide awake.

The boys watch a film almost every evening.

The thought made him sit up, turn on the light and open his notebook. He read through what Jonas had said with fresh eyes and blinked in surprise, because his almost-sleeping brain had worked through all those random memories and come up with a possible solution to the mystery of Jonas and Africa.

Gerlof picked up a pen with trembling hands and wrote down one word so that it wouldn't go out of his head by morning. Then he reached for the phone book. He needed to speak to someone, an old acquaintance from the local history society.

He found the number and keyed it in. The person at the other end picked up after only three rings, and Gerlof spoke quietly, so as not to wake his grandsons.

'Good evening, Bertil – it's Gerlof Davidsson.'

'Gerlof? Oh . . . good evening.'

'Am I disturbing you? Were you asleep?'

'Not at all – I stay up late in the summer. We've been sitting out on the veranda, my brother and I, so it's absolutely—'

'Good,' Gerlof interrupted him. 'It's just that I have a question that might sound a bit odd. But it's important, and it's about the Marnäs manor house. Are you still running things up there?'

'I am – I can't get out of it.'

'I'm looking for someone who had a summer job there five years ago, selling tickets. A young man, but I don't know his exact age – just that he was young.'

'Five years ago? '94?'

'That's right. Can you think of anyone who fits the bill?'

Bertil didn't say anything for a moment.

'The only person I can remember who had a summer job was Pecka. He would have been about twenty back then . . .'

'Pecka?'

'That's what he called himself, but his real name is Peter, Peter Mayer. He worked for us for one summer, then he moved on.'

'Do you know where to?'

'He had lots of different jobs. As far as I remember, he joined the crew of a fishing boat for a while, then he worked at a couple of campsites and in a grocery store. I don't think things worked out too well for him; he had some problems with his temperament, and disciplinary issues, if you know what I mean.'

'I think I do,' Gerlof said. 'One last thing . . . Do you have a list of the films you've shown at the manor house?'

'Not here, but there's one in the office.'

'Could I have a look at it?'

'Of course,' Bertil said. 'I'll drop by in the morning.'

'Thank you, Bertil – thank you very much.'

Gerlof said goodnight and ended the call. Then he went back to his notebook to write down a name he had never heard before: PETER MAYER.

Then he turned off the light and went back to sleep.

Jonas

Jonas had finished sanding for the day and had treated himself to a dip in the pool afterwards. As usual, he was alone. Nothing that had happened over the past few days had changed that. Casper had gone off on his moped; he hadn't really seemed to care when Jonas finally told him that his old rubber dinghy had sunk. Dad was at the restaurant, and Mats and Urban were working down at the Ölandic.

There were, of course, boys of approximately his own age in the village. Kristoffer was a year younger, and perhaps a little childish, but he was still a pretty cool companion. After his swim, Jonas cycled over to the Davidssons' cottage.

'Jonas!'

As he walked in through the gate, he saw Kristoffer's grandfather Gerlof in his usual spot in the garden. He waved his little notebook at Jonas.

Gerlof seemed bright and cheery this Wednesday, as if he was bursting with news. Jonas went over to him, and Gerlof started talking right away.

'Kristoffer's inside, you can go and see him in a minute, but I just want to show you something first. I wrote something down after we'd had our chat yesterday. It's about the ship, and the man you saw on board. Would you like to see?'

Jonas didn't really want to think any more about the ghost ship, but he didn't have much choice.

'Good. Here it comes.'

Gerlof held out his notebook and pointed to three words written in pencil, in shaky handwriting. Jonas leaned forward and read, '*The Lion King*'. He read it twice, then looked up at Gerlof.

'It's a film,' Gerlof said. 'I've only seen it on video with my grand-children, but it's been on in the cinema, too . . . Do you remember it?'

Jonas nodded; he had seen it several times. 'It's about animals in Africa,' he said. 'A father lion is killed by his brother and thrown off a mountainside. And there's loads of music.'

'Exactly,' Gerlof said, looking pleased. 'It was when you said the word "Africa" . . . During the night, I got the idea that the man who was after you might have been working in a cinema when you and your brother went to see *The Lion King*. I checked with an acquaint-ance who's involved in showing films on the island, and it was on at the manor house in Marnäs five years ago, in the summer of '94. Were you here then?'

'I think so.'

'Good. Because Marnäs manor house is a big red building, made of wood. Just like the one you described to me.'

Jonas remembered now. He had been seven years old that summer; Mats had been twelve. Dad had taken them up to Marnäs, but he hadn't stayed for the film, he had just dropped them off and picked them up afterwards. So they had gone to the cinema on their own, for the first time ever. They had gone into the building and up to the ticket office, and . . .

It was all coming back to him now.

'Yes, that's where he was. The man from the ship, he was sitting in a little kiosk, and he sold us our tickets.'

'Good,' Gerlof said again. 'And I managed to find a name . . . There was only one young man who worked in the cinema that summer, so I think we can identify him.'

He paused and leaned forward. 'But if I tell you, will you promise not to tell anyone else?'

Jonas didn't look too sure, but he agreed.

'His name is Peter, Peter Mayer. But he's known as Pecka. Do you recognize that name?'

Jonas shook his head. 'The man on the ship didn't tell me his name.'

'No, of course not. But I looked in the phone book this morning, and there's a Peter Mayer who lives up in Marnäs.'

Jonas stiffened. There was a sudden chill in the evening air. 'So he lives here . . . on the island?'

'Yes, if that's him. But there's nothing to worry about, Jonas. He doesn't know who you are.'

Nevertheless, Jonas's heart was pounding. Marnäs wasn't far away; you could cycle there in half an hour. Casper went there on his moped virtually every day. And the man with the axe lived there.

'We just need to find out more about him,' Gerlof went on. 'You said he mentioned an old man, an American?'

'Aron,' Jonas said.

'Aron,' Gerlof repeated thoughtfully.

Jonas wanted to tell Gerlof about the figure he had seen by the cairn the previous day, the figure that reminded him of the man on the ghost ship – but now he was no longer sure whether he might have imagined it.

They sat in silence for a moment, then Gerlof looked down at his notebook.

'Right, Jonas. I'll try to find the American, too. If he exists.'

Gerlof

Tilda's phone was still engaged. Gerlof had things to tell her, but he hung up. He knew that it wasn't against the law for a private individual to look into things, but he thought it was time to let her know what he had found out about Peter Mayer. And the mysterious Swedish-American.

Gerlof thought about the period of mass emigration from Sweden to the United States, the great exodus from Sweden that had lasted from the 1840s into the 1920s and beyond.

These days, as the summer residences in Stenvik kept on getting bigger and bigger, and all the shiny, expensive cars zoomed along the coast road, it was easy to forget how poor this area had been a hundred years ago. Poverty had reigned throughout the whole of Sweden – a remote country in the north without any great wealth. Hunger and lack of work had driven a fifth of the population overseas, mainly to America.

Öland and America were linked by all those journeys – first of all, the journey to the new country, then the journey home. Most of those who returned were poverty-stricken; the odd one had made it and was rich.

Gerlof didn't know of any emigrants who were still alive, so he picked up the phone again and called someone who might just have the answer. Bill Carlson in Långvik was the only elderly American he knew; Bill was an interested descendant of genuine emigrants from the island.

A young Swedish relative answered, but he quickly called Bill in from the veranda.

'Yeah?'

'Hello Bill, it's Gerlof Davidsson.'

There was a brief silence at the other end of the phone, then an enthusiastic 'Gerlof! Hello-o! How are you?'

'I'm fine.'

'How's your little boat?'

'Well, we're working on her . . .' He cleared his throat and went on. 'Bill, I need your help with something. I'm looking for an American.'

'An American?'

'Yes. I think he's on Öland at the moment, but I don't know where.'

'Good luck with that. There are more of us than you might think in the summer. I was in the grocery store here in Långvik yesterday, and I met a whole bunch of kids from Washington who—'

'This is an old man,' Gerlof broke in. 'A Swedish-American who might be called Aron. He comes from northern Öland, I think – at least, he seems to be familiar with the coast around here. And I think he's interested in ships.'

'Doesn't ring any bells. Anything else?'

'No . . . but he seems a bit of a dubious character.'

Bill laughed quietly. 'You mean he's a criminal?'

'Maybe. I don't know him.'

'There were all kinds of emigrants,' Bill said. 'Have you heard of Oskar Lundin from Degerhamn?'

'No, who was he?'

'An old Swedish-American from Chicago . . . I met him one summer many years ago, and he claimed he'd been a driver for the Mafia back in the thirties. For Al Capone. Lundin said he used to drive Capone to meetings, until he was arrested and locked up in Alcatraz.'

'Is he still alive, this Lundin?'

'No, he's every bit as dead as Capone. Most of those who came home are dead now.'

Gerlof sighed. 'You're absolutely right.'

'But some are still alive,' Bill said. 'We're meeting up for lunch on Friday.'

'Who's meeting up for lunch?'

'Those who've come home to northern Öland . . . Those of us who are left. There's always an annual get-together for all Swedish-Americans at the Borgholm Hotel, just after midsummer.'

'And does everyone come along?'

'Who knows?' Bill said. 'But I've got something I can show you, if you want more names. It's taken from the church registers – it's a list of everyone who emigrated from Öland during the twentieth century. My cousin has been to the House of the Emigrants in Gothenburg to do some research; he got the list from their archive.'

'That would be very useful,' Gerlof said. 'And this lunch . . .'

'It's usually very good. You're welcome to come with me.'

'Really? I'd love to, but I'm not a Swedish-American, Bill. I've never even been to America.'

'Don't you have any emigrants in the family?'

'Well, yes. . . my grandfather's two brothers. They set off across the sea in the early 1900s. One ended up in Boston and became quite wealthy; the other is supposed to have died on the street in Chicago. That's the closest I can get.'

'In that case, you can be an honorary homecomer,' Bill said.

'Thank you.'

'People won't ask you many questions anyway. They'll just go on and on, like windmills. All they want to do is talk about their own stories and adventures.'

'Then I'm happy to listen,' Gerlof said.

The Homecomer

Everyone seemed to be carrying around their own little telephones these days. Everyone except the Homecomer. He had to rely on the public kiosks that still stood in the squares and picnic areas on the island, and he was standing in one of those kiosks right now.

He keyed in a number, and a hoarse male voice answered, sounding suspicious.

'Hello?'

'Wall?'

'Yes . . .'

'Do you know who this is?'

'Yes . . .'

The arms dealer's voice was slurred, as if he had been drinking all day.

'I'd like to do some more business with you,' the Homecomer said.

'We need to sort out the last lot first,' Wall said. 'What the hell did you do with the ship?'

The Homecomer was silent.

'Nothing that can be undone,' he said eventually.

'Exactly. Pecka called me yesterday; he was really shaken up. He told me you sank her.'

'Yes. We had no choice . . . There was poison gas on board.'

Wall didn't speak; the Homecomer heard him swigging something at the other end of the line, then he said, 'So you want to come here and do some more business?'

'Yes. And I've got money now.'

'Tomorrow evening,' Wall said.

The Homecomer put the phone down. He thought about the bunker not far from Villa Kloss, then about a man he had once met, a man who had made rocks fly through the air.

The New Country, April 1932

'We have to be prepared to make sacrifices,' Sven says. 'You do understand that, don't you?'

Aron looks at his sore hands and says nothing. Sven's hands are in just as bad a state as his own. The skin is cracked, the nails are coming away from the flesh, there are cuts along almost every finger. They're actually quite lucky, because some of the other workers have already lost a couple of fingers. It's the mud and the rocks that destroy the hands, the sticky mud that hides beneath the grass, keeping the rocks firmly in place. The workers stab at the ground with their spades, trying to gain some leverage, but the clay and the rocks refuse to give way.

Life in the new country consists only of sleep and work.

Every night they sleep in a kind of hut with twenty other men, or perhaps more, on beds that are not beds. Sven's is made up of three empty boxes, while Aron's slightly shorter one is a few planks of wood balanced on two sawhorses.

Every day is full of digging, from morning till night. Sven, Aron and the other immigrants are building a canal through the forests, or perhaps a wide ditch. Aron doesn't really know which, he just keeps digging. There are poles in the ground to show where they have to dig, a straight line leading towards the mountains on the horizon, and Aron doesn't think about the eventual goal. He just keeps toiling away with his spade, but over and over again it gets stuck in the unforgiving ground. He tugs, he pulls, he sobs. He digs and digs.

Winter turns to spring, and they carry on digging.

One day when the snow has melted, the work suddenly gets easier. An energetic man in a black cap arrives from the direction of the railway, pushing a cart containing some wooden boxes. He greets the workers with a cheery wave, and when he hears that some of them are Swedish he raises his hat to them.

'*Ruotsi!*' he says, using the Finnish name for Sweden before continuing in Swedish. 'I come from Esbo in Finland, but I became a mining engineer and wanted to get out and see the world. This is a fantastic country, isn't it?'

Sven nods, but Aron just stands there.

The man looks around. 'Any stubborn rocks you want to get rid of?'

'Definitely,' Sven says.

There are always huge rocks. Some of the older workers point out several waiting up ahead.

'Excellent, in that case allow me to demonstrate a little magic trick!' the man from Esbo says, lifting the first wooden box off the cart.

Aron helps him to carry the rest, and watches as he takes fat sticks wrapped in oiled paper out of the boxes.

'Ammonal!' he shouts, gathering the men around the nearest rock. He picks up the sticks. 'These are my boys, and they're going to work together . . . Put them on the opposite side of the rock from the direction you want it to go in, bury them deep in the ground so they have something to kick against and press the detonator against the fuse. But slowly! You have to treat these boys as tenderly as if they were your very own cock!'

The men burst into raucous laughter, then fall silent. They all watch with tense anticipation as the man borrows a pickaxe and makes a row of holes for the dynamite underneath the rock. He shows them in which direction to point the sticks, and how to pack them tightly in order to achieve the best possible effect.

Then the man lights a metre length of black fuse wire and, when it begins to spark and crackle, he makes everyone move back. A long way back.

The ground shakes. A cloud of smoke and fire erupts, and the rock is hurled in the air. It's like magic! The men cheer and the man raises his cap once more.

'Ammonal! Dynamite is the future!'

*

The man from Esbo teaches them how to blow up rocks, but he soon moves on, and it's back to the spades. Aron almost wishes he had never met the mining engineer, never found out that something called dynamite even existed. He doesn't want to know that there are balls of fire that can move mountains, when all he has is a spade.

As the days grow warmer, the mud dries out and digging becomes easier. But then the mosquitoes arrive; the air is filled with them in early summer. Clouds of mosquitoes sweep in across the forest, whining around Aron's ears, crawling up inside his sleeves, or biting right through the fabric of his shirt. His face swells up, his skin itches and throbs from all the bites. The mosquitoes get in his eyes and his nose, even in his mouth, where they taste sweet, like blood.

Sven makes them each a hat of birch bark to protect them from both the mosquitoes and the sun. And then he picks up his spade and carries on digging.

'We mustn't give up,' he says. 'After all, this is what we wanted, isn't it?'

Aron doesn't say anything.

He never wanted to dig in the new country; he wanted to be a sheriff.

When they are given soup during their short break in the middle of the day, hundreds of mosquitoes land on the warm liquid, at first swimming and then slowly, helplessly, sinking. Aron crushes them with his spoon and shovels the lot down. He chews ferociously, with his eyes shut; he wants to murder the mosquitoes. Murder every last one.

Jonas

Jonas was back at Villa Kloss. He wasn't going to think right now, at least not about Peter Mayer. He was going to work.

He fetched the sander and plugged it into the socket on Uncle Kent's decking. Then he switched it on and carried on sanding, one plank at a time. Slow and steady, just as his father had taught him. Every scrap of grey had to be removed from the wood, leaving it pale and fresh. Only then would he be able to start brushing in the oil.

Jonas worked on his knees, his forehead shiny with sweat. The sun was burning down and he really didn't want to think about it – but that name kept echoing through his mind. *Peter. Peter Mayer. Mayer. Peter.* He knew he couldn't talk to anyone, but the name Gerlof had given him just wouldn't go away. The man on the ship, the man who had killed people with an axe.

Peter Mayer. Sold the tickets for The Lion King. *Lives in Marnäs.*

'How's it going, Jonas?' His father had slid open the glass door and was looking down at him. 'Are you getting on OK?'

Jonas nodded.

'Are you enjoying yourself?'

Jonas didn't know what to say. He tried to smile, but his father must have seen something in his expression. He stepped outside.

'Are you missing Mum?'

'A bit . . . But it's all right.'

Jonas carried on sanding.

'So what is it, then?' his father said.

Jonas switched off the machine. After a few seconds he said, 'Stuff's been happening.'

'Stuff? What are you talking about?'

156

'Something happened . . . on Monday evening.'

'Monday? When you were at the cinema?'

Jonas should have kept quiet, but he felt a kind of pressure in his chest when his father stared at him.

'I didn't go to the cinema,' he said eventually. 'I stayed at home.'

His father came and stood beside him. 'I don't understand.'

'I went down to the shore and took the dinghy out. And something happened.'

The thing that had happened was too big to keep inside, and he ended up telling his father about *everything* he had seen out in the Sound. He spoke slowly at first, then faster and faster. He told him about the ship, about the living dead, about the man who had chased him. The man who might be called Peter Mayer.

His father listened carefully. He was a good listener; he had never laughed at anything Jonas had told him. And he wasn't laughing now.

'OK,' he said. 'So now I know. Thank you for telling me, Jonas.'

That was all he said. He didn't seem in the least bit disturbed by the story, just thoughtful. After a while, he seemed to reach a decision.

'Everything's fine. You can go and play.'

'I'm working,' Jonas said. Then he thought about the woman he had spoken to at Gerlof's house. 'Are we going to contact the police?'

'Of course . . . Soon. I need to think.'

His father looked away, over towards the water, as if he were slightly embarrassed. Then he went back indoors.

Jonas was worried; he had promised Mats that he wouldn't say anything about the cinema trip to Kalmar, and he had promised Gerlof that he wouldn't tell anyone about Peter Mayer. 'Promise not to tell anyone else,' Gerlof had said, but that was exactly what Jonas had done. He couldn't keep his mouth shut.

All he could do was carry on working. Stop thinking.

After an hour he had finished about a fifth of the decking. The wood looked almost new, clean and fresh in the sunshine. No chips.

He was quite proud of himself.

As he straightened up, he saw a big car turn off the coast road. It was Uncle Kent, in a white cap and oversized sunnies. He opened the door and waved.

'JK, come over here for a minute!'

Jonas made his way over. Uncle Kent got out of the car and was already talking by the time Jonas reached him.

'Your dad called me a little while ago, JK . . . He said something exciting had happened to you the day before yesterday.' Kent crouched down so that they were face to face. 'He said you were on board a big ship, and you met a guy called Peter Mayer.'

Jonas didn't say a word.

'Is this true?' Kent demanded.

Jonas nodded slowly.

'Interesting.' Kent held Jonas's gaze. 'In that case, let me explain. We had a ship in the dock at the Ölandic over midsummer, delivering a cargo of fish. It left a couple of nights ago, without informing us. We thought that was very strange.'

Jonas thought about the dead seamen, but still he didn't say anything.

Uncle Kent went on. 'And this Peter Mayer: he calls himself Pecka, and he worked at the resort as a security guard last summer . . . so I'd like to speak to him. But I want to be sure that it really was Pecka you saw on board that ship, JK. Do you think you'd be able to identify him?'

Jonas hesitated, but Uncle Kent smiled reassuringly.

'It's fine,' he said. 'Pecka lives in Marnäs. I have an address for him there, and I'd just like a word with him. But first of all I need to be sure . . . Could you come up there with me?'

Jonas thought for a moment, then nodded again. He opened his mouth to speak, but Uncle Kent ruffled his hair.

'Excellent! In that case, we'll pop up and see him this evening.' Kent straightened up. 'There's a fair on in Marnäs, so it will be really busy. We'll just have to hope he's at home.'

Kent got back in the car, and Jonas watched as he reversed out on to the coast road.

There was nothing for it but to go back to his sanding. But things just didn't feel right to Jonas.

Look for the man from the ship? And speak to him? But what if he had the axe with him?

Lisa

No champagne, no pissed guests. Just a golden sunset and a warm breeze at a little outdoor bar and restaurant in Stenvik.

Lisa wasn't spinning any discs this Thursday evening. She was sitting on a stool with her guitar resting on her knee and a microphone in front of her. The microphone was the only thing she could see clearly, because the sun was in her eyes.

She wasn't wearing a wig tonight, because she wasn't a DJ. She was a troubadour, playing folk songs. It was completely different from spending half the night in the DJ booth. The sound was nowhere near as good, for example – she had nothing more than one small speaker, and the wind coming off the water swept away quite a lot of the music.

She preferred the old Swedish songwriters such as Evert Taube, Dan Andersson and Nils Ferlin, but the audience often demanded more modern masters.

'Play Ace of Base!' a girl's voice yelled out.

'I don't know any of theirs,' Lisa said.

'What about Markoolio, then?' one of the guys shouted.

Lisa picked up her guitar. It was after nine, and time to finish off.

'I'll play you a song I do know,' she said. 'It was written by Tomas Ledin, and it's all about how short the summer is . . .'

She was behaving herself this evening. There was no way Lady Summertime could be let loose among ordinary holidaymakers with her long fingers. She was after the fat wallets that belonged to the rich, so that she could give them to the poor. Well, to Silas.

At quarter past nine she had finished the gig, as the blood-red sun hovered above the horizon.

Lisa needed bread and milk, but the shop next to the bar had closed at eight o'clock. It was run by an elderly father and his son; their name was Hagman. The bar itself was owned by her employers, the Kloss family; it was a small but intense workplace: two Finnish waitresses picked their way among the tables, and in the kitchen a Canadian chef presided over pizza dough and jars of pesto. Kent Kloss wasn't responsible for this place, thank goodness; it was run by Niklas, his younger brother, who kept a low profile and spent most of his time on the till; the staff didn't need his constant supervision.

Lisa put away her guitar and headed for the exit. Niklas Kloss smiled at her, and she quickly asked, 'Did it sound OK?'

'Absolutely.'

'In that case, I'll be back on Monday.'

'Good – I'll look forward to it.'

He didn't really seem to be listening; he was looking over towards a big car that had just pulled into the car park and was standing there with its engine ticking over.

The driver got out, and Lisa saw that it was Kent Kloss. He waved to his brother, and Niklas walked towards him.

The wind carried odd words across to Lisa.

'. . . former employee,' Kent said.

'. . . don't want to talk about . . .' Niklas responded.

'. . . have a chat . . .'

'. . . ought to call . . .'

'. . . rather go round there . . .'

After a while, Niklas got into the car, looking both grim and stressed. Kent quickly slid behind the wheel and drove out of the car park.

Lisa could see a boy in the back seat, one of the Kloss children; he glanced at Lisa as the car pulled out on to the main road. He didn't look too happy either.

As she walked back to the campsite, carrying her guitar, the sun had just gone down, leaving only a glow in the sky and making the clouds look like red fire above the horizon. Or streaks of blood.

The coast quickly darkened. Lisa headed towards her caravan, wondering why the Kloss brothers would allow a young boy to be out so late at night.

Jonas

Marnäs lay on the west coast; it had a number of shops and the white, medieval parish church. It was too big to be a village and too small to be a town, but people gathered there anyway. There was an off-licence, a harbour with several fishing boats and a police station that was open for a few hours every Tuesday.

Jonas really liked the shops in Marnäs, but there was no chance of visiting them tonight. It was almost nine thirty; it was twilight and the shops were shut. However, the fair was in full swing and had attracted plenty of people.

The funfair had been set up in the harbour area next to the square, with brightly coloured carousels and stalls selling burgers and sausages. There were lots of cars, and Uncle Kent couldn't find a space on the square, so he parked in a disabled bay behind the harbourmaster's office.

'We won't be long,' he said. 'I'll just have to pay the fine if we get a ticket.'

Niklas didn't say anything; he didn't seem particularly happy this evening. But Uncle Kent carried on talking as the three of them got out of the car: 'We'll go over to Mayer's place and ring the doorbell, see if he's at home.' He looked at Jonas. 'If he's there, JK, and if you're sure he was the guy you saw on the ship, then we'll have a little chat with him, find out what happened. But you don't need to stay around for that . . . OK?'

Jonas nodded. His heart was pounding, but he also felt as if he had grown since this morning. He was suddenly at the centre of everything. He was important – he was a witness.

The three of them walked past the harbour and the funfair. Jonas looked at the flashing lights and caught the aroma of grilled sausages and fresh popcorn. He would have loved to look around the stalls, buy some sweets and check out the second-hand videos, but Uncle Kent marched on, shaking his head.

'Look at all this crap,' he said. 'Marnäs is a real magnet for people peddling cheap tat in the summer. It's all sell, sell, sell.'

Once they had passed the fair, he increased his speed and turned into a narrow side street. He led the way to a couple of apartment blocks north of the harbour, with a view over the dark-blue Baltic.

'Number eight, that's where he's supposed to be living,' he said. 'Second floor.'

He opened the door, held it to allow Jonas and his father to go in, then let it close behind them.

The cool stairwell felt eerily silent.

Kent set off up the stairs. 'Keep behind me, JK,' he said quietly. He was moving more cautiously now, and didn't switch on the light. Niklas stayed at the back, as if protecting their line of retreat.

They reached the second floor and saw two doors. MAYER was on a handwritten label on the left-hand door. Jonas's pulse rate shot up when he saw it; he felt as if the name were leaching evil into the stair-well.

But Uncle Kent didn't seem in the least concerned. He stepped forward and pressed the doorbell. For a long time.

Jonas was even more frightened when he heard the sound of the bell; he felt as if he were back on board the ship. He noticed a peep-hole in the door, just like the one they had at home in Huskvarna. Perhaps someone was standing there, spying on them.

Peter Mayer. The man with the axe.

But no one answered the door. Uncle Kent waited, rang again, waited. Eventually, he sighed. 'Damn,' he said. 'No one's home, JK. We'll have to go back to Villa Kloss.'

Jonas was relieved. A little disappointed, perhaps, but mainly re-lieved.

They left the building; it was even darker now. The streetlamps around the harbour had come on and the people visiting the fair looked even more shadowy.

Jonas moved a little distance away from his father and his uncle so that he could look at the rides. They ought to let him have a go on

162

something now, maybe the dodgems or the cannonball, but he knew they wouldn't.

Beside the harbour was Moby Dick, the only pizzeria in Marnäs. Jonas had eaten there with Mats and their father the summer before last. The place was packed tonight, of course. There were tables outside and every one was occupied, with people drinking and laughing and smoking. Sunburnt golfers in white caps and blue polo shirts, sailors in blue jackets, cyclists with helmet hair.

Summer visitors. Jonas couldn't take his eyes off them.

A tall guy in a black denim jacket was moving between the tables, carrying a takeaway pizza; he had a shaven head and his eyes were darting all over the place.

Jonas stared at him for a long time.

Time had slowed down; his heart was thumping.

He made himself look away after a while, as if everything was perfectly normal – but he was absolutely certain who he had seen. He stopped, turned around and gently tugged at his father's arm.

'There,' he whispered.

'What?'

'It's *him*.'

Niklas stopped. 'Who?'

'The man from the ship.'

'You mean Mayer? Where?'

Jonas tilted his head in the direction of the pizzeria, where Peter Mayer had just reached the pavement. He was about to walk past them, heading down towards the harbour.

'Kent!' Niklas called out.

'What?'

'Over there.'

Niklas pointed, and Kent turned his head. He spotted Peter Mayer and stopped dead.

A second later, Kent took off, straight across the street. 'Hey!' he shouted. 'Pecka!'

The man looked over his shoulder and froze for a few seconds. Then he began to move in the opposite direction, faster and faster. Away from the crowd and from Kent Kloss.

'Hang on!' Kent yelled. 'I just want to . . .'

At that point, Peter Mayer dropped the pizza box and fled – but he

163

was running away from his apartment block, heading west with long strides, away from the lights. He didn't look back.

Jonas watched as Uncle Kent also broke into a run, following Peter Mayer down the street.

'I'll get the car!' Niklas shouted.

Uncle Kent nodded, and kept on running.

Niklas placed his hand on Jonas's shoulder. 'Come with me, Jonas.'

Jonas was intending to obey and took a few steps behind his father. Then he hesitated in the crush on the pavement, and on an impulse turned back. He wanted to see what happened; he decided to follow Uncle Kent. He set off slowly, then began to move faster.

'Jonas!'

He heard his father calling him but didn't stop.

He felt good as he ran. He wasn't the quarry tonight, he was the hunter. A member of the Kloss family.

He moved through the shadowy crowd, but Kent was wearing a pale windcheater and was easy to see. Jonas watched as he ran across the street, heading west. Away from the shops and houses. Jonas could just make out another figure, his shaven head shining.

Jonas ran after them, as third man.

Soon there was no one else around. Jonas passed the last building, then the last streetlamp, and carried on into the darkness.

It was cold here, and pitch black until his eyes adjusted. Jonas blinked and saw grey shadows up ahead.

Uncle Kent was passing the church. Peter Mayer stopped by the roadside, looked around, then disappeared into the birch forest.

Kent leapt across the verge and followed him.

When Jonas reached the same spot, he saw a path leading through the trees, so he, too, leapt over the verge and on to the path.

The deep-green darkness of the forest closed around him with a faint soughing. But he could hear other sounds among the trees: the cracking of twigs. The birches surrounded him like grey pillars; he zigzagged between them and increased his speed.

Suddenly, the forest fell away, and Jonas found himself in a meadow, or an unploughed field. It was covered in grass and illuminated by a cracked light up in the sky – the white moon, which was almost full.

He saw two figures moving in the moonlight, one pursuing the other. They were on the far side of the field, where the forest began again, and both quarry and hunter disappeared among the trees.

Jonas followed them, and found another path. He was tired now, but scared and excited at the same time. Tonight, he wasn't alone, as he had been on the ship. His father wasn't far behind, and Uncle Kent was somewhere in the forest.

He carried on along the path, hearing crashing noises in the undergrowth. And now there was also a swishing, like the wind. It was the sound of cars driving past on the main road between Borgholm and the villages to the north.

Jonas listened and kept his eyes on the path so that he wouldn't get lost.

All of a sudden, he heard a shout; it sounded like Uncle Kent.

He stopped.

Another shout, louder this time.

Then a screech, but not from a human being – he was sure it was car tyres on tarmac.

The sound ended abruptly, then there was silence for a few seconds. Then more shouting, a confusion of voices in the darkness, and car doors opening and closing.

Jonas stood motionless on the path, listening hard.

More cracking and creaking, and heavy breathing. Someone was coming towards him.

A shadow loomed out of the darkness.

'JK? Are you there?'

Uncle Kent.

'Yes, I just wanted to see if—'

But Kent interrupted him sharply: 'You shouldn't be here.'

Jonas didn't know what to say.

Uncle Kent strode past him, puffing and panting.

'Did . . . did you catch up with him?' Jonas asked.

But Kent didn't reply, he just walked across the field and took the path leading back to Marnäs.

Jonas had no option but to turn around and follow him. He still didn't know what to say, but eventually he caught up with Kent among the birch trees and said, 'So you didn't catch him?'

'No,' Kent snapped. 'He's gone.'

He kept on walking.

At long last they emerged from the forest, jumped over the verge and were back on the road.

In the light of the streetlamps, Jonas noticed that Uncle Kent had acquired a twitch just below his left eye, as if a little muscle there were conducting an exercise session all by itself.

Kent stopped again, turning his full attention on Jonas. 'Did you see anything back there?'

'Like what?'

Uncle Kent took a deep breath and set off again. They continued in silence until they heard a shout: 'Hello?'

It was Jonas's father. He was waiting for them just past the church, with the car parked at the side of the road.

'What happened?' he said.

Kent went up to him, very close, and spoke so quietly that Jonas could barely hear him. 'There was a car.'

'A car?'

Uncle Kent nodded. 'It was heading straight for Mayer.'

'And?'

'I don't know,' Kent said. 'I don't think things went too well.'

Niklas looked worried, but didn't ask any more questions.

They all got in the car and let out a long breath in the silence. Niklas started the engine. 'OK . . . Let's go home.'

Once they were on the main road, Jonas noticed lights to the south. A short distance away, perhaps a hundred metres, several cars had stopped, and there were people standing around them. He saw flashing blue lights and people in high-visibility jackets moving about on the road.

Niklas indicated left, but Kent shook his head. 'Not that way. Turn right and we'll go via Långvik. The coast road is better tonight.'

Niklas turned right.

Jonas looked back. He realized that there must have been a serious accident, but now they wouldn't be able to see what had happened. If anyone was hurt.

The flashing blue lights disappeared into the distance.

After a kilometre or so, Niklas turned off the main road and on to a narrower track leading to the coast.

Kent leaned back. 'There you go,' he said. 'I expect we'll find out what happened from the news . . . We're not going to talk about this.'

'As usual,' Niklas said.

Jonas didn't say anything; he just sat quietly in the back, looking out of the window. They were surrounded by darkness now.

But what did Uncle Kent mean? Were they not going to talk about it to the other members of the family? Or to the police?

Gerlof

Just as Gerlof was getting ready for bed that night, he heard about a fatal accident in northern Öland. It was on the local radio news at midnight:

'And so to Öland. A twenty-four-year-old man was killed earlier this evening on the B136 just outside Marnäs. The initial police report suggests that he stepped out in front of a car heading south. The victim was taken by ambulance to Kalmar, where he was pronounced dead. The driver, a man in his fifties, is suffering from severe shock . . .'

The newsreader didn't name the dead man, and Gerlof's only reaction was the same as usual: the Department of Transport ought to lower the speed limit on that road. It was wide and straight all the way down to Borgholm, tempting many to drive far too fast. Perhaps he would write a letter to the paper. Suggest they turn it back into a dirt track.

He switched off the radio, then he turned off the light. Tomorrow he would be travelling on that very road, in order to attend a nostalgic lunch in Borgholm.

The next day, he found himself sitting at a long table with a group of men and women of his own age, people who had returned home, experience etched on their faces. They were swapping emigration stories, and Gerlof didn't want to be left out:

'My father had a cousin in Böda whose brother emigrated to America. One evening, when this cousin was just about to go to bed, the room was suddenly filled with the smell of death. Both he and his wife were aware of the same appalling stench. Eventually, they managed to get to sleep, but at dawn the cousin woke up and thought he saw his brother standing by the bedroom window – and he realized that his brother over in America was dead.'

He fell silent. A few people around the table laughed at the story, as if it were funny.

Nine men and two women had gathered for the Swedish-Americans' lunch at the Borgholm Hotel and were enjoying fried halibut with tomato compote.

Gerlof had arrived after a short walk around the town which had once been his home port as the skipper of a cargo ship. These days, he didn't recognize a single face on the streets, which were packed with tourists.

He had stopped down by the quayside for a little while, remembering the forest of masts that had once dominated the skyline. These days, the jetties were lined with countless modern plastic boats but the harbour itself looked run-down, with gaping holes in the brickwork and huge cracks in the quays themselves.

At least the historic hotel was well maintained, and Gerlof loved the light, airy restaurant. The food was excellent, and the floor was made of polished limestone, which one of his ancestors might have hewn out long ago. Beautiful.

However, he spent most of his time looking at his lunch companions. They spoke in a mixture of English and Swedish; they all seemed to understand both languages. A round of Swedish schnapps was ordered, and their stories quickly grew more bizarre.

'The food here is good, but when I used to go fishing in Alaska we'd catch halibut weighing two hundred kilos . . .'

Ingemar Grandin had come all the way from San Pablo, California. One of the ladies was called Nordlof and came from New Haven, Connecticut. Others were from Minnesota, Wisconsin and Boston.

It turned out that only three of them had actually emigrated from Sweden. Their parents had taken them to America when they were only children; the rest had been born in the USA, but their parents were originally from Öland.

None of them looked as if they had driven Al Capone around the streets of Chicago, Gerlof thought, or hijacked a fishing boat.

They moved on to the local patisserie for coffee and cakes, and suddenly the stories took on a more sorrowful tone. Perhaps the schnapps was kicking in. They were no longer talking about how big the new country had been but how hard life had often been for the immigrants.

'Lots of them used to carry Swedish papers and maps around in their pockets . . . They were homesick all the time, but they just couldn't afford a ticket home.'

'Yes, it was very difficult for those who couldn't settle in the USA. Endless hard labour. Particularly forestry work – that was crazy, really dangerous.'

'That's right – I've seen old lumberjacks who've lost both arms and legs . . .'

At the end of the gathering, Bill Carlson gave Gerlof some folded sheets of paper. 'This is the information you wanted from the House of Emigrants.'

'Thank you.'

It was a typed list of names and dates. At first, Gerlof was a little confused, but then he remembered that Bill's cousin had amused himself by collecting the names of local emigrants from the church records. He noticed that it contained names only from the island's northern parishes, and only from the last hundred years, but it was enough.

He ran his finger down the list, and stopped abruptly:

Aron Fredh, b. 1918, Rödtorp, Alböke parish
Sven Fredh, b. 1894, Rödtorp, Alböke parish

They had left in May 1931, according to the records. There were a number of later emigrants from both the forties and fifties, when Swedes no longer went by ship to 'America', but flew to the 'USA', but Aron and Sven must have been among the last of the main wave of emigrants.

The name Aron had caught Gerlof's attention. It was the name Jonas Kloss had heard on the ship, of course. But the name of the place also rang a bell.

Aron from Rödtorp?

Suddenly, he remembered, and leaned eagerly towards Bill: 'I recognize this one,' he said, pointing to the name. 'I think Aron from Rödtorp was a boy I worked with for a little while, up in the churchyard in Marnäs . . . He talked about going to America at the time, and the following year I heard that they'd actually gone, he and his father. But I don't know how they got on over there.'

Bill looked at the list. '1931 . . . So they went after the Great Depression. It wasn't a good time for new Americans; there was so much unemployment, among other things. I should think it was pretty tough for them.'

'Indeed,' Gerlof said.

He looked at the group of elderly Swedish-Americans and wondered if Aron Fredh had ever come back home.

The Homecomer

When the Homecomer went back to the arms dealer on the eastern side of the island, he went by car, alone. He parked about fifty metres from Wall's cottage and waited for a little while, watching and listening. But there wasn't a soul in sight.

The sun was low in the sky behind the car, making the grassy shore glow bright green, with the deep blue water beyond. It was idyllic, yet something didn't feel right.

He opened the car door and heard the geese cackling nervously down by the shoreline. Otherwise, all was quiet. He got out and took in the expanse of the Baltic Sea, with Gotland beyond the horizon. And the faded red cottage in the foreground.

'Hello?' he called out.

But no one came to the door this evening.

As he approached, he could see that it was ajar. Slowly, he pulled it open a little further and shouted again. 'Hello? Anyone there?'

The geese cackled once more, but that was the only response.

No, this didn't feel right. The Homecomer moved more stealthily. He took a quick look around the rooms on the ground floor, but soon realized that Einar Wall wasn't at home. So why was the door open? That didn't tally with Wall's caution on his previous visit.

The skiff floating on the water didn't look right either. The Homecomer noticed it when he stepped outside. It looked as if there was someone in it.

He walked towards it. The wooden boat had been up on the grass the last time he was here, but now it was in the water, with no mooring rope.

It wasn't a person in the boat but large, brown birds perched on the gunwale. Their weight was making the skiff bob up and down.

Not geese, but birds of prey, with ravens and jackdaws circling around them.

The Homecomer stopped at the water's edge. The birds flapped their huge wings nervously but didn't fly away.

He realized they were sea eagles – enormous birds with powerful hooked beaks, leaning down from the gunwale to peck at something in the bottom of the skiff. As the ravens came closer, the sea eagles raised their heads like snakes, then resumed their pecking.

They were eating something. Lumps of meat, presumably.

One of them had got hold of something white and was pulling it upwards, and the Homecomer saw that it was a hand. A lifeless human hand. The bird opened its beak, and the hand fell back into the boat.

The Homecomer stood motionless beneath the vast expanse of the sky for a few seconds, then he waded into the water, yelling at the birds and eventually scaring them off. By that time, he had almost reached the gunwale and could see into the boat.

Einar Wall was lying there on his back, flat out on the narrow wooden planks with an almost empty bottle of Explorer vodka beside him.

The Homecomer recognized parts of the arms dealer's clothes, but nothing else.

There was nothing else to recognize.

The eagles' beaks had done their work, and Wall's face was no longer there.

The Homecomer let go of the gunwale and backed away. He had seen dead bodies before; he was used to it. He made his way back to the shore and stood there with wet shoes, staring at the skiff.

Finally, when he had pulled himself together, he went into the house to try to find what he had come for. The cottage was a treasure chest now.

Wall had boasted that the police had been there, searching for guns, but had found nothing.

The Homecomer set to work, and he had better luck. Guns were his forte; he knew what they weighed; he could almost smell them. Methodically, he went through every piece of furniture in every room, and when he checked a rectangular dowry chest upstairs and saw that it contained old blankets, the weight made him suspicious.

It was too heavy.

The guns weren't among the blankets; they were right down at the bottom, hidden under a false base.

The first was an old long-barrelled Husqvarna with five boxes of Gyttorp cartridges. The ammunition looked good, but the rifle itself was worn.

The second was a modern Beretta. Beautiful.

The Homecomer held the guns up to the window and studied them one at a time; he liked a weapon that fired well, with reliable ammunition that killed the quarry quickly, if the marksman did his job.

Guns on the island had been very poor when he was a boy and had led to many accidents. In those days, a number of old hunters were still trying to shoot seabirds with muzzle-loading firearms and worse; it often took three or four shots before the bird was dead.

The Homecomer had never needed more than one shot to kill something or someone, not even when he was a boy. The ability to kill instantly was partly about having a good weapon and being stone-cold sober, but it was mostly about remaining calm and having a steady hand.

He carried both guns downstairs. He ought to leave right now, but there was a bunch of keys hanging in the kitchen. Padlock keys.

He picked them up and went out to the boathouse. Many boathouses on the island were secured with nothing more than a piece of rope, but Wall's was furnished with a steel bar and a sturdy padlock. Had the police checked out here?

After some trouble, the Homecomer found the right key and opened up.

The stale smell of seaweed rushed towards him. He could see why; the place was full of fishing nets, hanging from poles attached to the ceiling.

In one corner he spotted a glass bottle: CHLOROFORM. He put it by the door and continued searching.

Right at the back, beneath piles of old nets that stank to high heaven, he found a couple of wooden boxes marked with a yellow sticker. He carried them out into the light.

The boxes had been carefully nailed shut. He thrust an old fish-gutting knife under the lid and forced the first one open. The contents were exactly what he had expected. He replaced the lid, wrapped his treasures carefully in a blanket and took them over to the car.

He glanced over at the skiff and the birds one more time. The sea eagles were back on the gunwale, bending down to eat. The ravens were waiting their turn. Soon the birds would have torn Wall's body to pieces, bit by bit. All the Homecomer could do was call the police, perhaps. Anonymously, of course, from a phone box.

He got in the car and drove off.

The New Country, November 1933

Aron is lost. Winter has returned to the new country, and everything is white. Empty and white. Mountains in the distance, forest close by, wide expanses of snow. And then the wide trench, slicing through the landscape like a dark-brown wound.

The mosquitoes have gone now that cold covers the wilderness, but life for Aron and Sven is not much easier.

Their home is a ramshackle hut where weary workers from at least ten different countries gather every night. All the immigrants eat dry bread and a thin meat soup around the iron stove, then fall into bed, often sharing, top to tail.

The hut stinks like an old stable. The labourers stopped washing when the water froze, which was several weeks ago.

Aron hears the wind howling on the other side of the thin wall and thinks about Öland, about the shore and the rocks he used to stand on in the sunshine, about the days when he would go out shooting with his grandfather, about the evenings when his mother would tell him stories, him and his sister, Greta – but these are faint childhood memories.

He is fifteen years old now. He has started to mix up the old language and the new, strange, foreign words that seep into his head and come out of his mouth, faster and faster.

It's not just that he is older – he has started to change, to turn into a foreigner. There is no mirror in the hut, but he can feel fine hairs beginning to sprout on his cheeks and chin, a downy beard that is gradually getting thicker and stronger.

Every morning he wakes in the cold, surprised that he is still able to move. If the stove has gone out during the night, it is his job to

176

relight it – if there is any wood left. He pushes in a few sticks and manages to get it going. At the same time he hears Sven and the other occupants of the hut slowly beginning to move, coughing and grunting.

One morning an older man (Aron thinks he might be German) two bunks away doesn't wake up. Someone shakes him, but quickly draws back. The German is as stiff as a board.

'Heart attack,' Sven says quietly.

Aron looks at the dead man and thinks of Gilbert Kloss, who collapsed and rolled into a grave on a sunny summer's day. His heart had stopped, too, but that was from fear.

The German is carried out and buried far away, out of sight, beneath a wooden cross. No one wants to think about him any more. He is dead.

Aron is determined to survive. In spite of the work, in spite of the cold.

Whether the stove is burning or not, the hut never feels warm. All those frozen joints and muscles struggle to thaw out. Icicles hang from the ceiling, frost creeps down the walls. There is a thermometer nailed to one of the huts; it often shows minus twenty-five degrees.

But still they have to go out. Time to work, to break fresh ground. They trudge through the snow beneath the fir trees; they shovel, fell trees, hack their way into the frozen ground, all because the trench must keep on growing.

The long white days in the ditch become routine.

Sven works just as hard as everyone else, but he has almost stopped talking in the cold. Sometimes he takes out his wooden box, checking for the thousandth time if there is any snuff left. Then he mutters something with his head down, and carries on hacking.

Occasionally, he comes to life in the hut in the evenings, but that's not necessarily a good thing. He stares around wildly and raises his hand to Aron in the darkness, ready to strike if he asks the wrong question – but Aron has almost caught up with Sven and merely stares back. He is tall, and he is too tired to be frightened of Sven, so he stands his ground, his legs apart; he has started to defend himself.

If Sven hits him, he retaliates. It feels good to strike back.

Jonas

'How are you getting on?' his mother asked.

Jonas kept the receiver pressed to his ear, not knowing what to say. He had things to tell her, about the ghost ship and the hunt for Peter Mayer, but he didn't dare speak. He didn't know who might be listening. Uncle Kent had said they mustn't talk about what had happened, and he could turn up at any moment. This was his telephone, on a table by the window in his house.

'Fine,' he said eventually.

'Is Dad behaving himself?'

'Yes.'

'Are you homesick?'

'A bit.'

'I miss you and Mats.'

Jonas had realized by now that Peter Mayer was dead, but Uncle Kent had been just the same as usual at breakfast, chatting and joking with Mats and their cousins.

Niklas had been less talkative, but then he was always quieter than Kent.

'Only four weeks to go, then you'll be back in Huskvarna,' his mum said.

Jonas was trying not to think about Huskvarna. *Four weeks.* A whole month.

The line was crackly and his mother's voice sounded a little tinny, so Jonas asked, 'Are you at home?'

'No, I'm in Spain, in Malaga. I told you I was coming here after midsummer – don't you remember?'

Jonas didn't remember that at all, but now he knew that he couldn't

178

go home even if he wanted to. The house was empty; he was stuck here at Villa Kloss.

'When will you be back?'

'In a week. I'm going to do some travelling first.'

Jonas heard the answer, but he was barely listening; he had been looking out of the window and had noticed a movement over by the cairn.

The grey-haired man was standing there next to the stones, his hand resting on the cairn. Jonas peered through the glass, but the reflection of the sun on the water in the Sound made the man look dark and blurred.

'Jonas? Are you still there?'

'Yes . . . Yes, I'm here.'

He blinked. And saw the man begin to make his way down. It almost looked as if he were sinking into the ground behind the cairn.

'Guess what I bought today, Jonas!'

'Dunno.'

'A Spanish present. But I'm not telling you what it is . . .'

Mum went on and on, but suddenly she decided the call was getting too expensive. She would phone again soon. And she loved him.

Jonas wondered if she was alone in Spain, but he didn't want to ask.

'See you soon!'

'OK.'

Slowly, he put the phone down. The ridge was deserted now.

He wouldn't think about any of it. Not about Mum in Spain, or what had happened in Marnäs, or the cairn ghost.

He would just get on with his work.

Fifteen minutes later he was back on the decking, already hot and pouring with sweat. He could hear the sound of splashing and cheerful voices from the jetty, while he was on his knees working hard to clean each plank. Sometimes it was easy, sometimes it was hopeless. The far end in the northern corner was mouldy and dark grey after years of neglect, and he couldn't bring back the pale colour, however hard he tried.

He paused and looked over at the ridge. The grey-haired man hadn't reappeared, but he saw a boat moving around out in the

Sound. It was Uncle Kent's launch, circling in the sun beyond the gill nets.

Urban, Mats and Casper were jumping and diving from the stern. They looked like dark shadows against the sparkling water, but the biggest shadow, Kent, was standing by the gunwale hauling in the line. Someone had just been water-skiing.

Kent had asked Jonas at breakfast if he wanted to join them, but he had said no.

He just wanted to carry on sanding, and to stop himself thinking. Stop himself remembering. But when he closed his eyes he could see Peter Mayer glancing over his shoulder in terror at Uncle Kent before he fled into the darkness. Into the forest and out on to the road.

Jonas wiped the sweat from his brow. Waved a fly away from his ear.

The waters of the Sound sparkled, the launch continued to zoom around in circles.

By the time he had sanded twenty planks, Jonas felt as if he were going to faint; he had to go and cool down.

The pool looked inviting, but he grabbed his trunks and went down to the shore. He took a detour via the cairn to check it out, but no more rocks had fallen down. There was no one in sight. The cairn ghost had gone.

He ran down the stone steps, past the dip and on to the shore. The summer sun was so bright here among the rocks that it could easily blind you. Jonas kept his eyes lowered so that his baseball cap shaded his face.

'Hi, Jonas!'

Aunt Veronica was waving to him, treading water about ten metres out. She was a good swimmer and would forge along with powerful strokes, her legs kicking strongly.

'Hi.'

'How was the fair last night?'

'Good.'

'Lots of people?'

'Yes . . . quite a lot.'

Jonas didn't want to think about the fair, or the pursuit in the darkness and the screech of tyres. He slipped off his shoes and stepped out on to the rocks, but almost let out a scream – they were red-hot.

180

'Put on some flip-flops, Jonas!' Veronica shouted.

Jonas didn't reply; he just gritted his teeth and made himself keep going.

He waited until Veronica had started swimming again, then he changed into his trunks and went and stood by the water's edge. The air was hot and still, but occasionally a cool breeze blew in off the Sound. Öland was a windy place. Sometimes the winds were as hot as in some far-flung desert, sometimes they were bitterly cold. The surface of the water was also constantly moving, and right now it was full of the foaming backwash from Uncle Kent's shiny launch. The boat was still whizzing around beyond the gill nets. No one was water-skiing at the moment, but the three boys were sitting in the stern in their trunks. And Kent was at the wheel, straight-backed and in control.

Jonas saw him turn and say something to Mats and their cousins, and they all laughed. Then he caught sight of Jonas, and waved.

'Hi there, JK!'

He was smiling, as if nothing had happened last night.

'Why don't you go out with the boys?' Veronica called. 'Have some fun!'

Jonas gazed at the shadowy figures in the boat. At Kent, who had chased Peter Mayer out on to the road, and at Mats and their cousins, who hardly ever told Jonas what they were going to do.

He shook his head. 'I'd rather stay here.'

Gerlof

'I heard about the death,' Gerlof said.

'Which one?' Tilda asked.

'The hit and run. The young man.'

Tilda didn't say anything, and after a moment he went on, 'Has there been another death here on the island?'

After a moment, she said, 'There has, yes.'

'Oh?'

'Do you know Einar Wall?'

'I know who he is,' Gerlof said. 'An old fisherman who lives on the east coast, just like you, but to the north of Marnäs.'

'Tell me more.'

'I don't know much more . . . I should think he must be a pensioner. He's always been a fisherman and a hunter, but he's done plenty of other things that were considerably less respectable. He's the kind of man people whisper about.'

'So he was a bit of a dodgy character, in other words?'

'The fish he sold was probably more popular than Einar himself. But I've never done any business with him. He's a good bit younger than me – between sixty and seventy, I'd say.'

'He *was*,' Tilda said.

'Is he dead?'

'We had an anonymous tip-off on Friday evening to say that he was lying dead outside his cottage. And he was. We think it happened that day, or the previous night.'

'How did he die?'

'I can't tell you that.'

Gerlof knew that he shouldn't ask any more questions, so he simply said, 'And the hit and run?'

'Wall's nephew. He was hit by a car on the main road . . . Peter Mayer.'

Gerlof gave a start. 'What did you say?'

'Peter Mayer. He was twenty-four years old; he ran out in front of a car the night before Einar Wall died. He was Wall's nephew; apparently they were very close. So we're looking into the connection, wondering if one death perhaps led to the other . . . That's why I was curious to find out what you knew about Wall.'

Say something, Gerlof thought.

But he didn't. He should have told Tilda about Peter Mayer some time ago, but he hadn't got round to it. What could he say now? Perhaps it was just a coincidence that Mayer had been hit by a car just after Jonas Kloss had identified him, but . . .

'We can talk more later,' he said. 'I have to go. John's picking me up.'

'Are you going on a trip?'

'Not really – we're just going for coffee,' Gerlof explained. 'With a gravedigger's daughter.'

Not all farmers on the island had been blessed with such extensive property as the Kloss family; Sonja, the daughter of Roland Bengtsson the gravedigger, was married to a retired farmer who had owned no more than half a dozen dairy cows, a few fields of potatoes, and a straw-covered stone barn which housed a small flock of chickens. The farm had been sold, and now Sonja and her husband lived in Utvalla, in a small house on the east coast overlooking low-lying skerries with a healthy bird population. Beyond the skerries lay only the Baltic horizon, like a dark-blue stage floor stretching towards eternity. Or at least towards Russia and the Baltic states.

But Gerlof wasn't looking at the sea as he eased his way out of John's car. He was looking north. It wasn't very far to Einar Wall's cottage from here; it was probably only a few kilometres away, behind a series of inlets and headlands.

Gerlof had called Sonja and invited himself and John over for coffee. You could do that kind of thing on the island with people you knew, and he had known Sonja for years.

There were suitcases in the hallway; Sonja and her husband were flying to Majorca the following day. However, they were pleased to welcome their guests. Gerlof's first question concerned their late neighbour.

'No, we didn't hear a thing that evening,' Sonja replied. 'We didn't see anything either – there's a pine forest between us.'

'Wall was a tricky customer,' her husband said. 'We knew he sold fish and game, but I think he sold other things as well. If you were out that way, you often saw strange cars coming and going. The drivers always looked grim – they never waved, which isn't a good sign.'

'And he drank, of course,' Sonja said. 'I suppose that's what killed him . . . His heart probably gave out in the end.'

'So he had a heart attack?'

'That's what we heard – that he was sitting drinking in his boat and he collapsed in the heat.'

'That sounds plausible,' Gerlof said.

Silence fell around the coffee table. So far, they had just been chatting, even though the subject matter had been quite serious, but Gerlof really wanted to talk about Sonja's father.

'Sonja, I'm not sure whether you know this,' he began, 'but I worked with your father in the churchyard when I was young. It was only for a short time, but he was very kind to me.'

'Oh – when was that?'

'In 1931, and there was another young boy there, too, whom Roland seemed to be keeping an eye on . . . I think his name was Aron, Aron Fredh.'

Sonja and her husband exchanged a quick glance. It was obvious they recognized the name.

'Aron and my father were related,' Sonja said at last. 'Dad looked after him from time to time.'

'So you were also related to Aron?'

'Distantly, yes. It wasn't actually my father who was related to Aron's family; my mother and Aron's mother, Astrid, were cousins.'

Astrid Fredh. Gerlof made a note of the name.

'But none of them is still alive?'

'No, they're all gone. Astrid died in the seventies; she'd left

Rödtorp by then. Aron had a younger sister, Greta, but she had a fall at the home in Marnäs last year and died.'

Gerlof vaguely remembered the incident, but it hadn't happened on his wing and, unfortunately, falls were far from uncommon among the elderly. You had to be very careful with those shiny floors and rugs.

'Where did Aron and his family live?' he asked. 'On the coast?'

'They lived over to the west . . . at Rödtorp, next to the Kloss family's land. Astrid and Greta stayed there more or less until the end of the thirties, but Aron and his stepfather went to America.'

Gerlof was taken aback – not by the fact that they had gone to America, but by the relationship.

'Stepfather? So Sven wasn't Aron's biological father?'

Sonja glanced at her husband once more. 'Sven came to the island as a farmhand at the beginning of the twenties,' she said. 'Aron and Greta had already been born by then.'

Gerlof noticed that she didn't mention who their real father was.

After a brief silence, John spoke up. 'Do you happen to know where Sven and Aron went when they got to America?'

'Goodness, I've no idea. It's almost seventy years ago, after all.'

'They didn't write home?'

'Not letters,' Sonja said. 'But there might be a postcard from them in my father's collection . . . Just a minute.'

She left the room and returned with a dark-green album, which she handed over to Gerlof. It was old and worn, with gold lettering on the front: POSTCARD ALBUM.

'My father inherited it from his father,' Sonja explained. 'They both collected postcards, although neither of them received very many over the years. We used to send them to Dad . . . Our postcards from Majorca are at the back.'

Gerlof slowly leafed through the album. He liked postcards; as a ship's captain, he had sent many to his daughters from various harbours around Sweden.

The Spanish cards at the back were in bright colours, with blue seas and a yellow sun. As he moved towards the front of the album, the cards were older, more faded and less exotic. They featured views of 'Gefle Esplanade' or 'Halmstad – Grand Hotel'.

But one of them was different, and Gerlof stopped and read the words on the front: 'Swedish-American Line SS *Kastelholm — Carte Postale*'. Beneath the text was a picture of a magnificent steamship of the type he had sometimes encountered while sailing the Baltic.

'This could be it,' he said, carefully removing the postcard.

There was a short message on the back, written in pencil in a sprawling hand:

Thank you for everything, Uncle Roland. We have arrived at the docks and will soon be going on board. This is a picture of the ship that will take us from Sweden to America, but we will be coming back.
   Look after Mother and Greta. Goodbye.
   Love from Aron

It was obviously a card from an emigrant, presumably sent from Gothenburg, but it revealed very little, apart from the fact that Aron could spell. The date was unclear, but Gerlof thought he could make out '1931' over the stamp.

He put down the card. 'Aron says they're coming back.'

'Yes, but they never did. And, as I said, we didn't hear from them again. I used to visit Greta Fredh from time to time, and occasionally I would ask if she'd had a letter from her stepfather or her brother, but she never had . . . not a word.'

Unless of course she was lying, Gerlof thought. Out loud, he said, 'We often heard stories about the emigrants who were successful and could send home plenty of dollars, but all those who ended up in the gutter just disappeared.'

Sonja nodded, looking a little upset. 'I just hope they had a better life in the USA, because the place they lived in at Rödtorp was just dreadful – little more than a grey shack. And, of course, Sven never had any money. He was a semi-invalid; his foot had been crushed.'

'So how did he make a living?'

'He did a bit of everything, as people who didn't have a farm of their own had to do back in those days. He worked as a miller's labourer, and went around the flour mills in the area.'

John glanced discreetly at his watch – it would soon be time for his evening rounds at the campsite – so Gerlof put down his cup.

'Thank you for the coffee; it was nice to talk to you. Could I possibly borrow the postcards for a few days?'

'We'll be in Majorca for two weeks, so you might as well hang on to them until we're back,' Sonja said.

Gerlof had one more question, but it wasn't about Aron. It was about the sound of knocking from inside a coffin. However, he didn't really know what he wanted to ask Sonja. It was her father who had heard the sound, along with Gerlof, and now Roland was lying in the churchyard, too.

In the end, he said, 'In that case, we'll head home and let you get on with your packing.'

Jonas

Kristoffer wanted to hang out, so Jonas was back in the Davidssons' garden. When he walked through the gate, he saw that Gerlof was sitting on his chair with his straw hat perched on his head, just as he should be.

The garden was quite small, but Jonas preferred being here to being at Villa Kloss. He could relax here.

But Gerlof's voice was sharper this evening. He sounded more like a sea captain. 'Good evening, Jonas. Come over here for a moment.'

Jonas slowly walked over to join him. Gerlof leaned forward, using his stick for support, and fixed him with a penetrating gaze. 'Peter Mayer,' he said. 'You remember that name?'

Jonas's heart gave an extra thump. Then he nodded. Gerlof looked so serious.

'And have you mentioned it to anyone else, Jonas?'

Jonas didn't know what to say. He wanted to sit down and tell Gerlof *everything*, absolutely *everything*, about the trip to Marnäs and Uncle Kent and Peter Mayer running across the field towards the road. And about the shouts and the screech of tyres.

But what would happen then? Yesterday, Casper had actually let him have a ride on the back of the moped, and Jonas knew he couldn't tell on Uncle Kent. So he shook his head.

'No. No one.'

'Do you know why I'm asking you about Peter Mayer?'

'No,' Jonas said quickly.

Perhaps rather too quickly. Gerlof waved away a fly, keeping his eyes fixed on the boy. 'You seem a little tense, Jonas. Is everything all right?'

'Not really.'

'What's the matter?'

Jonas took a deep breath. He had to say *something* about his fears, so he decided to reveal one of them. 'The cairn. It's haunted.'

'Oh?' Gerlof didn't sound in the least bit afraid.

'I've seen the ghost. It actually came out of the cairn.'

'Did it?' Gerlof smiled at him. 'I heard there was a dragon living in there. Twelve metres long from nose to tail, and bright green.'

Jonas didn't smile back. He was too old for fairy tales, and knew that dragons didn't exist. There were other things to be frightened of, but not dragons.

Gerlof's smile disappeared. He leaned more heavily on his stick and got to his feet. 'Come with me, Jonas. We're going for a little walk.'

He set off slowly but resolutely, with Jonas close behind.

At the far end of the garden a small path led through the under-growth and into a meadow. They followed the path for some thirty metres, then Gerlof stopped.

'Look over there, Jonas.'

Jonas turned his head and saw a square tower of sun-bleached wood in a clearing not far away. He knew what it was – a windmill. There was another one behind the restaurant, but that one was red and looked almost new. This one was derelict, with unpainted walls and wind-damaged sails.

'You mean the windmill?'

'No. Over there.'

Gerlof was pointing to the right of the windmill with his stick. Jonas looked, and saw a pile of round stones lying half hidden in the long grass.

'You see that? Those stones are the cairn . . . The *real* cairn, which was raised over some dead chieftain back in the Bronze Age.'

'The real cairn?'

'Yes. Your ancestors Edvard, Sigfrid and Gilbert Kloss dug out the cairn in the twenties. They thought there was ancient treasure under the stones. I don't know if they found anything, but while they were digging they decided the cairn would look better on the ridge, in front of their land . . . More "National Romantic".'

'What does that mean?'

'It's something that was fashionable in those days . . . People liked to worship ancient monuments. So the brothers fetched an ox cart and transported several loads of boulders to the ridge and shifted half the cairn.'

Jonas didn't say anything, he just listened.

'So the new cairn opposite Villa Kloss isn't a grave,' Gerlof went on. 'Haven't you noticed the old bunker set into the rock?'

'I've seen the door,' Jonas said. 'It's down in the dip.'

'Exactly. But do you think the army engineers would have been allowed to build a bunker under the cairn, if it was a real ancient monument?'

Jonas shook his head.

'They wouldn't,' Gerlof stressed. 'But because it's not a real cairn, it was fine.' He glanced over at the stones again, and added, 'If there's anyone who ought to be afraid of the ghost, it's me . . . When I was little, I was told that if you walked past here, invisible arms would reach out and grab you, and squeeze the air out of your lungs.'

'Are you scared?' Jonas said quietly.

Gerlof shook his head. 'I think there's an explanation for most things that seem frightening. In the old days, people used to hear ghosts screaming out on the alvar at night, but it was just hungry fox cubs, sitting in their dens and calling for food.'

Jonas felt a bit better now. Gerlof had an answer for everything.

They walked back to the garden. Jonas checked the legs of his trousers to make sure he hadn't picked up any ticks from the grass, but he couldn't see any.

Gerlof sat down and closed his eyes, as if the conversation was over. But Jonas hadn't finished. 'I've seen someone standing by the cairn. Several times.'

Gerlof opened his eyes. 'I believe you, Jonas. But that was a real person. A tourist, perhaps.'

'But he was like you . . . really, really old. And he just disappeared.'

'What did he look like?'

'He had grey hair and a white beard. He was dressed in dark clothes. Just like the man in the wheelhouse.'

Gerlof peered up at him. 'Are you all right, Jonas?'

The boy shook his head.

'I know you have horrible memories,' Gerlof said. 'You've had a terrible experience. Something dreadful happened to me one summer, when I was fifteen years old. I saw a man have a heart attack and die right in front of me. But everything passes – that's the only consolation. We get older, and happy memories push away the horrible ones.'

Jonas wondered when he would find those happy memories.

Gerlof

Gerlof's grandsons and Jonas Kloss had cycled off to the sweet shop, and Gerlof had gone indoors to avoid the mosquitoes' evening assembly.

He gathered up some empty glasses the boys had left on the coffee table, then flopped down in the armchair next to the telephone. He was very tired.

He was getting nowhere. Not with Peter Mayer's death, at any rate.

And the elderly American? What could he do to track him down? He picked up his notebook, licked his finger and started to leaf through the pages. He read through what he had written during his lunch with the Swedish-Americans, and over coffee with the grave-digger's daughter, paying close attention to every detail.

Speculation about Sven and Aron Fredh from Rödtorp. A question jotted down: 'Whereabouts in the USA did Aron end up?' But the line below was blank because, apart from the postcard before their departure, Sonja and her father had never heard from their relatives again.

'I just hope they had a better life in the USA,' Sonja had said. 'The place they lived in at Rödtorp was just dreadful – little more than a grey shack . . .'

He thought for a little while, then called Sonja. She answered quickly, but sounded stressed.

'You obviously haven't left yet,' Gerlof said.

'No, the bus to the airport leaves in a couple of hours.'

He got straight down to business.

'Sonja, I've been thinking about something you said when we came over for coffee . . . You said the Fredh family lived in a grey shack on the coast, at a place called Rödtorp.'

'That's right. Astrid Fredh had been given the tenancy of the croft by the Kloss family. It was deep in the forest, where the Ölandic Resort is now.' Sonja paused, then added, 'The Kloss family knocked it down, and I don't suppose anyone remembers the name these days. All the old names are disappearing, one by one . . .'

'You're right,' Gerlof agreed. 'But why was the place called "Rödtorp", which suggests it was red, if it was actually grey?'

Sonja responded with a dry laugh. 'It had nothing to do with the colour of the paint. It was the way Sven used to talk when he was working in the mills that led people to come up with that name.'

'And what did he talk about?'

'How can I put it . . .? He was an agitator. He used to go on at length about the blessings of socialism. That was what Sven believed in . . . He had become a committed socialist during his military service in Kalmar during the First World War. When he came to Öland and became a farmhand and worked in the flour mills, he became even more passionate about his views. Some say he became a communist in the end.'

'So he talked about politics in the mills and on the farms?'

'Yes, I think he liked to spell out chapter and verse, so to speak. But there was a lot more politics in the air in the thirties than there is now; there were both communist and Nazi summer rallies here on the island. There was trouble from time to time; they used to tear down each other's flags. And the Kloss brothers wouldn't tolerate any political talk. Sven quarrelled with them, too.'

Gerlof remembered – the political disputes had been a good reason to stay at sea, where the talk was of wind and weather and cargo rates.

'Thanks for your help, Sonja. Enjoy your holiday.'

He hung up and went into the bedroom, where the gravedigger's postcard album lay on the bookshelf. He sat down and found the black-and-white postcard from Aron Fredh. Read the brief message once more, then gazed at the picture on the front. The white ship, SS *Kastelholm*, at the quayside in Gothenburg. Sweden's gateway to America.

His eyesight was better than his hearing, and he took a closer look at the picture. Not so much at the ship, but at the quayside and the surroundings. The background was blurred and unfamiliar; a grey morning mist hovered over the water, and the only other vessel in the harbour was a steamship on its way out to sea, with deciduous trees and stone buildings beyond. No derricks, which was a little strange, since his own recollection of Gothenburg in the thirties was of an entire forest of derricks . . .

Suddenly, he recognized the port with a strange sense of déjà vu, because all at once what had seemed so unfamiliar was very well-known; he had been there many times.

He picked up the phone again.

'John, have you finished your evening rounds at the campsite?'

'Yes. Anders has gone off to do some work on the gig; I thought I might give him a hand.'

'I'll come with you if you can pick me up,' Gerlof said.

'Of course.'

Gerlof rang off, then made another call. To the National Maritime Museum.

John arrived fifteen minutes later, but Gerlof couldn't wait; he had something to tell his friend before they set off, and drew him on to the veranda.

'I've found something out, John.'

'Oh, yes?'

'Sven Fredh, Aron's stepfather, was a communist.'

John blinked, his expression vacant. The word 'communist' was no longer so loaded these days.

'Don't you understand?' Gerlof went on. 'Sven was a revolutionary; he was hardly likely to travel to America. Communists weren't exactly popular there. Immigrants from Europe weren't really welcome anyway after the Wall Street Crash, least of all troublemakers and "Bolsheviks".'

'No, but he could have kept quiet about his views when they got to immigration control in New York.'

'They never got to New York,' Gerlof said. He held out the post-card from Aron. 'This isn't Gothenburg docks. That's Stockholm in the background.'

'Stockholm?'

Gerlof nodded.

'It's not easy to recognize the ship's surroundings, but this evening I suddenly realized it was Skeppsbron in Stockholm. And what was the destination of ships sailing from Skeppsbron in the thirties? Was it America?'

'No,' John said. 'It was Finland. We used to go there sometimes before the war, and we saw them loading.'

'Exactly, but there were also ships that went further . . . SS *Kastelholm*, for example.'

'She went to America. It says so on the postcard.'

Gerlof shook his head.

'The *Kastelholm* was owned by the Swedish-American Line, but they also had European routes. I rang the Maritime Museum in Stockholm just before you arrived, and one of the curators looked up the *Kastelholm* on their computer database. She sailed the Baltic in the early thirties . . . all the way to Leningrad.'

John was listening, but looked puzzled.

'Aron and Sven didn't go to America,' Gerlof continued. 'They went in the opposite direction, to the country that no longer exists . . . the Soviet Union.'

John stared at him. He was beginning to understand.

'So the new country wasn't in the west . . . but in the east?'

'Yes. For some Swedes that was the case . . . for those who dreamed of the revolution and a classless society.'

'But what happened to them out there?'

'I don't know. Those were troubled times in the Soviet Union, and Stalin became increasingly paranoid, so anything could have happened . . . What do you think became of Aron?'

John didn't say anything, so Gerlof went on. 'He certainly didn't end up working for Al Capone, at any rate.'

High Summer

I am not saying that life is good
I would rather say that it is bad
but I am not saying that either.
I need only three tools:
a set square, a pair of scissors and a knife
so that I can measure and cut
what can be measured
and what can be cut.

The rest the night can measure
And the creatures that emerge at that time of the day.

Lennart Sjögren

The New Country, October 1934

Aron's boots leak; they are always wet. He is standing in the soft mud outside the row of grey huts that seem to cower beneath the fir trees. He is staring at Sven, who has finally told him the truth.

'So we're not in America?'

'No.'

'Then where *are* we?' asks Aron, afraid of the answer.

'We're in a different country,' Sven explains. 'The ship brought us across the Baltic, to a city called Leningrad, and we have travelled north from the coast.'

Aron is aware of that; there is no sea here. Only forest. But there is a great deal he doesn't understand.

'So Hibinogorsk isn't in America?'

Sven shakes his head. 'It's in northern Russia, by a mountain called Hibina.'

Aron is still staring at him, and Sven goes on. 'Russia is part of a union, just like America, but this one is known as the Soviet Union.'

Aron has heard of Russia, and he vaguely remembers the word 'Soviet' from some lesson at school, but it means nothing to him.

'But you said . . .'

'I said we were going to the new country. That's where we are now: in the east, where the sun rises. The sun and the wealth that comes with abundance.'

Aron says nothing, but he is thinking about the fact that he had nothing but a piece of black bread for breakfast. One small piece. He looks around the mining town, at the grey huts and the muddy streets.

'America is not the Promised Land,' Sven says. 'It is the kingdom of evil. The poor and the blacks are hunted down like dogs in America. They are captured and hanged from trees so that the rich white folk can use them for target practice, just for fun. Do you really want to go there?'

Aron doesn't reply.

'No, you don't. I can see it in your face. You want to stay here, where everyone works side by side.'

'I want to go home,' Aron says eventually. 'Back to Rödtorp. I wrote and told Mum we were coming home.'

'She doesn't know that.'

'She does.'

'She knows nothing,' Sven says, shuffling unsteadily to one side. 'I never posted the letters.'

Aron can't believe his ears.

'In any case, we can't leave the Soviet Union at the moment,' Sven says quietly. 'We can't afford it. We *will* leave this country and go home . . . but not yet.'

Aron has been listening to the same thing for the past three years. The same empty promises. As far as he is concerned, his stepfather, the proud Swedish worker, has begun to shrink.

The Soviet Union? Aron tries to find out more about this country. He has started to understand the language now, the Russian language that he thought was American, and he can hold a conversation of sorts with the workers in the camp.

He is also allowed to go to school for a few hours each day. Aron is studying with a Russian teacher, herr Kopelev. He listens and repeats the words, and learns the language much faster than Sven. He can swear in Russian, and he can reel off such high-flown phrases as 'Comrades, a groaning table awaits you after the world revolution!' and 'Do not allow your possessions to consume you, Comrade – private property is the root of all evil!'

But what everyone talks about is food. Including Aron – he dreams of Swedish food. Plaice, salted and fried. Eel, smoked and oily or boiled and firm. Potatoes, grated potatoes. Pork. Minced salt pork. Grated potatoes and minced pork turned into Öland dumplings, steaming hot.

Everyone talks about food, all the time. Rumours spread in Russian, and one morning down in the ditch he passes them on to Sven.

'People are starving. Dying on the streets.'

Sven stops digging and looks at him. 'What are you talking about?'

'That's what I've heard. There's no food.'

'Where? Where are these people starving?'

'In the south. In Kraine,' Aron says, wiping his nose with his glove.

'Ukraine,' Sven corrects him.

'That's it . . . Ukraine. There are farms there, so that's where the food ought to be, but there's none left. The soldiers have taken all the produce.'

'It's not soldiers who take the food,' Sven says, driving his spade into the mud. 'It's the wealthy farmers who hide it, then eat at night.'

'But all the cows are dead,' Aron insists, 'so they've started slaughtering their children. They'll eat anything down there.'

'Don't listen to that kind of nonsense.' Sven leans closer. 'I'll tell you a story about Stalin.'

'Who?'

'The leader. The captain who steers this whole ship, Josef Stalin.' Sven looks up at the pale sky, then back at Aron. 'Twenty years ago, he was the one who led the struggle against the old guard, the Tsar and his followers. On one occasion, he was arrested by the Tsar's police and sentenced to a beating. He was to run the gauntlet between two rows of police officers, standing ready with their barbed whips. Do you know what Stalin did then?'

Aron shakes his head.

'Before he moved forward to accept his punishment, he picked a blade of grass and placed it between his teeth. Then he began to walk. Stalin didn't run between the whips – he *walked*. He took his time, as if he were strolling through a meadow. And when he reached the end, with his back covered in blood, he opened his mouth and showed the last police officer the blade of grass. There wasn't a toothmark on it. So, although Stalin was beaten that day, he still won. Do you understand?'

Aron nods.

'That's how strong we have to be if we're going to get through this,' Sven says, straightening up for a moment. 'Start digging.'

Aron makes no move to obey him. 'I'm not like Stalin.'

Sven looks sharply at his stepson. 'But you can be.'

The Homecomer

The Homecomer was sitting in his car in a deserted lay-by with an open wooden box on the passenger seat. The box could have contained tins or jars, but it was marked with a yellow sticker and the words DANGER – EXPLOSIVES!

Inside, there were twenty sticks of pale-yellow plastic explosive. Side by side. Fast asleep. Encased in protective wrapping. There were also detonators, and the rolls of plastic cable were fuse wire.

All of this belonged to him now. Wall no longer needed anything.

The Homecomer hid the boxes under a blanket, then got out of the car and went over to one of the picnic tables. There was no one around; all the other cars just went whizzing by until, eventually, an old yellow sports car pulled in. He recognized the car, although the driver was different. Rita was sitting behind the wheel, and there was no sign of Pecka.

She got out and slowly came over to join the Homecomer. He raised a hand in greeting, but she just gazed blankly at him. Her eyes were red from crying.

Something was wrong.

'Where's Pecka?'

Rita merely shook her head. 'Gone,' she said.

'Gone?'

'He was hit by a car . . . on Thursday night.'

The Homecomer stared at her. 'Where did it happen?'

'On this road . . . a bit further north. He only went out to get us a pizza . . . A couple of smartly dressed guys rang the doorbell while I was waiting for him, but I didn't answer.'

'Smartly dressed?'

'Two men and a boy.'

'Kloss,' the Homecomer said. 'The Kloss brothers. And the boy who saw Pecka on the ship. One of them must be his father.'

Rita looked down, unable to suppress a sob. The Homecomer sighed. 'Pecka's uncle is dead, too.'

'Einar?'

'That's right. I found him outside his cottage; he was lying dead in his boat. So Kloss must have been to see him, too.'

Rita sat down. For a moment, the Homecomer felt as if he had his daughter sitting beside him, but he pushed the thought aside.

'Einar must have heard about Pecka,' Rita said quietly. 'He was very fond of Pecka. They were almost like father and son.'

They sat in silence for a little while; the Homecomer was thinking about fathers and sons, about Pecka and Wall and all the others who had died. The world was full of them.

After a while, Rita stood up. 'We can't stay here any longer,' she said. 'We've got to get out.'

'That's exactly what the Kloss brothers want,' the Homecomer said. 'They think they've won.'

Rita glanced over at the road, down towards the coast and the Ölandic Resort; she seemed to be thinking something over.

'There is something we could do,' she said after a moment or two. 'For Einar Wall and Pecka.'

'Oh?'

'It's something he talked about . . . something he was planning when he got the sack from the Ölandic, before he and Wall decided to go for the ship instead.'

'An attack on the Kloss family?'

Rita nodded. 'He said he was going to ruin their business. Get his revenge. Pecka was going to make sure that no one wanted to stay at the Ölandic Resort. They would lose millions . . . He told me exactly what he was going to do.'

The Homecomer also got to his feet. He gave a brief smile. 'Let's do it.'

Gerlof

At the beginning of July, a shimmering heatwave had moved in across the island. The sun rose above the Baltic Sea at half past four in the morning, and by seven any trace of the night's chill had disappeared. At nine, the heat out on the alvar was almost overwhelming. Some birds, like the cuckoo, had already fallen silent.

Gerlof realized that, up to now, the summer had merely been warm. This was *heat*, with glaring sunshine from a white sky making the air quiver, and not a breath of wind.

Like many other villagers, he preferred to spend time down by the shore, where there was at least the hint of a sea breeze. Sometimes John was there too, sanding down the gig or replacing a rotten plank.

Gerlof was sitting in the shade of the boathouse in a low deckchair, wearing his straw hat. 'I won't be here for much longer,' he said to John.

John wrinkled his nose and carried on with his work. 'You've been saying that for years.'

'I didn't mean that,' Gerlof said quickly. 'I meant physically, down here in the village. Both my daughters will be arriving with their families soon, and there's not enough room in the cottage. So I'll be moving back up to the home in Marnäs.'

'When?'

'Next weekend . . . In ten days.'

John looked at *Swallow* and shook his head. 'She won't be ready by then.'

'I know,' Gerlof said gloomily. 'And I'm not sure how often I'll be able to get down to the village. But my thoughts will be with you.'

204

Otherwise, his thoughts were mainly occupied by two young boys: Aron Fredh and Jonas Kloss.

Not that Aron was a boy any more, if he had survived the trip to the Soviet Union, but that was how Gerlof pictured him. A young boy in the sunshine, standing by a freshly dug grave. Had the knocking sound from down in the ground scared him that day? Gerlof assumed it had; he remembered a tall, gaunt man had come to fetch Aron from the churchyard. His stepfather, Sven, the committed communist.

Then he thought about Jonas Kloss, another frightened boy. He had also been scared by ghostly goings-on, but Gerlof wasn't convinced that it was only his fear of the cairn ghost and his experiences on board the ship that had made Jonas so tense.

He suspected that Jonas also had family problems.

When John had finished working on the gig for the day, Gerlof slowly made his way back up to the garden. But the sun was too strong; he couldn't sit outside any longer.

After a while, one of his grandsons helped him to set up a parasol. It provided shade for him and a small part of the garden, but the rest of the lawn was looking very much the worse for wear.

Gerlof took out his handkerchief and wiped his brow. It was twenty-eight degrees in the shade. Plants were dying, animals hiding away.

A few species of bird seemed to be enjoying the warmth and the light. When Gerlof looked inland he saw a shadow high in the sky: a hawk searching out rodents in the grass down below. Its wings were spread wide like black sails, and it hovered above the alvar, circling effortlessly.

Gerlof wondered whether the hawk was happy, experiencing such freedom.

Or perhaps it wasn't free at all.

Just hungry.

Gerlof was hungry, too; he went inside for a bowl of yoghurt with cinnamon. The phone rang while he was standing in the kitchen. It was Tilda, with news.

'We've heard from the coastguard.'

'About the ship?'

'No, it's still missing. But they've found a body out in Kalmar Sound – a seaman.'

It was the summer heat, Gerlof thought. As the waters of the Sound warmed up, bodies floated to the surface.

'Was he from the *Elia*?'

'Possibly. The Kalmar police are dealing with the matter. He had ID on him, so they're checking it out.'

'Good,' Gerlof said. 'I'm checking out a few things, too.'

He heard Tilda sigh, but carried on anyway. 'I'm trying to track down the old man on the ship . . . The American, if that's what he actually was.'

'According to Jonas Kloss, he was a Swedish-American,' Tilda said.

'Yes, but if he's the person I think he is, then he emigrated to Russia, not America. That fits in better with what was going on at the time. And, if that's the case, his name is Aron Fredh.'

'I don't recognize the name,' Tilda said. 'But let me know if you find him.'

'It's not easy. There are far too many people on the island at the moment.'

'Tell me about it,' Tilda said drily. She was silent for a moment, then added, 'The discovery of the body means that we're going to have to question Jonas Kloss. And this time it will be a formal interview, not just a chat.'

'At the station?'

'We'll probably do it at his home, if he feels safer there.'

But does he? Gerlof thought. Out loud, he said, 'I'd like to be there, if that's all right.'

Tilda laughed. 'Hardly.'

But Gerlof refused to give in. 'I can be . . . what did you call it? A witness, an independent observer to make sure that everything is done properly.'

After a brief silence, Tilda said, 'In that case, the boy would have to agree.'

'I think he will.'

'And you'd only be allowed to sit there,' Tilda stressed. 'You wouldn't be allowed to say a word, or to talk about it afterwards.'

'I can do all that.'

'Really?' Tilda sounded far from convinced.

Jonas

'We're having visitors, JK,' Uncle Kent said.

He was standing straight-backed in the heat on the decking, and he looked far from pleased. He was gazing out at the deserted coast road, and Jonas could see the corner of his left eye twitching slightly, just as it had done that evening in Marnäs.

He had tried to avoid his uncle as much as possible after that evening but, as he was working on the decking right next to the front door of the house, it wasn't always possible. Uncle Kent walked past him morning and evening. Sometimes in a suit, sometimes in shorts and a T-shirt. Sometimes he said a quick hello, sometimes he seemed too stressed even to notice Jonas.

This evening he was wearing a dark-grey suit and had stopped on his way from the car to tell Jonas about the impending visit.

'Who's coming?'

Kent looked at him, weighing him up. 'The police,' he said. 'They're coming here tomorrow evening, JK. They want to talk to you.'

'What about?'

Kent turned his attention to the Sound. 'They want to discuss the mysterious ship you claim you saw out there. Nothing else . . . So all you have to do is answer their questions. And I'll be there the whole time.'

Jonas glanced at the house and saw two heads through the panoramic window: his brother, Mats, and his cousin Urban were sitting on the sofa, watching TV. He knew that they knew he'd told the truth about the cinema visit; they hadn't said anything to him, but they *knew*. And he was still waiting for some kind of retribution.

'Is that all right, JK?' Kent said.

Jonas nodded and turned to look in the other direction, at the coast road and the ridge. There wasn't a soul in sight. The cairn was still there, of course, but there had been no sign of the ghost over the past few days. It was as if Gerlof's revelation that the cairn wasn't a real grave had frightened it away.

'One more thing . . . Do you know what a *player* is, JK?'

His uncle leaned closer. His shirt was unbuttoned beneath his jacket, and Kent was wearing some kind of male fragrance, as heavy and cloying as alcohol.

Jonas shook his head.

'A player is someone who's part of a business enterprise, or perhaps a game of some kind. There are small players and major players . . . and you are a small player in a very big game. Do you understand?'

Jonas nodded hesitantly.

'Good.' Kent blinked and lowered his voice so that he was almost whispering in Jonas's ear: 'And you know what your father did, don't you? Why he wasn't around last summer?'

Jonas nodded again.

'He's back with us now, so everything is all right.' Kent leaned even closer. 'But if you got the idea that you're a major player, JK, and you decided to tell the police about the evening when we went to Marnäs . . . well, they might just decide to take him away again. Is that what you want?'

Jonas shook his head.

'Nobody wants that,' Kent said. 'So you give them basic answers to their questions about the ship, but don't tell them anything else. OK?'

'OK.'

'Good. If you do that, we can win this game.'

Kent straightened up, patted Jonas on the shoulder and went indoors. A little while later, Jonas heard the treadmill start up.

The Homecomer

The farm was illuminated by a single floodlight attached to a pole high above the barn. The rest was in darkness, full of the sounds of animals lowing and bleating and thudding against the wooden walls. An old silo loomed up against the sky like a blunt-nosed rocket.

It was Friday, and even though a large farm never closes down, tonight it was likely to be less busy than usual. The working week was over; everybody wanted some time off.

But not the Homecomer. He crouched in the shadow of the silo, keeping quiet and still as he waited for Rita, who had disappeared in the direction of the barns, carrying a plastic bucket.

'Won't be long,' she had said, without asking for any help.

The Homecomer waited. The night air was warm and dry, with the faint smell of dung. He looked around, at the silo and the barn and the new machines. There were still those on the island who made a good living from farming, he realized. Perhaps the old-fashioned smallholdings had all disappeared.

He heard soft footsteps on the grass and saw a slender figure coming towards him – Rita, moving quickly and quietly.

'There you go,' she said, sounding out of breath. 'Nobody saw me.'

The bucket was no longer empty. It was heavy and full to the brim, its lid firmly closed. It was impossible to see what was inside.

The Homecomer took the bucket and looked at the other object Rita was carrying. It was a red plastic box with some kind of long hose. 'What's that?'

'A high-pressure pump. Which means we have everything we need.'

He nodded. 'Time to visit the Kloss family, in that case.'

The New Country, May 1935

'We can go home now,' Sven says at the beginning of summer, when the ground has dried out and it is easier to dig. 'Home to Rödtorp.'

Aron looks at him. 'Is that true?'

'It's true. I've handed in my passport to the office, and the secretary has sent it to Leningrad. Soon it will come back with the right stamps for the journey, and then we can go.'

Aron believes him. *Now*, he thinks. *Now.*

But the days of summer pass, and there is no sign of the passport.

The only thing that does arrive is an increase in food rations, so that Aron no longer shakes with hunger every morning and night. There is an abundance of berries in the forest this summer, and wagons deliver plenty of meat and apples.

But, just as the food pours into the camp, people begin to disappear.

One of the first to vanish is Michail Suntsov, an old labourer from Minsk who lives in the room next to the one occupied by the Swedes. Suntsov has told Aron extraordinary tales of life in the Soviet Union and has whittled him a beautiful fighter plane from birch wood, which Sven has hung up above their beds.

But one day Suntsov is gone. As they set off in the morning to carry on digging, some strange men in uniform are waiting for him. They take him aside and speak to him, and Suntsov doesn't turn up to work that day.

He is simply not there any more. His bed is empty and, when Sven asks the others in the room, no one knows what has happened. Or perhaps they do know, but no one is talking.

Those who whisper too much also disappear. This almost always happens at night. They are taken away in the darkness by uniformed men who are no more than shadows in the room. The workers are led out, alone or in twos, and they are never seen again.

And there is still no sign of Sven's passport.

Autumn comes, bringing back the cold. The grass is covered in frost and the ground is hard.

Sven gradually loses his determined expression; his eyes begin to flicker from side to side. His back is bent, and his limp is worse than ever.

'We're going home anyway,' he assures Aron. 'I've written to the Swedish consulate in Leningrad, explained the situation . . . told them we're not free to travel as we wish. So things will soon be sorted out.'

But he sounds less than certain.

And nothing happens. The days pass, the first snow falls, they carry on digging.

One day, Sven is called into the office after work. Aron watches him go, sees the door close. Sven is in there all evening, or so it seems.

When he returns to the hut, he sounds stressed. 'They had my passport,' he says. 'They've had it all the time. And the letter, the one I wrote to the consulate . . . They keep all letters; they've also confiscated letters from Sweden.'

He slumps down on the bed and goes on, 'They're talking about crushing the conspirators.'

'What does that mean?' Aron asks. 'What's a conspirator?'

Sven shakes his head and looks over at the closed door of the office. 'I shouldn't have handed in my passport,' he says to himself. 'I shouldn't have done that.'

He sits there, mumbling to himself. Aron goes to bed and gazes up at the model plane hanging from the ceiling. The only proof that Suntsov ever existed.

He closes his eyes and tries to sleep. He still has his own passport; he keeps it in his pocket and never shows it to anyone.

Sven is still sitting on the edge of the bed, but Aron falls asleep.

He is woken by a hand on his shoulder. A hard hand in a leather glove, shaking him.

'Up!' he hears in Russian.

It is an order, issued quietly.

Aron opens his eyes and sees three men standing in the hut. A tall man by his bed, and two others over by the door. They are all wearing dark coats and caps, some kind of field uniform.

'Up!' the man with the leather gloves says again, dragging Aron out of bed.

The floor is ice cold. The man picks up Aron's clothes and boots and throws them at him.

'Come with us.'

Aron gets dressed and is led silently out of the hut, half asleep and feeling lost – but then he sees that he is not alone. Another man is being led outside.

Sven. They have woken Sven, too.

A fourth man in uniform is standing in the snow beside a black car, a number of documents in his hand. Aron can see that one of them is Sven's passport, but the man doesn't give it back, and nor does he introduce himself. He simply reads out both their names, slowly and in Russian.

'Is this you?'

Sven nods.

'In that case, you will come with us.'

They are pushed into the back seat of the car, with a guard on each side, so that Aron has to sit on Sven's knee. The car drives away from the labour camp, into the darkness.

Sven moves cautiously, putting his mouth close to Aron's ear. 'Keep calm,' he whispers in Swedish.

'I am calm.'

'It's important. We have to keep calm.'

But Sven seems anything but calm; his upper body is twisting and moving back and forth, as if he is in pain.

Aron does feel calm. He is surprised to find that he is almost enjoying the trip. This is the first time he has ever been in a car, and somehow he has the sense that he is leaving all his troubles behind. Sven keeps his eyes lowered, but Aron gazes around, studying the gun belt the man next to him is wearing. A black pistol butt is sticking up out of a holster, but he can't see what model it is. A Mauser? He's heard that the Soviet police usually carry Mausers.

He suddenly remembers his dream: to be a sheriff in America.

It is a long journey through the darkness, but Sven says nothing, and Aron keeps quiet, too.

Eventually, they see lights. Floodlights, on top of a black structure looming up above the forest – a watchtower, Aron realizes.

He can also see barbed wire. The car drives in through an open metal gate, which is then closed behind them. It pulls up in front of a low stone building, and Sven and Aron are led out of the car and in through a doorway.

A guard carrying a machine gun takes them down a long corridor with a cement floor, past a series of closed wooden doors.

They can hear sounds all around them, muffled thuds and loud cries.

The soldier opens one of the doors. He gives Aron a shove. 'Get down there,' he says.

He steps aside, and Aron sees a flight of wide stone steps plunging down into the underworld.

Gerlof

Gerlof has never visited the Kloss family – he has never even set foot on their land. The garden consists of a sparse but attractive rockery with viper's bugloss and juniper bushes sheltered from the road by a stone wall. Side by side beyond the wall lie two single-storey houses that look like boxes made of pine and glass, flanked by garages and smaller guest chalets.

Back in the fifties, Gerlof could have bought a plot of his own on the coast road, but he had turned down the opportunity. He had been a ship's captain in those days and hadn't wanted to see a single drop of seawater when he wasn't working, which was why his cottage was where it was. Out of sight of the water.

John gave him a lift, but it wasn't a member of the Kloss family who met him when he got out of the car. A middle-aged woman with short grey hair and a steady gaze was waiting on the drive.

'Gerlof Davidsson?'

'That's right.'

He had never met the woman, but he recognized the firm handshake and the look in her eyes – she was a civilian police officer. Perhaps it was also her sensible clothing; in spite of the fact that it was a warm evening, she was wearing a dark skirt, a white blouse and a cardigan.

'Cecilia Sander. I'm with the County Police – I'm responsible for conducting interviews with children, and I'm here to talk to Jonas Kloss. I believe you're acting as an independent observer?'

'That's right,' Gerlof said again.

'You know what that involves?'

'Yes. I listen and remember.'

'Good.' Cecilia Sander turned around and headed towards the house furthest south. 'Everything's arranged. We're in here.'

Gerlof followed her across the recently sanded wooden decking to a sliding glass door, then into a large room with a polished stone floor and pale wooden panelling. It was wonderfully cool indoors; concealed fans in the ceiling seemed to be doing an excellent job.

Veronica Kloss was standing by the door, wearing jeans and a white top. Her dark hair tumbled around her shoulders; she smiled and held out her hand. 'Gerlof?'

'Good evening . . . We've met before,' he said, hoping she would remember.

'Really? Where was that?'

'Up at the home in Marnäs, when you came to talk about the Kloss family, and the story of the Ölandic Resort.'

'Yes, of course, I was there last summer,' Veronica said. 'It was very enjoyable . . . A lot of elderly people have so many stories to tell.'

'To those who are prepared to listen,' Gerlof said.

He relaxed and allowed himself to be led further into the room, past a treadmill and a wine rack.

Several people were seated on sofas around an oak coffee table. There was more tension in the air in here. He recognized Jonas Kloss, who looked more stressed than anyone else. His Uncle Kent was sitting beside him, with a healthy tan; he was wearing a light-brown summer jacket.

There were also three teenage boys smartly dressed in shirts and dark-blue jeans. Jonas's brother and cousins, Gerlof assumed.

A younger woman was moving around the table, pouring iced water; at first Gerlof assumed she was another sister, but when she said, 'You're welcome,' in broken Swedish, he realized she must be the housekeeper. Some people could still afford such a luxury.

'Right,' Cecilia Sander said, sitting down at the end of the table, where she could see everyone. 'Let's get started. It would be best if just Jonas and one member of the family stays; the rest of you can go.'

'In that case, I'll stay,' Kent Kloss said quickly. 'I'm his uncle. His parents aren't here.'

He smiled at the police officer, but she didn't smile back.

'Where are they, Jonas?' she asked.

'Mum's at home . . . She lives in Huskvarna. Dad's here, but he . . .'

215

Jonas paused and looked at his uncle.

'He's working in our restaurant,' Kent Kloss explained. 'He has to be there, otherwise we lose our alcohol licence.'

Jonas didn't say anything.

'OK, Jonas,' Cecilia Sander said, opening her notebook. 'Let's have a little chat.'

She glanced at her papers, then went on. 'One evening towards the end of June, the twenty-eighth, you were supposed to be going to the cinema in Kalmar. But that didn't happen, so you went down to the shore instead.'

'Yes.'

'Why didn't you go to the cinema?'

'Because I was too young for the film that was on. I wasn't allowed to go with them.'

Kent cleared his throat and leaned forward. 'The older boys cooked this up behind our backs – needless to say, it wasn't the right thing to do. We've spoken to them about the way they treated Jonas, and they're all very sorry.'

Cecilia Sander listened carefully to what he had to say but kept her eyes fixed on Jonas. 'So you went down to the shore. What happened then?'

Jonas glanced around the table. 'I . . . I saw a ship coming towards me . . . when I'd rowed out a little way in the dinghy.'

'Can you tell me what happened next?'

'She was called *Elia*, the ship I mean . . . I climbed on board.'

He started to tell the story Gerlof had already heard twice. It was a slow process, but it was impressively consistent.

Cecilia listened and made notes until the end of the story, when Jonas had jumped overboard and made his way ashore, then she reached into her bag and took out a number of photographs.

'I'm going to show you a rather unpleasant picture now. I'm telling you so you're prepared. It's the photograph of a dead man who was found floating in the Sound a few days ago, five nautical miles to the north . . .'

She held up a picture of a chalk-white face with closed eyes and a thin beard. A man in his fifties, wearing overalls. The face was swollen; Gerlof could see that he had been underwater for some time.

216

'Do you recognize him?' Cecilia Sander asked.

Jonas glanced at the photograph, looked away, then back, this time for longer. He nodded. 'He was on the ship . . . He was the one who was lying by the hatch.'

Cecilia nodded. 'He's German, and his name is Thomas Herberg,' she said. 'His wallet was in his pocket, so we were able to identify him.'

No one said a word, so she picked up another picture. 'And the ship you boarded, the *Elia* . . . could this be her?'

Gerlof leaned forward. The photograph had been taken at an angle from the front, and showed a small cargo ship with a black-painted hull and two wooden structures on deck. He felt quite proud when he saw that it was very similar to the drawing he had done in the boathouse, with Jonas's help. The big difference was that the ship in the photograph was safely tied up at a quayside.

'Yes . . . I think so,' Jonas said.

Gerlof glanced at Kent Kloss, who had looked at the picture then immediately turned away to gaze out of the window.

'You got part of the name right,' Cecilia said. 'She's actually called *Ophelia*, and she's an old cargo ship from Hamburg.'

She turned the picture over and added, 'Thomas Herberg was the captain.'

Ophelia, Gerlof thought. Not *Elia* – but perhaps the crew had painted over part of the name?

'I have some more pictures,' Cecilia Sander said, lining up four more. They were photographs of young men, aged between twenty and thirty. They were all staring into the camera with serious expressions, and Gerlof thought the pictures looked like police photographs. He didn't recognize any of the faces, but Jonas quickly pointed to the fourth man.

'I recognize him – that's Peter Mayer. He was the one who suddenly appeared, the one with the axe.'

'So you know his name? Have you seen him elsewhere?'

Jonas nodded. 'At the cinema in Marnäs,' he said at once. 'When I was little . . . He was selling the tickets.'

Cecilia Sander made a note. 'And is that the only time?'

Jonas glanced over at his uncle, who stared back. Then he looked at Cecilia Sander and nodded.

'OK,' she said. 'In that case, I have just one final picture, Jonas. Have you ever seen this person?'

It was an enlarged and slightly blurred photograph of an elderly man with a grey beard; he was wearing a black jacket and staring straight into the camera. Gerlof could see part of a wooden sign behind the man; he recognized it as the name of the unit on the first floor at the residential home in Marnäs, just below Gerlof's unit.

Eventually, he recognized the man, too: it was Einar Wall, fisherman and suspected arms smuggler. But Wall had lived in a cottage on the coast, not in the home, so why had the picture been taken there? Did he have a relative in Marnäs?

Jonas shook his head. 'No.'

There was a brief silence as Cecilia Sander finished making notes, then she looked up at Jonas.

'Good,' she said. 'We've finished then. You'll receive a printed copy of this interview so that we're all in agreement on what was said here today . . . And if there's anything else, I'll be in touch. Thank you very much, Jonas.'

Jonas gave a brief nod and got to his feet. He almost ran to the glass door leading out on to the veranda; Gerlof could see he was glad it was all over.

The Homecomer

It was late on Friday evening, and the Homecomer wiped the sweat from his brow in the cramped kitchen as he tightened the last water pipe. The plastic bucket Rita had brought from the farm was standing beside him; it was empty now.

He and Rita had driven into the Ölandic Resort with the bucket and the high-pressure pump, and no one had stopped them. Presumably they looked like campers – an elderly father and his daughter, or possibly granddaughter.

Unscrewing the pipe work had taken quite a while, giving the two of them time to have a chat. Rita had talked about her family. She had no contact with her parents, and her brother worked in the far north of Norway, so she had come to Öland the previous autumn to try to find a new life. And because of Pecka; they had met at a music festival.

'What about you?' she said. 'Do you have family in the USA?'

'I never said I was in the USA,' the Homecomer replied. 'I was in the Soviet Union.'

'Which no longer exists,' Rita said. She didn't ask any more questions.

At last, everything was done.

'Here we go,' Rita said, switching on the pump.

The Homecomer took a step back and listened to the low hum. This was the beginning of the nightmare for the Kloss family.

Everything was heading towards its conclusion now. That was how it felt. Pecka and Wall were dead. His wife was dead, too – and he might not have long left either.

The Homecomer looked out of the window.

He saw the campsite with its rows of tents and chalets, but he was thinking about a prison camp.

The New Country, December 1935

Life is work. The sleep of exhaustion and hard work; nothing else.

Aron and Sven are trapped. They are prisoners by night and slaves by day; they are never free. They labour with axes and saws along with Matti, a tall, thin Finn, and Grisha, a short, stocky Ukrainian. They fell fir trees from morning till night and drag the logs down to the river. There are no horses yet – while they are waiting for the horses to arrive, the men have to act as beasts of burden.

Where are they? Somewhere in the north of the Soviet Union, that's all they know. This is where they were sent, after brief questioning and instant verdicts.

Documents were produced, stamped, copied. Aron could read Russian well enough by now to realize that he and Sven had been convicted of sabotage and sentenced to eight years in a labour camp.

What is sabotage? They have no idea.

But the punishment is work: even more work.

After a few days in a crowded cell near the court, they were transported by night to a train, where they were pushed into a wagon lined with wire cages full of prisoners. They were given a little soup, and the train began to move.

They travelled for hours, perhaps days. The cold got more and more intense. There were no windows in the wagon, just cracks in the walls, but they presumed they were heading north.

There was no toilet either, just a hole in the floor which soon froze over. After that, the prisoners just had to squat down in the darkest corner. After a while, there was a stinking pile there, growing bigger with every visit.

From time to time, the train stopped and more prisoners were hustled into the cages. They were guarded by young men in uniform, soldiers with rifles and sub-machine guns. Aron looked at them, remembering how it had felt to hold his very own gun when he was a little boy.

'Have you seen the knives attached to the barrels?' he whispered to Sven.

'Those aren't knives,' Sven said wearily. 'They're called bayonets.'

Aron was amazed. 'So they can use their guns to shoot someone, and stab them as well?'

Sven didn't reply, he just leaned back against the wall and closed his eyes. Aron sat alone by the wire mesh, staring at the guns.

Eventually, the train stopped, and this time it didn't move off again. When the doors opened, it was twilight. The prisoners were brought out on to a snow-covered platform; they were lined up and marched off. Straight into the forest.

Aron's first sight of the camp was a bundle of clothes powdered with snow in a great big pile by the side of the track. Then he saw a blackened hand sticking out of the pile like a claw and realized he was looking at a heap of dead bodies.

'They don't bury people here,' he said.

Sven didn't respond, but another prisoner behind them mumbled something in Norwegian; he said the ground was frozen solid.

Everything was frozen here.

The second thing Aron saw was a fence covered in ice, with shadows sitting or lying by some of the posts – enormous chained dogs. Further away, there was a watchtower, three storeys high, overlooking a row of low huts.

They were taken into one of the huts; the place was already packed. Aron glanced out through a cracked window at a white world. Beyond the fence and the snowdrifts there was dense coniferous forest, and far away on the horizon he could see high mountains.

Trees.

Mountains.

Aron has seen more trees and more mountains this winter than in his whole life. There were no mountains on Öland, and hardly any trees; here in the new country, huge trees reach up to the sky every-where you turn.

The landscape outside the camp is utterly desolate, and bitterly cold. The snow has settled early. The white days in the forest beyond the fence become routine, but every other week they are allowed a bath.

They learn that the camp is only a couple of years old; the prisoners built it themselves. There was nothing there but an empty field when the first prison colonies arrived after a long march. They dug holes in the ground to sleep in, then built small shelters, and finally proper huts.

About fifty prisoners from ten different countries live in Sven and Aron's hut. When they are not working, they all gather round the stove, which is nothing more than a rusty barrel that gives off hardly any heat. They eat dry bread and thin meat soup, and two or three men squash together in each bed.

Aron hears the wind howling outside the hut and thinks about the storms on Öland, but these are distant childhood memories; he feels like an adult now. He is seventeen years old.

He wakes up, kills a few bedbugs, then gets up. If there is any wood left he pushes a few sticks into the iron stove, lights it and hears Sven and the other men slowly begin to move around.

Almost every morning someone goes to wake some lie-a-bed but finds a cold body that will never move again.

Death picks his way among the bunks, and Aron quickly gets used to the sight of blue lips and frozen eyes, a stiff body being carried out of the hut. No one has the energy to wash the corpse, so it joins the rest, like a log on a woodpile.

Time to get to work.

The brigade marches out into the forest at seven o'clock every morning, then the men are divided into smaller groups. They are accompanied by a foreman, but Sven and Aron hardly ever see him. The groups are sent off with an axe and a two-man saw to fell trees then drag the logs down to the river.

The logs float away, but there is no escape for the prisoners. There is nothing around them but endless forests and snow, with rumours of bears and wolves.

And there is no point in going on strike, or trying to cheat the system. The logs on the riverbank are counted at the end of each day, and any group that fails to fulfil its quota receives reduced food rations. Less food means death, sooner or later.

So they chop and haul and drag, and they are always, always cold. The work helps to keep their arms and legs warm, but their hands are ice cold. Sven has managed to buy boots and gloves with hardly any holes in them for himself and Aron; other prisoners have to make do with bits of cloth wrapped around their fingers and toes.

Matti the Finn has no gloves, no protection at all for his hands. His reserves of fat are beginning to run out; he is so cold that he no longer even shakes. Aron can see that the fingers on his left hand are white and covered in ice; they have turned into a solid lump. Matti is trying to work, but he is moving as if he is in a trance.

'Have a rest, Matti,' Sven says. 'When we get back this evening you can thaw out.'

Matti leans on a pine tree but becomes more and more confused. He starts speaking Finnish, and after a while they can hear him singing quietly to himself.

The others keep on working. They have to meet their quota.

But in the twilight Matti is suddenly nowhere to be seen. Aron, Grisha and Sven have chopped down a tree; when they look up, they see only meandering footprints in the snow. Sven follows the trail, but loses it in the darkness. They shout for Matti in all directions, but there is no reply.

They search and search, until the whistles summoning them to gather for the march back to the camp echo through the trees. They have to leave, without Matti.

The foreman yells and swears when the prisoners have been counted and it becomes clear that one is missing, but there is nothing he can do except lead the column back to the camp.

That night, the temperature outside is minus eighteen degrees. Aron listens to the wind and thinks about the endless forest. About Matti.

The next morning, the brigade marches off once more; the men are divided into groups and head for their work stations. Thin snowflakes are falling, but the forest is silent. They pick up their saws.

But then they hear someone singing loudly among the trees. The language is Finnish, and they recognize the voice.

'Matti!' Sven shouts.

He stumbles away, and Aron follows him.

The sound of the song leads them to Matti. Eventually, they find him at the bottom of a tall pine tree, slumped in the snow, holding his fists up in front of him; they are two clumps of ice. Small, thin mushrooms are sticking up out of the snow all around him in a wide semicircle.

'Matti?'

Sven rushes forward and gives his comrade a shake, but there is no response.

Matti is no longer listening; his eyes are frozen shut, and he is singing at the top of his voice.

Slowly, Aron walks over to the pine tree. He looks at the strange semicircle in the snow; he can't understand how mushrooms can grow in the middle of winter.

Suddenly he realizes what the mushrooms are.

They are fingers.

The Finn has snapped off his frozen fingers and arranged them in front of him in the snow.

Matti goes on singing, bellowing with his eyes tight shut.

Aron stares silently at the fingers. Ten of them, pointing accusingly up at the sky.

Matti is taken to the sick bay for a speedy amputation of his hands and feet, but it doesn't help. He dies the same night.

Something turns to iron inside Aron that day. The softness is gone, and the suffering around him no longer affects him so deeply. He notices the sick and the dying in the camp but lowers his head and keeps on walking.

Both he and Sven become more cautious in their dealings with other prisoners in the camp, but new groups are constantly arriving. And many of them are eager to talk.

For a few weeks they work with an American, Max Hingley from Chicago, who came to the new country as a committed communist at the end of the twenties and ended up as a slave labourer on a canal-building project two years later. They work together in the forest every day, then suddenly Hingley is gone. The word is that he was taken from his hut during the night and sentenced by a troika the very next day. No one knows why.

'I suppose they thought he was a spy,' someone says.

'A spy?' Sven says. 'But Hingley was a committed communist.'

There seem to be new rules now. And new opinions to replace the views that are dead and gone.

A young Soviet prisoner joins their brigade and is placed on its northern outpost, in the Swedes' little group. He introduces himself as Vladimir Nikolajevitch Jegerov; he tells them that he is one year older than Aron and comes from Kiev in the Ukraine. He explains that he has such a long name because it is normal practice to take the father's name as one's middle name.

'But call me Vlad,' he says. 'That's easier for a foreigner.'

'Call me Aron,' Aron says in Russian.

In a brigade full of silent men, Vlad is talkative. His mother was Russian and his father Ukrainian, but both are dead now. It was the great famine that took them, two years ago. Vladimir was sentenced to four years in a labour camp for hiding half a loaf. He misses Ukrainian bread, both white and black.

'I also miss the stewed meat we used to have,' he says. 'And the apples, the apricots, the potatoes, the sugar, the cream, and those wonderful sweet cherries . . .'

Aron listens open-mouthed. Dribbling. He had decided not to make any friends, but when Vlad talks about food, he could listen to him for ever.

Vlad has learned to survive in the camp. He has made himself a pair of boots from birch bark, his padded jacket has no holes in it, and somehow he manages to hold on to his sheepskin hat in spite of all the thieves. He also has a stock of paper and his own pen, and he teaches Aron how to write in Russian.

There are many new letters to get to grips with, and some letters that Aron recognizes don't sound the same here, but slowly he learns the alphabet. He writes a Russian word in the way he thinks it would be written using Swedish letters, while Vlad writes it in Russian. Then they compare.

After almost three years, Russian is the language of everyday life for Aron. He speaks Swedish only with Sven, and those occasions are becoming increasingly rare.

Vlad has somehow managed to hide away a fresh onion, which he shares with Aron. While they are eating he says that he saw Max Hingley being taken away by men in grey uniforms. They were from the secret police, the GPU, and they came in the middle of the night.

'It was because he was a foreigner.'

Aron stiffens, clutching a piece of onion in his hand. 'A foreigner?'

'The secret police assume all foreigners are spies.'

They munch on the onion in silence, and after a moment Aron says, 'I'm not a spy.'

'Are you sure?' Vlad smiles and leans forward. 'You ought to become a Soviet citizen . . . you and Sven. You ought to get yourselves Russian passports, then you can travel freely when you're released.'

'We don't want to become Soviet citizens,' Aron says. 'We want to go home.'

Vlad nods. 'But you have to get out of here first. Then you can go home.'

'Yes, but how do we do that?'

'You take passports from those who don't need them.'

At first, Aron doesn't understand. 'But surely everyone needs their passport?'

Vlad shakes his head. 'Not if they're *fitili*.'

Fitili means candle wicks. It is the word used to describe those who will soon be extinguished – the dying prisoners.

Aron listens, and thinks things over.

He talks to Sven that night, in the darkness between the bunks when the other prisoners have fallen asleep, when they are snoring and snuffling loudly.

Aron whispers in Swedish, passing on Vlad's warning and his advice.

'He means . . . steal a Soviet passport?' Sven whispers back when Aron has finished. 'Turn thief in order to become a citizen? Is that what he said?'

Aron nods. 'Take a passport. From a dying candle.'

They stare at each other in the darkness, listening to the snores and snuffles.

Gerlof

The interview at Villa Kloss was over; everyone had begun to get to their feet. It took the longest for Gerlof, who was there in his capacity as an independent witness, but he was deliberately being slow. He had remained silent while Cecilia Sander was questioning Jonas, but had kept an eye on Kent Kloss the whole time. The owner of the Ölandic Resort was smiling now, as if he had won a tennis match.

Gerlof wanted to wipe that smile off his face, so as he leaned on his stick for support he looked over at Kent and said quietly, as if he was just chatting, 'By the way, I saw your dredger passing by Stenvik back in the spring . . . I presume it was on the way down to the Ölandic?'

In fact, it was John who had seen the dredger out in the Sound, but Kloss didn't know that.

He nodded. 'Yes, we had to clear some mud.'

'From the bottom of the harbour?'

'That's right.'

Kloss wasn't really listening; he glanced at his watch.

'I know there's a harbour at the resort,' Gerlof went on. 'It started off as a narrow steamboat jetty and was converted into a cargo dock after the war . . .'

Kloss didn't say anything; he was already moving away from the table. But Gerlof stuck out his walking stick, almost barring Kent's way, and asked, 'Do you use the cargo dock?'

Kloss stopped and looked at him. 'Well, you say cargo dock – it's really just an old stone jetty that we've shored up with concrete.'

'And you keep it in working order?'

'Yes – as I said, we usually do some dredging in the spring; otherwise it just silts up.'

'So what's the depth by the jetty?'

'A few metres . . . Three, maybe?'

Gerlof waved his stick at the picture of the *Ophelia*, which was still lying on the table. 'That's deep enough,' he said. 'I should think the draught of that ship is around two metres. So she could easily have been moored at the Ölandic's jetty.'

Kent Kloss stared at him. Gerlof definitely had his attention now. He went on, 'No one down in Borgholm seems to have seen her, and since the waters off this part of the coast are so shallow, there aren't many other harbours. So was she in your cargo dock?'

Kent Kloss didn't say anything, but now Cecilia Sander was also beginning to show an interest. She had gathered up her papers, but suddenly she looked at Kent. 'Was she *your* ship?'

Kent Kloss turned to face her, and answered tersely, 'The answer is no. Not really.'

'You mean you don't know?'

'She wasn't *ours*, I do know that . . . but it's possible we might have been using her.' Kloss lowered his gaze. 'We had a ship in the dock at midsummer, but I don't remember her name . . . She was delivering cargo; we'd rented part of the hold.'

'For what?' Cecilia Sander demanded.

Kent looked down at his hands and studied his nails. 'For . . . food supplies,' he said eventually.

'It was fish,' Gerlof said. 'Wasn't it?'

'Fish, exactly. They brought fish from the Baltic to our restaurants. They unloaded over the midsummer holiday, then they left.'

'You must have had some contact with them?'

'Not since then.' Kent Kloss shrugged, but Gerlof thought it was an act, that he was making an effort to appear relaxed. 'And it was our kitchen manager who dealt with the delivery. I didn't even know what Captain Herberg looked like; all I have is the phone number of the company in Hamburg.'

'And have you seen the ship's log?' Sander asked.

'I'm sorry, I haven't,' Kent said.

Sander jotted something down in her notebook. She nodded to herself, but didn't seem entirely satisfied.

Gerlof wasn't satisfied either. A delivery of fish from overseas. Perhaps that sounded logical at this time of year, but was it that simple?

He looked out of the window and saw Jonas on the decking, talking to a middle-aged man in a jacket. The man's expression was serious and, occasionally, he glanced over towards the house. Jonas's father, Niklas, Gerlof guessed.

'We'll be in touch,' Cecilia Sander said as she left. She looked straight at Kent Kloss and added, 'We'll be working with Customs and Excise and with the coastguard on this case.'

Gerlof followed her outside. The sun had almost disappeared, but the heat was still there. At least Kloss had a big blue pool in which to cool off.

Jonas was already hard at work; he had switched on a small sander and was moving it over the decking with long, even strokes. His father had disappeared.

Gerlof turned and saw Kent Kloss standing by John Hagman's car. John had wound down the window, and they were talking. They stopped when Gerlof reached the car. Kloss stared at him; the self-assured look was back in his eyes. *Just you try*, it seemed to be saying.

Five minutes later, John started up the car and reversed on to the road.

'I see you were chatting with the enemy,' Gerlof said.

'Kloss isn't an enemy. Just a rival,' John said.

'What did he want?'

'He was asking if I had any elderly guests staying on the campsite.'

'You must have, surely?' Gerlof said. 'You've got your regulars, haven't you?'

'Of course. And then he wanted to know if there were any elderly men on their own, someone who might not have stayed here before in the summer. New faces. There are a few; he asked me if they were from overseas, but I haven't a clue.'

'So he's looking for elderly foreigners? Just like us.'

'That's right. He wanted me to tell him which caravans they were staying in, but I can't do that. I can't betray the confidence of my guests.'

'Of course not,' Gerlof said, in spite of the fact that he had been thinking of asking John exactly the same thing. 'What do you know about Kent's brother?'

'His name is Niklas.'

'Indeed. And what else do you know about Niklas Kloss?'

'Not much,' John said, glancing back at the coast road. 'He runs the restaurant, but I don't see much of him. It's Kent Kloss who's around most of the time, and sometimes their sister, Veronica.'

'It was the same today,' Gerlof said thoughtfully. 'Kent Kloss was there while the boy was being interviewed. It should really have been Jonas's father, but he seemed to be hiding.'

'Niklas Kloss is the black sheep of the family,' John said. 'If you believe the gossip.'

'What's he supposed to have done?'

John nodded in the direction of the houses on the coast road. 'He also inherited a plot of land here, but he couldn't afford to build on it, so after a few years he sold it. Gambling debts, apparently. And then of course he ended up in jail.'

'Did he? What for?'

'No idea. Fraud, maybe, or theft . . . It's not very long since he came out.'

Gerlof nodded pensively. 'In that case, I can understand why he avoids the police.'

The Homecomer

The second weekend in July, there wasn't a cloud in the sky over Öland; from morning till evening, the island was bathed in light and warmth, and the sun attracted visitors from all over southern Sweden. This was when the real wave of tourists arrived from the mainland. The holiday season was well under way. There were no traffic jams, as there had been at midsummer, but from Friday to Sunday a steady stream of cars and caravans passed over the bridge before dispersing all over the island, from north to south.

The beaches were packed with people during the day, the campsites and hotels at night. Summer cottages were opened up, barbecues set up, lawnmowers hummed into life. For the next few weeks, every road, every electrical supply cable and every sewage outlet on the island would be used to its maximum capacity, until calm returned in August.

The holiday complexes were also full to bursting, as were the nightclubs. This was the most important month of the year for the Ölandic Resort outside Stenvik.

The Homecomer was standing in a picnic area just off the main road, watching the cars pass by. Rita was beside him; she looked tired but resolute. She tilted her head in the direction of her own car: 'Well, we've done what we had to do . . . I'll be on my way.'

The Homecomer nodded, thinking once again that he could have been her father or grandfather. He took out his wallet and removed a wad of notes. 'A bit more from the ship,' he said. 'Where will you go?'

She took the money but made no attempt to count it. 'Copenhagen,' she said. 'I've got friends there. I'm going to stay out of the way for a while . . . What about you?'

'I'm staying here on the island,' the Homecomer said.

'How long for?'

'Until I die.'

Rita smiled briefly, as if he were joking. 'Thanks for everything.'

She gave him a quick hug, then walked away. Heading for new adventures.

The Homecomer remained where he was. Several cars had stopped, and the picnic tables were beginning to fill up with people. He knew that the Kloss family would be looking forward to the arrival of all the tourists.

The Ölandic Resort was ready. But no one except the Homecomer and Rita knew that disaster was on its way to the complex. It was already creeping through the ground.

The New Country, February 1936

The day when disaster strikes is just like any other working day.

There are four of them in the forest: Aron, Vlad, old Grisha and Sven. They are shifting logs, and on this particular occasion they have an old horse to help them. His name is Bokser, and he drags the sledge down to the river and back again. Bokser is half dead; he has scabs as big as saucers on his neck, but he still has to work. He is the third horse the commandant has requisitioned from a farm to the south of the camp; the first two froze to death. The meat tasted like dry bacon.

Bokser is a luxury, and no one knows how long they will be allowed to keep him. Other brigades don't have a horse; the prisoners have to pull the sledges instead.

The four of them work hard, felling trees and loading up the logs; they are behind with their quota. They are always behind. The trees would have to fall down by themselves in their thousands for them to catch up. There should have been seven of them in the brigade today, but two are sick and one is in solitary confinement, accused of trying to cheat the system.

The logs are lying on the ground. Vlad counts to three, then he and Grisha and Aron lift them on to the sledge, one after the other, and Sven secures them with a chain. Grisha whines and complains after each one. They have done all this thousands of times before.

Aron's movements are mechanical; in his mind, he is on the shore down below Rödtorp, where the sun is shining and the waves murmur among the rocks. Where the sand is soft and you can go for a swim whenever you like.

'Aron,' Sven says quietly.

Aron blinks, and he is back in the cold, the endless exhaustion. He turns his head and sees Sven standing by the sledge laden with logs; there is a strange expression on Sven's face. A resolute expression. His hands are moving, turning something around and around.

Then everything falls apart. The world shakes and shatters.

'Look out!' Sven yells in Swedish.

Vlad is still bending down next to the sledge, but Aron begins to move. He realizes what is happening. The chain has come off, and the logs are moving. Nothing can stop them now.

'Vlad!' Aron shouts.

At the same time, he jumps back, and almost gets away. He hears the crash as the first log falls off the sledge, but the end of it catches his shoulder, dislocating the joint.

The next log strikes him, knocks him to the ground and hits him in the face.

Aron feels no pain. He feels only the power, the weight of the tree trunk pressing him down into the snow. He sees the rest of the logs rolling down, long and black against the sky. They bounce on the frozen ground like millstones, crushing everything in their path, but by some miracle every single one misses his head, and they go rolling down the slope.

He can hear Grisha's voice shouting through the racket. Bokser neighing frantically. They have both survived.

But somewhere under the logs is Vlad. Vladimir from the Ukraine. With his warm coat and his sheepskin hat.

Aron knows he is there, but he can't see Vlad. His eyes are swollen shut. When the pain from his broken bones takes over his entire body, Aron is no longer there. He has gone away, drifted off into unconsciousness as if it were the sea, gently lapping on the shore near Rödtorp.

aron
aron
Aron!

Faint noises in the darkness, echoing shouts that sound like his name. He can hear them, but he doesn't want to go back.

Aron opens his eyes. No, he isn't lying on warm sand, he is lying in the snow among the fir trees. And a huge shadow is looming over him.

'Aron! Can you hear me?'

It is Sven's voice, full of energy. He shouts right in Aron's face. 'We're going to do it! We're going to swap!'

Sven bends down and Aron feels hands on his body. Hard blows that make his broken ribs throb with agonizing pain.

'Stop it,' Aron whispers.

But Sven won't stop.

'We have to hurry up, Aron . . . I've sent Grisha to get help. They'll be here soon – we have to hurry!'

Aron feels someone pulling off his clothes. It is Sven, his hands tugging at buttons and laces.

'We're swapping over!'

Aron stops listening; he turns his head to the side and vomits. Into the snow, and all over his upper body, which is now naked.

Then he loses consciousness once more.

Aron wakes up to a faint light. He is lying on something soft, but it isn't snow. He is in a bed.

'Vladimir Jegerov?' a voice says beside his bed.

Aron turns his head and sees a nurse. She is pale and thin; she is a prisoner just like him, but at least she works indoors.

The nurse smiles; she has kind eyes.

Afterwards, he can't remember whether he nods in response to her question, but she goes on. 'You've been in an accident involving some logs, Vladimir. Your right leg is broken, and so is your nose. Your shoulder was dislocated, but we managed to put it back. You were lucky . . . One of your comrades wasn't so fortunate.'

'Who?'

The nurse holds a steaming cup of tea up to his lips.

'A foreigner,' she says. 'A young Swede . . . The logs rolled over him like a tank. He was crushed to death.'

Vlad, Aron thinks. But he doesn't say a word, he just sips his tea.

'You'll be in here for a while,' the nurse says. She smiles again, and leaves him.

Every movement hurts, but Aron slowly raises his left hand and feels his face. The shape is different; it is swollen and covered in scabs. Crushed and numb. He lifts the sheet and sees splints on his right leg. He is wearing underpants and felt boots, but they are not his own. They are Vlad's.

Aron closes his eyes. No point in thinking about it.

Sven did this. He loosened the chain and released the logs. He swapped their clothes.

This was his plan: Aron the foreigner would become Vlad the Soviet citizen.

Someone coughs. Aron turns his head and discovers that he is lying in a crowded hospital hut with at least thirty other men. There isn't much room, but there are lamps and stoves and it is light and warm.

And the sheets might not be clean but they are *sheets*, and he can't see any bedbugs. The tea is real, not ersatz. And there is a plate of freshly sliced onion by his bed.

He has heard rumours about this in the camp: that prisoners who are injured or fall seriously ill are very well cared for.

It's strange, but all he can do right now is rest between the sheets, enjoying the sensation.

He relaxes.

Vlad is dead, but it is Aron who has ended up in paradise.

Lisa

Lisa hadn't felt well that morning. She didn't have a temperature, but she was weak and shaky. Lady Summertime had done her sixth gig at the hotel on Friday night, and it had been extremely lucrative. The club had been packed, she had filled it with smoke and, in the darkness, three wallets and two mobiles had found their way into her bag. However, the credit cards lay untouched; she had been too exhausted to drive down to Borgholm to deal with them.

Lady Summertime had stuck to water all evening, but Lisa was still unsteady on her feet when she got up in the caravan the next morning. It felt like a stomach bug, as if something were in the process of waking up down there. She only had a sandwich for breakfast, but she felt bloated and full. She went down to the shore with her swimsuit and a towel, but she stayed away from the water, dozing in the sun instead.

Several days of shimmering heat had brought crowds of people to the shore, and Lisa felt almost hemmed in by all the beach towels and summer bodies. Kids, clutter and chaos everywhere. The stench of suntan lotion was worse than ever, the holidaymakers yelled and screamed to one another in the water, beach flies buzzed around, trying to get into her mouth. Lisa swallowed and closed her eyes.

By lunchtime, she had had enough and made her way back to the caravan. Several times she stubbed her toes on the stony ground; her feet weren't cooperating, somehow. Was she dehydrated, in spite of all the water she'd drunk at the club?

Her mobile was lying on the bed; she'd forgotten to take it with her to the shore, and she saw that Silas had called twice. Shit. But she didn't have the energy to ring him back.

She had a sandwich with no butter for lunch, then got back into bed for a few hours and drifted off to sleep. When she raised her head the interior of the caravan was oppressively hot, even though the sun was quite low over the sea. It was quarter past six; the whole day had gone.

Time to get up, have a shower and head for the May Lai Bar.

She was there by half past seven, but didn't feel any better. Her case of vinyl albums was as heavy as lead as she trudged down the stairs, panting and pouring with sweat.

Dinner was available in the hotel kitchen, but she didn't go there. She filled up her water bottle in the ladies' room, put on her wig and her make-up and emerged as Lady Summertime. A somewhat shaky DJ.

She entered the booth and started the show. No cheerful shout-outs over the microphone tonight. Summertime put on a track without saying anything at all and switched on the disco lights. She had a long shift to get through; all she could do was grit her teeth and look happy.

No, there was no way she could look happy.

But she carried on working, and after nine o'clock the cellar gradually began to fill up. Earlier than usual – a typical Saturday night with lots of people. The temperature was rising, and the bartender was happy to supply anyone who was thirsty with water from his soda pistols.

But the bar staff also seemed to be moving slowly this evening, as if they were sleepwalkers who'd taken too many tablets. And, in spite of the crowd, there wasn't much action on the dance floor; most people were hanging around at the sides.

Summertime glanced at the tempting wallets and purses sticking up out of the pockets of shorts and jeans, but she didn't feel up to going after them. She could hear Silas muttering in her head, but this evening she just concentrated on playing music, focused and determined.

She kept on drinking water, but it didn't make her feel any better. Her stomach was like a gurgling washing machine with worn cogs. It went round and round, refusing to settle.

Summertime swallowed; she could feel her false eyelashes starting to come away because she was sweating so much. She tried to keep her balance at the mixer desk.

At some point after ten o'clock, she just couldn't do it any more. Her stomach started to bubble, and Lisa knew her body sufficiently well after twenty-four years to realize that an eruption was imminent. Something had to come out, one way or another.

She couldn't stay in the booth, so with trembling fingers she put on the longest track she had: the Beach Boys favourite 'Here Comes The Night', which lasted almost eleven minutes. Then she backed away from the decks. It was OK, hardly anyone was dancing, and she definitely had to get to the ladies' toilets.

But the door was open and there was a long queue stretching back into the cloakroom – and as Lisa pushed people aside in a panic and forced her way in, she saw a young girl in a white blouse, with an equally white face, leaning over the hand basin and bringing up yellow liquid in a seemingly endless cascade. Into the basin, over her blouse, splashing up on to the mirror. Lisa could hear similar noises from inside the cubicles, a chorus of retching.

She swallowed hard to keep the vomit down, and turned away. It was happening; her stomach could no longer tie itself in knots, and it was ready to get the show on the road.

The apocalypse was coming. Any minute now.

'Excuse me,' she gasped. 'Excuse me, could you move, please . . . I have to get through!'

Several girls in the queue weren't listening; the sounds from inside the toilets had made them start throwing up, too. They were bent double, vomit all over their bags and shoes, their hair limp with sweat. It was like a gastric ward in the middle of an outbreak of salmonella. Stinking pools on the tiled floor, revolting smells in the air. Total chaos.

Lisa broke away from the queue and ran for the door. She needed a bush to squat behind, or a car if the worst came to the worst. But the stairs were too far away, she wasn't going to get there, wasn't going to make it outside.

The world was spinning, the cramps in her gut were sheer agony. Far away, she could hear the thump of the Beach Boys track, like a beating heart.

She spotted the door to the VIP room next to the stairs and rushed towards it.

'Hey, you!' a voice said behind her.

A fucking security guard. But Lisa couldn't talk now; she simply opened the door, saw a load of suits sitting around the table but, most important of all: an ice bucket. She bent over it and opened her mouth.

It was disgusting, it was embarrassing, but at the same time it was liberating. Just to open her mouth and let it all out.

Behind her she heard 'Here Comes the Night' die away; it was followed by a deafening silence.

Unprofessional, Summertime thought. A black mark.

But Lisa was too ill to care. She lifted her head from the rapidly filling ice bucket, took a deep breath, then threw up again.

Jonas

Jonas was woken late on Saturday night by strange grunting noises from the guest chalet next door. Agonized moans, suppressed groans. Then he heard a thud, a glass door sliding open, then more groaning and coughing behind the chalet.

He listened in the darkness. It sounded like Mats out there; was he sick?

Jonas turned over and tried to get back to sleep, but it was impossible. It was too hot, and the moaning and groaning were still going on outside.

Eventually, he got up and opened the door. The night air was still warm, with not a breath of wind. A slender moon shone down on the Sound.

'Mats?' he called out quietly.

He got a groan in response and took a couple of steps away from the door. He saw his older brother crouching in the shadows; Mats was on the grass with his head down, like a defeated footballer. He was a pathetic sight and, oddly enough, this made Jonas feel incredibly fit and healthy. He raised his voice: 'What's wrong? Are you sick?'

Mats slowly raised his head. There was a pool on the grass beneath him, a pool that shone in the moonlight. 'Jonas . . .' he said. 'Can you fetch me some water, bro? From the house?'

Jonas went into Uncle Kent's house, into the kitchen, and found a bottle of mineral water in the fridge. When he got back, Mats had managed to stand up, but his head was still drooping.

Jonas passed him the bottle. 'Have you been on the beer?'

Mats shook his head. 'I've been cutting the grass over at Ölandic . . . I don't know what this is.'

Then he staggered back into his chalet with the water, without saying thank you. Jonas went back to bed; he still suspected that his brother had been out partying.

But that probably wasn't true, because when he got up in the morning *everybody* was sick, or so it seemed. Only Jonas and Paulina were up for breakfast. The chalet doors and bedroom doors were closed – total silence reigned in Villa Kloss, for once.

Uncle Kent came into the kitchen after a while, just as Jonas was tucking into a cheese sandwich.

They stared at one another. Jonas hadn't dared to ask his uncle if he had said the right things during the interview with Cecilia Sander, but she had gone away and hadn't been in touch since, so surely that meant things had gone well?

'Good morning,' Kent said eventually, but his voice was quiet, and Jonas could see that his uncle wasn't feeling too good either. His face was grey, in spite of his tan.

He didn't say any more; he opened the fridge and took out a bottle of juice. Grapefruit juice. He looked down at the pale-yellow liquid and seemed to be giving it some thought before finally taking a couple of cautious sips.

The telephone rang; Kent went over and answered it. 'Yes?'

He listened for a long time, then said wearily, 'You're joking. You *are* joking?'

He listened again.

'OK,' he said at last. 'Yes, I've got some problems with my gut as well . . . It's like Montezuma's Revenge. We'll have to bring in extra staff. *Someone* must be OK, for fuck's sake? So bring in whoever you can get hold of. What about the guests?'

There was a protracted silence.

'Right, well, clean up as best you can. Everyone will have to pitch in . . . Have we got a suction pump?'

Silence again.

'OK, I'll be in right away.' He sounded exhausted.

He poured the rest of the juice down the sink, then turned to Jonas.

'JK, if your aunt turns up, tell her we're in a hell of a mess. There's some kind of gastric epidemic over at the resort. It's affecting the

243

staff, and the guests too, apparently. The toilets are starting to get blocked, so I have to get over there. Tell Veronica she can reach me on my mobile.'

Jonas nodded. 'Mats is sick too,' he said. 'He's been throwing up.'

'*Everybody*'s sick,' Kent said. 'Aren't you, JK?'

Jonas shook his head.

'But you might be,' Kent said. He threw a final poisonous glance at Jonas, as if the whole thing were somehow his fault, then he was gone, lumbering towards his car.

Jonas made himself another sandwich. It was a bit odd, but he felt perfectly fine. He wondered whether to go over and see Kristoffer.

Tomorrow was the beginning of a new working week. The decking would soon be finished, beautifully sanded and stained dark brown with Chinese wood oil. Then he would get paid. And in a week's time he would start work over at Aunt Veronica's house, which would mean he was slightly further away from both the cairn and Uncle Kent.

The thought cheered him up, because there was something bad quivering in the air this summer. Something much worse than gastroenteritis.

Gerlof

Swallow was slowly beginning to regain her former beauty, with the help of new boards and strong-smelling creosote. Gerlof had brought a flask of coffee down to the gig by the boathouse, where John and Anders were busy painting the hull on this warm evening. John looked suspiciously at the coffee as Gerlof poured it out.

'Have you boiled it properly?'

Gerlof stopped in mid-movement. 'What are you talking about?'

'You have to boil your drinking water, Gerlof.'

'Why?'

'There's an outbreak of gastroenteritis all along the coast,' John explained. 'People have ended up in hospital. It's a real epidemic. Haven't you read the paper?'

'Not yet,' Gerlof said as he carried on pouring the coffee. 'I feel perfectly all right.'

'Stenvik doesn't really seem to have been affected,' John said. 'The problem is mainly at the Ölandic Resort.'

'That's unfortunate.' Gerlof sipped his coffee. 'Right in the middle of the high season, too . . . It's a bit of a disaster, I'd say.'

'Absolutely. Apparently, the sewage disposal system on the campsite has broken down, things are so bad . . . and people have started to leave. They're packing up their tents and caravans and heading home.'

Gerlof had expected John to look pleased, but he knew that if something was bad for one campsite, it was bad for all of them. People who went home because of a bad experience in a holiday village or campsite usually bad-mouthed the whole island.

He liked standing here in the glow of the setting sun, with a warm breeze blowing in off the Sound. But he wouldn't be here for much longer. In five days, he was due to move back into his room at the residential home in Marnäs, and in a way the summer would be over, as far as he was concerned. It would be much more difficult to get out and about.

Which was a shame. This might be his last summer in the village.

Gerlof swatted a fly away from his cheek and looked to the south. The inlet was quiet. A few people were swimming by the jetty, and there were still plenty of sun-worshippers on the beach.

A short distance away, he could see the cairn, and thought about what he had told Jonas. *That's not the real cairn.*

Then he screwed up his eyes; something wasn't right.

'The bunker door is open,' he said.

John stopped what he was doing. 'What are you talking about?'

Gerlof pointed to the other end of the inlet, at the debris the stonemasons had left behind on the rocks above the shore.

'The door of the old bunker . . . it's open. It's usually closed, isn't it?'

'That's right,' John said. 'The army fixed a padlock to it many years ago. I haven't checked, but I should think it's still there.'

Gerlof saw signs of movement; a figure emerged from the bunker, but he was too far away for Gerlof to be able to make out any details.

He thought back to what Jonas Kloss had said about the man who suddenly appeared by the cairn, then simply disappeared.

'Perhaps he's a phantom soldier,' he said.

The Homecomer

The Homecomer walked slowly out of the bunker and into the diminishing warmth of the sun. He secured the door with a padlock he had brought from Einar Wall's collection.

His back was stiff and aching. He had been stooping beneath the low concrete ceiling for over an hour. It had felt like being back in that endless ditch in the Soviet Union.

He had managed to get into a rhythm, digging inside the bunker, but it was a slow process. Behind each rock he dug out there seemed to be two more, bigger than the first. The ground here on the island consisted of more stones than earth. He drove the pickaxe into the wall, prised out stones and earth that came rattling down, then repeated the same movement two hundred times or more during the course of an evening, toiling away like a miner in a prison camp.

The sweat was pouring off him on this warm evening; his arms ached.

Outside, in the bottom of the dip, he stretched his limbs, looking to the south. He couldn't see the Ölandic Resort from here, but he thought about the hum of the high-pressure pump he and Rita had used down there. It had done its job.

He glanced to the north. The shore was almost deserted by now, but there were still a few holidaymakers by the jetty. Perhaps they had come from the Ölandic, escaping the problems with the water in the resort.

On the other side of the inlet, he could see a couple of old fishermen by a boathouse, painting a wooden gig. It was a peaceful scene, and it made the Homecomer think of his grandfather, who would

247

always work on his nets and boats in the evenings at Rödtorp, totally absorbed in the task.

A sense of peace.

He could go over to the old men, talk to them, swap stories. Find a little serenity, just for a while. But he knew who he carried inside him. Sooner or later, Vlad would emerge, and he was always on his guard.

The New Country, March 1936

Aron is eighteen years old. He wears his dead friend Vlad's warm clothes, sleeps in Vlad's bunk and eats out of Vlad's mess tin. Some of the prisoners know or suspect that he is not really a Soviet citizen, that his name is not Vladimir, but Sven has managed to keep them quiet. So far.

Old Grisha is the biggest problem. Grisha *knows*, and he wants money to maintain his silence.

'Ready money,' he says to Aron one evening when they are alone. 'Real roubles. Otherwise, I'll go to Polynov.'

Vlad merely nods. Polynov is the commandant, a moustachioed former police officer who struts around with a riding crop when he inspects the prisoners. But Polynov is interested in only two things: an orderly camp and strong vodka.

Grisha is the only one who cares about money. He is the last capitalist in the camp.

Capitalists deserve to die.

Aron has to do something, but he can't ask his stepfather for help. Sometimes, he can meet Sven's eye in the exercise yard, but he dare not speak to him. Sven is a foreigner.

Nor can he visit Vladimir's grave. Vlad was buried with the other prisoners who had died, in an ever-growing cemetery in the forest to the south of the camp. There is no cross over the grave, but on one of the walls in Aron's hut Sven has carved ARON FREDH 1918–1936 next to hundreds of other names. For appearances' sake.

Sven looks thinner and shorter each time Aron sees him. His stepfather reminds him of a restless dog, constantly moving. He sidles along by the huts, staring at people. If one of his fellow prisoners happens to say the wrong thing to him, there is always trouble; Sven spits or throws a punch, but he usually hits nothing but thin air. He can't even fight any more.

Had Aron really been afraid of his stepfather when he was little? Now, as Vlad, he isn't afraid of him at all. Sven is like an old mongrel among a pack of young dogs.

Sometimes, he sneaks into Vlad's hut and hides little notes to Aron in his bed, written in Swedish. This is incredibly dangerous. Vlad rips them up and eats the scraps of paper; he daren't even read what Sven has written.

Sven's plan to make Aron a Soviet citizen has worked but, like Vlad, he no longer believes they will be able to escape from the new country.

How could it happen? How could Sven and Aron ever get away?

First of all, they would have to get through the barbed wire surrounding the camp, past the guards. Then they would somehow have to find their way through the vast Russian forests, through the snow and the cold. Through a country where, according to the rumours, citizens receive one hundred roubles if they go to the police with the severed hand of a fugitive.

It is too risky. And eventually it becomes impossible, because, one day, Sven is gone.

Aron assumes he was taken during the night, just like all the other foreigners. One day, there is no sign of him in the exercise yard, and when Aron looks in his hut he sees only an empty bed. Two days later, another prisoner has taken it over, because it is closer to the stove.

This happens all the time, of course; prisoners simply disappear. Someone comes for them during the night, and they are taken away. No one asks questions.

Vlad keeps quiet. He doesn't care about foreigners.

But Sven is Aron's only link with his home in Sweden, and he has to find him. He tries searching for Sven in different parts of the camp but is met with silence and frightened looks.

Only a white-haired farmer from Karelia gives him a thin smile one day as they stand in the mud in the yard.

'Pfff!' he says, blowing air through his lips and making his moustache quiver. 'Pfff . . . and they're gone. All foreigners end up as a fart in the wind. They are convicted of spying and sent up a chimney. You know that, don't you, Swedish boy?'

Inside Vlad, Aron recoils. 'Sven isn't a spy,' he says.

'He's been convicted by the troika,' the farmer says. 'No foreigner escapes.'

Aron doesn't say anything, and the farmer leans forward and lowers his voice. 'I've spoken to Grisha. He told me what you did in the forest. You swapped clothes, didn't you? What a miracle . . . A dead Soviet citizen came back to life!'

Aron clenches his fist. 'Shut your mouth,' he snarls. 'I don't know what you're talking about.' Vlad is beginning to take over.

'You don't know what I'm talking about?' the farmer says. 'Well, perhaps Polynov would want to know.'

He is still smiling beneath his moustache, so Vlad takes a step forward and punches him right on his hairy upper lip.

Unfortunately, it isn't a very hard blow; he is too tired. The farmer merely shakes it off, then he measures up to Vlad and punches him back, almost as ineffectually.

They circle around one another. It is a pathetic fight, like a stumbling dance in the mud, but it attracts a crowd, and soon a ring of yelling prisoners forms around them.

In the end, a guard steps in and separates them.

It is over. Vlad's chest is aching from a hard blow with an elbow, and he has managed to graze the farmer's cheek.

The guard calls over a colleague, and Vlad and his opponent are taken away to see Polynov.

Polynov is the king of the camp.

It is a strange feeling, being led into his office. It has a well-scrubbed wooden floor; there is a small collection of wine in a cupboard on the wall and there is even a rug.

Commandant Polynov looks like a fat toad sitting on his throne, which is a rickety wooden chair. On the desk in front of him is a half-empty glass of vodka and an old army revolver. Hanging on the wall are two framed portraits, one of Jagoda, the chief of the secret police, and one of the president, Josef Stalin. In his mind's eye, Aron sees Stalin, the great leader, with a blade of grass in his mouth.

'What's happened?' Polynov asks, sighing over the trail of mud the prisoners are leaving on his floor. 'Why were you fighting? Haven't we broken you yet?'

'Comrade Commandant,' the farmer says, pointing to Vlad. 'He started it.'

'That's not true,' Vlad responds. 'The Kulaks just love fighting, everyone knows that.'

'Shut up, you little bastard!' the farmer yells.

The commandant plays with the revolver as he listens wearily to the prisoners' bickering. 'Enough,' he mutters.

Polynov gets to his feet, suddenly stone-cold sober. His gaze bores first through Vlad, then the farmer. He places the gun on the desk in front of the two prisoners. 'Sort this out among yourselves.'

Vlad stares at the cracked wooden butt of the revolver. He doesn't really know what the commandant wants.

But the farmer understands and wipes the blood from his cheek.

'Comrade Commandant,' he says in an authoritative tone of voice. 'I have important information which I feel I must pass on to you.' He points to Aron. 'This prisoner is not what he claims—'

At that moment, Vlad picks up the revolver. It seems to fit perfectly in his hand. The farmer must be stopped, whatever he is thinking of saying about Aron, so he places the barrel of the gun on his fellow prisoner's chest and pulls the trigger.

A sudden recoil through his hand, a loud bang, and the farmer is lying on the rug, twitching like a rag doll, staring up at the ceiling.

Vlad takes aim and fires again, but the only sound is a dry click.

Polynov reaches out and takes the revolver. 'There was only one bullet.'

He nods, and the guard steps forward with his rifle, aims it at the farmer's chest and fires.

The world stops.

'. . . Ukrainian?'

Aron turns his head. The commandant has asked a question.

'So you're Ukrainian?'

Aron takes a deep breath and straightens up, almost standing to attention. He is calm now; he allows Vladimir Jegerov to come forward.

'I am a Russian Ukrainian, herr Commandant. My father came

from Stalingrad and my mother from Kiev, but they are no longer with us.'

'Why are you here?'

Vlad answers without hesitation. 'I hid a loaf of bread for my little sister to eat, herr Commandant. She lived for another week because of that loaf.'

'So you stole bread from the state? And they didn't shoot you?'

'They sent me here, herr Commandant,' Vlad says. 'I have five months left to serve.'

'Good,' says Polynov. 'You can certainly shoot.'

Vlad grows even taller as the commandant continues. 'We have too many idiots among the guards. Untrained drunks. They keep on missing when they fire.'

'I don't drink,' Vlad says.

The commandant glances at his bottle of vodka, then he bellows, 'Jakov!'

The head of the guards enters the room, and Polynov points to Vlad. 'A new recruit for you.'

Jakov steps forward. He is short but sticks his nose in the air just centimetres from Vlad's chin. 'Your first order, Comrade.' He jerks his head towards the farmer's body. 'Fetch a couple of prisoners. Bury him after dark.'

Polynov goes over to a cupboard and takes something out. 'This is a Winchester that the Tsar's bandits had stashed away . . . It's old, but it works. Wear it over your shoulder so that everyone can see it. If you lose it, you're back on hard labour.'

Vlad does not lose the rifle. He has been a Swedish prisoner in the camp; now he is a Soviet guard and can feel the weapon straightening his spine.

There are many advantages to his new role – on the very first day, he is allowed to collect five kilos of potatoes, but he does not have permission to leave the camp. However, he can move around more freely, and he has an important task to carry out.

The following evening, he is on guard duty, patrolling the fence, and he arranges to meet Grisha by the furthest huts. Grisha creeps along in the shadows behind the buildings; Vlad stands and waits just a few metres from the fence.

253

But Grisha is wary. He won't come out into the light, so Vlad takes something out of his pocket. It is a paper bag, rustling in his hand. 'Dried apricots and fresh tobacco,' he says quietly.

At last Grisha steps forward. He takes the bag, slips it inside his jacket. Fruit and tobacco are hard currency, but he still seems disappointed. 'Is that all?'

Vlad shakes his head. 'I've hidden the money over there.' He nods towards a dark spot further along. 'Five hundred roubles . . . If you promise to keep quiet about me, it's yours.'

Grisha looks at him. A guard earns about eight roubles a day; five hundred is a fortune.

But he still has doubts.

'What about the dogs?'

Vlad smiles. 'Can you see any dogs? They're over by the main gate tonight.'

Grisha is still standing behind the hut, undecided.

Vlad has had enough; he shrugs wearily. 'Please yourself . . . I'll take the money if you don't want it.'

And he sets off along the fence. He is holding his breath, watching for a movement out of the corner of his eye.

And there it is.

Grisha is old, but he moves fast. He rushes past Vlad, heading for the fence post where the money is supposed to be.

When he is two steps away from the fence, Vlad raises the rifle to his shoulder.

'Prisoner trying to escape!' he shouts.

Then he aims at Grisha's back and fires. Once, twice.

It's like shooting a seal.

Other guards come running, but Vlad has aimed well. All they can do is prod at the body, then return to their own posts.

Grisha will be left there by the fence for a few days, as a warning.

Lisa

It took forty-eight hours of a sky-high temperature, an unbearable stench and a distinct shortage of toilet paper in the caravan but, eventually, Lisa began to feel better. Slightly better, anyway. After throwing up in the VIP room, she had somehow managed to drag herself back to the caravan, where she had collapsed into bed and spent all night vomiting helplessly. The gastroenteritis turned her into a five-year-old, a five-year-old with a temperature, dizzy and confused.

She spent Sunday lying in a daze.

By Monday, she was able to move, keep down a little water. Blink at the sun outside.

By Tuesday, she was almost back to being an adult. Her stomach ached, but it was calmer now. She couldn't eat anything, but at least she managed to get out of bed.

Toast. She ought to have some toast, but she just didn't want any. Paulina was fine and had called in with several bottles of mineral water; Lisa drank some, then waited. Her stomach gurgled rather worryingly, but nothing came back up. She drank a little more and gazed out of the window.

It was still summer out there.

She had cancelled only one gig at the May Lai Bar. Nobody at the hotel seemed to care, because the whole complex had been affected by the same sickness bug.

And now it was over. Although that wasn't quite true, because the news had spread.

*

The May Lai Bar was virtually empty that night. Lisa thought the whole resort felt a bit like a ghost town as she drove down to the hotel. The campsite was just a huge field, with the odd tent and caravan here and there; the long rows of campers had gone. Apparently, lots of people had taken one look at the headline in the local paper – RESORT STRICKEN BY GASTROENTERITIS – and had quickly packed up and gone home. Or moved to other large campsites on the island, where there were no bugs in the water.

But how could one complex be affected, and not the rest?

Anyhow, the show at the Ölandic must go on, so Lady Summertime stepped into her booth at nine o'clock. She felt like a little bird back in her cage as she put on the first record and picked up the microphone. 'Good evening, everybody! Lady Summertime is here with all your favourites. Let's go – it's the Bee Gees with "You Should Be Dancing"!'

Her voice echoed through the club as if it were an empty waiting room; she sounded weary and mechanical, and nobody took any notice of the Bee Gees. A few shadowy figures were sitting at the bar with tall glasses, but there was nobody on the dance floor. And it stayed that way. Nobody wanted to move tonight.

Lady Summertime did her job, anyway.

At twenty past eleven, she glanced up from her decks and saw a mobile phone lying next to an empty glass on one of the high oak tables along the right-hand wall, which cheered her up no end. There was also a pair of black sunglasses; Summertime looked around, but there was no sign of the owner. Turning back to the decks, she did a smooth segue from Fleetwood Mac to Elton John while covertly keeping an eye on the table. The phone was still there, partly hidden behind the glass. It was small and black, probably one of the latest Ericsson models. The table was triangular, fixed to the wall at chest height. She wouldn't have to bend down to pick up the phone, she could just reach out and . . .

Who'd left it behind? A rich guy? A poor girl? She hadn't noticed who had been standing at that particular table, which was unprofessional.

Her shift was almost over. She put on 'Sweet Dreams' by Eurythmics, still watching the table. It was as if she had developed tunnel vision; Summertime could see nothing but the mobile, apart from the odd quick glance at the guests dotted around the room.

No one appeared to be looking at her.

When there were two minutes left of the track, she switched on all the flashing white spotlights, dimming the wall lights, and sent a curtain of smoke swirling across the dance floor. Then she quickly slipped out of the booth, as if she were going to the loo.

But instead she moved into the room.

No one by the door, no security guards. The customers at the bar were chatting to each other, apart from one, who was talking to Morten, the Danish bartender. And there was still no sign of anyone near the mobile. Summertime was only two metres away from it now. Three short steps through the white smoke. Then two more, and she was standing by the wall. She turned in a single elegant movement, hiding the table from view while at the same time sweeping her hand across and picking up the phone. A second later, it was safe in the pocket of her denim shorts.

She looked around and saw that one of the doormen had come into the club. It was . . . what was the guy's name? Lisa couldn't remember, and he was too far away for her to be able to read his badge. He wasn't looking in her direction at the moment, but what about a few seconds earlier?

If that were the case, surely he would have come over to her by now?

The phone felt heavy in her pocket, but she couldn't dump it now. She had to get back to the booth.

She put on her headphones. 'Sweet Dreams' was almost over, and she couldn't allow a single second of silence. She mixed to Lou Reed's 'Perfect Day', a quieter track to slow things down. A few couples actually got up to dance; perhaps someone would find the love of their life tonight.

Halfway through 'Perfect Day' a skinny girl in a black dress came in and went straight over to the table by the wall. The table where the mobile had been.

Summertime saw her, but did nothing. The girl picked up the glass, looked at the table, bent down and peered at the floor, gazed around the club.

257

Summertime pretended she hadn't noticed her; she adjusted her headphones and bent over the decks.

The girl went over to the bar and spoke to Morten. He shook his head but reached under the counter for his own mobile. The girl nodded and took it.

Summertime glanced over at the door. The security guard was still there, but she was hidden by the door of the booth, so she took the stolen phone out of her pocket, slowly, slowly. She held it lightly between the fingers of one hand and with the other she picked up a couple of LPs and put them in the case under the table. At the same time, she reached out and slipped the phone through the gap at the bottom of the pane of glass at the front of the booth.

Just before it disappeared from view, it started flashing and vibrating. The girl had used Morten's phone to call her own number, of course. She was gazing around the room, in spite of the fact that the music was drowning out the ringtone.

Summertime put on another slow number, 'Don't Give Up', even though her shift was now over. She was nervous, she wanted to look busy.

The mobile was flashing away. After a minute or so, a couple swaying around the dance floor just a couple of metres away noticed it. The man bent down, picked it up and answered, sticking his finger in his ear so that he could hear. He looked over at the bar, where the girl was waving her hand. He went over to her and Lisa watched the end of the pantomime:

Thank you so much, where did you find it?

On the dance floor.

Thanks again, I looked everywhere . . .

The phone had been found, the drama was over. And so was Lisa's shift. The last notes died away and she grabbed the microphone.

'That was Peter Gabriel and Kate Bush with "Don't Give Up". Never give up, people! Lady Summertime isn't giving up either; I'm just taking a little break until midnight, making way for our live band, The Fun Boys, who will be playing out on the terrace . . .'

She took off the headphones. She would go up to the hotel kitchen for something to eat before she started again in half an hour.

On her way out, she nodded to the tall security guard and gave him a relaxed smile. His name was Emanuel, according to his badge. He looked down at her and nodded back, but Lisa couldn't read his expression.

Gerlof

There was a dull, rumbling noise outside Gerlof's garden, silencing the insects and muffling the birdsong. He turned his head and could just make out a big, black shadow behind the trees on the village road.

Nothing else happened for a long time. The sun carried on shining, the shadow stayed where it was, the rumbling noise continued.

Gerlof was tired, and his legs were aching, but after a while he got up and went over to the gate.

There was an enormous car out on the road, with tinted windows. One of those SUVs, built to withstand a collision with a traffic island or a pushchair in the city. A plethora of chrome and glass sparkled in the sunlight.

The driver's window slid down, and Gerlof saw Kent Kloss sitting there, one hand resting on the leather-covered steering wheel, his mobile pressed to his ear.

Kent obviously had two cars. Gerlof opened the gate and slowly made his way over to the car.

'Hello there,' he said. 'Thanks for the other day.'

They hadn't seen each other since Jonas's interview at Villa Kloss.

'No, thank *you*,' Kent said.

He looked tired, and made no move to switch off the engine.

'Did you want something, Kent?'

Kloss nodded. 'I've come to pick up JK.'

'JK?'

'Jonas . . . my nephew. I've come to take him home.'

Gerlof didn't move. He had no intention of fetching Jonas.

'How are things over there?' he asked instead.

'Absolutely fine. It's just as hot as it is here.'

'I meant at the resort,' Gerlof said. 'I hear you've had some problems down there.'

Kloss lowered his gaze. 'That's right – gastroenteritis. It's been chaos all weekend . . . But the toilets have been cleaned and everything's fine now.'

'And the guests?'

'They're coming back,' Kent said quickly. 'One by one.'

But he looked far from convinced and started revving the engine impatiently.

Gerlof wondered what Kent was really doing here. Why did he need to pick up his nephew in the car? Did he want to keep an eye on him?

'Any news about the *Ophelia*?' he asked.

'Sorry?'

'The cargo boat you hired.'

Kent looked down at the sea. 'Not as far as I know,' he said. 'She's disappeared, but . . .' He paused, then added, 'I'm trying not to think about her.'

'No,' Gerlof said. 'After all, she was being used to move contraband.'

Kent took his foot off the accelerator. 'What did you say?'

'You were smuggling alcohol on board the *Ophelia*.'

Kloss stared at him and shook his head. 'We were transporting fish,' he said, revving the engine once more in what could be perceived as a threatening manner.

'Smuggling alcohol is an ancient occupation,' Gerlof went on. 'Not only on Öland; it used to go on all along the coast throughout southern Sweden. Do you remember Algoth Niska?'

Kloss didn't say anything, so Gerlof went on, 'When I was young, Algoth and his gang used to sail out into international waters and meet up with ships from Poland and Germany. They would buy vodka for one or two kronor a litre. Tobacco, too, and sometimes arms. They would bring the whole lot back to the island and hide it all over the place, in boathouses, wells, under piles of logs . . . even in shelters way out on the alvar.' He looked down at Kent Kloss. 'What happens nowadays?'

'No idea.'

'I'm sure it's tempting to sell the alcohol on,' Gerlof said. 'When the high season begins, the police keep a close check on bottles brought *on* to the island over the bridge, but they don't monitor vehicles as they leave. So once you've unloaded the cargo from the ship, the contraband can be transferred to cars and distributed that way. Am I right?'

Kent managed a thin smile. 'As I said . . . the *Ophelia* was carrying fish.'

'I'm sure there was some fish on board. An old cargo that you could show Customs . . . but that was a mistake. She had no refrigeration unit, so the fish went rotten in the heat. That was fine as long as the hold was left open, but when someone battened down the hatches the crew suffocated.'

Kent took his foot off the accelerator again. 'We're looking into the matter,' he said. 'There are one or two security guards at the Ölandic who have turned out to be somewhat unreliable . . .'

'Like Peter Mayer?' Gerlof said.

'He no longer works for us; he was dismissed last year. Another guard disappeared at midsummer.'

'And Einar Wall? Do you know him, too?'

'Only in a business capacity . . . He supplied a small amount of fish and game to our restaurants.'

Gerlof was beginning to suspect what had happened at midsummer. A small group of people knew that there was a cargo ship with cash on board moored at the Ölandic dock, and those people had come up with a plan. Einar Wall had been part of the group, along with his nephew Peter Mayer and an old man who had returned home from overseas. They had decided to rob a ship that was being used to smuggle contraband, and that was exactly what they had done.

But things hadn't exactly gone according to plan.

'Peter Mayer died on the main road,' Gerlof said. 'And Einar Wall died not far from his cottage.'

He hadn't asked a question, and Kent's only response was to rev the engine yet again.

But Gerlof hadn't finished. 'You ought to be careful, Kent. Things could happen.'

Kent looked up at him. 'Are you threatening me, you doddery old fool?'

It was quite an amusing insult, but Gerlof remained serious. He shook his head. 'Not me. It's someone else who constitutes a threat.'

'Who do you mean?'

Gerlof took a risk, and said the name that was spinning around in his head: 'Aron Fredh.'

Kent's expression was grim, and Gerlof knew that the name meant something to him. After a few seconds, Kent smiled wearily. 'Aron Fredh . . . that's another story.'

'Is it?'

'Aron Fredh was a snotty kid who went off to the USA with his stepfather, Sven, who was another loser.'

'Was he?'

'Absolutely,' Kent said. 'Sven Fredh was supposed to move the cairn for us, but he cocked it up completely.'

'Sven built the cairn?'

Kent nodded. 'Sven Fredh moved the stones down to the coast back in the twenties, along with my grandfather and his brothers. But the whole thing fell down . . . it almost landed on top of Sven, and it crushed his foot. They had to start all over again, and they gave Sven the sack.'

Gerlof listened; this was news to him. He raised his voice above the noise of the engine. 'I've met Aron.'

'This summer?'

Kent was interested now, but Gerlof shook his head. 'When I was young . . . in the summer of 1930. Aron Fredh and I worked in the churchyard together, digging a grave.'

Kent leaned forward. 'In that case, you should be able to find him, Gerlof. You know what he looks like.'

'Not now. I'm too old.'

'But you have a good memory, in spite of your age . . . I mean, you remember ships and people and all kinds of things. You could make some money out of this.'

'Money? Why is Aron Fredh so dangerous?'

But he didn't get a reply. The gate squeaked behind him; Jonas had emerged from the cottage. The boy approached the car, looking at his uncle the way a dog looks at its master.

'Time for dinner, JK,' Kent said.

Jonas nodded and got into the car.

Kent gave Gerlof one last long look. 'Perhaps we'll speak again,' he said. He put the car into gear and drove off.

Gerlof watched him go. It had been an interesting conversation, but of course he realized that, although Kent Kloss had said quite a lot, he had admitted nothing.

Jonas

The Chinese wood oil was dripping from his brush, and the sweat was pouring down Jonas's face. He swept the brush back and forth across the decking. When he had done four planks, he took a break and drank at least half a litre of water (guaranteed clean bottled water) before resuming his task.

Only a few planks left, then he could go for an evening swim. Uncle Kent's decking would soon be finished; next week, he would move over to Aunt Veronica's and do the same thing all over again.

The sight of wood ingrained with dirt and the smell of Chinese oil – that was what this summer meant to Jonas.

As the sun began to sink towards the strip of land on the horizon, he decided to call it a day. He let out a long breath; he would go for a swim, then he was free for the evening. Uncle Kent had announced that he would be holding an inaugural barbecue to celebrate the newly renovated decking, but Jonas didn't want to be there. He had a feeling that Uncle Kent was somehow keeping an eye on him. He had picked Jonas up in the car from Kristoffer's earlier on, even though Jonas was perfectly capable of walking home on his own.

He fetched his trunks and went across the coast road, out on to the deserted ridge.

For the first few days after midsummer, he had avoided going down to the shore alone. His fear of the water hadn't completely gone, but he had no intention of letting it get the better of him.

The blue viper's bugloss coming through the stones had started to dry out and turn dark purple. The grass was yellow, and the bushes had begun to lose their leaves. Only the cairn looked unchanged, apart from the fact that another rock had fallen down. How many were lying on the grass now – was it ten or eleven? Jonas quickly walked past, without stopping to count them.

He ran down the old stone steps that led to the dip, then on to the shore. It was only about fifty metres but, halfway, he suddenly stopped.

He had heard something down in the dip. From the old quarry, where the stonemasons had left behind a V-shaped wound and broken rocks.

A scraping noise, over to the right. Jonas looked, but all he could see was pink rock and grey gravel. No people.

But the noise came again, several times. It sounded as if someone was hacking rhythmically at the ground, with either a pick or a spade.

No, not at the ground. *Under*ground.

Jonas couldn't see very far, because there was a large rocky outcrop jutting out in front of him. However, if he stepped down into the bottom of the dip, he would have a better view.

The ground was very uneven here; he was wearing his old trainers, so he had to be careful, occasionally jumping from stone to stone. There was some kind of thorny bush growing through the gravel and clutching at him, but he managed to wriggle past. Now, he could see further.

There was a metal door set in the rock, almost directly below the cairn up on the ridge.

The bunker. Now he remembered. Gerlof had mentioned it, too.

He vaguely recalled from previous summer holidays that the bunker had always been secured with a rusty old padlock – but now the door was open. And that was where the scraping noises were coming from.

Someone was in there.

Not the cairn ghost, he knew that. Gerlof had said there was no ghost.

So he moved a little closer. He had never seen inside, but he and Casper had played outside the door, winding each other up and wondering if there were dead soldiers in there.

The noise continued.

Jonas took one more step. Now he was only a couple of metres from the entrance to the bunker, and he could see the sun shining on a dusty cement floor. But the light reached only a short distance; beyond that point, it was pitch black.

He listened hard. Perhaps Mats and their cousins had opened the door? They had been at home during the day, but he didn't know where they'd gone after that. They never bothered to tell him what they were doing.

Were they sitting inside the bunker in the darkness, watching him right now? If so, he couldn't risk looking like a coward. If he turned away, he would do it quickly and resolutely, as if he had something important to do.

Or perhaps he would stay. Walk right up to the door and see what was in there. He took one step, and waited. The noise from inside had stopped.

So he took another step.

There was a wide block of stone in front of the door, like some kind of threshold. Jonas didn't stand on it but leaned forward so that he could stick his head into the bunker. He held his breath and listened.

The air was very still, with a musty smell. He was looking into a small room, with another narrow doorway at the far end, where the sunlight didn't reach. The first room contained only one piece of furniture: a rickety wooden table. One of the legs was broken, but someone had used a block of stone to keep it more or less level.

There was something on the table.

Jonas blinked and looked again; it was still there. Small and flat, thinner at one end.

Now he could see what it was: a gun.

Jonas suddenly forgot that he wasn't supposed to go inside the bunker; he was too curious. Was it a real gun?

He stepped inside, on to the cement floor. He reached out and picked up the gun.

It was very heavy – and old: the wooden butt was covered in scratches. But it was definitely a real gun.

He looked up; he had heard a slight noise, a faint scraping, and he held his breath again. The sound was coming from the inner room, from the darkness. Someone was in there.

The ghost?

Jonas had to get out.

He quickly wrapped the gun in his beach towel and backed out of the bunker.

He decided not to bother going for a swim; he wasn't hot any more. He made his way back through the dip and up the steps, back on to the ridge, still clutching his treasure from the bunker.

He ran past the cairn, across the road to Villa Kloss and back to his own little chalet. He closed the door and drew the curtains, then sat down on the bed to look at his acquisition.

A real gun.

The Homecomer

The Homecomer was standing in the darkness in the bunker's inner room. He was still holding the pick, but it was resting on the ground. He had used it to break through the cement wall at the back, where there were the most cracks, and now there was a pile of earth and stones at his feet. However, he still had a few metres to go before he was far enough in, right under the cairn.

There was no treasure there, he was well aware of that. But he kept on going anyway.

As he was just about to raise the pick, he heard a noise behind him.

He stopped and held his breath. He could hear a faint shuffling from the outer room, like cautious footsteps, and he realized he hadn't closed the door. But it was evening; no one should be down in the dip at this time of day. And since the bunker was hidden from the coast road and the houses on the other side, he knew that no one had seen him go inside.

Perhaps it was a mistake to work here while the sun still hovered over the Sound, but it was a question of time and energy. He couldn't do everything at night.

Now it sounded as if the person in the other room had turned around and was on their way out.

The Homecomer tried to relax; his legs were beginning to stiffen up.

Silence descended, but he didn't move for several minutes. Finally, he put down the pick and edged towards the door.

The outer room was empty. The metal door was half open.

The sunlight enabled him to see the bare surface of the rickety wooden table – and then he remembered what he had done. He had put the Walther there. He had wanted to keep it free from dust and dirt, so he had left it there while he broke down the wall.

And now the table was empty.

The Homecomer had committed the ultimate sin for any soldier: he had lost his gun.

Fortunately he had another.

The New Country, July 1936

At the beginning of the year, all Party membership books must be renewed with a photograph. Enemies of the state who have somehow acquired a false identity will be unmasked in this way, and will be purged – but Aron calmly settles down in front of the camera in the office. A photograph is nothing but an advantage as far as he is concerned. He has stolen Vladimir Jegerov's name and life, and with his own Party book Vlad becomes even more credible.

Afterwards, it feels odd to see the photograph once it has been developed; Aron has not looked in a mirror for several years. He sees a hardened young man with a broken nose and a red scar running across his forehead. He doesn't recognize himself; it is Vlad that he sees.

Vladimir has not only become a member of the Party, he has also been given a domestic passport and a guard's uniform. This almost makes him a free man; he can move around without restrictions outside the camp, and he has moved into a small room in the military barracks that is actually warm. An old *babusjka* prepares his food each evening and takes care of his uniform. Trying to keep his boots clean and shiny in the spring mud and the summer dust is a hopeless task, but Vlad has found two pairs and alternates between them.

He has only one rifle, but he never lets it out of his sight, and he cleans it meticulously every night. It must always be in good working order.

After a few months, the spring begins to make its presence felt even in the north of the Soviet Union. Some of the prisoners go crazy and hurl themselves towards the light. Towards the fence. Vlad does not hesitate: he positions himself with his legs wide apart and shoots them.

And he is good at it.

He has shot seven prisoners by the fence since Grisha. All trying to escape. Commandant Polynov has praised him for his vigilance and has even given him a bonus of one hundred roubles.

A wood-fuelled crematorium has been built at the far end of the camp; the bodies are dealt with there.

In the summer, the heat pushes through the forest, and the camp becomes drowsy. The prisoners work more slowly, but there are also fewer escape attempts.

There is a sense of peace in the Soviet Union, in a way. The Kulaks and the class enemies have been broken, and all foreign spies have also been removed. Perhaps the future is here at last.

But at the beginning of July, a new vice-commandant arrives at the camp, a lieutenant. His name is Fajgin, and he has come from somewhere in the south, wearing a new uniform and a spotless cap.

Polynov gathers the guards in his office, but it is Fajgin who speaks, with fire in his eyes. The emblem of the NKVD, the People's Commissariat for Internal Affairs, is on his shirt collar; it shows a sword striking down a serpent.

'We have important news,' the lieutenant says. 'More enemies have been unmasked in the south, both in the towns and in rural locations. More than ever.' He leans across the desk. 'This is a huge conspiracy, involving thousands of people.'

'Kulaks?' asks the guard next to Vlad.

'We have got rid of the Kulaks,' Fajgin replies. 'These enemies are even more dangerous. They are Trotskyites. Intellectuals. Fanatics.'

'Is this war?' someone else asks.

'Yes. This is war. But not on the streets. These enemies hide, they try to blend in and look like us. Be like us. Then they strike, through sabotage and disturbances. Or murder, which is what they did to Kirov.'

The guards stand in silence. *Kirov.* They all remember the murder of Sergei Kirov, the leader of the Leningrad Party organization, two years ago. Kirov was both popular and respected, one of the few leaders who could challenge Stalin. Suddenly, he was dead, shot by a madman.

Fajgin rests his clenched fists on the desk and goes on. 'They have a plan, drawn up by the traitor Trotsky. He is directing them from outside our country; they are ready to die for him.'

Trotsky. So many names for Vlad to keep in his head. Wasn't Trotsky a friend of Stalin? Evidently not.

Fajgin gives a little smile for the first time, and points to a folder in front of him. 'And, believe me, they will die. We have lists of those who are on their way here by train, and details of how they will be dealt with . . . The Trotskyites will have their own building here in the camp.'

There have been punishment blocks with barred windows for a long time in the camp, and this is where many of the new prisoners from the south end up when the trains deliver them. The new block that is built behind them is different. It is called the Sty, even though there are no pigs in the camp. It is a long, low building with thick timber walls, and it is right next door to the crematorium. The innermost room has a sloping floor.

The new arrivals are sorted into two categories, according to Fajgin's list: the first or second category. The second is the largest group; they are set to work in the brigades.

Those in the first category remain in camp. They are allocated a special platoon of guards, who are issued with new Mausers. Vlad is not selected for this group; he still has his old Winchester and continues to spend the long shifts patrolling the fence.

But he knows what is going to happen inside the Sty.

The work is carried out at night.

A wind-up gramophone begins to play patriotic marching music when a Trotskyite is taken into the innermost room. The music is very loud, virtually drowning out any other sounds.

However, sometimes Vlad is on duty outside the Sty, and he hears the shots echoing through the timber walls. The shots come at regular intervals, every night.

Not everything has been thought through; they should have added another door or some kind of hatch at the back of the Sty. As it is, all the bodies have to be transported to the crematorium through the front door, long after midnight, when the summer night is dark enough.

In the mornings, grey smoke rises from the chimneys.

But there are too many enemies this year; the trains just keep on coming.

The number of Trotskyites swells to a flood. Summer turns to autumn, and the emaciated rag dolls are all over the camp, staggering around.

In September, Vlad and a dozen or so other guards are summoned to Commandant Polynov's office, where Fajgin is also waiting. Fajgin's chin is up, but Polynov's head is drooping. He looks very old; his face is swollen, with dark hollows under his eyes. He finished off his wine collection long ago.

Vlad also notices that the portrait of Jagoda has been removed. Stalin's picture is still there, but there is another face beside him. A younger man, with an expression as merciless as Jagoda's.

'Our commissariat has a new leader,' Polynov says quietly, nodding towards the portrait. 'His name is Comrade Ezhov. Jagoda has been arrested . . . he was caught reading Trotskyite literature.'

The commandant sighs. 'The putrefaction is spreading. We need more firing squads.'

He picks up a bottle of vodka and takes a long swig. He is very drunk.

'We will be getting more work,' he goes on. 'A lot more work. All of us. We have to clear it . . . cleanse it from . . . from . . .'

He falls silent, as if he has lost his way. Fajgin takes over.

'The Sty and the crematorium are no longer adequate when it comes to dealing with Category One prisoners, and we cannot start piling up corpses inside the camp. We have to find a better solution, so we are going to organize a special place for our most dangerous enemies, the Trotskyites. We are going to clear the ground and pre-pare a gravel pit for them deep in the forest, where no music will be necessary.'

Gerlof

Gerlof was posing in the churchyard, leaning on his stick in front of a clicking camera. He wasn't entirely comfortable with the situation, but it had been his decision. It was all in a good cause, he told himself.

The plan was to lure Aron Fredh from wherever he was hiding.

He looked up at the photographer, who was also a reporter. Bengt Nyberg was a veteran on the local paper, which carried stories about most of the things that happened in the north of the island.

'I noticed you wrote about the gastroenteritis outbreak,' Gerlof said.

Bengt looked quite pleased. 'Yes, down at the Ölandic. I think they wanted to keep it as quiet as possible, but it was a bit of a scoop for me. Hundreds of people were affected . . . The whole of their sewage system was knocked out by the amount of use their toilets were subjected to.'

'But you didn't come down with it yourself?'

'No, I avoided the water. And it seems to have been very localized . . . They think it was in the pipes in the complex itself, that some kind of parasite got into the system.'

'Dear me,' Gerlof said. 'And right in the middle of the high season.'

'Yes, it's bad news for the Kloss family,' Bengt said. 'But good for the other campsites.'

They fell silent. Gerlof gazed around the churchyard, at the neatly mown grass and the rows of gravestones around the church. He had been visiting this place for seventy years, and many new graves had appeared. His wife and all of his older relatives had ended up here.

He turned his attention back to the reason he was here, and the

275

story he wanted to tell. 'It happened somewhere around here. I can't say exactly where, but I know we were standing fairly close to the wall.'

Bengt took a few more pictures of Gerlof pointing dramatically at the graves with his stick. Then he lowered the camera. 'So which grave was it?'

'I don't remember. I dug quite a lot of graves that summer. But it was in this area . . .'

He was lying, of course, but he didn't want to name the Kloss family in the newspaper. He didn't think Kent Kloss would appreciate that.

'But I remember what I heard,' he went on. 'Three sharp knocks, then three more . . . And that was when we stopped filling in the grave. We brought the coffin back up and called Dr Blom. He turned up on his bike, but there was nothing he could do.'

'He was dead?' the journalist asked. 'The man in the coffin?'

'As dead as a doornail.'

Gerlof looked around again. It was just as warm and sunny today as it had been all those years ago; it was a strange feeling. As if a whole lifetime hadn't passed at all. He remembered exactly where they had stood, the priest, the doctor, the Kloss brothers, and Bengtsson the gravedigger slightly behind the others. And Aron Fredh, further away.

Nyberg took one more picture and jotted something down in his notepad. He seemed satisfied, and looked up at Gerlof. 'Well, that's certainly a hair-raising story . . . A summer mystery.'

'So are you going to write about it?'

'Yes, I'll put something together. It won't be very long, but we'll have a picture and a short article. Material like this is very useful when it comes to filling an empty column.'

'And when will it be in the paper?'

'I don't know,' Nyberg said. 'Tomorrow, with a bit of luck, although we're not exactly short of news this month, even though it is holiday time.'

Gerlof assumed he was talking about the deaths of Einar Wall and Peter Mayer the previous week. He leaned forward. 'You're welcome to say that I'd like to hear from any witnesses.'

'Witnesses?'

'Yes, anyone else who remembers the knocking. Anyone who was in the churchyard that day. They can get in touch with me.'

Bengt Nyberg nodded, without asking who Gerlof thought these witnesses might be, after some seventy years.

They parted company at the church gate, after Nyberg had revealed what the headline was likely to be. It was less than subtle:

GERLOF STILL HAUNTED BY KNOCKING FROM THE GRAVE

You could call it sensationalism, but Gerlof was still pleased when he opened the paper two days later. The article was in a prominent position, and he thought plenty of people would read it. He knew that everyone else who had heard the sound of knocking on that day was long dead.

Everyone except himself, and possibly Aron Fredh.

Lisa

A settled stomach was what everyone needed. Lisa felt pretty good this morning; the sun was shining and life felt better. She should have known it wouldn't last long.

About an hour after she had woken up, she went down to the shore. The rocks were warm beneath her feet. She carried on out on to the jetty, right to the very end, and jumped in without hesitating. The sandy seabed was soft and the water was warm, over twenty degrees, and she stretched out with a sigh of pleasure. Closed her eyes, floated along, chilled out. No worries.

She swam back and forth not far from the jetty until a large group of children arrived for their swimming lesson and started splashing around. She got out and went back to the campsite.

When she saw her caravan, she realized something was wrong.

It was moving. The door was ajar, and it was rocking slightly.

Lisa slowed down but kept on walking. She remembered an old saying: Don't go knocking if the trailer is a-rocking.

But if a caravan was rocking when it ought to be empty, surely you should check it out?

Lisa didn't knock, she simply opened the door.

'Hello?' she said quietly.

It was dark inside, and she couldn't see properly after being out in the sunshine, but she clearly heard a voice: 'Hello, Summertime.'

It was a male voice. It sounded calm, but Lisa's stomach turned to ice. Something was wrong. She didn't climb the steps into the caravan but leaned forward and stuck her head around the door so that she could see as far as the bedroom area.

A tall figure was sitting in the middle of her narrow bed.

Kent Kloss, wearing white shorts and a red top. He nodded to her, and she realized that he had opened her bag.

Her DJ bag. Kloss was slowly going through her vinyl LPs. He hadn't got very far yet, but he was making steady progress.

'Come on in!' he said with a smile. 'Make yourself at home!'

Lisa stepped inside, but this certainly didn't feel like home. The caravan was hot and cramped and seemed to be quivering around her. She dropped her beach bag and gave him a quick smile in return.

'Hi, Kent . . . How did you get in?'

He was still smiling. 'I have a spare key. We own this caravan – don't you remember? We allow you to live here, as our employee.'

The last sentence sounded slightly threatening. Lisa didn't quite know what to do, so she nodded.

'I wanted to see if everything was OK,' Kent went on. 'So I came in, and I was curious. I love old dance music, so I thought I'd have a look at what you've got.'

'Fine by me,' Lisa said. 'Those are the LPs I play over at the club . . . I've got nothing to hide.'

His response was instant. 'Haven't you?'

She shook her head, moved a step closer.

Kent carried on flicking through the records, then suddenly jerked his head towards the bed beside him. 'And what about all this?'

Lisa looked down and saw a small pile at the foot of the bed. Wallets and purses, which of course she recognized. And the mobile phones next to them.

Her entire haul from the May Lai Bar was lying on the bed for all to see. Kloss had already found it.

'They were among the records,' Kent said. 'I presume you were hiding them?'

Lisa didn't say a word.

I can explain – that was probably what you were supposed to say under the circumstances.

She knew she looked guilty. She didn't have a chance, but she made an attempt to sound both honest and bored. 'Oh, those . . . I found them in the bar. People lose all kinds of stuff in there. I asked if any-one owned them, but no one came forward. So I brought them back here . . . but maybe someone saw me in the club and misunderstood.'

Kent Kloss stared at her. 'You're right, someone did see you. It was

Emanuel, one of our security guards. He saw you pick up a mobile phone from a table on Tuesday night.'

Lisa took another step towards him. 'I found that one, too.'

'I'm sure you did. And now I've found you.'

Kent Kloss got to his feet. Perhaps he was just irritated; he moved closer to her.

'I've met all sorts over the years,' he said. 'Campsite security guards who steal from chalets, bartenders who help themselves out of the till, light-fingered cleaners in hotel rooms . . . I know the score.'

Lisa was aware of a strong smell emanating from him, but it wasn't aftershave. Kent stank of booze, and there was a menacing glint in his eye.

'Are you working for him?' he said quietly.

'For who?'

The slap came without warning, striking her hard and fast across the nose and cheek, and she staggered backwards. She stumbled over her beach bag and ended up on the floor. The caravan was rocking like a ship on stormy seas.

Kloss didn't wait for her to recover. 'Is that what you're doing? Are you spying on us?'

Lisa blinked, felt her nose. 'Who would I be spying for?' she said, trying to get up.

'Don't move!'

Kloss took a deep breath, gathered his strength and kicked her hard in the thigh. The pain was horrendous; Lisa whimpered, but didn't move. She could hear her own shallow breathing in the silence that followed. She reached up to her nose and felt drops of warm blood.

'I don't know who . . . who you're talking about.'

'Don't you?' he sneered.

Lisa released Lady Summertime, who snapped, 'You and your family steal from the guests, too.'

'Do we?'

She nodded. 'Fourteen hundred for a bottle of champagne, Kent. Sparkling wine that's probably smuggled in for fifty kronor a bottle . . . Isn't that daylight robbery?'

'Don't change the subject. One of us has a problem here, and it's not me.'

280

Summertime braced herself for another blow, but went on: 'Call the cops, then.'

Kloss looked down at her. 'Not yet.'

A blood vessel was throbbing on his suntanned forehead; he remained motionless for a few seconds, then relaxed. He took at step back and sat down on the bed, legs wide apart, leaving his crotch exposed.

'There's something you can help me with,' he said.

Lady Summertime considered giving him a swift kick, right there in the middle. But Lisa pushed her aside. She got up cautiously, still expecting him to hit her again, but nothing happened. Kent Kloss had vented his anger, and he hadn't called the police.

He glanced out of the window, as if to check that no one could see him, his fingers drumming on his thighs. Eventually, he spoke. 'A man has come over to the island this summer, and he's . . . he's caused some problems. I didn't know who he was at first, but now I do. His name is Aron Fredh.'

He was looking closely at Lisa, as if she might react to the name. But she'd never heard of Aron Fredh. Would Kent hit her again if she said the wrong thing?

'OK,' she said. 'Aron Fredh.'

Kloss looked down at his tanned hands. 'I don't know what he looks like; he's keeping a low profile . . . but I need to find him. I think you might be able to help me track him down. He's here somewhere; I think he might be staying over at the resort, on the campsite or in a chalet under a false name. He must be, because he managed to poison our drinking water, and that can only be done from inside the complex.'

Poison our drinking water. Lisa had extensive experience of the effects of that particular event.

'The Ölandic Resort is enormous,' she said. 'How am I supposed to find him?'

Kent was smiling again now. It was as if the slap and the kick had never happened. 'You snoop around, of course . . . After all, that's what you're good at.'

Lisa let out a long breath. 'So you just want me to find this man, among all the guests, when you haven't a clue what he looks like?'

'He's an old man, we know that, but in good shape for his age.

And he's probably alone. That description fits a number of men at the resort; we'll tell you where they're staying and, when their caravans or chalets are empty, you go and check them out. Discreetly.'

'When they're empty?'

'Of course . . . We don't want the guests to know what's going on.'

'And how will I know when it's safe?'

'The security guards will keep an eye on things. Most caravans and chalets are empty in the middle of the day.'

Lisa didn't have much choice. 'What am I looking for?'

'Anything unusual. Guns, balaclavas, bundles of cash. You'll know when you see it . . . This is no ordinary holidaymaker.'

'And then I'm free to leave?'

Kloss got to his feet.

'We'll see. You're not going to be arrested, anyway. And you can carry on gigging for the time being . . . as long as you keep your fingers to yourself.'

'And what if I get caught snooping around?'

A victorious smile spread across Kent's face. 'You've already been caught, Summertime. That's why you're going to do this.'

Gerlof

There had been a few comments on the newspaper article about the knocking from the grave, and Gerlof was still hoping that it had been read by the right person. It was a bit like a personal ad. If Aron Fredh was still on the island, of course.

He sat down to wait for visitors. These were his last few days in the cottage; after the weekend, he was going back to his room in the residential home in Marnäs.

But on Friday he had a visit from a murderer. Not the one he was looking for this summer, but a murderer he himself had tracked down many years earlier.

Gerlof was in the garden as usual, in the shade of the parasol. It was always open these days; the heat of the sun was merciless.

His hearing aid was switched on, and suddenly he heard a rustling sound behind him, in the meadow. Footsteps, definitely footsteps. Gerlof turned his head, and a few seconds later the man appeared among the juniper bushes, wearing jeans and a shirt and loafers. He stopped on the other side of the boundary, in the tall grass. Gerlof recognized him.

This was the man who had killed his grandson.

The visitor remained where he was, and they looked at each other for a few seconds. Gerlof was glad his daughter Julia wasn't in the village today.

'Good afternoon,' the man said quietly.

'Good afternoon.'

Gerlof wondered if he ought to be afraid, but he wasn't. Not at all. This murderer didn't look dangerous, just tired and pale in the sunshine. Much older. And he had nothing in his hands.

So Gerlof nodded to him. 'Come and sit down.'

The man walked slowly across the garden and sat down on the opposite side of the table.

'So you're out,' Gerlof went on.

The man shook his head. 'I haven't been released. I'm out on parole. My first unsupervised outing, so I wanted to call round and . . .' The man fell silent and looked around, over towards the gate and the cottage, then asked, 'Are you alone?'

'My grandchildren have gone for a swim. My daughters haven't arrived yet.'

The man seemed to relax, at least until they heard a loud buzzing and a hornet appeared. Gerlof knew that their sting could be dangerous, but they were less aggressive than their smaller relatives. Perhaps their size made them calmer.

The hornet zoomed past, and in the silence that followed Gerlof asked, 'So how long are you out for?'

'Twenty-four hours. The probation service releases prisoners in stages. First of all, for just a few hours, then a little longer . . . if you behave yourself.'

'And have you behaved yourself? Are you cured?'

The man looked down at his hands. 'Cured . . . How am I supposed to know that?'

'I'm sure you know how you feel,' Gerlof said. 'Whether you're at peace with the rest of the world.'

'I've tried,' his visitor said. 'I've had the opportunity to talk about . . . about my thoughts.'

'So all that hatred is gone?'

The man nodded and looked up. 'Do you hate me, Gerlof?'

Gerlof looked away. 'That's exactly what I'm wondering.'

He met the visitor's gaze, searching for anger, but he found none. Only weariness. He changed the subject.

'Niklas Kloss,' he said. 'Have you heard of him?'

The man nodded. 'He's one of the wealthy Kloss siblings, isn't he? The owners of the Ölandic Resort?'

'Yes, but Niklas is the black sheep of the family. He's been in prison.'

The man nodded again, as if he recalled the story. 'Not where I was. I've never met him.'

'But you've heard of him?'

'There's always talk . . . I know why he was inside. Smuggling . . . on a massive scale. He was caught by customs with a truck full of spirits from Germany, worth millions. Kloss wasn't driving, but he was the one responsible. So they say.'

Gerlof picked up on the last three words. 'You don't believe it was him?'

'I think it was more likely to be his older brother, Kent Kloss. But Niklas went down for it; he got a couple of years. That's all I know.'

'I'm not surprised,' Gerlof said.

'No. People have always smuggled booze and tobacco across the Baltic, but the quantities are greater now. It's difficult to understand who's going to consume the amount that comes in. It will soon be like medieval times, when Swedes drank several litres of beer every day.'

'But I don't suppose it all stays on the island.'

'No, some of it is probably transported over to the mainland.'

The man fell silent. Gerlof thought that, for a little while, he had felt as if he were chatting to just anyone, as if the man were an ordinary visitor – but every time there was a silence, the tension was there again.

'It was brave of you to come here,' he said eventually.

The man didn't respond, so Gerlof went on, 'I hope you can come back . . . To the island, I mean.'

'That's my goal,' the man said. 'To come home. Prison . . . that's not a home.'

Gerlof had made a decision.

'You asked if I hated you. I think it would be miserable to sit here in the sun, towards the end of my life, hating people.'

The man nodded; perhaps he was relieved. He got to his feet and gazed around the garden. 'I'll go back the same way I came, past the old mill . . . and the cairn.'

'They're still there,' Gerlof said.

He raised a hand to wave, and his visitor was gone.

The Homecomer

It was late in the evening, and the Homecomer was reading the local paper. It was on sale in the shop at the Ölandic Resort, and he had been buying it in order to follow the problems with the drinking water. However, he had found another interesting article in yesterday's paper. The headline had caught his attention:

GERLOF STILL HAUNTED BY KNOCKING FROM THE GRAVE

He looked at the photograph again and saw an old man leaning on his walking stick among the graves in a churchyard. Marnäs churchyard. The man had told the reporter an old story.

The Homecomer recognized the man after all the years that had passed, and he remembered the open grave.

He shivered, even though it was still warm down by the sea. He could feel the dead reaching out, clutching at him with invisible hands.

Terrifying noises echoed inside his head.

The sound of knocking from inside a coffin.

He had never been back to that churchyard, not in seventy years.

He felt alone. He *was* alone. Pecka and Wall were dead. Rita had left the island. He missed his wife and his child, but of course there was no way he could see them.

The road was dark and deserted.

The Homecomer didn't have a telephone of his own, so he was standing in a kiosk. He had called Directory Enquiries to ask for Gerlof Davidsson's number. He picked up the receiver and keyed it in.

The New Country, November 1936

The Trotskyites are standing in a line, silent and frozen. The wind is bitterly cold, but they are wearing only their dirty underclothes, so that none of them can hide any kind of weapon. Spindly legs, trembling arms. They are not only undressed, their hands are bound with wire. Sometimes a metre-long rope binds two prisoners together, so that when one of them falls his or her neighbour is almost pulled down, too. But not quite.

Vlad has noticed that, when an enemy falls forward, the man or woman attached by the rope always struggles to remain upright, standing with their feet wide apart and fighting to keep their balance. Often, they take a step to one side, as if the enemy who is still alive wants to get as far away as possible from the one who is already dead.

It is strange, Vlad thinks as he lowers the Winchester, that an enemy wants to live as long as possible. Even if it is only for a few extra seconds on the edge of a newly dug grave, where death is already clutching at them.

A deserted gravel pit – this is where the prisoners are transported to from the camp, in a steady stream of trucks. This is where they are lined up and shot, in a forest south of the camp, north of Lake Onega.

The end of the world.

Vlad is happy to get out of the camp, but the battle against the Trotskyites is no easier out here than it is in there. Arctic winds blow across the sand, and the young NKVD guards accompanying him just want to get the day's work done and go back to the barracks.

Vlad is wearing two freshly laundered linen shirts, a well-worn but warm army greatcoat and sturdy new boots. He is protected from the wind, and the job he has to do makes him even warmer. He raises the rifle, takes aim, fires and lowers it, over and over again.

The guards are standing three paces away, with their guns trained on the prisoners. The most effective method would be to walk right up to each one and place the barrel of the gun against the back of the neck, of course, but operating from a short distance away means that the person firing the shot does not get dirty.

In Vlad's opinion, it ought to be impossible to miss even from three paces away, if you hold the gun steady. But a guard will move the gun surprisingly often, so that the enemy is hit in the back, or the shoulder, or not at all. The prisoner jerks, but remains standing.

This is bad. Vlad never misses. He is in charge here, which means he is the one who has to step forward and fire a second shot.

On these cold autumn days, many of the prisoners seem to be foreigners, immigrants from the west who came to seek their fortune in the new country: Polacks, Germans, Canadians. A few Americans, some Norwegians and an endless stream of Finns. Sometimes, as Vlad raises his gun, he sees a prisoner turn his head. In spite of the fact that all hope is gone, someone starts pleading for their life, offering love or money, or simply begging for mercy.

Occasionally, he hears muttered prayers in Swedish or Finland-Swedish. Aron would like to stop and listen.

But Vlad does not listen to the enemy; he simply takes aim and silences the flow of words.

The guards have brought white cabbage, tinned meat and vodka to the gravel pit, and while a team of prisoners is busy shovelling sand over the bodies Vlad and his men can sit down and eat. After his time in the labour camp, he has built himself up with regular, decent food, but he still doesn't drink alcohol. He gives away his ration to his colleagues. This makes him popular, but it also means that the aim of some guards is even worse after their break.

At the end of this particular day, a black car sweeps into the gravel pit. Commandant Fajgin steps out, accompanied by two other men. One is short, the other tall.

Fajgin stands swaying by the car for a moment. He is the camp commandant now; Polynov was dismissed because of his drinking, but Fajgin has not learned from this. He has started to work his way through his predecessor's stock of vodka. Right now, he is talking and gesticulating, but his two companions appear to be treating him like thin air. They step forward to watch the last prisoners fall.

Vlad recognizes the shorter man: Grigorenko, a local Party secretary. The tall man is younger, thirty-five or forty, and is wearing a neatly pressed NKVD uniform with four stripes on the collar tab. A major.

Eventually, the trio begins to move towards the grave and the guards.

'Attention!' Fajgin bellows.

So this is an inspection of men and weapons. Perhaps the major has been instrumental in sending prisoners to their final destination and wants to see how they are dealt with.

But, in fact, he wants more than that.

Vlad realizes later that Fajgin must have boasted about his being a crack shot, because he jerks his head in Vlad's direction. The major stops in front of Vlad. He has a dark-blue scar running across his forehead, possibly from a blow with a sabre during the civil war. He looks Vlad and the old army greatcoat up and down with a critical expression, then turns his attention to the battered rifle, still warm in Vlad's hands.

'You never hesitate, Comrade?'

'No, Major.'

'You are always on your guard against the enemies of our country?'

'Yes, Major.'

'You work hard and sleep well?'

'Always, Major.'

The officer nods. He reaches out a black-gloved hand and draws Vlad to one side, away from the others. 'Are you happy here in the north, Comrade Jegerov, in the cold and the wind?'

Vlad understands that he can be honest on this occasion, so he shakes his head.

'The People's Commissariat needs more people in Leningrad,' the major says. He makes a point of turning his back on Fajgin, and adds, 'We need people with a steady hand, people who can do their job. People who are sober.'

'I drink nothing but water,' Vlad says.

289

'Comrade Jegerov,' the major says, leaning closer, 'do you know what *chernaya rabota* is?'

'No, Major.'

'It is secret work in Leningrad. Black work. Hard work with long hours, often at night, in the fight against the enemy.'

Vlad stands up very straight.

Leningrad. The big city. And the gateway to Aron's homeland.

He is ready.

Gerlof

It was Saturday evening, and Gerlof was in his cottage, after spending another oppressively hot day in the garden. His head and body felt stupefied by all the long, sunny days. They sucked all the energy out of both him and nature.

He was just about to go to bed when the phone rang, which was unusual at this late hour. The boys were in their rooms, so Gerlof picked up the receiver and answered quietly, 'Davidsson.'

His hearing aid was still switched on, but there was only silence in his ear. No voices, just a faint rushing sound in the background.

'Hello?'

Silence.

Who would call at this time of night and not introduce themselves? It was unlikely to be John, or either of his daughters. Gerlof began to suspect who was on the other end of the line.

'Aron?' he said.

There was no reply, but he was still convinced.

'Aron,' he said again, more firmly this time. 'Talk to me.'

After a few long seconds, a male voice spoke in his ear. 'So you remember the knocking.'

Gerlof swallowed in the darkness; his mouth was suddenly dry. It was an old man's voice on the phone, but it was as hard as granite. The voice of a battle-scarred soldier.

He took a deep breath. 'Yes. And so do you.'

'I do.'

Gerlof waited, then went on. 'You were frightened that day, when you and I were standing in the grave on the lid of the coffin. We were both frightened, weren't we?'

Another silence, then the voice spoke again. 'Kloss was knocking because of me.'

'What do you mean?' Gerlof said.

'He wanted to scare me away.'

'Why?'

There was no reply, but he heard something else in the background, a faint buzzing sound. Some kind of electrical machine had been switched on near the phone, and the buzzing was accompanied by a muted metallic whinnying.

Gerlof continued, 'Edvard Kloss died when a barn wall came down on top of him. I've always wondered if it fell over by itself, or if someone gave it a helping hand . . .'

He paused, but there was still no response.

'According to the gossip, it was one of his brothers. Either Sigfrid or Gilbert had loosened the props that were holding the wall up, and gave it a push when Edvard was standing in the right place . . . But, of course, it could have been someone else. Some disgruntled worker.'

The rushing sound and the strange buzzing were still going on.

'I found out recently that your stepfather, Sven Fredh, used to work for the Kloss brothers, and that he moved the old cairn for them. But that didn't go too well, did it?'

'It fell down,' the voice said. 'The brothers were on Sven's back all the time; they really got to him, and he couldn't work out how to arrange the stones. They started rolling towards his legs, and he ended up with a limp for the rest of his life.'

'And Sven wanted compensation from Edvard Kloss?'

'Yes, but of course Kloss insisted it was Sven's fault.'

'You were injured, too, Aron . . . I remember the day we met up in the churchyard – you had a long scratch on your forehead. How did you get that, Aron?'

Silence.

'It's so long ago,' Gerlof said. 'I think you can tell me now.'

For the first time, the voice at the other end of the line sounded stressed. 'It was after the barn wall had come down. When I crawled in underneath it.'

'So you were there that night?'

'Yes. But I didn't bring the wall down on top of Edvard Kloss.'

'In that case, it was Sven,' Gerlof said. 'He brought the wall down, then he sent you in to get Edvard's wallet. Is that what happened?'

'Yes. Edvard had to pay.'

'Pay what, Aron?'

'What he owed Sven for his crushed foot . . . and for my mother.'

Gerlof listened, trying to think. 'So he had harmed Astrid in some way?'

'Harmed?' the voice said quietly. 'You could say that.'

Gerlof didn't ask any more questions. He had already suspected who Aron Fredh's father was; it wasn't the first time a serving girl had ended up pregnant by the master of the house.

'So Edvard Kloss was your father. Was he your sister Greta's father, too?'

'Everyone knew,' the voice said. 'But he always denied it.'

Gerlof sighed. 'I know you feel bitter towards him, Aron. But Edvard's grandchildren have nothing to do with these old grievances. You do realize that, don't you?'

Once again, there was a long silence before Aron spoke. 'Those grandchildren took the croft away from me. They took everything I had here.'

Now it was Gerlof's turn to keep quiet. What could he say?

'And you took a ship from them,' he said eventually, 'and the crew suffocated in the hold . . . How could you do that?'

When the voice eventually spoke, there was no trace of regret.

'The crew were criminals. And they weren't supposed to be on board; I had to move them below deck. But it was Kloss's ship, with plenty of cash, and that was what mattered. So we took the money and sank the ship.'

'Where is she?' Gerlof asked.

'Far out in the Sound. Five nautical miles north-west of Stenvik.'

Gerlof sighed again, even more heavily this time. 'Don't make any more trouble, Aron.'

The voice didn't speak for a while, but when it did reply it was every bit as hard as before. 'I'm doing what I've learned to do. I had to make my way out into the world and learn how things are done . . . I became a soldier.'

'In Russia,' Gerlof said.

'In the Soviet Union. I was a soldier in the new country.'

'But the war is over now, Aron. There's plenty of help available;

you don't have to keep on making mistakes. Otherwise, you'll be hearing that knocking sound for the rest of your life.'

'I don't need any help. I haven't got long left.' Aron sounded worryingly sure of himself.

'What are you going to do now, Aron?' Gerlof said eventually.

The only reply was a click.

Gerlof slowly put down the phone; his hand was shaking. He reached out to open the veranda window, to let in some cool, fresh air.

Out there in the darkness, he could hear the bush crickets chirruping, but he couldn't see any shadows moving around. The trees, the grass and the plants were resting now, after another trying day in the sun.

Gerlof knew that the plantlife on Öland was tougher than any soldier. Nature would always have the upper hand. If the earth and the plants were in good shape, there would be food. If not, people would starve.

Most things were sparse and tough on the island. There were no plentiful resources to be extracted, and no one had ever discovered oil or a goldmine. Tourism was no more than a moderate success; there were no plans to open enormous hotels or casinos with the aim of creating a Swedish Las Vegas.

It was hard to make a fast buck here and, as a consequence, Öland had escaped the invasions of fortune hunters or armies which had destroyed so much in other defenceless places around the world. There was plenty of sunshine and stone and there were many hardy plants on the island, but not much else.

For which Gerlof was very grateful.

He was also glad that a strong leader hadn't suddenly appeared, demanding that everyone should report on their neighbour for their own good. Gerlof and his fellow islanders had therefore managed to avoid the difficult decisions which others had been forced to make in uncertain times.

There were a number of guns here, of course, but, fortunately, not many. Nor was the population divided into different sects or tribes, each believing they had a right to more power and higher status than others, and therefore any disputes had been restricted to local village issues. People had argued about land, but those quarrels had never gone beyond harsh words or court judgements.

The island had been lucky, on the whole.

But now there was a problem.

Gerlof closed the window before any mosquitoes found their way in, and picked up the phone again. He felt sleepy but wanted to make one call.

John answered almost right away, and Gerlof got straight to the point. 'Aron Fredh rang me.'

'Did he now? Where was he?'

'He didn't say . . . but it sounded as if he was outdoors, in a phone box.'

'Well, there aren't many of those around.'

'No,' Gerlof said. 'And the interesting thing was that I could hear something in the background . . . a kind of humming. Or maybe rattling, with a faint whinny from time to time. I couldn't work it out, but I've been giving it some thought, and I think it might be an electric horse.'

'An electric horse?'

'You know, one of those rides for children – you put money in and it moves around for a while.

John was quiet for a moment. 'There's a phone box by the shop down at the resort . . . I think they've got some rides there, too.'

'You mean Aron is staying at the Ölandic? Well, they do say you should keep your friends close and your enemies closer . . .'

'Did he sound sorry?' John wanted to know.

'Not in the slightest. But at least we talked; we'll just have to hope that he calls again, even if I am moving back to the home on Monday.'

'I'll give you a lift.'

'Thanks, John. Goodnight.'

Gerlof put the phone down, then went and sat on his bed to think things over.

An old soldier had come home to the island, hell-bent on revenge, spreading fear all around him. No one knew who he was, and no one knew *where* he was either. As long as it was high season, as long as Öland was packed with summer visitors, he could move around freely. Who could stop him?

The Kloss family?

Gerlof?

Lisa

Lisa didn't have a gig on this hot Sunday, but of course she had a different kind of job to do for Kent Kloss. She was supposed to snoop around the Ölandic Resort, looking for a particular man.

A man who was old but apparently dangerous.

At around two o'clock, she parked her car by the hotel and walked over to the top campsite. She was wearing shorts and a yellow T-shirt, just like an ordinary holidaymaker. A white baseball cap pulled well down over her eyes and a pair of oversized sunnies meant that she could carry out her task without anyone noticing. She hoped.

The first time she had seen the Ölandic Resort, towards the end of June, the expanse of grass that made up the campsite had been fresh and green, but since then the sun had blazed down almost non-stop. Now the grass was dry and yellow, almost brown in places, and the short blades crunched underfoot as she moved among the caravans.

The campsite felt a bit like a burning desert, quivering in the heat. But following the previous week's outbreak of gastroenteritis there were plenty of empty spaces, and Lisa could see several families packing up and getting ready to leave. She wasn't interested in them, of course, but in the guests who were staying.

She was hunting for golf balls in the grass.

It was Kent Kloss's idea, and she wasn't sure whether it was brilliant or completely stupid: he had placed a white ball next to each caravan or chalet that he wanted her to investigate. As if the balls had just happened to land on the campsite . . .

So Lisa kept her eyes on the ground, and after about fifty metres she spotted the first flash of white in the yellow grass. It was next to a fairly new caravan with a small awning.

She stopped a few metres away and glanced around. There was no one nearby.

A risky business, she thought, and wished she could have worn her wig, like Lady Summertime.

She was nervous. Even if the security guards had been told to leave her alone, the occupants of the caravan might turn up. What was she supposed to say then – that she was cleaning?

If the neighbours saw her, she could pretend that this was her caravan and simply walk in. Which would be fine until the real owner appeared.

Lisa couldn't just stand here, so she stepped inside the awning and tried the door. Locked. In which case there wasn't much she could do except peer through the window. Very quickly.

She pressed her forehead against the glass. What was she looking for?

'Anything unusual,' Kent Kloss had said.

A gun, perhaps, or bundles of notes.

But all she could see was a neat and tidy interior, much tidier than her own caravan, with folded towels and a small pile of books. Empty worktops. No guns.

So she moved on, and found another golf ball at the end of the same row. This caravan was silver-grey and bigger than most of the others; it was almost as broad as hers was long.

The door inside the awning was ajar – only a fraction, but it was obviously not locked.

Going inside was extremely risky.

She looked around. The long expanse of grass between the rows was completely deserted.

OK. She stepped inside.

A fat black fly was buzzing against the windowpane; it rested for a few seconds, then started up again. It wanted to get out into the sunshine, but Lisa didn't dare open the window. She didn't dare touch anything, and kept on glancing outside.

Still no one in sight. But if you didn't lock your door, you weren't far away. She didn't have much time.

She noticed a grey blanket on the bed; it looked as if there was something small and round underneath it. She didn't really want to go that far inside but decided to take a chance. She took three quick steps over to the bed and pulled back the blanket.

The puppy was a dachshund. It had been fast asleep; it gave a start, leapt up on its short little legs and started barking at Lisa.

She backed away in a blind panic, out through the door; she closed it behind her and scurried away across the grass, her cap well pulled down.

The barking died away, but it was several minutes before her heart began to slow down. Fortunately, no one was taking any notice of her.

Only the holiday village left now. There were a couple of suspect older guests staying there, according to Kent Kloss, so Lisa might as well check them out while she was here. She walked down towards the water, past a small grove of ash trees, and reached the chalets.

There was a golf ball lying outside the third one in the first row, as if a player on the course had somehow pulled off a diagonal shot right across the campsite and through the trees.

The chalet looked closed up and empty, but Lisa moved carefully anyway. She stepped up on to the little veranda and tapped on the door. After a short silence, she heard a thud, then the door opened and a man in very small red trunks and with an equally red face peered out. He was in his seventies, tall and thin and completely bald.

'Yes?' he said.

Lisa stepped back, but immediately regained her equilibrium.

'Oh, hi,' she said. 'I was wondering if you had any soap powder? I'm staying just over there, and I've run out.'

The man stared at her; he looked as if he'd only just woken up.

'No.'

'OK, no problem.' Lisa beamed at him. 'Bye, then.'

Then she was gone, hurrying away as fast as she could. Had she seen anything suspicious? No. She hadn't seen anything at all.

The other interesting chalet was two rows down, twenty metres closer to the water. One last white golf ball shone out in the grass. She picked it up as a souvenir, then went up to the door and knocked gently.

No answer.

She glanced around, then pushed down the handle. And the door opened.

Nothing else happened. She stuck her head inside.

'Hello?'

No response. No barking dog, and the bed was empty. If she saw a blanket, she certainly wasn't going to lift it up, but she might as well have a quick look.

The place was neat and tidy; the bed had been made, and there was a suitcase next to it, but no sign of any other personal effects. Oh yes – there was a rucksack on the worktop in the kitchenette, next to over a dozen bottles of mineral water and some kind of red pump.

The rucksack was made of black leather and looked full.

Lisa always found suitcases and bags tempting, of course. There might be anything in there. Money. Jewellery. Rubbish.

She checked once more to make sure there was no one behind her, then slipped inside the chalet. She took off her sunglasses, went over to the worktop and opened the rucksack.

It contained a couple more bottles of water and a man's clothing: rolled-up flannel shirts, jeans, sweaters. But she could also see something pale down at the bottom; it looked like wood. She took it out.

A wooden box. A snuff box? It was old and scratched.

And there was something else underneath it; a shiny metal tube was sticking up, and at first Lisa thought it was some kind of pipe. Then she realized she was staring at a gun.

A revolver.

She didn't pick it up. She backed away, still clutching the box. She just wanted to get out of the chalet; she had seen enough, and she had no intention of getting caught again this summer. She didn't feel safe, because if the door had been left unlocked, perhaps the occupant had just popped out for a few minutes and . . .

She turned around and shot outside.

There was no one in sight. Lisa kept her head down and moved about thirty metres away, to the edge of the forest. She stopped in the shade of a tall ash tree and took out her mobile.

'Kent Kloss.'

His voice was loud and authoritative, but she spoke quietly. 'It's Lisa Turesson.'

'Yes?'

'I think I've found something.'

'On the campsite?'

'In one of the chalets – the last one. I've just been in there, and I . . .' She fell silent.

She saw an old man; he had appeared from behind the trees and stopped in the shade. And he was looking at her.

Lisa recognized him. At first, she couldn't work out where from, and then she realized that she had seen him from approximately the same distance a few weeks ago, at midsummer. The man had been standing out on the rocks by the shore, in the fenced-off part of the resort.

He set off towards the chalet she had just left. Lisa was horrified when she saw that she hadn't closed the door behind her. It was standing wide open, like a warning signal.

The man disappeared inside.

'He's here,' she whispered. 'He's back.'

'Keep him there,' Kent Kloss said. 'We're on our way.'

Lisa stood there, not knowing what to do. *Keep him there?* How the hell was she supposed to do that?

After less than thirty seconds, the man emerged from the chalet.

'I can't,' she said into her phone. 'He's leaving.'

It was definitely the man from the shore. Aron Fredh, if that was his name. An old, white-haired man with a compact body; he looked strong, in spite of his age. He was moving fast, away from the chalets and up towards the car park. In seconds, he was hidden by the trees.

'Stop him,' Kloss said in her ear.

'I can't,' she said again.

She didn't move. Aron Fredh had a revolver in his rucksack, and she had taken enough risks already today.

She opened her left hand and looked at the object she had taken from the chalet. A small wooden box. She turned it over; there were stains on the bottom. Snuff, perhaps, or oil. Or blood.

Gerlof

The cottage was full of people again. Lena and Julia had arrived with their husbands for two weeks' holiday with the children. They had all had morning coffee, and his daughters had helped Gerlof pack his bags, so now there was nothing left to do before he set off for Marnäs. He had glanced at his phone from time to time, but it had remained silent all morning.

John Hagman looked at him. 'Ready to go?'

Gerlof nodded. 'Back to the institution.'

As they drove away from Stenvik and the cottage, Gerlof watched the bright landscape passing by and wondered if summer was over as far as he was concerned, anyway. Time passed so quickly during this late phase of his life.

The residential home was bathed in sunlight, its windows shining. The car park was empty, and the place felt deserted when he walked in. At first, he couldn't understand why, then he realized that many of the staff were on holiday.

Most of the residents were still there, of course, dozing in the heat. As he passed the coffee bar, he saw Raymond Matsson sitting at a table with a younger relative who had come to visit. The relative must have been in his fifties, but could well be a grandchild, as Raymond himself was ninety-seven years old.

The relative leaned forward and yelled in a voice that sounded as if it were coming through a megaphone, 'Have you eaten today, Raymond?'

'What?' Raymond raised his head. 'Beaten? Who's been beaten?'

'No, Raymond, I'm asking you . . . have you *eaten*?'

Gerlof moved on, without waiting for Raymond's answer.

It shouldn't be like this, he thought; younger people shouldn't be yelling at the elderly. Raymond ought to be sitting there talking about his long life, about everything he had learned from having experienced almost the whole of the twentieth century, from horse-drawn carriages to space shuttles. But perhaps Raymond had nothing to say in spite of all that, no wisdom to share.

What did Gerlof have to tell?

Only that both the summer and the century had gone so fast. The six weeks he had been away from here, on parole in the summer cottage, had felt like six minutes.

He followed John, who had unlocked the door of his room and carried his suitcase inside.

'Gerlof!'

He heard a voice behind him as he was about to go in. It was Boel, the supervisor of the home, and she was smiling. She even winked at him.

'So you couldn't stay away any longer?' she joked.

Gerlof nodded. 'I gave up.'

'Now it's my turn to escape,' Boel said. 'I'm going on holiday on Friday; my husband and I are off to Provence.'

'Have a lovely time.'

'What about you?' Boel said. 'Have you had a good rest?'

'Yes, I feel fine. I take after my grandfather.'

'So, he was big and strong, like you?'

'Tough rather than strong,' Gerlof said, launching into a story. 'When my grandfather was eighty years old, he was out fishing all by himself one day, just off Blå Jungfrun. A storm blew up and his skiff capsized. But my grandfather wasn't afraid; he simply swam ashore, towing the boat behind him, then lay down underneath it on the shore. He couldn't light a fire, because his matches were wet, so he lay there for three days with no food, all alone, as the storm raged and his clothes slowly dried out. When the wind dropped he rowed home to Stenvik, and he was perfectly fine.'

'Impressive,' Boel said.

'He was a good role model,' Gerlof said. 'And I've been working on my gig this summer.'

Boel stopped smiling. 'Don't even think about going out in it on your own. Not at your age.'

302

She moved on, and Gerlof went into his room. John was pulling up the blinds.

Everything looked just the same as usual. The long plastic mat was still there in the little hallway, the bathroom was clean, and all the framed diplomas that gave him the right to command a ship at sea were in their proper places on the walls.

The telephone was still there, too. Gerlof went over and picked it up and got a signal straight away. Good.

'I've told Julia and Lena that if anyone rings the cottage asking for me they're to pass on this number.'

John nodded; he knew exactly who Gerlof meant.

'What else are you going to do?'

'It's back to the bottle for me, I think.' Gerlof pointed to his desk, where he was working on another ship in a bottle. This one was a two-masted schooner; he had almost finished whittling the hull, and the next job was the masts and the rigging. Then came the tricky task of getting the ship in through the narrow neck.

But he would also have plenty of time to think about Aron Fredh.

Gerlof could try to persuade himself that Aron had done what he came to do and had left the island, but he didn't believe it. Not as long as Kent Kloss was still around.

Lisa

Kent was sitting in Lisa's caravan, weighing the old wooden box in his hand. Lisa was perched on her bed, as far away from him as possible. Kloss didn't look well; there was a hunted expression in his eyes. And he stank of booze again this evening. Of a lot more than one Cosmo.

He looked at her. 'So this was in the rucksack in his chalet?'

'Yes.'

'And you saw a gun in there, too?'

Lisa nodded.

'What kind of gun?'

'I don't know . . . a revolver?'

Kent's expression was far from pleasant. 'You should have taken that as well.'

'I didn't have time.'

He stared at the box and sighed. 'Aron Fredh registered as Karl Larsson when he rented the chalet. He paid cash, and didn't give a home address. That meant he could stay at the Ölandic, go anywhere he wanted, and spy on us . . . But if he comes back, we'll have him.' He glanced up. 'What else did you see in the rucksack?'

'Not much . . . Some clothes, and several bottles of water.'

Kent smiled wearily. 'I'm not surprised he had his own water; after all, he'd poisoned ours . . . We know how he did it now.'

'Did what?'

'How he caused the gastroenteritis epidemic,' Kent explained. 'He brought a high-pressure pump in with him, then all he had to do was unscrew the pipes in the chalet, then pump water polluted with dung all through our system.'

304

'It affected the staff, too,' Lisa reminded him.

'Yes, but the guests were his priority.' Kent rubbed his eyes, as if he hadn't slept for several days. 'We've purified the water now, but of course a lot of people have already left. So this is a lost season, as far as we're concerned . . . A complete waste of time.'

Lisa looked at him. 'Why did he do it?'

'What?'

'I mean . . . He must really hate you.'

Kent's eyes were weary and red-rimmed, but his expression was dark. 'That's not something you need to concern yourself with,' he said. 'That would be a mistake.'

'OK.'

Kent stared at her for a long time, then he glanced down at the wooden box again. 'I've seen this before.' He pointed at the double cross burned into the bottom. 'This is our house mark. My grand-father had one exactly the same; all three Kloss brothers had a snuff box made of apple wood. But Sigfrid's and Gilbert's are on a shelf in my kitchen. Edvard's was missing – until now.'

He weighed the box in his hand and added, 'Sigfrid, my grand-father, always carried his box with him. I assume Edvard did the same.'

'So what does that mean?'

'It means that Edvard Kloss had this box with him when he died. And that Aron Fredh was there, and took it.'

In the silence that followed, Lisa considered asking how Edvard had died – whether Aron Fredh had murdered him, perhaps – but she decided to say nothing.

Kloss was beginning to look quite pleased. 'At least he's on the run now. We're watching the chalet, so he can't come back there.'

'Maybe he'll leave the island,' Lisa said.

Kloss didn't reply. Lisa was relieved when he got to his feet and moved towards the door. She still remembered the slap he had deliv-ered, and she couldn't relax when Kent Kloss was around.

'So we're done?' she said.

Kloss stopped in the doorway. 'Not exactly.'

'What do you mean?'

'We haven't finished yet.' Kloss was smiling, but the hunted look was still in his eyes. 'Keep working,' he said. 'I'll be in touch.'

He walked out and shut the door behind him.

Lisa stayed where she was, feeling the walls of the caravan closing in on her. The heat was oppressive; it felt as if some kind of explosion were imminent.

Jonas

There wasn't a sound. It was quarter past ten, and the sun had gone down; a white half-moon was drifting slowly across the Sound, occasionally veiled by thin, wispy clouds. The heat along the coast had been swept away by a cool sea breeze this evening.

Jonas was lying in his little chalet, listening to voices chatting and laughing on the coast road. Boys' voices, but deeper than his own.

It was his brother, Mats, and their cousins. They were down on the ridge with some of their friends from other houses in the village. They all had their bikes and mopeds with them; the older boys met up in different places every evening – down by the restaurant or the jetty, or up by the main road.

Jonas had given up trying to keep tabs on them. He was lying on his bed on top of his very own secret: the gun he had found in the bunker. He still hadn't told anyone about it, not even his dad.

He didn't know if he could trust his father.

Or whom he could trust, in fact.

The laughter outside continued. Jonas ought to get to sleep, but it was impossible. The air inside the chalet was too warm, and he felt wide awake. Eventually he sat up, reached under the mattress, felt the butt of the gun and pulled it out.

It was big and heavy. He felt as if he had grown in stature, just from holding it.

He tucked the barrel into the waistband of his trousers at the back, then pulled on his shirt. He left it loose, just like the gangsters in films did to hide their guns.

Then he went out into the night.

It was dark, but still mild in spite of the breeze. Dry summer air, with the scent of flowers and herbs.

He could see the group of boys over on the ridge, still laughing. He walked through the garden in front of Villa Kloss, picking his way among a series of marker posts that had been driven into the ground; someone was obviously planning a building project. He crossed the coast road, feeling the gun rubbing against his back with every step he took.

As he got closer, he could see that there were five boys in the group. He recognized Mats, who was sitting on his bike. His brother seemed to have grown taller since midsummer, as did Urban and Casper.

The boys fell silent as he approached.

'It's your kid brother,' someone said.

Nobody said hello, but they all turned to look at him.

Perhaps this was the moment to produce the gun, but Jonas didn't do that. He just went over and stood between Mats and Casper, as if he were one of the gang.

The boys resumed their discussion; apparently they had been talking about girls.

'Of course they ought to shave,' someone said.

'Under the arms, anyway.'

Someone laughed. 'And in other places!'

'I shave under my arms, too,' Mats said firmly. 'I mean, you can't have a girl lying with her head on your arm if you haven't shaved there . . . She'd feel as if she had a grizzly bear in her face!'

They were all laughing now. Jonas had nothing to say; he was an outsider.

But he did have one advantage.

He took a step forward and stood next to cousin Casper. He fumbled behind his back and got hold of the gun.

'Look what I've got,' he said quietly to Casper.

He pulled out the gun. He had intended to hold it up so that everyone could see, but it was too heavy, so he just held it in front of him, with the moonlight shining on the barrel.

Once again, they all turned to look at him, and the conversation about girls came to an abrupt end.

'It's a gun,' he said, in case anyone hadn't realized.

A hand reached out, but he moved the gun away. 'I found it,' he said.

'Don't do anything stupid,' Mats said.

Jonas shook his head – he was in control. He would just press the trigger a little bit, a little bit more . . .

Suddenly, a bright light swept over the group. 'What's all this?'

There was a familiar voice behind the light: Uncle Kent's. He must have come up from the shore; he was carrying a torch.

Jonas lowered the gun. He would have hidden it behind his back, but it was too late; Uncle Kent had already seen it.

'Give it to me.'

It wasn't a polite request. He was already holding out his hand, and he took the gun off Jonas.

Kent drew him aside and leaned closer. Jonas could smell alcohol on his uncle's breath.

'It looks real. Where did you find it?'

What could Jonas say?

'Down in the dip,' he said eventually.

'And whose is it?'

'Don't know.'

Kent pushed the gun into his waistband, just as Jonas had done.

'Show me, JK,' he said. 'Show me exactly where you found it.'

The boys were all looking at him now; he was definitely the centre of attention. There was nothing to say; he set off along the ridge and down the stone steps. Kent followed him, lighting the way with his torch.

When they reached the dip, Jonas turned north and led Kent to the door of the bunker. It was closed and locked.

'It was here,' he said.

'By the door?'

Jonas shook his head. 'The bunker was open.'

Kent shone the beam of his torch on the rusty metal door and the padlock.

'So someone has a key . . .' he muttered. 'Unless they've changed the lock.'

He went over and tugged at it, but it didn't move.

'There was someone inside,' Jonas said. 'It sounded as if he was digging.'

'Digging? Someone was in there digging?'

Jonas nodded, and Kent stood in silence for a moment, then straightened up. 'OK,' he said. 'Good. Let's go home.'

Kent turned and made his way back to the stone steps. The gun was still tucked in his waistband, as if it belonged to him now.

The Homecomer

Trapped and frightened . . . The Homecomer had dreamed the old dream again, the nightmare about a little boy being forced to crawl in beneath the barn wall.

'*In you go,*' Sven had growled, sweaty and stressed in the forest. '*Get in there and fetch his money.*'

Into the darkness. Aron had crawled in over the cold earth, in beneath the hard wooden wall. Past the nails reaching out for him. One of them had scratched his forehead, but he had kept on going.

Towards the body.

Edvard Kloss, his real father, who was lying there underneath the wall.

Trapped. Motionless.

Aron had felt something hard in Edvard's trouser pocket: a wooden snuff box. He took it, and fumbled in the other pocket, where he found a fat wallet and pulled it out.

At which point the body twitched. There was a whimpering sound, and a hand closed around Aron's arm.

Edvard Kloss was still alive.

Aron had panicked in the darkness. He raised the hand holding the wooden box and struck at the body. Hit his father on the head, on the temple, several times. Over and over again.

Edvard fell silent, and the hand around Aron's arm lost its grip.

The Homecomer woke in the car with a start.

His father was gone. He was alone.

The morning sun was finding its way through the birch trees and had reached the car, but its rays did not warm the Homecomer. He remembered too much.

They had found the chalet where he was staying at the Ölandic; he had got away with only his rucksack, nothing more. He had had to leave his shoes, clothes and two guns. And Kloss had stolen Sven's snuff box.

He couldn't go back. Nor could he sleep in the car any longer – his old bones were too stiff. If this was his last week on the island (and that was how he felt), then he needed to be well rested.

He needed a proper bed.

He had to find a new hiding place, somewhere in or near Stenvik.

It was seven o'clock, and the summer's day had begun. Cars and trucks were starting to zoom past along the main road.

The Homecomer started the car. He pulled out of the car park and headed north.

Right now, he was on the run, but it was only temporary.

The New Country, May 1937

After six long years, Aron is back in Leningrad as a new man: Vladimir Nikolajevitch Jegerov. Back by the wide bay leading out into the Baltic Sea – the bay that was the gateway to the new country for Aron and Sven.

Back then, they stayed in a hotel, but now Vlad is living in the barracks while he waits for a single room of his own.

Vlad the soldier has not brought very much with him when it comes to mementoes of the long, hard years in the north. A Party membership card, a uniform, a few minor scars on his face and a torso pitted with the marks left by scratching countless mosquito stings and louse bites. And his name and citizenship, of course. It has become Aron's name now, his whole identity: Vlad Jegerov. The Swede within him is carefully locked away.

The old concrete buildings in Leningrad are not as tall as he remembers them. The city seems low, stretching out along the banks of the shining River Neva, but new palaces exuding power have been built in honour of Stalin.

Vlad's workplace is not as beautiful as the palaces, but it is substantial and impressive. It is Kresty Prison, a red-brick five-storey building surrounded by a wall four metres high and built in the shape of a huge cross. On each floor the corridors run straight through the prison, with rows of cell doors on each side. There are thousands of prisoners behind those doors, twenty or thirty men in each cell. Very little noise seeps out, and it takes a death scream to persuade the guards to open them.

The cellar is also soundproofed. That is where Vlad will be working, in the innermost interrogation room. The air is thick with the smell of sweat and blood and cheap cleaning products, and the doors are even more impressive.

The new colleagues Vlad encounters in the corridors are tall and grim-faced, but they have a certain style and elegance; they move gracefully in their dark-blue NKVD uniforms. They glance at his grey coat and worn boots and smile at one another. Vlad realizes he is a country bumpkin.

'Come in, Comrade Jegerov.'

His new commanding officer, Captain Rugajev, welcomes him into his office and offers him tea and a piece of dried black pudding. The captain carefully studies the new guard's Party membership book and other documents, giving Vlad the chance to look around the room.

He sees Stalin gazing into the future on the wall behind Rugajev, of course. To the right of his portrait is a poster featuring a Soviet worker dragging a long, venomous serpent out from under a stone, with the caption 'We will eradicate spies and saboteurs!'

Eventually, Rugajev nods and hands back the papers. Then he smiles at Vlad's scruffy uniform, just as amused as everyone else in Kresty. He gets to his feet.

'Look in here, Comrade.' Rugajev opens a cupboard, which is full of neatly pressed uniforms and shiny leather boots. 'We were issued with new outfits in the spring as a reward for our hard work. Choose one that fits you.'

Vlad quickly glances along the row and picks out a uniform. Rugajev hands over a gun belt with a leather holster, and a brand-new pistol. A Mauser.

'There is a great deal of night work here in Kresty Prison.' The captain nods towards the portrait on the wall. 'Our leader works late into the night, and so do we.' Then he nods towards the picture of the worker and the serpent. 'And that is our job, day *and* night. But you were hunting down our enemies up in the north, weren't you, Comrade Jegerov? All the time?'

Vlad nods. He understands what the Mauser is for.

'Can you type, Comrade?'

'No, Captain.'

'Then learn. You will be conducting many interrogations, and they must be documented and filed. Go and see Comrade Trushkin in the morning.'

Before he does anything, Vlad changes his clothes in one of the guardrooms. He takes off his old uniform and puts on his new black boots, billowing blue trousers with sharp, dark-red lines, a light-brown jacket, the leather gun belt with the Mauser in its holster and, finally, the wide peaked cap with a brown band around it and the red star in the centre.

He looks in the mirror and lifts his chin, like a sheriff. Now he fits in here. He is ready.

And there is a lot of work, just as Rugajev said.

The first prisoner Vlad interrogates is an emaciated, worn-down man who is fetched from his cell in dirty underclothes; he was arrested for crimes against Article 58 of the Soviet Penal Code, which is always used when charging enemies of the state.

Vlad positions himself on the cement floor just a metre away from the prisoner, his legs wide apart. Perhaps Rugajev has given him something simple to start with, because this man is already broken. Fear shines in his eyes when he is placed in the interrogation chair.

Vlad hears the rustle of papers behind him. He turns his head; he hadn't noticed, but an older colleague has entered the room and sat down at a desk over by the wall. He is there to record proceedings and is feeding a sheet of paper into his typewriter.

It is time. Vlad looks at the prisoner. 'Tell me about your crimes,' he says quietly.

The man starts talking almost before Vlad has finished, his head drooping. 'I am a Trotskyite. At the beginning of the year, I decided to sabotage several machines that were absolutely essential for production at my tractor factory in Charkov. I threw hammers and chisels into the machinery, and it was only thanks to the intervention of a quick-thinking foreman that a total shutdown was avoided.'

'What else did you do?'

'I recruited several other workers to my Trotskyite group, in order to increase the incidence of sabotage within the factory.'

'And who are these individuals?'

The saboteur starts reeling off names, and the typewriter clatters into action.

They are given a dozen or so names.

When the saboteur has finished, he seems relieved. He looks up at Vlad. 'I am evil,' he says. 'Aren't I?'

315

He is still looking at Vlad, who does not reply.

Aron doesn't know what to say either.

The typewriter has stopped clattering. In the silence that follows, the last sheet of paper is removed, and the typist hands it to Vlad.

It is time for the saboteur's signature.

Vlad holds out the document and the prisoner signs it with a trembling hand.

As Vlad watches him sign the confession, he feels better. Standing erect in his new uniform in front of an enemy of the state is terrific. Getting him to admit his crimes is a small but important victory in a major war.

After completing his first few shifts, Vlad begins to learn how to type. How to feed the paper into the roller, how to tap out the words. Comrade Trushkin teaches him with patience, one key at a time.

Grigori Trushkin is a couple of years older than Vlad, a Russian worker's son who, like many other guards, was trained in the Young Pioneers and Komsomol. He was only four years old when the Bolsheviks brought down the Tsar; he remembers nothing other than the Communist government. After leaving school, he was forged into a young OGPU soldier when the wealthy farmers had to be broken at the beginning of the thirties. Trushkin can discuss Marxism and class struggles without any problem, but he also enjoys chess, and loves to play Stravinsky's *Rite of Spring* on his gramophone, in spite of the fact that it has been banned for many years.

'Stravinsky came from my home town,' he says proudly.

Trushkin takes Vlad out and about in Leningrad, and does what Sven never did with Aron: he allows him to discover the city.

The heels of their boots tap loudly on the wide, cobbled streets of Leningrad, and their blue uniforms make them highly visible. They are never stopped by the police and asked to show their identity papers, not once. They merely nod, like colleagues. And all around them on the pavements, ordinary citizens lower their voices and glance away nervously.

Vlad feels good when he is with Grigori Trushkin. So does Aron. They wander along the quayside by the River Neva and visit a dimly lit teahouse, eventually ending up in a smoky restaurant where vodka glasses are frequently raised – but Trushkin doesn't drink as much as many of his colleagues. He prefers hot chocolate.

Later, in a grocery shop in the city, Vlad finds anchovies and smoked eel from the Baltic. He buys some pieces of fish and savours every mouthful – and suddenly Aron is thinking of the island across the sea, and his own shore.

He ought to get in touch, write home to his mother. But it's impossible, of course. Countries outside Russia are full of spies, and anyone who is in contact with foreigners also becomes a spy. Letters are much too dangerous.

After three months' hard work, Vlad is given a reward by Rugajev: a watch, presumably confiscated from an enemy of the state. He places it on his left wrist so that he will know what time it is when he is interrogating prisoners or writing up reports.

The pressure is increasing from above, with constant demands to elicit more and more names.

Comrade Trushkin conducts interrogations that are at least as harsh as anyone else's, but one evening, as Vlad is about to run and catch him up a few blocks to the north of Kresty, he sees Trushkin stop by a park bench, then bend down and drop something on the ground before quickly moving on.

Vlad walks up to the bench and picks up an envelope addressed to a woman in Leningrad.

He stares at the name: Olga Bibikova. He recognizes the address; he has written it down himself after an interrogation.

Maxim Bibikov's wife. But Bibikov is dead; he got a bullet in the back of his neck three days ago.

Vlad doesn't understand, so he hurries along and catches up with Trushkin. 'Comrade.' He holds up the letter. 'What's this?'

Trushkin looks, and smiles like a shy schoolboy. This is unusual.

'It's just a letter.' He grabs the envelope and slips it in his pocket. 'I leave it in a dry spot on the street in the hope that someone will find it and post it.'

'But why?' Vlad asks. 'What kind of letter is it?'

Trushkin laughs, quietly and nervously. 'It's just a message.'

'About what?'

'I wrote and told Bibikov's wife that he died of tuberculosis,'

Trushkin says. 'So that she won't have to keep wondering what's happened to him.'

Vlad looks around; there is no sign of anyone else in a blue uniform. Vlad wants to move on, but Aron makes him stay, ask more questions. It transpires that Trushkin has written a series of anonymous letters to the relatives of those who have been executed, informing them that their husband or father has passed away following a heart attack or a lung infection. Short letters, admittedly, but still . . .

'It saves them wondering what's happened,' Trushkin says again, with a shrug. 'It's just to give them peace of mind.'

Aron nods silently, but Vlad is furious. *Letters are dangerous.* They leave a trail. And he knows that this is wrong, writing letters and sympathizing with the enemy.

'Stop writing them,' he says to Trushkin. 'Immediately.'

Sympathy is the wrong attitude – it means the battle is lost.

Vlad refuses to participate in this particular battle, in spite of the fact that anxious wives and parents regularly turn up at the prison. They stand there with warm clothes and food parcels for the prisoners, pleading for help. As a guard, Vlad is used to it. He listens to them, his face expressionless, and gives the response he has been taught to give: '*Razberemsja.* We will take a closer look at this case.'

Silently, he wonders, how can these people still be at liberty? They are related to criminals; they should all be arrested. This does happen frequently, but there are still many left out there.

Why haven't we seized all our enemies yet?

Vlad must not lose his grip, not here at Kresty in his uniform. If a woman with frightened eyes stops him in the street, perhaps with a child in her arms, he simply stares her down and goes on his way.

And if she won't give up, if she calls after him and catches him up, he stops, plants his legs in their shiny boots wide apart, and replies, 'I'm sorry. Your husband has been moved elsewhere.'

Which is always true.

Gerlof

As the sun blazed down on the landscape outside the windows, Gerlof drifted around the corridors of the residential home. It was cool and airy inside, and it was easy to get about. There were no raised thresholds, no stones, no clumps of grass – but it was lonely. Very little happened.

He had few visitors. John was busy with the shop and the campsite, and Tilda was away on holiday. His daughters popped in, but they were always on the way to somewhere else.

There was a poster by the main door advertising a course that was due to begin in August: 'Make Friends with the Net'. Gerlof assumed it didn't have anything to do with learning to fish.

He missed the talks they had during the rest of the year. Veronica Kloss had come in to talk about her family history, and it had been really interesting. Now, of course, he knew quite a lot more about the Kloss family than she had mentioned that day.

There was a small library in the home, so he went down there and found a book by an Anglo-American historian, Robert Conquest, about the Soviet Union in the thirties. He borrowed it and took it up to his room. He wanted to know what kind of life Aron and Sven Fredh had encountered when they reached the new country, and the title of the book made him fear the worst. It was called *The Great Terror*.

One quiet Friday towards the end of July, Gerlof took the lift down to the ground floor. It was just as cool and quiet down there. Using his walking stick for support, he made his way slowly along the corridor. Greta Fredh's room had been almost at the end, if he remembered rightly. It was now occupied by someone called Blenda Pettersson, according to the name on the door.

He remembered what Aron had said on the phone: 'They took everything I had here.' He had meant the croft by the shore. Nothing else. Hadn't he?

Gerlof looked at the nameplate, but didn't knock.

'Hello there – are you lost?'

A dark-haired, tanned young woman was smiling at him; she was wearing a red uniform and was obviously a temporary member of staff.

Gerlof shook his head and introduced himself. 'I live upstairs,' he said. 'I'm just having a little wander round, calling in on my neighbours.'

'Oh, I see. Our residents down here tend to spend most of their time in their rooms; the heat makes them very tired. Do you know Blenda?'

Gerlof shook his head again, but the girl had already opened the door. 'We can go in, I need to check on her anyway . . . Hi, Blenda!'

Gerlof felt like an intruder, but followed her anyway.

He walked into a small apartment that was almost an exact replica of his own: a hallway with a worn plastic mat, a spacious bathroom with an adapted shower on the left, and a bedroom beyond the hallway. A woman with thin white hair was slumped in an armchair.

Gerlof couldn't work out whether she was awake or not. The girl chatted away to Blenda, but got no response. She tidied the bed, filled a glass with water and set out several tablets. Then the visit was over.

But Gerlof lingered outside the door. 'The lady who used to live in this room before Blenda . . . Greta, wasn't it?'

'Greta Fredh, that's right. She died last summer, when I was filling in over the holidays. It was in the middle of August.'

'Did she have a fall?' Gerlof asked, vaguely remembering something Sonja Bengtsson, the gravedigger's daughter, had told him.

'That's right.' The girl lowered her voice, as if Death might be listening. 'Greta fell and hit her head in the bathroom. The lock might as well have been glued shut; we had to send for a locksmith to let us in . . . but by then it was too late.'

Gerlof looked at the door. 'Did Greta have any visitors? Any relatives who sometimes came to see her?'

The girl thought for a moment. 'Veronica Kloss used to come and read books and magazines to her . . . You know, the woman who runs the Ölandic?'

Gerlof nodded. He knew very well. 'But they weren't related, were they?'

'Greta sometimes claimed they were, but she was very confused towards the end.'

'Any other visitors?'

'Not as far as I know. Not while she was alive. Her brother was here a couple of times earlier this summer, but I think he was just collecting some of her things.'

Gerlof gave a start. 'Did this brother tell you his name?'

'Yes . . . Arnold.'

'Aron,' Gerlof said.

'Oh yes, Aron. But he didn't say much; he was very quiet.'

'What did he look like?'

'Old, but in good shape. Tall and broad-shouldered . . . He seemed to have lots of energy, even though he must have been getting on for eighty.' She looked at Gerlof, and quickly added, 'Mind you, that's no age.'

'Age is all in the mind,' Gerlof responded.

He thanked the girl and set off along the corridor. He saw the name 'Wall' on the room next door. Ulf Wall. Who was that? The father of Einar Wall, who had been murdered? Perhaps, because the picture of Einar Wall that the police had shown him seemed to have been taken just here.

Ulf Wall's door was firmly closed. Gerlof didn't knock; he kept on going. He was desperate for a cup of coffee, and he could only get one back in his own section.

Jonas

Uncle Kent was wearing a black T-shirt and khaki camouflage shorts; he was almost behaving like a soldier, marching up and down in front of the family and staff at Villa Kloss – and for the first time in days he looked quite pleased with himself, Jonas thought.

'The alarm is triggered by a motion sensor,' he said. 'It's switched off using a remote control. You have one minute to deactivate it once you step on to our land. It's also millennium-proof, so it will work after New Year.'

Jonas listened to Kent's presentation, surrounded by Mats and their cousins, Aunt Veronica, his father, Paulina and a gardener who had only just started working for the family. His name was Marc, and he came from somewhere abroad; he was muscular and very tanned.

They were gathered in the garden at the front of the house, which currently looked like a moonscape. The grass, the shrubs and the viper's bugloss were gone; everything had been ripped up and replaced with fine gravel. Over the past few days, Jonas had realized what the temporary markers that had appeared the previous week were for.

They had now been replaced by a dozen small posts, buried in the ground with only a couple of centimetres showing. They were made of black plastic, but Jonas thought they looked like the wooden poles in a gill net.

'Sensors', that's what Kent called them. He reminded everyone several times that they were extremely sensitive, then pointed to a panel next to the garage.

'This is the control panel for the external alarm. You use one code to activate it and a different one to switch it off.'

He pointed towards the house.

'The control panel for the intruder alarm is on the wall just inside. You open the door and switch it off. It covers the guest chalets as well.'

He gazed at the assembled group. 'Good,' he said. 'So now we have both an external and internal alarm to guard against intruders; everyone will be given the codes. Any questions?'

No one said anything. All Jonas wanted to do was slip away.

'What about the hares?'

Jonas looked around; his father had put up his hand.

'I'm sorry?' Kent said.

'There are hares all over the place at night,' Niklas went on. 'Won't they set off the alarm when they run across the garden?'

'Yes,' Kent said. 'Which is why we're getting a fence next week. One and a half metres high, all the way round Villa Kloss, with an automatic gate. The hares won't get over that.'

Aunt Veronica was standing slightly apart from everyone else; she had remained silent so far. She wasn't in camouflage gear, just a pale-green dress, and now she was shaking her head. 'I'm not having some kind of Berlin Wall around my part of the property,' she said.

'It's quite a low fence,' Kent insisted. 'Even the boys will be able to see over it.'

Veronica stared at him. 'Our family is not going to hide.'

'No, but we do need to protect ourselves until things calm down. This isn't just a petty quarrel between neighbours, Veronica.'

Her eyes narrowed. 'Don't do anything stupid.' With that, she turned and went back to her own house.

Kent ignored her; he took several small pieces of paper out of his pocket and addressed the group once more. 'Good, that's everything, then . . . Come and collect your copy of the alarm codes.'

Jonas joined the queue; as he was waiting, he looked over at the cairn. It had been quiet there for the past few days; one or two tourists had stopped to gaze at the stones, but there had been no sign of an old man.

'Can you see anything, JK?'

Jonas turned his head and saw Uncle Kent smiling at him. He was holding out a piece of paper, and Jonas took it. 'No,' he said. 'Not a thing.'

Kent glanced down at the road. 'I know someone is watching us,' he said quietly. 'An old man who sometimes sneaks into the bunker . . . But we're going to take care of that particular problem.'

Lisa

'Are you feeling all right?'

Lisa was playing her guitar at the restaurant in Stenvik. It was Saturday night, and the place was more or less full; there were a couple of empty tables inside, but the outside tables were packed. Presumably, most people were there for the beer and pizza and the view over the bay rather than for the music, but it didn't matter.

The odd '*Yeeaah* . . .' drifted back to her.

'Good to be here!' she said into the microphone.

It was all a bit of a cliché, but it *did* feel good to be there, even if her voice was starting to sound hoarse after several weeks of shout-outs and singing, constantly trying to make herself heard above the hum of conversation. It was much nicer to be out here in the evening sun by the sea, rather than down in the cellar in the nightclub. Any pleasure in playing Lady Summertime over there had completely disappeared.

Here in the village, her audience consisted only of ordinary holidaymakers who wanted to relax. Playing records in the May Lai Bar had been something completely different over the past week; it had felt like playing in a tomb. The upper-class brats who had been there at the beginning of July, throwing their money around, had moved on to Gotland or Stockholm, leaving the place empty and much too quiet.

However, here at the restaurant, there were people to entertain, and she was enjoying herself.

'Thank you!' she said in response to scattered applause. 'And now here's a song by Olle Adolphson, which you just might recognize . . .'

It was a warm evening with a golden sunset. Lisa brought out the old Swedish songs about the beauty and fragility of the summer, knowing that all this would soon be over. It was almost August. The summer was short, there was no denying it. Life wasn't that simple; you couldn't just drift around doing whatever you wanted while the sun was shining.

She had less than a week left in Stenvik, then she would be going home, back to the city and its exhaust fumes. Back to Silas, to answer his questions about why she hadn't sent any money, and what she was going to do about it.

The setting sun was in Lisa's eyes, but she tried to focus on her audience. Most tables were full, but right at the back she could just see a man on his own, with a glass of water in front of him. He was only a dark shadow against the sun, but he was nodding in time with the music.

Was it the man from the campsite? Was he watching her? Did he want the wooden box back?

Concentrate, she thought.

She closed her eyes and sang, trying to forget about the man. Otherwise, she would lose it.

She managed two more songs, with her eyes shut. When she looked up, the man had disappeared.

'Thank you!' she shouted, and it was over. She slid off her stool and made her way into the darkness of the restaurant.

Niklas Kloss was standing by the till. He had seemed tired and distracted over the past week, moving at a completely different speed from the waiters and waitresses and spending most of his time hanging around by the chiller cabinet. She presumed that the outbreak of gastroenteritis at the Ölandic had given the whole Kloss family sleepless nights.

'Well done,' he said.

That was it. Time to go home. But as Lisa left the restaurant, someone stepped out of the shadows. A slim figure, moving quietly across the gravel.

'Lisa?'

It was Paulina, and she was smiling a little uncertainly. 'Nice music,' she said.

'Thanks.'

Lisa wondered how long Paulina had been standing there listening.

326

Why hadn't she sat down at one of the tables? Was she shy, or didn't she have any money?

'You are going back now, Lisa?' she said, nodding towards the campsite.

'Yep,' Lisa said, picking up her guitar case. 'Back to the caravan for a rest before my last gigs.'

Paulina walked beside her in the darkness, past the maypole with its withered garlands. As they were crossing the coast road, she jerked her head towards Villa Kloss and said quietly, 'He has a suggestion.'

'Oh yes?'

Lisa didn't need to ask who 'he' was – Kent Kloss, of course.

'He has a job for you. For us,' Paulina went on.

'Another gig?'

'No, a different kind of job . . . here in the village.'

Lisa looked at Paulina. 'What does he really want? Is he exploiting you?'

Paulina gazed at her for a moment, trying to work out what Lisa meant, then she shook her head. 'No,' she said. 'I'm not like that. I just work for him.'

She sounded so definite that Lisa was sorry she had asked the question and quickly changed the subject. 'So how did you get the job here?'

'An advert. He put an advert in lots of newspapers, and I answered.'

'Just like me,' Lisa said with a sigh.

Paulina looked at her. 'He's going to talk to us soon. He wants more help.'

'I know,' Lisa said wearily. 'I've already helped him, down on the campsite.'

She knew that this wasn't a request for help, of course. Kent Kloss didn't make requests. He gave orders.

'He'll pay,' Paulina said.

'Will he, indeed? And is this job legal?'

Paulina didn't say anything, and Lisa shrugged. Legal or not, she had her price.

'OK,' she said. 'In that case, maybe I'll help him one last time before I go home.'

The Homecomer

There was a hotel in the village on the coast to the north of Stenvik – a huge white colossus not unlike the Ölandic Hotel, right by the harbour in Långvik.

The Homecomer pulled into the car park, then went into Reception. A young girl in a white blouse and shorts who looked as if she was about to go and play tennis welcomed him. He smiled at her.

'Do you have any vacancies?'

'We had a cancellation yesterday evening,' the girl said, looking at her computer. 'It's a double room.'

'I'm on my own, but I'll take it.'

'Excellent.' The receptionist entered something into the computer. 'Do you have some form of ID? A driving licence?'

The Homecomer stared at her. He hadn't been asked for anything like that at the Ölandic.

'No,' he said. 'Nothing Swedish . . . I'm from overseas.'

'So you have a passport?' the receptionist said. 'We have to register overseas guests.'

The Homecomer didn't say anything.

Register. That meant they would contact the police. Or Kloss. Had Kent Kloss asked them to keep an eye open for him?

'It's in the car,' he said in the end. 'I'll go and get it.'

He backed away and hurried out of the hotel; he could feel the receptionist watching him the whole time.

He got in the car and drove away. Out of Långvik, up on to the main road. There were lots of cars there; it was easy to blend in, become one of the crowd.

Then he suddenly remembered a hiding place where he could stay. He had been there before.

A place near to the Kloss family property but still out of the way.

He turned off the main road, constantly checking in his rear-view mirror. No one.

The New Country, February 1938

Aron has turned twenty, and this year is full of work and news. From the cellar in Leningrad, he hears radio reports of political trials and major purges of Party officials in Moscow. But Vlad himself is promoted to the rank of lieutenant within the NKVD.

This brings privileges. Each month, Vlad receives a book of coupons that he can use to shop at Insnab, the new shop for employees of the state, which sells foreign goods and clothes.

His new rank also brings respect. As an NKVD man, Vlad wears his uniform in the street, attracting brief glances from his fellow citizens – deferential looks from *babusjkas*, admiration from small boys. He stands for law and order, a symbol of security in a world full of enemies.

But there is a great deal of work. Night work. With Captain Rugajev, Comrades Trushkin and Popov, and all the rest.

The interrogation of the prisoners often takes place in shifts, down in the cellar, with posters on the walls displaying slogans such as 'Towards the future with Communism!' and 'Carry out your task with Soviet honour!'

Vlad and the other interrogators grow tired, and tiredness makes them violent, but at least they are allowed to rest sometimes. The prisoners are never allowed to rest. A prisoner who must be broken is placed on a hard chair in bright light and is bombarded with questions, often day and night, non-stop:

'Why are you spying for Japan?'

'Why didn't you raise your glass in a toast to the Party?'

'Why did you laugh at that particular joke?'

The questions are endless.

So is the stream of prisoners. Higher powers in Moscow have established that there are thousands of enemies of the state, perhaps millions. Every NKVD commissariat has been issued with a quota of people who are to be deported and executed, which means that people must be arrested.

The black vans go out every night, picking up more and more enemies of the state and delivering them to the prison. Sometimes they are dressed in expensive furs, sometimes in flimsy pyjamas. Sometimes they have small children in their arms, or following behind them in tears.

Late at night, Aron occasionally hears knocking in the darkness of the cellar, a protracted, quiet tapping. It unsettles him, but every time he approaches the rhythmic sounds they stop.

'It's a kind of language,' Trushkin explains.

'A language?'

'The prisoners are talking to one another from cell to cell, tapping out a code on the wall.'

'Oh?'

'We try to stop them,' Trushkin says, 'but they just carry on knocking.'

Aron relaxes slightly. It is people who are knocking.

The prisoners are processed as if they are on a conveyor belt; everything is organized to be as quick and easy as possible.

All prisoners are examined, stripped naked, their bodily orifices are searched, then they are immediately taken down to the cellar, shaking and terrified. Vlad stands there in his uniform, his black boots firmly planted on the cement floor, and Aron hears him ask the same questions over and over again:

'Why have you been slandering the Party?'

'Why did you sabotage the machinery?'

'What are the names of the agents you recruited?'

When Vlad's voice begins to grow hoarse, one of his colleagues takes over.

Comrade Trushkin never tires as an interrogator, no matter how long his shift, and Vlad regards him as a role model. Trushkin hurls himself at every prisoner, spitting out question after question:

'Why did you join the Trotskyites?'

331

'Why do you want to leave your homeland?'

'Why didn't you think about your children?'

Sometimes, other prisoners are brought in, those who are already broken, to help persuade intractable saboteurs to admit to the crimes of which they are accused.

Sometimes, prisoners who suffer from claustrophobia are locked up in particularly confined spaces, where the walls and ceiling seem to close in around them. Shivering prisoners are put in ice-cold cells; those with a fever are sluiced down with cold water. Torture is an approved interrogation method, and a *dubinka*, a rubber baton, is used on their backs and the soles of their feet.

There are many methods, but the goal is always the same: to obtain a written confession, the scribbled signature at the bottom of the notes taken during the interrogation, scrawled in ink which is often mixed with drops of blood.

The confession provides proof that the interrogation has gone well. Proof that the enemy is guilty.

Vlad writes down all the names they gabble. Names, titles, crimes.

Then the notes are read and signed by the criminal.

And after that: *Vysshaia mera*. The ultimate punishment under the law.

The bullet.

The death chamber in the cellar is also used as a barbershop. When the prisoners are led in, they never know what is coming, because the prison authorities have decided that the executioners and the barbers should wear the same uniform.

The door has extra soundproofing and is firmly closed. A gramophone in one corner plays energetic marching music at full volume. The back wall is white and looks harmless, but in fact it is a sheet of plasterboard with timber and a thick layer of sand behind it to catch the bullets.

The prisoners' fate becomes apparent only when they are forced to stand in a white square on the cement floor, facing the wall, but by then it is too late. Four or five seconds of stillness as the music plays, then the executioner steps forward and fires.

And the gramophone keeps on playing.

Captain Rugajev often selects Vlad to serve in the death chamber, and Aron knows why: his aim is perfect. Many of the guards are less than adept with a pistol and have to use two bullets, sometimes even three. But Vlad takes careful aim.

If it is not possible to shoot a prisoner – perhaps because the body will have to be shown to some foreign diplomat afterwards – then a chloroform mask is placed over the face, and a doctor administers a fatal injection so that the death looks like the result of a sudden heart attack.

After a long shift, the floor must always be washed. Some of the cleaners cannot be trusted, so occasionally a prisoner is given the job, but often the guards have to do it themselves.

One evening, Trushkin and Vlad are working together in the cellar, with a stiff brush and a hosepipe.

'Do you know what we are, Comrade?' Trushkin asks as he sluices down the walls. 'It's just come to me.'

'No,' Vlad says. 'What are we?'

'We are like a small part of a combine harvester,' Trushkin says. 'Do you know what that is?'

Vlad shakes his head.

'It's a fantastic machine. They've started appearing on the *kolkhozy* instead of sickles and scythes. I saw one trundling along outside Moscow last year.'

'What does it do?'

'Everything! It's a single machine that does everything in the fields – the work that one or two hundred farmers would have done. And, of course, it never gets tired!'

Aron pictures a human monster striding across a field, so he asks, 'What's it made of?'

'Iron bars, metal drums and rotating cogs and wheels.'

'And a scythe?'

'Knives,' Trushkin explains. 'Long rows of knives, so the crop is cut down and fed into the thresher, where the grain is separated from the chaff. Then all you have to do is start baking bread . . . And when I saw it rolling along, I thought that our organization is like a combine harvester, driven by Comrade Stalin.' He rinses away the last traces of blood from the corner of the cellar. 'You and I are the knives.'

Aron brushes the water away. A combine harvester? But it is not

333

enough to thresh the grain, it must also be *crushed* in order to obtain flour.

Trushkin never tires of the threshing process in the cellar, but after a long, hard summer, at the end of July 1938 he is sent away on a well-earned holiday by the Black Sea. Vlad continues the nightshifts without him.

'What state are you spying for?' he asks.

'What is your codename?'

'Who recruited you?'

There seems to be no end to the interrogations, or the paperwork.

Aron's only consolation is that the struggle cannot continue for ever. Peace must surely come soon, and the croft on the island across the Baltic Sea will still be there, waiting for him. The croft and the shore, his sister and his mother. He will go home, when the last enemy is gone.

But they keep on coming. On the night of 4 August 1938, a prisoner is brought down to the cellar with a bag over his head and a coat draped around his shoulders. The bag is nothing new as far as Vlad is concerned; it happens often in the summer when the nights are light and the transportation of enemies has to be carried out more openly.

Otherwise, this prisoner looks like all the rest. He is wearing stained underclothes beneath the coat and his legs are covered in cuts and bruises.

'Number 3498,' the clerk says, inserting a new sheet of paper in his typewriter.

Vlad is ready. Three buckets of ice-cold water are standing by the wall and the *dubinka* is lying on the table. He quickly pulls the bag off the prisoner's head – and stands there holding it in his hand.

It is Trushkin.

Comrade Trushkin, Aron's friend, is sitting on the chair in front of him.

Trushkin doesn't say a word; his lips are cracked, but he looks at Vlad. He is staring straight into Aron.

Aron turns to his colleague. 'I don't understand,' he says.

'What don't you understand?'

334

Aron looks back at Trushkin. 'I don't understand why he has been brought here. Why we have to . . .'

The clerk picks up a document and reads, 'Prisoner 3498 has been in contact with the relatives of enemies of the people. He has sent letters to them.'

Aron clears his throat, looks into the prisoner's bloodshot eyes. Comrade Trushkin knows where he is: at the start of the hard road leading to a full confession. He knows that the chair on which he is sitting will get wet, that the floor beneath him will soon be covered in stains.

'Anything else?' Vlad asks over his shoulder.

'Indeed. He was planning a coup from within the organization when they picked him up down in Sochi. He was the spider at the centre of a web of foreign spies . . . I'm sure we will get plenty of new names tonight.'

Aron nods stiffly. His colleague adds, 'You two know one another, don't you?'

'What?' Aron says.

'You and Trushkin. You used to go drinking together in your free time, didn't you? You're friends, aren't you?'

Vlad shakes his head. 'That is incorrect.'

The room falls silent. He is expecting Trushkin to say something, to open his mouth and protest, but it doesn't happen. Trushkin merely stares blankly at him.

'That is incorrect,' Vlad says again. 'We are not friends.'

Aron wonders if anyone has the cellar under surveillance. An ear pressed to the door? An eye peeping in through a gap? One of his commanding officers could walk in at any moment, wondering what they're doing, why nothing is happening – so he walks resolutely up to the prisoner, removes his coat and pulls up his vest. Trushkin's back is still milky white, free of cuts and bruises.

'Let us begin,' Vlad says.

He suppresses Aron's whining objections. They both know that Trushkin was wrong: they are not parts of a combine harvester down here in the cellar. They are parts of a windmill. They work at the millstones, and Stalin is the master miller. But the mill is driven by the wind, and right now the wind is blowing so hard across the new country that no one can stop it. Not even Stalin.

The quota of enemies must be met, new names are needed, and Vlad can see that Trushkin understands this. They must both do their duty now.

Trushkin is looking down at the cement floor. Only his back is visible.

Aron crawls away, but Vlad steps forward.

He picks up the *dubinka* and begins the interrogation.

Jonas

Uncle Kent's wooden decking looked brand new, in Jonas's opinion. He was very pleased with himself. It was time to move on to Aunt Veronica's decking; the only thing left to sort out between him and Kent was his wages.

The money.

He had put it off as long as possible, and now it was late evening. Eventually, he went over to the house. There was a faint light showing in the windows of the living room, so he slid open the glass door.

It was hot and stuffy inside; the fans were turned off. Jonas could see bills and sports gear all over the floor and the bag of golf clubs had fallen over just by the door. He listened but couldn't hear a thing. He was reaching out to switch on the main light when a voice said, 'Don't put the light on.'

Jonas stopped and peered into the room. The TV wasn't on, but someone was sitting in the armchair in front of it.

The cairn ghost, he thought. The cairn ghost has come into the house.

'Evening, JK – how's it going?'

Jonas recognized Kent's voice and took a couple of steps across the stone floor.

'Fine . . .' he said. 'I'm due to be paid today. For the decking.'

Kent nodded slowly. 'Absolutely. Come over here.'

Jonas slowly moved closer and saw Uncle Kent get up, swaying slightly. There was an empty bottle on the table.

Kent smiled and took out his wallet. 'There you go, JK.'

Jonas went over and took the money. 'Thanks.'

'You're welcome,' Kent said, patting his forehead. His fingers were ice-cold. 'Are you happy here, JK?'

Jonas nodded.

'Good,' Kent said. 'That's good. I like people to be happy at Villa Kloss.' He looked around. 'I've always been happy here. We used to have some wild parties back in the day, me and Niklas and our friends . . . We used to bring girls down from Stockholm and crack open the bubbly. I had a water bed in those days, as big as the swimming pool. We'd party around the clock sometimes. Have a little nap in the sun in the morning, then start all over again down on the shore at lunchtime.'

He looked at Jonas and wrapped his hand around the back of the boy's neck. 'But there is one thing I can tell you, JK, and it's important. Are you listening?'

Jonas felt as if his whole body had gone rigid, but he managed another nod.

'One thing I've learned,' Kent said, 'is that there's always clearing up to do after a party. The longer you party, the more clearing up you have to do. Can you remember that?'

Jonas held his breath, then said, 'OK.'

'Well done, JK.' Kent removed his hand. 'I realize you might have been wondering about what happened near Marnäs the other night . . . me, too. But I only wanted to *talk* to Mayer, ask him what he was up to. Last season, he stole money from us so, obviously, we had no choice but to sack him. And then this year he boarded our ship in the Ölandic dock, locked the crew in the hold and cast off. So I wanted to speak to him, but he ran away from me, straight through the forest and out on to the road. And then a car came along and . . .'

Kent looked out at the alarm system in the garden and sighed. 'Everything's going to be fine. Things have been a bit messy over the past few weeks, what with all the problems we've had in the complex, but it's all right now . . . He's not going to get to us. We'll retaliate.'

Jonas didn't say anything. He was thinking about the gun Kent had taken. He edged slowly backwards, away from the hand.

Uncle Kent turned away and sat down again. Jonas kept moving towards the door, past the bills and the golf clubs.

Kent looked around. 'Where are you going, JK?'

'Just outside.'

'Don't leave the garden,' Kent said. 'We have to stay here now; the alarm system will protect us. It's safest here, inside Villa Kloss.'

Jonas slid open the glass door and quickly stepped out on to the decking, almost bumping into Aunt Veronica, who was on her way into the house.

'Hi, Jonas – still up and about?'

He smiled at her.

'You're starting work over at my place tomorrow, aren't you? That's great – I need lots of help!'

Jonas nodded. He was looking forward to it, too.

Veronica glanced into the room, spotted Kent and lowered her voice. 'How's he doing?'

'OK . . . I think,' Jonas said.

'He's had a lot to deal with.'

'Yes.'

'I'll just pop in and see him . . . Sleep well, Jonas.'

She went inside and closed the glass door.

Jonas walked across the decking, past the small, faint lights. He looked back through the big window into Kent's living room. Veronica had gone over to the armchair and was shaking Kent, saying something Jonas couldn't hear.

Kent muttered a response, but Veronica kept on talking, a serious expression on her face.

Slowly, Kent sat up. He listened to his sister and nodded, without saying anything else.

Jonas stopped spying on them and went back to his own chalet. He was exhausted.

Lisa

It was Thursday night in the May Lai Bar, the midnight hour, and Lady Summertime had only an hour of her shift left. Thank goodness. The purple wig was making her head more and more itchy.

This was Summertime's penultimate gig at the club, and it hadn't gone well. The place wasn't even half full and the atmosphere was non-existent. The dance floor was deserted and, on top of all that, Lisa felt as if she were being watched up in her booth.

Which she was, of course. The security guards were around all the time, and she suspected that Kent Kloss had told them to keep an eye on her.

Lisa bent over the mixer desk; she was making sure Summertime behaved herself. There would be no more little excursions on to the dance floor, and she was keeping her fingers to herself. Staying on the right side of the law was the sensible thing to do, but the excitement had gone.

Half an hour after midnight, Kent Kloss himself arrived, which was unusual, and sat down at the bar. He ordered something from the bartender, slapped a few regular customers on the back and chatted with a couple of the guards who came over to him. Lisa noticed that he was drinking only mineral water; he carried on chatting and laughing, but he didn't even glance over at the DJ booth. Not once.

Lisa started to feel nervous. Lady Summertime was fumbling with the controls, and the transitions between tracks were anything but smooth.

Eventually, the agony was over.

'Thank you and goodnight,' she said after the last song, 'The End' by The Doors.

And that was that. No one applauded; the remaining guests finished off their drinks and wandered out into the night. A thick cloud of weariness hovered just below the ceiling.

It's the heat, Lisa thought, but she knew that wasn't true. There's no atmosphere in a half-empty club. She gathered up her records, finishing just as the last guests left the room. But before she could follow them, Kent Kloss came over.

'Hi, Summertime. Need any help with your bags?'

'I'm fine, thanks.'

She shook her head firmly, but he followed her up the stairs anyway. They emerged into the warm air and headed for her Passat. A small black shadow flitted past across the night sky – a bat, hunting for insects.

'Are you behaving yourself?' Kent said when they reached the car.

'Absolutely. I'm being positively angelic.'

'Keep it up. Don't do anything stupid.'

Kent seemed to be stone-cold sober, but he had stopped smiling when they left the club.

'At least we've been lucky with the weather this summer,' he said. 'Everything else has gone to hell in a handcart, but the sun is shining.' He looked over at the brightly lit hotel and added, 'Eight pallets of vodka and Russian champagne . . . Know anyone who might be interested?'

Lisa shook her head. 'How come?'

Kent smiled wearily. 'That's how much we've got left. Eight pallets, unsold. We had a major delivery by ship at midsummer, but we've sold only half the amount I'd calculated. It was the gastroenteritis . . . We'd have earned two million this summer, tax-free, if he hadn't added water polluted with dung to our system.'

Lisa didn't reply; she just looked at her watch. It was gone two o'clock. 'I have to go,' she said.

Kent moved a step closer. 'Has she spoken to you?'

Lisa unlocked the car. 'You mean Paulina? Yes, she has.'

'And you're in?'

'That depends.'

'On what?' Kent's voice had a harder edge now.

Lisa knew she had nothing going for her, but decided to give it a try anyway: 'Then can I go home?'

'You can go home if you do this,' Kloss said, 'or wherever the hell you like. I won't go to the police. No one will come looking for you.'

Lisa nodded. 'OK. What do I have to do?'

'I want you to watch. I want you to keep watch on Villa Kloss, you and Paulina. Aron Fredh is bound to turn up there, I'm certain of it . . . and you know what he looks like.'

'And what will you be doing while we're keeping watch?'

Kent opened the car door for her and leaned closer. 'I will be setting the trap.'

Gerlof

The telephone in Gerlof's room rang after coffee time on Friday morning, and he picked up the receiver with a certain amount of trepidation.

'Davidsson.'

'Gerlof?'

He recognized both the voice and the accent. It was someone who had come back home to Öland, but not the person he had been hoping to speak to.

'Good morning, Bill,' he said. 'How are things in Långvik?'

'Fine, but it's time to say goodbye. The summer is over . . . I'm heading back to Michigan tomorrow.'

'That's a shame. My boat isn't quite ready yet.'

'In that case, we'll have to take her out next summer.'

'Maybe,' Gerlof said. 'If I'm still here.'

Bill laughed. 'We're going to live until we're a hundred, Gerlof.'

'Look after yourself, Bill.'

'I always do,' the American said. 'By the way, did you get hold of that guy you were looking for?'

'Yes, I found him. But it turns out he didn't actually come from the USA; he was in the Soviet Union.'

'Oh yeah? What was he doing there?'

'Who knows? . . . But I suppose he believed in a better future in the workers' paradise.'

'I guess so,' Bill said. 'Like Oswald.'

'Oswald who?'

'Lee Harvey Oswald. He went to the Soviet Union at the end

343

of the fifties, then changed his mind and came back home with a Russian wife and a young daughter.'

It took a few seconds before Gerlof remembered the events in Dallas. 'You mean the assassin,' he said.

'That's right, the gunman who shot JFK,' Bill said. 'But I don't suppose your guy is planning anything quite so terrible.'

'Absolutely not,' Gerlof said, feeling anything but certain.

The Homecomer

Aron was sitting right at the top of his new hiding place. He had made himself at home as best he could, with blankets and a thin mattress, and he had slept well for the last few nights.

He felt safe, strangely enough, like an eagle in its nest at the top of a tree. He could see out towards the bay and the Sound, and inland as well.

This evening there were fluffy white clouds scudding in across the island. Some of them resembled human heads, others distorted monsters.

He could see the children gathering on the shore for their swimming lessons and holidaymakers running along the jetty and jumping into the water, from morning till night.

He could see cars coming and going.

He noticed that some visitors had already started shutting up their summer cottages, getting ready to head back home to the mainland.

The sun would carry on shining for a long time, but summer in the holiday village was almost over.

He gazed out across the Sound. The waves were tipped with white this evening, licked by the wind. The sea was immense and powerful, constantly moving.

Aron's dream was to die here by the Sound. He wanted to look out across the water, then close his eyes, with peace in his heart. And perhaps it would happen, if he stayed close to the sea for the time he had left, and kept away from his enemies until it was time to face them.

He would be ready. Everything was prepared.

Slowly, Aron began to climb down from the tower, past his bed on the ground floor, out through the door and down the steps. His car was hidden among the trees a short distance away.

He was heading up to Marnäs for one last conversation with Gerlof Davidsson.

The New Country, 1940–45

The war against the counter-revolution has been long and hard, and Vlad is very tired.

So many are gone now. Denounced and condemned. There is a constant insistence that every enemy who is unmasked must give the names of more enemies, who in turn give even more names, like an ever-growing mill wheel.

They have crushed so many.

Trushkin has been shot.

Teachers and scientists have also been shot.

Homosexuals and soldiers have been shot.

Poets, porters and priests have been shot.

So many.

Captain Rugajev, Vlad's first commanding officer at Kresty, was removed by Zakowski, the top man in Leningrad. Zakowski was then shot by Jagoda, the NKVD Chief of Police; the following year, Jagoda was executed by his successor, the vodka drinker Nikolai Yezhov, a bloodthirsty individual who soon ended up in Lubyanka Prison, condemned to death by the new leader of the NKVD, Lavrenti Beria.

Vlad's new commanding officer at Kresty has survived for several months in his post. His name is Karrek, and he is a hard-bitten old soldier from the First World War. Major Karrek doesn't say much, but he always carries a little notebook with him. It is said that he jots down any rumours about his men. Karrek continues to administer the ultimate punishment under the law down in the cellar, often by his own hand.

Trucks trundle away every night, transporting the bodies to a military area outside the city. Vlad has heard that enormous excavators are needed to dig mass graves big enough to accommodate all the corpses.

To think that there were so many enemies, so many traitors.

Vlad is certain that no one suspects him of being a Trotskyite, or an imperialist, or any other kind of traitor to his country. He is loyal to Stalin, to the Party and to his commanding officer; he is no enemy of the state.

He is clean.

And yet. The fear and the doubts are there when he goes to bed, and the walls press in around him. What is Karrek writing down in his notebook? Vlad is terrified of turning up at work one day and being met by evasive glances, by the realization that no one is calling him 'Comrade' any longer. After all, he was once a foreigner, and sometimes he isn't completely convinced that he is not a spy.

He remembers his friend Vladimir, and the question he asked up in the north when Aron said he wasn't a spy: 'Are you sure?'

Is he? Aron sees what goes on in the cellar, he notices and remembers everything – doesn't that make him a kind of spy? Perhaps he is spying for some foreign power that has yet to get in touch with him. If Sven was a spy, perhaps Sven's secret plan was to place Aron in the Party, so that other agents would be able to contact him later.

These dark thoughts always come at night, when he is lying in his bed. He sees bloody faces floating in the darkness, he listens for the sound of knocking. He waits for the sound of a car stopping outside the building, for footsteps hurrying up the stairs. Loud banging on the door, like knuckles against a coffin lid.

There are sometimes footsteps in the stairwell, but so far no one has come to his door.

What can Aron do, while he waits?

Nothing. He just has to let Vlad get on with his work. Day and night, nothing but work.

On 4 May 1940, Vlad is called into Karrek's office. The major is sitting at his desk with his notebook in front of him. He gives a brief nod.

'Come forward, Jegerov.'

Vlad steps up to the desk. He notices a bowl of pickled gherkins, but Karrek doesn't offer him any. He merely leans back and studies Vlad. 'How are you?' he says.

'Very well, Major.'

Karrek adjusts his cufflinks. 'I have been called to Moscow to serve in Lubyanka Prison. I am to take over as the commandant. It is a great honour. I need to take a number of men with me, and I have selected the very best.'

At first, Vlad doesn't understand, but then he stands to attention.

Three months later, Major Karrek is transferred to Moscow. He takes Vlad and two others with him to the capital.

They arrive in a city where a certain air of calm has descended after all the trials and purges. There is far less suspicion, and everyone seems relieved that the threat of war has been removed, now that the Soviet Union and Nazi Germany have become allies.

Perhaps the future has arrived, Vlad thinks. At long last.

The summer of 1941 is scorching. Aron finds it oppressive, as if a thunderstorm is coming. And the storm breaks at midsummer.

On 22 June, Hitler invades the Soviet Union in a lightning attack that sweeps aside all opposition. Polikarpov aircraft are shot down by swarms of Messerschmitts. German Panzer divisions advance across the wheatfields of the Ukraine.

The railway line between Leningrad and Moscow is cut on 21 August. Kiev falls on 26 September.

Aron cannot go home to Sweden now, not even if he is granted safe conduct by Stalin himself.

He is trapped in a country where, for the first time, everyone is affected by the war. There is no bread. Sugar is rationed, so is soap.

A quarter of the population joins the Red Army, but they are unable to drive back the fascists. During 1941 alone, the Soviet Union loses almost three million soldiers.

At the end of October, the Germans are outside Moscow. Kalinin in the north and Kaluga in the south have already fallen. Shops and abandoned apartments are looted. Moscow's sixteen bridges and Stalin's dachas are mined. Stalin himself prepares to leave Moscow, but on 18 October he eventually decides to stay and sleep on an underground train.

General Zhukov assures him that the city can be held.

The NKVD is given free rein to execute deserters and workers who attempt to flee. Vlad is one of those operating out in the streets, just behind the fortifications.

The German army stops to rest and to prepare the final onslaught on Moscow, which is a mistake. Four hundred thousand well-rested Soviet troops, together with a thousand tanks and a thousand planes are on their way from the Far East on special trains. They arrive at the end of October, and gather outside Moscow.

At the beginning of November, Stalin holds a military parade in the besieged city in order to stiffen the resolve of his people and to boost morale. Vlad helps to carry chairs from the Bolshoi Theatre for members of the Politburo. He hears the leader give an inspiring speech about the defence of the mother country, with music provided by the NKVD ensemble.

That night, the temperature drops to arctic levels as if to order, and in the middle of November Zhukov launches a counter-attack. On 5 December, the Red Army manages to stop the progress of the Germans.

Slowly, the war turns for the Soviet Union, but the cost is incalculable. Over eight million Soviet troops perish in the conflict. In addition, almost ten million civilians die of starvation or in Nazi massacres.

The NKVD is reorganized after the war. The prison service is placed under the jurisdiction of the Ministry of Internal Affairs, the MVD, while counter-espionage and the hunt for class enemies becomes the remit of the Ministry for State Security, the KGB. Vlad moves to the KGB.

Moscow gradually begins to thaw out after the winters endured during the war; there is more food, and people have more time to enjoy themselves. Vlad has been living in the same small apartment for five years now, in a block for employees of the state. There is a communal bathroom, but he has his own kitchen. He is not well paid but has been able to buy himself a car after the war, a brown Pobeda. He goes on several outings, but never to the north. Never to the place where the old camps lay.

When he has a free evening, he sometimes goes to the Bolshoi. He chooses the cheapest seats right at the back, and watches a play or a ballet.

Vlad often has to work at night, long shifts of twelve hours or more at the prison on Lubyanka Square. In recent years, a dirty stream from the great flood of the war has poured into Moscow's prisons: defeated officers, German scientists, Russians who allied themselves with Hitler, rebels from the Baltic states, diplomats who have been arrested and even more prisoners of war. They must all be interrogated, categorized, weighed and measured.

'Where exactly on the Eastern Front did you serve?'

'What kind of rocket boosters were you testing?'

'Are you prepared to work for us now?'

The cells fill up. The anxiety grows. Sometimes, in the mornings, the prisoners throw out a lifeless body when the door is opened. It might be a suicide, or an informant who has been beaten to death. Sometimes, the prisoners throw out their food as well, if they are on hunger strike. There are force-feeding procedures. Aron and another guard push two tubes up the prisoner's nose, then start pumping in milk. The prisoner can choose whether to suffocate or swallow. They all choose to swallow.

Vlad is in control, but Aron is tired now. He is tired of picking people up, tired of the interrogations, tired of being a guard. He is thirty years old, but often feels as if he were sixty.

The interrogations continue, the transportations continue, the shootings continue. Traitors are shot, deserters are shot, enemies are shot. Russians or foreigners, it makes no difference.

'Do you know why we put a bullet in the back of their neck?' Karrek asks late one night, after several glasses of vodka.

Aron and the other guards shake their heads. They've never given it any thought; they've just done it, year after year, bullet after bullet, even if the first shot wasn't fatal. Sometimes it took a second bullet when the prisoner was lying down. Sometimes a third. There are rumours that sometimes the sand that was thrown over a body kept on moving.

'You don't know?'

'No.'

'It's obvious,' Karrek says. 'Because the back of the neck can't stare at us.'

Gerlof

'I don't know how you have the patience,' John Hagman said.

'It keeps my hands flexible,' Gerlof replied.

He was sitting at the table opposite John, concentrating on finishing off the rigging for a clipper, the classic *Cutty Sark*. It was a fiddly job, using wire hooks and thread and thin yardarms made of toothpicks.

When the very last tiny knot had been tied, he let out a long breath.

'I don't really understand it either, John,' he admitted. 'And I haven't even got a customer for this one, I've just—'

He was interrupted by the sound of the telephone. He stared at it, then pulled himself together and picked up the receiver.

'Davidsson.'

'Good evening,' a voice said quietly.

Gerlof recognized it; he was more prepared this time. He nodded to John.

'Good evening, Aron. How are you?'

'Fine.'

'I'm not,' Gerlof said. 'I've been reading a book, a history book about the terrible things that happened in the Soviet Union in the thirties. *The Great Terror*.'

'I don't read books.'

'But you're familiar with the Great Terror.'

There was no reply, and Gerlof went on, 'A million people were executed between 1936 and 1938 alone. Most were shot, according to the book. Others died under torture. A million, Aron, in less than two years.'

Still nothing.

'What were you doing during those years, Aron? You said you were a soldier, but what did you do?'

'I obeyed orders,' the voice said. 'I fought against Fascism.'

'But you're not a soldier any longer, Aron. You can give up now. You can start talking to the Kloss family.'

'No. There are too many dead.'

'Not here on the island,' Gerlof said.

'Yes. Here, too.'

'Where?'

The voice seemed to hesitate before answering. 'On Kloss land.'

'Who are you talking about?'

'A security guard,' the voice went on. 'He's buried under the cairn between the shore and Rödtorp. He was shot.'

As Gerlof listened, he remembered Tilda talking about a security guard who had gone missing at midsummer. 'Why are you telling me this, Aron?'

'Who else would I tell?'

Gerlof thought for a moment. 'I heard about your sister,' he said. 'I know that your younger sister died in the home at Marnäs last year, Aron. Was she your only family?'

'I have a daughter. But she's not here.'

'So you must have a wife, too.'

'Not any more.'

'What happened?'

The voice didn't respond.

'Goodbye,' it said eventually, and Gerlof heard a click at the other end of the line. He sighed and put down the phone.

So that was that. He looked at John.

'He's somewhere else now . . . I couldn't hear the same background noises. There was no whinnying horse this time.'

'The question is, why did he call you?'

'I suppose he wants some kind of contact, like everyone else,' Gerlof said. 'Everyone wants to feel human. Even murderers have that need within them.'

He stared at the telephone.

'Aron had a family,' he said. 'He talked about a daughter, and about a wife who isn't around any more. I think he's completely alone now, and that's not good . . . It felt as if that was our last conversation, as if he was just calling to say goodbye.'

When John had left, Gerlof picked up the phone again and called Tilda. She was back in Sweden, but didn't want to talk.

'I'm on holiday,' she said.

'It's about a police matter,' Gerlof said.

'As I said, I'm on holiday.'

'Unfortunately, this can't wait. The security guard who disappeared at midsummer – is he still missing?'

'As far as I know,' Tilda said.

'I've got some information.' He explained what Aron Fredh had told him about the body near Rödtorp.

At least Tilda was listening.

'I'll ask them to check,' she said. 'Where exactly is Rödtorp?'

'It's where the Ölandic Resort is now. Aron Fredh grew up there.'

'Inside the complex?'

'Yes, down by the water,' Gerlof said. 'So this will mean more hassle for the Kloss family, if what he says is correct . . . as I'm sure he's well aware.'

Gerlof could hear Tilda writing something down, then she said, 'We have to try and find this man.'

Gerlof sighed. 'Talk to Kent Kloss.'

Jonas

Something bad had happened. Jonas could feel it in the air around Villa Kloss.

He didn't speak to anyone, he just kept on working, and Veronica's decking was half finished. After several weeks on his knees, he had developed a routine when it came to sanding down and oiling the wood, and fortunately he was able to make much faster progress; there were only three days left of his summer holiday in Stenvik. Everyone seemed to be hurrying to get things finished before the summer was over.

Jonas hadn't seen much of his father; Niklas often worked late at the restaurant, and stayed in bed in the mornings. He emerged later and later with each passing day, wearing dark glasses, but he always had a smile for Jonas before he went off to work.

Mats was going home on Saturday morning, Jonas and Niklas on Sunday. Either Veronica or Uncle Kent would give them a lift to the station.

Jonas was hoping it would be Veronica.

He had a good view of Villa Kloss from the decking, and he could see brief family meetings here and there: Uncle Kent and Niklas had a lunch meeting by the garage, Veronica and Niklas had a chat afterwards by the pool, and later in the evening he noticed Kent and Veronica sitting on Kent's decking. Whispered conversations, every one.

Something had definitely happened – but there was still work to do and a blazing sun to bring him out in a sweat, so Jonas kept on slogging away.

At the beginning of the holiday he had been afraid that he would be lonely, but now he enjoyed spending time on his own during the day. Avoiding Kent and his cousins – even Mats and their father.

Urban and Mats got back very late from working at the Ölandic that evening. Urban went straight to his room, but Mats stopped to have a word with his kid brother. He crouched down on the decking and asked quietly, 'Have you heard, bro?'

'No, what?'

'The police have found a body. Hidden under a cairn.'

Jonas immediately glanced over at the ridge, but Mats shook his head. 'Not that one – another one, inside the Ölandic complex. The cops are all over the place.'

'Who was it?'

'A guy who worked for us, a security guard . . . I never met him, but he worked at the Ölandic.'

Jonas looked at his brother and wondered whether to tell him about the cairn ghost, but Mats straightened up. 'Anyway, that was my last shift.' He sounded relieved.

One by one, everyone returned to Villa Kloss. Jonas stood on the decking as the sun went down; he had the feeling that they were all keeping up a pretence in front of him. In spite of the fact that they chatted about the dry weather and the shortage of water and the fact that there would be no more swimming lessons after today, he knew that the adults were thinking about something else entirely.

The sun was cooled by the sea and became a red line on the horizon. Jonas turned around and saw Veronica sitting by the house with a glass of wine.

'Hi, Jonas,' she said.

He went over, expecting her to tell him about the body that had been found, but she just ruffled his hair.

'Tired?'

'A bit,' he said.

Veronica took a sip of her wine; she seemed to be thinking something over. After a moment, she asked, 'Has your father told you about our family, Jonas?'

Jonas shook his head. 'Not really.'

His aunt leaned back in her chair and gazed out across the coast.

'It's a fascinating story,' she began. 'It all started with a farmer

356

called Gillis, who acquired a lot of cheap land here on the coast in the nineteenth century. Everyone thought it was worthless, because after all you couldn't grow crops on the coast . . . but he just kept on buying more, and held on to it all his life. Then he passed it on to his three sons, Edvard and Gilbert and my grandfather Sigfrid, and after his brothers died, Sigfrid fenced off a large portion of the land and created what became the Ölandic Resort. So we've owned that land for generations. The Kloss family has lived here for as long as anyone can remember, I think. People have tried to take it away from us, but they have never succeeded.'

She twirled the wine glass around in her fingers. 'We should all be proud of our family. That's what I tell Casper and Urban, and it applies to you, too, Jonas.'

He nodded – but, to him, the family was just a series of names. He had no idea who Gillis and Edvard and Gilbert and Sigfrid were.

He said goodnight to his aunt and went off to his little chalet.

As he lay beneath the cool sheet he could hear a lone bird outside, a subdued song that gradually fell silent in the twilight.

And just before he fell asleep he heard quiet footsteps crossing the decking; it sounded as if Uncle Kent was setting the alarm, or perhaps sneaking off down to the coast road. Jonas closed his eyes and covered his ears with the pillow and the duvet. All he wanted to do was sleep.

The Homecomer

Aron knew they were getting closer.

They were bound to have discovered the body by now, if Gerlof Davidsson had believed him, but that meant the police would be concentrating on the Ölandic Resort.

After the telephone conversation with Gerlof, he had waited until the sun went down before leaving Marnäs and driving back to the western side of the island.

He could move around in the darkness now. It was long after midnight, and the dip down below the coast road was full of shadows.

Was anyone there?

Standing at one end, he wasn't at all sure. He could see the metal door of the bunker fifty metres away, and he listened hard to check if he could hear anything.

Silence.

Slowly and cautiously, he moved along the dip, just as he had for several weeks now.

The padlock was still in place; he took out the key and quietly unlocked the door. It squeaked slightly, but swung open.

He had finished digging the hole beneath the cairn, which was why he was being more careful than before. He no longer came here in daylight; he had become a nocturnal creature.

The moon emerged from a bank of cloud over the Sound, helpfully illuminating the entrance to the bunker as he looked inside. Everything looked fine, just as he had left it, his tools and the boxes in place.

A roll of electric cable lay just inside the entrance, and Aron picked it up and took it outside, closing the bunker door before he started paying out the thin cable behind him, concealing it under pebbles and larger limestone rocks.

Eventually, it was completely hidden. Good, he thought, as he straightened up.

Then he heard the sound of rustling in the darkness.

Someone had entered the dip at the far end and was moving towards him.

Aron wasn't prepared to take any risks at this stage. He quickly turned around and hurried away.

After ten metres, he was out of the dip and could see the campsite and the jetty. The Sound shimmered before him beneath an almost full moon, but he moved away, into the darkness beyond the shore. Across the coast road, past the festival site and in among the low-growing trees.

Only when he reached the shadows in the forest did he stop and listen. He couldn't hear any footsteps behind him.

And yet Aron could feel the blood surging through his arms and chest. His heart was pounding, damaged and worn after more than eighty years, but he thought it would go on beating for a little while longer.

He needed his heart to see out this week.

The New Country, October 1957

It is late autumn in Moscow, and Aron has just left a deathbed in a bedroom that is cramped and dusty and unbearable. Like many others, he has gone out on to the street this evening, scanning the sky for the Sputnik satellite, which is supposed to be whizzing around up there. A technological triumph. But the sky above him is dark grey.

His former commanding officer Major Karrek looked just as grey when Aron left him. Karrek has been at death's door for a long time, his body swollen from alcohol abuse, yet at the same time shrivelled like a mummy in his tiny apartment. A young nurse has visited him every day over the past year, but in the evenings Aron is alone with Karrek. No one else comes to see him.

Soldiers die alone.

So much has happened in just a few years. Stalin also died eventually, sick and alone in his bed, because no one dared to disturb him. The new leader is called Nikita Khrushchev and, in common with everyone who had held that position, he carried out a purge when he took over. Lavrenti Beria, Stalin's spymaster, was quickly condemned and executed and, once he was gone, Comrade Karrek had to leave his post. Karrek had done his duty as the governor of Lubyanka Prison, and no punishment awaited him, just a small state pension and total obscurity.

Karrek was evicted from his office, and he took it very hard. Only three years after Beria's death, Karrek's liver collapsed, destroyed by his drinking. The major was already thirsty beforehand, but once the great leader's protective hands were gone Karrek went into freefall in a sea of vodka, like so many who had worked for the security of their country and dedicated their lives to tracking down the enemies of the people.

Towards the end, there was a look of terror in his eyes. He seemed to be waiting for something.

'I've counted them, all those to whom I administered the ultimate punishment under the law,' Karrek whispered, staring at Vlad. 'You probably think that's impossible, but I had a number inside my head, and I kept a tally of every shot.'

Vlad didn't want to ask about the number, but Karrek coughed and went on. 'Twelve thousand, three hundred and five.' He lifted his right hand, the one that shook most after all the recoils. 'By this . . . this hand. How does that sound?'

'Incomprehensible,' Vlad said.

Karrek was still staring at him with glassy eyes, but Vlad lowered his gaze and looked at his own right hand. For the first time, Aron thought about what it had done, and how often.

Had the index finger pulled the trigger thousands of times? Definitely.

And how many blows to backs and feet and heads with the *dubinka*? The number was incalculable. Most of those who had suffered were men, but there were women, too. Never children, however. There were sadists within the organization who beat children, even killed them – but not Vlad. His limit was the age of fifteen. Or thereabouts.

Traitors and enemies of the people. They got what they deserved.

Karrek died with a sigh. He fell asleep quietly and peacefully in his bed, unlike the twelve thousand, three hundred and five.

It is October, and Sputnik is whirling around in space, spinning and bleeping.

Aron is walking around Moscow, every bit as alone as the satellite. However, he thinks he sees familiar faces everywhere on the streets, and that frightens him.

Last week, he was recognized outside Kursky Station; he is sure of it. A middle-aged woman stopped just a few metres away and stared at him with terror in her eyes. What had Vlad done to her? Used the *dubinka* on her back? Kept her awake for three days? Or had he just broken her son's arms, or shot her husband?

Aron doesn't remember.

Whatever Vlad did, it was in a good cause.

A higher goal, a better future. Vlad and his colleagues had worked hard down in the cellar, clearing away one enemy after another, always looking to the future.

Is this the future? Has it arrived?

Aron has his doubts. He walks the streets and thinks about running away. Going to the Swedish embassy, a building he has never been anywhere near, or to Ovir, the official bureau for visa issues and registration, and telling them everything.

It is evening, a cold autumn evening, and Vlad seeks refuge from Moscow's icy winds in an Azerbaijani restaurant not far from his apartment. He sits down at a corner table and orders vodka. He will have a kebab later, but the vodka is his main aim.

A chilled glass covered in condensation arrives, and Vlad drinks a silent toast to Stalin. Down with Khrushchev, the hypocrite who is himself up to his neck in blood.

He is drinking heavily for the first time in his life. The alcohol makes Aron feel sick, but Vlad orders one glass after another. When he has emptied his fifth and felt the vodka worm its way down into his belly, he looks up and sees his dead NKVD colleagues sitting at the table with him. They encourage him: *keep on drinking!* His stepfather, Sven, is sitting on his left; he and Aron are the same age now. Vladimir from the Ukraine is on his right, with shattered legs.

Old Grisha is there, too, and his stylish colleague Grigori Trushkin, whom Vlad interrogated for several nights until Trushkin was broken. But Trushkin is smiling and nodding at him. *Drink, Comrade! So many summers, so many winters.*

Vlad raises his glass to the dead, over and over again. He empties each glass methodically; he closes his eyes after the eleventh or twelfth and feels the room spinning. He is a satellite, spinning out into space.

This is what it's like. This is what it's like to be free and damned at the same time. Stupefyingly lonely, and increasingly drunk and sick.

Aron doesn't remember any more.

Does he get thrown out of the restaurant, muttering in Swedish, or does he stagger out of his own accord? All he knows is that, suddenly, he is on his knees on the pavement, with his head hanging down and saliva dribbling from his mouth.

He has to get home; he will freeze to death out here. So he tries to stand up.

Then everything goes black, and when he comes round he sees nothing but cobbles. He has fallen over.

Where is he? He has no idea. He loses consciousness again.

Darkness.

A hand is shaking his shoulder. A slender hand, and he can hear a woman's voice: 'Are you all right, soldier?'

Her name is Ludmila, and her middle name is Stalina, but she never uses it. She calls herself Mila, and she helps him home. Once she has got him into bed, he looks at her and tells her, or tries to tell her, that this is the first time he has ever been drunk. He never, ever drinks.

Mila doesn't believe him, of course.

'At least you're not aggressive,' she says quietly. 'A lot of men turn nasty when they're drunk.'

Aron is not aggressive, he promises her that. He is not dangerous. And he will never drink again.

Mila sits by his bed for a while. Gradually, he is able to see her more clearly; she is dark and pretty.

'What work do you do?' she asks.

Both Aron and Vlad hesitate. 'Civil servant,' they say eventually. 'What about you?'

'I'm a nurse.'

After a brief silence, Aron asks, 'Can I see you again? Do you live here?'

'My mother lives in Moscow,' Mila says. 'I'm staying with her for a week. I work . . . somewhere else.'

Aron realizes that she works with secrets, just like him.

Mila gets to her feet. 'I have to go.'

'I'd really like to see you again.'

Mila looks around the room. 'You have a telephone.'

'Yes,' Aron says. 'My office needs to be able to get hold of me sometimes.'

Mila smiles. 'I'll give you my mother's number. Give her a call and speak to her, and we'll see if she'll allow you to talk to me.'

Lisa

Kent Kloss looked tired; perhaps he had been drinking the night before. But he was sober now, moving animatedly back and forth and making Lisa's caravan shake.

'He was close last night. I could hear him creeping around down by the bunker, but he got away . . . Tonight, you two will be there, too, and we'll get him.'

We? Lisa thought. Was he including her?

But she didn't say anything; she just sat quietly on the sofa listening to Kent. Paulina was over by the door; she didn't say anything either.

Kent was on his feet as usual, his head almost touching the ceiling, and even though his face was pale and tired, there was an energy in his body. He kept opening and closing his fists, turning his head and listening, shifting position.

He had placed a black bag on the worktop.

'He's got a day,' Kent went on. 'Maybe two . . . Before his luck runs out.'

Lisa had heard what had happened, of course: a security guard had been found shot and buried in the resort. She was almost certain that it was the same man who had appeared in the forest on her first day here, but she had no intention of asking Kent any questions about the matter. This wasn't the time to reveal that she had met him just before he died.

Instead she asked, 'So what's he doing down there in the bunker?'

'He's spying,' Kent said. 'He's spying on me and my family. And he's using the bunker as his operational base.'

Lisa noticed that Kent had started using military terminology, but she kept quiet, and so did Paulina.

Kent unzipped the bag and took out two small items made of black plastic. 'You'll need these tonight.'

Lisa realized they were walkie-talkies. No surprise there – Kent Kloss liked his gadgets.

He glanced at his watch and went on, 'It will be dark in an hour. We'll meet on the coast road down below my house at ten, and I'll explain what you have to do. Bring torches and the walkie-talkies . . . Any questions?'

Lisa and Paulina remained silent.

For the first time in many years, Lisa wished the police would turn up. Knock on the door and start investigating the whole thing. But she knew that Kent Kloss didn't want the police anywhere near him, whatever he was intending to do to the man in the bunker.

Kent picked up the bag and opened the caravan door. 'Good. See you later. . . Wrap up warm – it could be a cold night.'

He stepped outside and shut the door behind him.

Lisa stayed where she was as the smell of Kent's aftershave gradually faded. 'Bollocks,' she said to the closed door. 'It's going to be a warm night.'

She looked at her walkie-talkie, which looked like a large black toy mobile phone. But Kent Kloss was serious, so no doubt it worked.

Then she looked over at Paulina, who was sitting with her hands clasped in her lap, a determined expression on her face. Lisa felt she had to say something. 'So we're going to do this?'

Paulina nodded. 'We are.'

'Why?'

Paulina was quiet for a moment. 'Sick mother,' she said eventually.

'Your mother is sick?'

Paulina nodded again, and Lisa asked, 'So Kent Kloss is paying you well?'

'Yes.'

'How much?'

'A thousand.'

'A thousand kronor?'

'Dollars,' Paulina said, taking an old tea caddy out of her bag. 'He give me a hundred already.' She opened the caddy and showed Lisa the notes.

'OK. Good,' Lisa said.

Paulina looked at her. 'And you? Why you do this?'

Lisa hesitated before answering. 'I have a relative who needs money.'

'Relative?'

'My father . . . my dad. He lives in Stockholm and he uses the street drugstore, if you know what I mean.'

Paulina obviously didn't understand.

'He's a junkie,' Lisa explained. She quickly got to her feet. 'OK, we'd better make sure we're ready.'

She wished she hadn't mentioned Silas. She just wanted to get away now, dump this last job and drive away from the island right now.

But she knew she had to stay.

The walkie-talkie was silent, but Lisa's mobile rang when Paulina had left. Lisa was lying on the bed. She stared at it for a long time without answering.

She knew who it was.

The phone kept on ringing: eight signals. Nine. Ten.

But Lisa didn't take the call. She just stared out of the window, where the fiery yellow sun was on its way down over the Sound. Eventually, the ringing stopped; Lisa stayed where she was.

After half an hour she got up, pulled on a dark jacket and covered her blonde hair with a black cap.

The sun had disappeared; it was time to go.

Gerlof

For the past week, Gerlof had been hearing stories about Veronica Kloss. How fantastic she was, how well she looked after the elderly.

'Incredible energy,' the staff in the residential home said. 'Never gave up. Happy to chat or to listen. Kept the old ladies going. Used to read to them.'

But if Veronica was so considerate, why hadn't she been here this summer? Gerlof knew that the Kloss family had had a number of problems to sort out down at the Ölandic, but even so . . . He hadn't seen her once.

Last summer, Veronica had been here almost every week. According to the temporary care assistant he had spoken to, Veronica had got on well with Greta Fredh, and had made several subsequent visits to read to Greta and the others.

Then Greta had died after a fall in her bathroom, and Veronica had stopped coming. Gerlof had talked to several residents who missed her and wished she would come back.

But why had she stopped? Was it only Greta who had been important to her?

The door of Ulf Wall's room was often ajar, but the room inside was dark even when the sun was shining down on the home in Marnäs, and Gerlof had resisted the temptation to call in. He didn't know much about Ulf, just that he was at least five years older than Gerlof, and might be the father of Einar Wall, the huntsman and arms dealer. And that he had been Greta Fredh's neighbour.

Finally, on the last day of July, Gerlof pushed open the door and peered in. 'Hello?' he said quietly.

At first there was silence, followed by a brief response: 'What do you mean?'

This question was rather difficult to answer, so Gerlof said nothing. He stepped into the hallway; the room was familiar because it was decorated and furnished exactly the same as his own, but it didn't smell quite as good. There was no movement in the air in here.

There was no movement in Ulf Wall either. He was wearing a grey cardigan, sitting in an armchair next to the window, which was covered by a roller blind.

Gerlof made his way slowly along the hall. 'Gerlof Davidsson,' he said.

The man in the armchair stared at him, and nodded. 'Yes. I know who you are, Davidsson.'

'Good.'

'You were in the paper a while ago.'

'That's right. And I heard about your son,' Gerlof said. 'That was a little while ago, too. My condolences. Einar was your son, wasn't he?'

Wall continued to stare at him, not moving a muscle, but after a moment he nodded again. 'But I've got two more,' he said. 'They're better behaved than Einar . . . they don't drink and they don't go poaching.'

There was nowhere for a guest to sit, so Gerlof remained standing, swaying slightly on his weak legs. 'I heard about your neighbour, too,' he said. 'Greta Fredh.'

'That's right – Aron's sister. She died last summer.'

Gerlof swayed even more. *Aron's* sister.

'So you know Aron Fredh?'

'We got into conversation,' Wall said. 'He was here a few times.'

'When was that?'

'Early summer . . . He came and had a look at his sister's room. Took one or two things with him.'

'And what did you talk about?'

'Greta, mainly . . . he wanted to know what had happened.'

'I heard she had a fall.'

Ulf Wall nodded once more. 'He wanted to know if any of the Kloss family had been around at the time.'

'The Kloss family?' Gerlof said.

'I told him what I knew.'

'And what did you know?'

'That she was here,' Wall said. 'Veronica Kloss kept on turning up for a while last year.'

'So I heard,' Gerlof said. 'She used to give talks and read to the residents. But she hasn't been here this year.'

'No, she stopped coming. After the accident.'

'When Greta fell?'

'Yes. When she died in the bathroom.'

'And the door was locked,' Gerlof said.

'Yes, Greta was very particular about locking the bathroom door. So that nobody could poke their head in.' Wall had a brief coughing fit. 'But Veronica Kloss was in there, too. She came out. I saw her running past my door.'

'Did you?'

'I did. And that's what I told Aron Fredh, too.'

Gerlof thought for a moment. 'Was your son Einar here at the same time as Aron?'

'Once, yes. They had a chat.'

'About the Kloss family?'

'About all kinds of things . . . Einar was furious with Kent Kloss – he was always trying to beat down the price of the meat and fish Einar supplied.'

Gerlof realized that something had begun here in Ulf Wall's room; it had started with a chance meeting between an arms dealer and a man who had come home. Two angry men with a common enemy.

'So do you think they might have done business together?'

'Very likely,' Wall said. 'But Einar didn't say anything to me about it.'

Gerlof couldn't stay on his feet any longer, and he was too polite to sit down on the bed, so he thanked Ulf Wall and left the room.

He paused in the corridor and looked at the room next door, where Greta Fredh had lived. He knocked on the door; no one answered, but he'd got into the habit of simply walking in, so he did the same again.

The old woman who had taken over the room was sitting there; she looked quite alarmed.

'Good afternoon.' Gerlof was slightly embarrassed at intruding like this, but he smiled and waved to show that he wasn't a threat.

He looked around; so this was where Aron's sister, Greta, had lived, and where she had died. In the bathroom, after a fall.

And the bathroom door had been locked – both Ulf Wall and the care assistant had said the same. It would have been impossible for anyone to push her over.

Gerlof was just about to leave when he noticed the mat in the hallway. He had one exactly the same – plastic.

And then he realized how it could have happened.

Veronica Kloss. Nice, kind Veronica, who came to the home to give talks. Who got involved with the residents, went to see them in their rooms, read to them. Last summer, until Greta Fredh was dead.

Gerlof turned and went out into the corridor.

'Hello?' he called out. There was no response, so he raised his voice like the former sea captain he was. 'Hello! Anyone there?'

A young woman appeared. She wasn't the care assistant he had spoken to before, but they were similar. 'What's happened?'

'This room,' Gerlof said, pointing with his stick. 'You need to cordon it off and call the police.'

The girl looked bewildered. 'Sorry?'

Gerlof tried to look as authoritative as possible and to sound utterly sure of himself. 'This is a crime scene. Greta Fredh was murdered in that room.'

Jonas

On Saturday, the sky was grey above Villa Kloss. There wasn't a breath of wind along the coast, but darker clouds were gathering over the mainland. It felt as if there was a storm on the way.

Jonas worked hard all day, brushing oil into Veronica's decking, and at quarter past seven in the evening he finished the very last section. His aunt had already paid him, and he had put the envelope containing the money under his pillow, along with his wages from Uncle Kent.

Jonas narrowed his eyes and glanced up at the sun as he put away the brush and the tin of oil. He didn't want to think about sandpaper, wood oil or decking ever again. He was thinking about the money now, and the fact that he and his father were going home. Veronica had promised to drive them tomorrow after lunch.

Mats had already left; he had caught the bus to Kalmar on the main road this morning.

Jonas cycled over to the Davidsson family's cottage to say goodbye, as was the custom when someone was leaving the island to go home. Kristoffer was there, along with his mum and dad, but Gerlof had moved back to the residential home in Marnäs.

Jonas rode home in the sunset, feeling a little disappointed; he was sorry not to have seen Gerlof one last time.

The summer was almost over but it was still mild, and Jonas left the door of his chalet open when he went to bed, to let in the night air. Needless to say, it was almost as warm as the air inside the room.

He looked at his watch one last time: nearly ten o'clock. The garden was darker than usual, because someone had turned off the lights around the pool and down by the drive. But the alarm was switched on; Jonas could see the green flashing diodes.

He slid down in his bed, the sound of the crickets filling his ears. He didn't think he would miss their loud chirping when he got back to town, although it was actually quite calming, a kind of rhythmic chomping from some invisible machine out there in the grass.

Suddenly, the crickets fell silent. Not for long, just a brief pause as if the needle on a record player had been lifted for a few seconds. And then they gradually resumed their song.

Was there someone out there? An animal? Or a person? Jonas listened for a while, but the crickets had returned to their usual rhythm.

He turned over, lay on his back. Through the white curtain, he could see the round moon suspended above the rocks and the Sound. Perhaps it was the full moon that was making the crickets sound so peculiar.

The bed was warm, but the sheets were lovely and cool. Outside, he could hear low voices; it sounded as if his father had come home from his last shift at the restaurant and was saying goodnight to Casper and Urban.

There had been no sign of Uncle Kent all day. Which was fine.

Jonas closed his eyes.

After a while, the voices fell quiet, then he heard footsteps and muted thuds from the other chalets as Casper and Urban went to bed, then there was silence.

The room seemed to get darker. Jonas slowly slipped away into the shadows of the summer night, as if a sooty grey fog had crept in under the door and wrapped itself around him. But he was tired, so very tired, and there was no danger here. No cairn ghost.

Only a guardian angel.

An angel was standing by his bed, tall and still. The angel placed a hand over his face, and whispered that everything was all right.

Sleep, just sleep.

The angel's soft white hand was still there. And that was fine, everything was peaceful. Jonas sank deeper and deeper, down towards the bottom of the sea.

A little part of him knew that this was wrong, that is was dangerous to sink this deep, but by that time he couldn't do anything about it.

The Homecomer

The three guest chalets stood side by side towards the back of the extensive plot that made up Villa Kloss. When the sun had gone down and the chalets were in darkness, there was no light here.

There was an alarm, but Aron knew the code, of course.

Silently, he opened the door of the chalet on the left. The room smelled of chloroform, thanks to the bottle he had found in Einar Wall's boathouse.

There was a boy lying in the bed inside. A white handkerchief soaked in chloroform had been placed over his face, so he was fast asleep. A deep sleep beneath a white mask.

Good.

Aron picked him up. The boy's breathing was calm and even as he was carried out of the chalet, across the grass and over to the far end of the garden, where a low wall ran alongside a narrow dirt track.

Aron stepped over the wall and on to the track. His car was parked a short distance away in the darkness. Keeping one arm around the boy's back, he opened the boot and gently placed the thin body inside.

Then he closed the boot and turned around to visit the boy in the next chalet.

There ought to be room for two boys in the boot, and the third one could go on the back seat. There was no danger of suffocation – they wouldn't be going far.

It was eleven thirty now.

In an hour, Aron would be back here on the coast for his final encounter with the Kloss family.

The New Country, 1960–80

Aron carries on seeing Ludmila, when she is not away because of her work. He misses her, of course, but he is more balanced now, a middle-aged man quietly working for the KGB. He has a new car, a white Volga.

It is slightly easier to travel now. The Soviet Union has opened up, slowly and cautiously, after the death of Stalin, and no one comes knocking late at night any more. Political dissidents are interrogated and imprisoned, but there are no longer any quotas involving thousands of class enemies. Aron's gun remains in its holster.

There are, of course, memories of the past, among both the hunters and the hunted, but no one talks about them. There is an old Soviet saying: 'Let he who mentions the past lose an eye.' People may no longer believe in a future paradise, but they want peace and quiet.

Mila continues to work as a nurse, but one particular job has made her ill. In the autumn of 1960, she travelled south, was away for several months and returned with fear in her eyes and a terrible cough. She has been coughing ever since, a dreadful rasping that is worst at night. And when she does manage to get to sleep, she sometimes wakes up with a start, screaming.

Aron doesn't ask any questions. Either Mila doesn't want to tell him what happened, or she's not allowed to, and that's fine. He has secrets of his own.

They get engaged in May 1961 and marry the following year. Not in God's name, but in the name of the state – a dignified, low-key ceremony at the Central Registry Office.

Aron and Mila can now move in together, but Vlad's tiny apartment is not suitable. A recently renovated two-room apartment is waiting for them on Petrovka Street.

Aron never thought he would be someone's husband but, at the age of forty-three, that is exactly what has happened. He just wishes that his mother and his sister, Greta, could see him now.

In time, they have a child, a daughter who is born in 1972, when Mila is thirty-eight years old. She is a much-longed-for baby, because Mila has had two miscarriages. Aron wonders if this is related to her illness.

The night before the child is due, Mila finally tells him what happened twelve years earlier. She tells him about the mass grave in the desert steppes that no one was allowed to talk about.

She even had to help with the digging. 'Everyone had to dig,' she says.

'A mass grave?' he asks. 'Who's buried there?'

'The engineers.'

And Mila tells him about the rocket launch on the great plain to the east of the Aral Sea, in October 1960. The night when her lungs were destroyed.

'I was at the hospital, several kilometres away, but we still felt the impact of the shockwave. At first, we thought it was the rocket lifting off, as planned, but that wasn't the case . . . We had no idea how badly prepared everything was, how those in charge ignored safety regulations in order to stick to the timetable.'

Things had become more and more hectic before lift-off, with the generals hassling the engineers. It was late at night, everyone was tired. So in the end it went wrong, very badly wrong. A short circuit in the system meant that the second-stage engines fired too early, detonating the fuel tanks below the first-stage engines while the launch pad was still crowded with people.

'The rocket started up without warning,' Mila says. 'It began spewing flames in all directions, then the fuel tanks exploded. A burning cloud billowed up into the night sky, and the whole launch pad was covered in fire . . . It annihilated those who were standing nearby and rolled like a burning wave towards those standing further away. They couldn't escape.'

Mila had been spared the sight of the firestorm, when many of those trying to run away got caught on the barbed-wire fence sur-rounding the area and turned into living torches.

But she saw everything afterwards. Everything.

'I went with one of the first fire engines to the scene of the accident to see what I could do for the injured on the spot and to arrange transportation to our hospital. We worked for several days among the smoking wreckage of the rocket and bodies charred beyond recognition. But we weren't allowed to say a word about the accident afterwards. Not a word. All the dead were hidden in a mass grave.'

Mila falls silent, then starts coughing. She coughs for a long time.

Aron sits by her bed, attempting to comfort her, but she shakes her head. 'It's indescribable . . . You wouldn't understand, you've spent your whole life sitting behind a desk . . . Have you ever seen a dead person, Vlad?'

At first, Aron doesn't say anything, but then he begins to speak. 'I haven't spent all my time sitting behind a desk. And I have seen people die.'

'Have you?'

Aron nods. He could spend several days telling Mila about the 'black work' he used to do, but instead he chooses to tell her about what happened one cold spring after Vlad had accompanied Major Karrek to Moscow. It was April 1940; Poland had fallen and it was the year before Hitler invaded the Soviet Union.

'I was a soldier and I was given a special task,' Aron says. 'It began with a train journey away from the biting winds of the city, travelling inland with an NKVD commando of trusted men from the prisons in Moscow and Leningrad, handpicked by Major Karrek. He was my commanding officer, and had a great deal of power. He led a unit that reported directly to Stalin.

'"We will be working in the darkness," Karrek explained to us. "Black work."

'No one on the train told us where we were going, and we knew we weren't allowed to ask questions.

'The railway line was newly laid. It stopped somewhere between Leningrad and Moscow, in a huge, gloomy forest.

'We got off the train and were transported further into the forest in trucks; eventually we arrived at a very basic barracks next to an extensive prison camp. I had seen high fences before, but behind this

376

fence I could hear foreign languages which I think were German and Polish – even though we were definitely still in the Soviet Union.

'On that first evening, Major Karrek changed his clothes. He put on leather gloves and dressed like a butcher, with a thick leather apron straining over his big belly to protect his green uniform, from his neck right down to his boots.

'He gave us a short talk:

'"We have been given an important task to carry out," he said. "We are going to shoot dogs that have been captured. A great many dogs . . . to ensure that they do not escape and tear our children limb from limb."

'Our black work was carried out indoors at night, next door to the camp, in a freshly dug cellar that was soundproofed with sandbags and logs.

'There were no desks. No one recorded proceedings.

'Comrade Karrek had brought special guns for the job; they were made by a German manufacturer – Walther. My role was to be in charge of the weapons, to be constantly at the ready with reloaded magazines.

'Comrade Karrek stepped forward in his butcher's apron. "Let us begin."

'My colleagues led the prisoners down into the cellar and over to the brightly lit part of the room, one at a time. I saw that they were soldiers, officers of some kind, but none of them had caps, and some were not wearing jackets. Their hands were bound behind their backs. They were not permitted to speak, but I could see that they were foreigners.

'Then I had to stop thinking and start counting.

'As soon as a prisoner entered the room, his legs were kicked from beneath him and he was dragged over to the wall by the logs on his knees. By this time, Comrade Karrek was already moving towards him with his gun raised, and in a single movement he took aim at the back of the prisoner's neck and fired.

'Five seconds later, my colleagues lifted the body and took it out through another doorway to a large flatbed truck.

'The floor was sluiced down and Karrek returned to the shadows. Everything was ready for the next prisoner.'

Aron falls silent, lost in the past.

'We worked through the night in that cellar. It was like . . . like a conveyor belt. Or a millstone, grinding away.

'Comrade Karrek allowed himself a small glass of vodka after every tenth execution. On some nights, my piece of paper was covered in tiny strokes, and Karrek had drunk more than twenty-five vodkas. All I had done was to load guns and count bodies, but after a ten-hour shift I was still completely exhausted.

'And Karrek's eyelids would be drooping as dawn broke, when the black work was almost over, but even the very last shots found their mark. Only when the last prisoner had been removed did he take off the stained apron and count the marks on my sheet of paper. The politicians who had planned all this insisted on a final tally each morning.

'I remember the smell of the forest when we emerged from underground; it was cold and fresh. But the stench of the cellar lingered on our uniforms when we returned to the barracks to wash and to sleep as the sun rose.

'The stench of gunpowder and blood.

'Early one morning, towards the end of our black work, a very drunken Karrek talked to us about *tjistka*, the necessary purge.

'"Every *tjistka* is difficult," he muttered, raising his glass. "But they pass. Soon, all our enemies will be gone, and then we can go home."

'And we did.'

Aron has finished his confession to Mila, but of course he has not told her everything.

He hasn't said anything about Sven.

Or about Comrade Trushkin.

His wife has listened, with one hand resting on her belly. She gazes at him for a long time afterwards, but not with disgust. Only sorrow.

'It was war,' she says. 'You wanted to win that war. You did what you had to do.'

Aron looks away. 'I was someone else back then,' he says. 'I wasn't myself.'

And then he takes a deep breath and at long last he tells her who he really is. He is not from the Ukraine, and his name is not Vladimir Jegerov.

'My name is Aron,' he says. 'Aron Fredh, and I came here from Sweden in the thirties.'

Mila is still listening, and she does not recoil in horror.

'I had to change my name and become someone else in order to survive,' he says eventually. 'But the executioner is gone now.'

Yes, Vlad is gone. He is dead. Aron is almost certain.

But he and Mila are alive, and twenty-four hours later they become parents.

Their daughter grows into a happy schoolgirl, tall and slender as a reed, with lots of energy. Aron loves his child; he plays with her for hours. When she is old enough, he begins to speak a little Swedish to her.

Mila sometimes goes out with friends from her army days, but Aron spends most of his time at home with his daughter.

He retires in the year she starts school. It feels as if a large part of Vlad's spirit leaves him on that spring day, never to return.

Aron visits the KGB veteran association occasionally, to catch up with former colleagues, but he grows tired of their melancholy nostalgia and his visits become more and more infrequent. He gains nothing from the quiet conversations, and the fear of being caught up in bonds of friendship has been with him ever since his days with the NKVD.

Aron takes it easy. He lives for the beautiful light over Moscow, for the sun drifting over the river and the parks – and for his wife and daughter.

And yet: one day he would like to show them his home at Rödtorp, and the shore.

Gerlof

'Kloss has installed a new alarm system,' John Hagman says.

'I can understand why,' Gerlof replies. 'They're afraid of Aron Fredh.'

John had picked him up from the residential home on Saturday evening; they had driven down to Stenvik, to John's little cottage, then on to the campsite, where John had collected the day's fees from the holidaymakers.

Now they were sitting in John's car south of the campsite, looking towards Villa Kloss. There were lights on in both houses, but Gerlof couldn't see any movement at the windows. The sun had gone down and no doubt the alarm was switched on, so he was reluctant to go and ring the doorbell.

'I understand him a little better now,' he said. 'Aron, I mean.'

'In what way?'

'I understand what drives him. The Kloss family have taken everything Aron Fredh had left on this island. Everything he has done this summer has been an act of revenge.'

'They should have spoken to one another,' John says.

'Yes, but I presume Aron did that before he left Russia. I should imagine he got in touch and told them he wanted his share of the inheritance, as Edvard Kloss's son.'

'An unknown heir,' John said.

'Two heirs,' Gerlof pointed out. 'Greta Fredh was Edvard's daughter, and Aron is his son. "Illegitimate children", as we said in those days, but still with a legal right to Edvard's land . . . Land on the coast around Stenvik, worth millions. This was bad news for the family and, even worse, Greta and Aron were entitled to claim their share of the Ölandic Resort.'

'If I know the Kloss family as well as I think I do,' John said, 'they would never agree to that.'

'No, and I think they made that pretty clear. They'd already demolished Aron Fredh's childhood home, and his sister, Greta, is no longer alive. Apparently, Veronica Kloss was the last person to visit her the day she died.'

'Interesting.'

'Exactly,' Gerlof said. 'I've been thinking about it ever since I discovered how much the staff at the home trusted Veronica Kloss. She was able to come and go more or less as she wished. And that was why she was able to kill Greta.'

'Do you know that for certain, Gerlof?'

'Well, it wasn't anybody else, at any rate. Greta Fredh was in her bathroom when she fell and broke her neck. And I'm told she always locked the door, so no one could have pushed her over.'

'But you think Veronica managed to get to her somehow?'

'Yes,' Gerlof said. 'There is a way to make a person fall over on the other side of a door . . . If they're light enough, and if you have strong arms. And if the floor is flat.'

John was listening, and Gerlof went on. 'There's a long, narrow, plastic mat in the hallway in every room in the home. I think Veronica put the mat in the bathroom, with one end sticking out under the door. When Greta had gone into the bathroom and locked the door behind her, Veronica stood on the other side and yanked the mat away. Then gravity did the rest . . . Greta fell and broke her neck, and Veronica could simply replace the mat in the hallway and leave the room.'

'So the murder weapon was a mat,' John said.

'It was still in Greta's room. I told the staff to put it somewhere safe so that the police can take a look at it. There could be fingerprints, or other traces. The mats don't get washed very often up there.'

'Did you call your own personal police officer?'

Gerlof sighed. 'Tilda, yes. Unfortunately, she wasn't very interested . . . she just said that fingerprints on a mat don't really count as proof. I think the only thing that would convince her is a confession from Veronica Kloss.'

'Not much chance of that,' John said.

'No. And that's why we're sitting here. Like two owls.' Gerlof glanced over at Villa Kloss and sighed again. It was almost ten o'clock, and he felt tired and powerless. 'What can we do?' he said. 'This is like one of those old disputes over land; it just gets more and more bitter. We've got Aron Fredh on one side, and the Kloss siblings on the other. This could end very badly.'

'Do you want to go home?' John said.

'Yes.'

John started up the car and set off along the coast road, away from Villa Kloss.

'Perhaps I could stay the night at your place,' Gerlof said.

'Of course.'

'Then we can try and have a word with the Kloss family tomorrow. When it's light.'

'Good,' John said.

But Gerlof didn't think there was anything good about it.

Lisa

What am I doing here? Lisa thought in the darkness down by the shore. How did I end up in the middle of all this?

She didn't really remember; she just knew what she had to do. Kent Kloss had set a trap for Aron Fredh, and she was part of it.

She lay pressed against the rockface above the entrance to the dip; she could hear the rushing of the sea behind her and was vaguely aware that her new friend Paulina was crouching on the edge of the rock on the other side. It was after midnight, which meant it was technically Sunday morning and the month of August had just begun. Lisa and Paulina had already been in position for over an hour.

The moon had risen, but its light didn't reach into the crevices in the rocks above the shore.

Kent had brought a powerful torch with him, and Lisa and Paulina had their walkie-talkies so they could alert him if anything happened. If someone approached the rocks, they were to press the 'send' button twice; if someone entered the dip, they were to press it three times.

Kent had hidden himself further along, somewhere near the bunker, with his camouflage jacket and his torch. Lisa thought he might be armed, too, possibly with a knife. It was just a feeling she had, the way he moved when he crept down from the ridge.

She couldn't see much at the moment; the area all around her lay in darkness, thanks to Kent. Once the rest of the Kloss family had gone to bed, he had turned off all the lights on the outside of the house and the lighting in the garden.

At first, Lisa couldn't understand why only Kent was down here with them; there was no sign of any other members of the family. Neither of his siblings, none of the boys.

But when she saw how silently Kent moved she began to realize that this was a mission he wanted to keep from the rest of them. He didn't want anyone to see what happened here tonight.

Only those who were a part of the trap.

Lisa and Paulina were each holding one end of a length of rope, which was attached to an old nylon fishing net concealed under a thin layer of gravel at the entrance to the dip.

When (or if) Aron Fredh appeared, they were to raise the net and pull it tight, blocking the narrow track.

'If he tries to run, he'll get tangled up in the net,' Kent had explained. 'Just like a fish.'

'And then?'

'Then we can relax and have a chat,' Kent had said, without explaining exactly who would be relaxing and chatting.

A cool breeze had begun to blow in off the Sound, and Lisa shivered. The height of summer was almost past; each night was a little darker and colder than the one before. Soon, she would be going home.

But, right now, she was here. She would get the job done as quickly as possible.

Absolutely nothing had happened since they began their watch, apart from the odd bat flitting past like a black rag in the darkness. They could hear the faint sound of the waves lapping down below; a boat occasionally chugged by out in the Sound – but nothing else. No old man had approached the dip.

Lisa cautiously stretched her upper body so that she wouldn't get pins and needles. She blinked. Waited. Wondered which street corner Silas was hanging around on tonight. Then she heard something.

Not footsteps in the night, just a low, muted sound. A boat engine. But this one was much closer than the others had been, and it wasn't going away. It was heading for the shore, slowing down just off the land belonging to the Kloss family. It seemed to have stopped; the engine was idling.

Lisa tried to twist around so that she could have a look, but she couldn't see a thing. Without the moonlight, the sea was completely black.

Then she heard more noises, much closer. The crunch of gravel.

Someone was very close to her, down in the dip. But it wasn't a man, it was a tall, slender figure. A woman.

'Lisa?'

Paulina's quiet voice. Lisa could see her only as a shadow in the darkness, the whites of her eyes shining. She must have left her hiding place and crept along the bottom of the dip; she was only a couple of metres away.

Lisa leaned over and whispered back. 'Paulina . . . What are you doing?'

The other girl held out her hand. 'Listen,' she said, pointing towards the Sound. 'Listen to me . . . Veronica Kloss is down there. She's fetched the motor launch.'

'The motor launch?'

Paulina kept her eyes fixed on Lisa. Her Swedish was much better now; she spoke with virtually no accent.

'The Kloss launch,' she said. 'Veronica and Kent are going to shoot Aron Fredh. They're going to take him out in the boat, attach weights to his body and throw him overboard.'

Lisa was trying to understand. 'You mean . . . You mean *murder*?'

Paulina nodded, then she reached up and grabbed Lisa's arm. 'We have to go,' she said. 'Right now.'

Lisa blinked. 'What?'

But Paulina didn't answer, she just kept tugging at Lisa's arm.

Eventually, Lisa got to her feet. 'Is he here?' she whispered.

Paulina shook her head. 'Come on!'

'But why?'

Lisa couldn't understand what the rush was, but Paulina wouldn't give up. She pulled even harder, and in the end Lisa dropped her end of the rope, swung her legs over the edge and scrambled down the slope.

Paulina turned away from her briefly, and shouted along the dip in a loud, shrill voice, 'He's got a gun! He's outside the bunker!'

A man's voice shouted in response, and Lisa saw a white light appear further along the dip. Kent Kloss had switched on his torch.

Lisa jumped down on to the gravel, managing to keep her balance. Paulina gave her a shove.

'Run!' she yelled. 'Now!'

The loud cry galvanized Lisa into action, and she ran. Away from the dip, down towards the water. Paulina was running behind her, pushing her on. Across the gravel, down to the shore.

Behind them, the beam of the torch swept across the walls of the dip and suddenly it picked up a powerful figure in the darkness.

It looked like the old man, Lisa thought. Aron Fredh.

But he wasn't down in the dip. He was standing up on the ridge, not far from the cairn. And he was holding something in his hand. Something shiny.

The Homecomer

It was time. Aron had left his car in the bathing area car park, at the far end of the inlet. Then he had walked south along the deserted coast road and turned off towards the cairn. He had crept silently through the long grass to the edge of the ridge, just above the entrance to the bunker. The cairn was now on his left, like a broad black cupola in the darkness.

He listened, and heard the throb of a small motorboat out in the Sound. Nothing else.

He moved on, keeping his eyes fixed on the ground. Finally, he dropped to his knees on the gravel at the very edge of the rocky outcrop.

Searching in the dark was hard, but after a couple of minutes he found what he was looking for: the end of the pale plastic tube he had run from the bunker and buried a few days earlier. It was sticking out from under a stone, protected from dust and moisture by a small piece of tape.

Aron removed the tape and carefully pulled a little more of the tube free of the gravel. It didn't look like a fuse, but that was exactly what it was. The modern kind was hollow, like a thin tube, and the inside was filled with highly flammable gunpowder. The fuse wasn't lit with a match but with a metal spark igniter. It was smaller than a pistol butt, and Aron was already holding it in his hand. He attached the igniter to the fuse, and slowly got to his feet.

He gazed down from his vantage point but saw only darkness. Then he heard a shout, echoing through the dip: 'He's got a gun! He's outside the bunker!'

It was a woman, and he recognized the voice.

Paulina.

Aron understood her warning, but didn't have time to react or move before the sky was suddenly lit up. A white light was switched on in the dip; it swept upwards in a broad arc and shone straight in his face.

'Aron!' a man's voice yelled.

Kent Kloss. He had a torch in his left hand and a gun in his right hand. An old gun that Aron knew very well. It was his own Walther.

Aron remained standing in the beam of the torch; he knew Kloss could see him. It didn't matter any more.

He nodded to Kloss, brought his hand into the light and felt the button under this thumb.

'Drop the gun!' he shouted. 'Otherwise, up she goes.'

But he was still too close to the bunker to risk pressing the button, and he hesitated a fraction too long.

'Fuck you,' Kloss said.

He raised the gun and fired. The bullet sped upwards in the darkness, and Aron reacted fast. He crouched down and shuffled backwards. He dropped to his knees again, then flattened himself on the ground; the second bullet whistled over his head.

Aron had dropped the igniter and the fuse. He began to feel around, and that was when he heard the crunch of gravel.

Kent Kloss had started to climb up out of the dip.

Where was the igniter? He saw it glinting in the grass but didn't have time to pick it up.

'Aron!' a voice yelled. 'It's over!'

Kloss had reached the top and was just a few metres away, waving his torch around. Aron could see that the gun was still in his hand. At any minute, he would spot his target, take aim and fire . . .

Aron reached out, but not for the igniter. There were plenty of sharp pieces of stone lying around among the gravel, and he picked one of them up.

He turned to face Kent Kloss, raising his arm ready to throw as hard as he could.

He was aiming for the torch.

Lisa

'Run, Lisa! Don't stop!'

Paulina was holding on to her arm, and she sounded so determined, so definite, that Lisa simply allowed herself to be dragged along, fleeing blindly through the night, away from the steep rocks and down towards the flat part of the inlet.

Lisa didn't slow down, but kept catching her toes on the bigger stones sticking up through the gravel; she almost fell several times.

'Wait,' she panted eventually.

When they reached even ground, she stopped to catch her breath; she could see the lights of the campsite, perhaps three hundred metres away. She looked back one last time and saw that Aron Fredh had been joined by another figure up on the ridge. Kent Kloss, holding his torch high in the air. They shouted at one another, and then they came together.

Two shadowy figures seemed to merge into one, fighting on the edge just above the bunker.

Paulina had also stopped and turned. She was just as breathless as Lisa, panting and staring up at the ridge, where the beam of the torch was still whirling around.

'I have to go back,' she said, taking a step towards the ridge.

'No!'

'Yes. He needs help.'

'Who?'

Paulina didn't reply, and Lisa grabbed her arm. 'He's dangerous!' she said, although she didn't really know which of the men she meant.

For a few seconds, they stood there motionless, engaged in a static tug-of-war. Lisa thought she was gaining the upper hand, persuading Paulina to change her mind and stay.

But it was already too late. The beam of light disappeared – had Kent dropped the torch?

It looked as if there was only one figure left. It was moving along the ridge away from the cairn, swaying unsteadily. Paulina stared at it and let out what sounded like a curse, in a foreign language. Then she suddenly shouted, 'Look out!' She pushed Lisa to the ground; Paulina was strong, and practically covered Lisa with her own body.

A few long seconds passed. The entire coast seemed to be waiting.

And then the silence was smashed to pieces, and chaos broke out. The darkness disappeared in a flash of yellow light, and the night was split in two by an enormous explosion.

The Homecomer

Aron had missed the torch with the stone, but he had hit Kent Kloss instead, on the right shoulder, and the sharp blow had made him drop the gun. Aron heard it land somewhere down below.

He didn't wait; he spun around and crawled along on all fours, away from the cairn, pulling the plastic fuse behind him like an umbilical cord.

The gun was no longer a problem, but Kent Kloss certainly was. He was like a wild animal now, younger and angrier than Aron.

'Stop right there!' he yelled. Kloss hurled himself at Aron, gripping his arm, pulling at his jumper. 'Stop, for fuck's sake!'

Kloss was growling and swearing, but Aron fought back and managed to pull away. He carried on crawling along the edge. Kloss kicked out at his legs to try to knock him over, but Aron gritted his teeth. He was a soldier now; he could deal with pain. He kept on going.

Just a few more metres . . . The igniter was lying on the ground, a little metal tube with a round button at one end. He reached out, so close . . .

He felt a hard blow on his back. Kloss loomed above him, the beam of the torch pointing downwards.

'Give it up!' he shouted, lifting his foot to deliver a vicious kick with his leather boot.

Aron grabbed hold of the boot and twisted the other man's leg like a joystick. Kloss lost his balance, his arms flailing. The torch flew out of his hand and the gravel crunched as he tried to regain his footing, but Aron didn't give him any time. He punched Kloss in the chest.

'Shit!'

Kloss screamed and seemed to hover for a second, clawing at thin air, before he fell backwards.

It wasn't a long fall, only a metre or so down a scree slope, but the landing was hard. Aron heard a dull thud at the bottom, followed by gravel rattling down on Kloss.

Aron was free now and quickly covered the remaining distance along the ridge. He picked up the igniter, which was still attached to the fuse.

Kloss would be back once he had found the gun. Aron didn't have much time.

He found a small hollow in the ground and lay down, flattening his body. He cupped his hands and held up the igniter. He knew that he was still close to the cairn – dangerously close, in fact.

He bent his head and pressed the button, producing a spark that ignited the thin layer of explosive inside the plastic tube.

The flame burned incredibly fast, faster than the eye could see. Moving at a speed of two kilometres per second, a lightning flash shot along the tube and into the bunker, where the spark ignited a series of detonators inside the hole that had taken Aron several weeks to dig out.

Deep inside the hole lay the main charge. The detonators did their job.

The month of August began with a dull roar over Kalmar Sound.

At quarter to one in the morning there was an explosion, a protracted boom that echoed across the bay. It could be heard as far away as the Småland coast and sounded like a thunderclap.

Aron was dangerously close. He pressed his body down in the hollow, less than fifty metres from the cairn; he had no idea whether he would survive.

The plastic explosive had been placed one metre down in the ground below the centre of the cairn, and the effect when it went up was as if a slumbering phantom had awoken and risen up from the depths of the earth.

Everything inside the bunker was destroyed.

The concrete walls cracked, the cement floor turned into gravel, and the locked metal door splintered into jagged shards that went whirling out into the dip.

The explosion caused a part of the ridge above the bunker to collapse and tumble down on to the shore. A huge rock trundled across the dunes like a steamroller, crushing the Kloss family's boathouse and everything it contained: fishing nets, deckchairs, life jackets and cool bags.

But the main force of the blast went straight upwards, where there was no concrete — just soft earth, loose gravel and all those rounded stones that Sven Fredh had once piled up to build a cairn on the ridge.

They were lifted from the ground, up into the night sky, scattering through the air as if a volcano had erupted. The smaller stones were carried out over the Sound, plummeting down into the water, where Veronica Kloss was sitting in the family's motor launch, waiting for her brother Kent to arrive with Aron's body. Veronica kept her eyes

393

shut and clutched the wheel as she heard the debris raining down on the boat; by some miracle, the boat escaped serious damage.

Aron stayed where he was, flat on the ground with his arms over his head; he could feel metal and stone whizzing past and landing all around him.

But most of the cairn went in a different direction: inland, in a dense shower.

Somewhere above the coast road, gravity took over from the blast, catching the stones one by one and dragging them downwards.

Gravel fell, earth fell. And the stones began to fall, too, like an invisible enemy in the darkness. Many of them headed straight for Villa Kloss, for the nearest house, which was Kent's.

They came crashing down in his garden, on his freshly sanded decking, in his swimming pool and on to the tiles on his roof.

Niklas Kloss was alone in the house. He was in bed in one of the guest rooms at the back, wide awake following the explosion. The windows had shattered, but as the sound of breaking glass died away he heard something else: a loud hammering on the roof. Tiles broke, rafters gave way.

Niklas lay there frozen in terror, waiting for the ceiling above him to collapse, but it held. Then suddenly the hammering stopped. An echo of the explosion bounced back and forth across the inlet, then that, too, faded away.

Everything went quiet.

In the dip below the ridge, Aron began to move. His clothes and skin were covered in dust, but he raised his head, realizing that he was still alive. Slowly, he got to his feet, thinking about the cheerful man from Esbo who had once taught him how to bury dynamite, how to adjust the angle. And how to set it off.

He glanced over at the coast road, at Villa Kloss, and saw black holes in the ground and in the roof.

The stones from the cairn had come crashing down like cannonballs.

Gerlof

John had been happy for him to stay over, and Gerlof had phoned the residential home to explain his absence. They had gone to bed at about eleven o'clock, but Gerlof hadn't been able to get to sleep. He kept on thinking about Veronica Kloss.

His thoughts went round and round in circles, but at last he dropped off into a deep and dreamless sleep – until, all of a sudden, the ground shook.

The foundations of John's little cottage vibrated, as if a tsunami had rolled through the bedrock. The windows rattled and the furniture shifted. Somewhere, a newspaper slid to the floor.

He heard John call out and stumble out of bed in the room next door.

Gerlof raised his head from the pillow and, at the same moment, he heard a dull roar. It was like a thunderbolt, but the sound didn't come from the sky; it seemed to come from the south-west. From the shore. And it was followed by a series of smaller bangs, as if objects were thudding down.

An explosion?

Gerlof had always been afraid of mines when he was at sea, but he knew this wasn't a mine.

He heard heavy footsteps. His bedroom door opened, and John appeared. 'Gerlof? Are you awake?'

'I am.'

'Did you hear the bang?'

'I did.'

They both listened for a moment, but everything was quiet. Very quiet.

395

John switched on the light, but nothing happened. The power was off.

'What shall we do?' he said, moving over to the window.

'There's not much we can do,' Gerlof said. 'It might have been gas cylinders . . . Can you see any sign of a fire out there?'

John shook his head. 'It's pitch dark.'

'In that case, as I said, there's not much we can do.'

'No . . .'

'Perhaps you could light some candles,' Gerlof suggested. 'And your old stove.'

'Good idea,' John said. 'I'll make some coffee.'

He hurried off to the kitchen. When John used to get stressed at sea, Gerlof had always given him a job to do. It calmed him down.

Gerlof stayed in bed, waiting for someone to phone or come knocking on the door, but everything remained quiet.

Something had happened in his village. Something terrible.

Aron Fredh, he thought. Aron had ramped up his war against the Kloss family, and Gerlof had been unable to stop him.

When he didn't hear anything else from outside, Gerlof began to sink back into the darkness. He didn't really want coffee. Not at this time of night.

Much later, after perhaps an hour, the sound of sirens began to approach from the main road, but by then Gerlof was fast asleep once more.

Lisa

Lisa had been pushed to the ground by Paulina, but she saw the explosion split the darkness. And felt it.

The glow was like an intense, golden-red sun on the ridge behind her, a sun that flared up and died away in a second. The next moment, she heard the roar and experienced something that felt like an earthquake. The ground beneath her vibrated, and the entire coast seemed to shake.

Ragnarök, she thought as she tried to crawl forward, away from the chaos. It was impossible, because Paulina was in the way, so she put her arms over her head to protect herself instead.

A shock wave swept over them, then came the debris. The gravel didn't reach them, but Lisa heard a cascade of tiny stones splashing into the water.

For a few seconds there was silence.

Almost complete silence.

Then came a series of loud noises up on the ridge, along the coast road and over at Villa Kloss. Something large and heavy was crashing down on to the ground, like the irregular beat of a bass drum.

The noise continued; Lisa could hear planks of wood creaking and breaking at Villa Kloss. The air was filled with great clouds of dust. She pictured a Roman warship out in the Sound, firing enormous rocks at the island. A cloud of black grenades.

'Come on!' a voice yelled in her ear.

A definite order. Paulina was no longer pressed against her on the ground; she was on her feet, tugging at Lisa's arms.

The crashing had stopped, but Lisa still wanted to stay where she was.

'Move!' Paulina insisted.

In the end, Lisa obeyed; she got to her feet and staggered north along the inlet, afraid of more flying stones. However, they hadn't reached this far; in the moonlight she could see that most had landed in the garden at Villa Kloss, and on Kent's house.

Lisa held her breath and stumbled on. Paulina was a shadow moving determinedly beside her, pressing on.

'What happened?' Lisa asked.

There was a smell of burning in the air now, and in the distance Lisa could hear the roof of Kent's house beginning to collapse as several load-bearing beams cracked under the weight of the rocks.

She couldn't see a great deal; the electricity seemed to have gone off all the way along the inlet. The village was in darkness, and she tripped over a root or a stone on the ground and almost fell; she couldn't even see her own shoes.

The explosion was still reverberating, but perhaps it was only inside Lisa's head.

'What happened?' she asked again.

The shadow beside her uttered one single word with great calmness, as if she had control over the chaos surrounding them: 'Ammonal.'

The New Country, April 1998

The Soviet Union has collapsed and Russia is an independent country, but it is a country that Aron Fredh does not recognize. Everyone in this new country is becoming more and more obsessed by money, or so it seems. Nightclubs have opened in the area around Lubyanka Prison where he used to work; men who shun the light park their black Mercedes nearby and step out with giggling teenage girls on their arm. Capitalist gangsters who would never have dared to show their faces in the days of the Soviet Union now go out of their way to be seen.

Aron and Mila's daughter is twenty-five years old, a dark-haired beauty who still lives at home. She samples the nightlife of Moscow sometimes, goes to nightclubs run by Westerners, but returns home disappointed. She is bored by the nouveau riche and their courtiers. Aron is glad, because this new Russia is a dangerous place, where capitalism is king and none of the old rules seems to apply. There are no new rules either. Young men are shot dead, girls are raped.

He rarely goes out. It is too stressful; there are too many big cars. Moscow is no longer his city, and that makes him sad. He longs for Öland, for the old world, where everything was so simple.

Mila doesn't go out either, but for different reasons. She can hardly breathe these days. Her lungs are worse than ever. Some days, she doesn't even get out of bed. Their home is filled with the sound of coughing and, eventually, Aron manages to get his wife to see a doctor, who sends her to a specialist clinic at the Pirogov Hospital.

She undergoes a series of tests and X-rays. The doctors confer in whispers. Finally, a consultant at the hospital explains the gravity of the situation.

'I expect your wife has been a heavy smoker?' he says to Aron when they are alone.

'Definitely not. But she was involved in a serious accident when she was young – a huge explosion involving poisonous gases, and a terrible fire.'

The doctor nods; now he understands. 'I'm afraid the diagnosis is incurable emphysema.'

'Incurable . . .?' Aron says.

'She needs oxygen,' the doctor explains. 'You have to make sure that she has a supply of oxygen, and the best possible care. Private care . . . You know how things are these days.'

Aron knows that private care in the new land costs money, like everything else. Lots of money. He has heard tales of ambulance drivers demanding hard cash from the sick and injured.

'What about overseas?' he says quietly. 'In . . . Sweden, for example?'

'They have excellent health care over there, and it could well be cheaper, but of course that only applies to Swedish nationals,' the doctor explains.

Aron goes home. Mila has been given her verdict. He thinks about Sweden, and Swedish health care. It's free to Swedes, no doubt to their families as well. Perhaps it is time to go back to Öland.

There is another reason why Aron is keen to get away. The archives from the days of Stalinism are being opened, and citizens of the former Soviet Union are trawling through mountains of documents, searching for the names of victims of the Great Terror. And for the names of those few executioners who are still alive.

Aron begins to think about changing his identity for a second time. Leaving Vladimir Jegerov behind. Going home to the old country, and taking Mila with him.

But he needs help. Someone who can confirm who he really is.

It is much easier to make overseas telephone calls from Russia now; there is no need to fill in any forms – but Aron does not have any numbers to call. He has no idea which members of his family are still alive.

However, one evening he picks up the phone to try to find out more. A helpful Russian operator finds someone by the name of Greta Fredh on Öland. She is living in a residential home for senior citizens, but she does have her own telephone.

The operator puts him through. He hears the phone ringing out, and after a moment a woman's voice says, 'Greta Fredh.'

The voice is old and weak, but Aron recognizes his sister. He begins to explain who he is, stumbling over the Swedish words and phrases.

Greta doesn't remember him. She doesn't know who he is. Against the background of a faint rushing sound, he tries to explain. That he emigrated to another country, that he is thinking of coming home. To Rödtorp, the place where they grew up, by the water between the island and the mainland.

Doesn't she remember?

There is only silence on the other end of the line.

'Aron?' his sister says at long last. 'Is that really you?'

'Yes, Greta. I'm coming home. To our croft.'

'Our croft?' Greta says.

'Yes. The Kloss family own land – lots of land – and we're related to them.'

'Kloss . . .' Greta says. 'That's right, Veronica is coming to the home to give a talk this summer. I'm looking forward to it.'

'Tell her you're a relative,' Aron says.

'I will.'

Aron thinks his sister is beginning to understand but realizes that her mind works slowly and that her memories are muddled.

'It's coffee time now,' Greta says. 'Bye, then, Aron. Goodbye.'

He puts down the phone, his hand trembling.

Mila is gazing at him from her bed. 'What about your other relatives in Sweden?' she says. 'The Kloss family?'

The Kloss family. Aron is indeed related to them; he is Edvard's son, even if his paternity was never acknowledged – it was such a closely guarded secret that Sven never spoke of it, and Aron's mother, Astrid, only ever hinted at it. And Edvard died rather than admit it.

But could the younger members of the family help out? Perhaps.

He nods to his wife and picks up the phone again.

A further conversation with the international operator reveals that there are several individuals with the surname Kloss who still live on the island of Öland. One of them, Veronica, also has a home in Stockholm. She was the person Greta mentioned.

Aron is given her address and telephone number, and glances over

401

at Mila. He has to make the call. He keys in the number with his index finger – his trigger finger – and waits.

After a while, a young man answers. His name is Urban Kloss, and it turns out that he is Veronica's son. He understands Aron's Swedish and confirms that this is the right family. They come from Öland, and spend the summers there.

But he doesn't seem to have any idea who Aron Fredh is.

Aron asks him to fetch his mother. Once more, he listens to the faint rushing sound as he waits. After a moment, he hears the cool voice of a woman: 'Veronica Kloss.'

Aron clears his throat and introduces himself, a little hesitantly, in Swedish. He explains who he is, where he is calling from.

'We're related,' he says.

'Related?'

As Aron goes on talking, his Swedish slowly improves. He tells Veronica about Rödtorp and the shore. About Edvard Kloss and Aron's mother. About travelling to Stockholm with Sven, then on to Leningrad. About the journey north, and the hard labour. He stops at that point; he doesn't want to tell her any more.

'But we are related,' he says again. 'I'm Edvard's son.'

Veronica has listened in silence; now she takes a deep breath. 'I have nothing to say to you.'

There is a click, and the connection is broken.

That's it. Aron sits there, lost for words, still holding the receiver. He looks at Mila, then back at the phone.

'She's gone,' he says. 'I suppose it all sounded a bit crazy . . .'

Mila nods. 'In that case, we'll go to Stockholm at Easter,' she says. 'When the air is a little warmer. We will go and visit your relative, young Weronikaya, so that you can speak to each other face to face.'

'Veronica. It's just Veronica,' Aron says.

He's not sure about this, but Mila is determined. 'Veronica, then. You can take your papers and the old snuff box with you, to prove who you are. That you are her father's brother.'

'Her father's stepbrother,' Aron says quietly.

'You're family,' Mila says firmly. 'We need their help; they have to give the croft and the shore back to you.'

Lisa

Paulina led Lisa on through the darkness by the shore, away from the shattered ridge, without stopping. Northwards, past juniper bushes and boathouses. They had almost reached the stone wall surrounding the campsite.

Lisa was expecting Paulina to head for her caravan, but instead she turned off towards the road. She stopped a few metres away from the roadside and waited.

Lisa looked at her. 'What's ammonal?' she said.

'Dynamite buried underground. He'd dug out a channel and placed the dynamite in it.'

Lisa blinked. She had so many questions it was difficult to choose one.

Paulina was looking south towards the dark Sound. They could still hear the throb of a motorboat engine, but couldn't see it.

Then came the sound of another engine, somewhat closer this time, and Lisa saw two headlights approaching.

A dark-coloured car was moving slowly along the coast road, coming from the south. It was probably her imagination, but she thought Paulina was smiling at the car.

'It's over, Lisa,' she said.

Paulina was strangely calm after everything that had happened; she seemed so different.

Lisa stared at her. 'Who are you?'

'I don't come from Lithuania,' Paulina said, still watching the car. 'I'm from Russia.'

The dark-blue Ford stopped beside them, the engine still running.

Paulina turned to Lisa and took her trembling hand. 'It's time to leave Öland,' she said. 'Go home, Lisa.'

Then she walked away. Lisa watched as Paulina covered the short distance to the coast road. The driver of the Ford had reached over and opened the passenger door.

Paulina got in.

Lisa could see by the interior light that the old man was sitting at the wheel. Aron Fredh. He smiled wearily at Paulina as she sat down beside him and gently stroked his cheek.

The car swung across the coast road. It drove past the restaurant and disappeared into the night.

Lisa was left alone by the campsite, where people had begun to emerge from their tents and caravans to gaze up at the damaged ridge to the south, murmuring to each other in their confusion.

She opened her right hand; Paulina had given her something as she was leaving. It was a thick roll of notes. Swedish banknotes.

She closed her hand around it and thought about Silas, her father. Silas would want this money. Silas needed this money. And that need would never end.

But she was tired of giving her father money to feed his drug habit.

She slipped the roll of notes into her pocket and set off. Slowly at first, then faster. She went to her caravan and packed up her clothes, her records and her guitar, then she did what Paulina had told her to do – left the island. She wanted to get home before the police turned up.

The Homecomer

Aron stopped the car on the way to the main road, and he and Paulina changed places. He looked back, down towards the inlet.

Everything was in darkness. His head was pounding after the explosion, but at least his hearing seemed to be intact.

'The cairn the Kloss family built is gone now,' he said in Russian. 'And their home and their boathouse. All gone . . . We've done what we came to do.'

Paulina looked at him. 'I thought you were dead, Papa. You were so close to the bunker, and I . . .'

'I always survive,' Aron said tersely.

Paulina nodded. 'And what about him?'

'Him', that was all she said. Aron had managed to meet up with his daughter in secret a few times over the summer, but Paulina had never mentioned Kent or Veronica Kloss by name.

'He's gone,' Aron said.

'But she survived,' Paulina said. 'She was down in the launch, waiting for him to bring down your body. He was going to shoot you . . . that's what they'd planned.'

'She survived? Veronica Kloss?'

'Yes. I heard the engine afterwards . . . the boat was moving away.'

She started the car and set off. Not south towards the mainland, but north, where there was no bridge. Towards the furthest point of the island.

They didn't meet any other cars, and when the road narrowed and the pine forest began Paulina turned on to a dirt track leading through the trees and switched off the headlights. It was almost two o'clock. Aron was exhausted, and every bone in his body was aching.

405

Paulina had cleared out her caravan and put her bags in the back seat earlier that evening. She opened one, took out two blankets and reclined the seats. They settled down in the darkness, and silence fell inside the car.

'We couldn't let the children come to any harm,' Paulina said after a while. 'You do understand that, don't you, Papa?'

Aron didn't respond at first. It had been his daughter's idea to remove the boys from Villa Kloss before the cairn was blown up. She had crept in and placed cloths soaked in chloroform over their faces once they had fallen asleep, and she had given Aron the alarm code.

'I know,' he said eventually.

The children, he thought. As Vlad, he had harmed many young people in the thirties. Eighteen-year-olds, seventeen-year-olds, perhaps even younger. He had interrogated them, beaten them, sent them off to the camps without turning a hair. Or he had made them orphans.

'What did you do with them?' Paulina asked.

'Who?'

'The Kloss children.'

Aron closed his eyes and lay back. 'I took them across the island and locked them in a boathouse.'

Paulina nodded. 'We'll phone someone in the morning and let them know,' she said, then added, 'My friend made it, too.'

'What friend?'

'Her name is Lisa.'

Silence fell once more; the forest was peaceful. After a few minutes, Aron could hear his daughter's calm, even breathing, but he couldn't get to sleep himself; his body was still throbbing and aching.

He must have dropped off eventually, because the sun was in his face when he opened his eyes, its rays shining between the tree trunks. Another glorious summer's day. Paulina shifted slightly beside him, but she was still asleep.

Aron blinked in the bright light, surprised that he had woken up. Slowly, he began to unbutton his shirt.

Before long, his daughter woke behind the wheel. They exchanged a few quiet words, then she started the car and they continued their journey north across the island.

In Byxelkrok, they saw the sea again, and stopped at the harbour hotel for a cup of coffee. The waitress barely glanced at them.

The police might well be looking for them in the south; there might be patrol cars all over Borgholm; they might even have closed the bridge – but here in the north, no one was interested in them.

There was a telephone kiosk down by the harbour in Byxelkrok; Paulina drove up to it and looked at her father. 'Are you going to call her now, Papa, and tell her where the children are?'

Aron nodded and got out of the car. He ambled over to the kiosk, picked up the receiver and held it to his ear, but he didn't make the call.

Instead, he turned his back on Paulina and opened his jacket with his free hand. There was a small tear in the fabric, stained dark red, but the wound was no longer bleeding. Not much, anyway.

It had taken several hours after the explosion for him to realize what had happened, but when he woke at dawn Aron had known that the throbbing in his belly wasn't normal. Silently, in order to avoid waking his daughter, he had unbuttoned his shirt and discovered a small, narrow wound in his right side.

Kent Kloss hadn't missed with his first shot after all.

He had a first-aid box in the car, and had dressed the wound with adhesive tape and a clean bandage to stop the bleeding, but his guts were hurting, and when he pressed with his fingers he could feel a piece of lead inside him.

Aron had been shot, for the first time in his life. It was almost funny, but he had to keep it to himself.

Paulina mustn't find out.

He put down the phone and slowly made his way back to the car. 'All done,' he said.

Paulina started the car and they continued northwards, heading for the last outpost: the harbour in Nabbelund and the ferry to Gotland.

'What did you do with the guns?' she asked.

Aron jerked his head towards a bag on the back seat. It had been filled with sticks of dynamite earlier on, but now it was almost empty.

'They're in there,' he said. 'I'll drop them over the side once we're far enough out.'

*

The Grankulla Bay inlet was surrounded by spits of land and low islets covered in dense forest, almost like a lagoon. Laange Erik, the tall white lighthouse, warned ships of shallow waters off the northern tip of the island.

Fortunately, the ferry to Gotland had made its way safely to the quayside and was ready for departure. Aron and Paulina left the old Ford in the car park and walked along the jetty. Aron felt the wind coming off the Baltic on his face. They went aboard; Paulina had booked their tickets all the way home. The ferry would take them to Visby; from there, it was a short flight to Stockholm, then on to Moscow.

Going home.

But of course this wasn't how Aron had expected it to end; he had intended to die on Öland, in the croft by the shore.

There was a cafeteria on the ferry, a small shop and a passenger lounge equipped with tables and chairs. They chose seats over in a corner, where no one could hear them.

Aron sat down carefully; his stomach was hurting. He looked out of the window to the south, as if he could see Stenvik and all the damage he had caused there.

Then he sighed and said to his daughter, 'I am a cleanser.'

Paulina was silent for a moment, then she said, quietly but firmly, 'Not any more. You've finished with all that, Papa.'

Aron looked at his hands. 'Cleansing and purging, that's all I was good at. It was the only thing I was praised for when I was young, so that's what I've done all my life. Apart from meeting your mother and taking care of you.'

'That was enough, Papa.' Paulina reached across and stroked his cheek. 'We're going home now; we can rest and eat good food. We're done with this country.'

She was efficient, as usual, focused, just as she had been when she had applied for the post with Kent Kloss – but Aron sensed a calmness in her after a stressful summer, and a kind of forgiveness, too.

He tried to relax. The quayside was empty now; everyone had either boarded the ferry or gone home. The Ford stood there abandoned; he had left it unlocked, with the keys in the ignition, so that anyone could take it if they felt like it.

Slowly, he got to his feet.

'I'm hungry,' he lied. 'Can I get you something?'

Paulina shook her head. He patted her cheek, allowing his hand to linger a fraction longer. Then he walked out of the lounge.

One minute to departure.

It was time to decide; Aron made up his mind. He went over to the locker and took out his bag, then made a beeline for the gangplank. He jumped ashore only seconds before it was removed.

A young sailor was standing on the quay, holding the last hawser. He looked at Aron in surprise.

'Changed your mind?'

Aron nodded. His stomach wasn't hurting quite so much now that he no longer needed to hide the pain. The sun was beginning to warm the air, and he was hardly shivering at all.

The sailor threw the rope on board, and the ferry began to pull away. The stretch of open water between the ship and the quayside quickly grew; soon it was too late to jump on to the deck, even if Aron had been young and fit.

He caught a last glimpse of Paulina's dark hair through the window. Her head was bowed, and she didn't see him.

The pain he was feeling now was the pain at the thought of never seeing his daughter again. But in her bag was the money Aron had taken from the safe on the *Ophelia* – over half a million kronor. She would have a good life without him.

Cumulus clouds were beginning to gather above the horizon in the west, grey and hammer-shaped, a forewarning of the bad weather to come in the autumn. A storm was on its way.

He turned his back on the water. There was plenty of time now. His daughter would be stuck on the ferry from Öland to Gotland for several hours.

Taking short steps, he made his way back to the car; he got in and let out a long breath. He threw his bag on the back seat and heard the guns inside clink together. As he thought about them he saw Veronica's face before him, with that cool expression. He saw her walking around the sunlit lawns at the Ölandic Resort, just as composed and triumphant as Lenin's widow.

Aron was dying. He didn't know how many hours he had left – but Veronica Kloss was going to live on.

Was she?

No, Vlad said inside his head. *No, she wasn't.*

He started the car and glanced over his shoulder at the bag containing the guns. Then he swung the car around and drove south.

Jonas

For the second time that summer, Jonas woke up in a boathouse, confused and blinking. But this place had thick stone walls, and he wasn't in a bed. He was lying on a pile of nets, fishing nets that were soft with age and stank of tar. The wind was howling around the boathouse, and he could hear the muted cry of gulls outside.

He realized that he wasn't alone. Casper and Urban were over by the wall, wearing pyjamas; when he looked down, he saw that he was in his pyjamas, too.

His cousins seemed as drowsy as he was, somewhere between sleep and wakefulness.

Jonas knew he had fallen asleep in the chalet, but he had vague memories of the night: a white angel by his bedside, a sweetish smell filling his nostrils. Then rough hands in the darkness.

He closed his eyes, dozed, waited. Someone had left bottles of water on a stool by the wall, and all three boys had a drink. A thin strip of light was visible through a narrow gap under the door, and eventually Urban got up. He pushed the wooden door with both hands, harder and harder, but it was sturdy and impossible to move. It must be secured from the outside somehow. Urban gave up and went back to his pile of nets.

The three of them sat in silence. Jonas had lots of questions, but no one had any answers. As the light outside grew stronger, Urban and Casper started talking to him.

They both had a headache. So did Jonas.

'It must have been some kind of drug,' Urban said quietly. 'They knocked us out while we were asleep.'

'I remember someone carrying me,' Casper chipped in. 'It was a man . . . an old man. But he was strong.'

The cairn ghost, Jonas thought.

They sat there in the semi-darkness for a long time. None of them had a watch. All they could do was wait. Jonas leaned against the wall with his eyes closed, listening to the wind and the birds.

Then he heard something else: the sound of a car engine nearby. He raised his head. 'Can you hear something?'

Casper and Urban listened, looking worried.

'Is it him?' Casper whispered.

'Dunno.'

The car drove right up to the boathouse, then the engine was switched off. They heard slow, heavy footsteps approaching through the grass.

The rattle of a padlock, the sound of an iron bar being removed. The door opened.

An old man stood there looking at them, his expression forbidding. Jonas recognized him; it was the man he had seen by the cairn.

Ten metres behind the man he could see a blue Ford.

The man had a black gun in his hand, pointing at the floor, but from the easy way he was holding it Jonas could tell he was used to it. The gun was a tool. He would take aim in a second if it became necessary.

'Out you come,' he said.

Jonas and Casper stood up and stepped out through the low doorway. The light was very bright outside; it felt like afternoon. Urban came out last, but the cairn ghost stopped him with his free hand, looking closely at him.

'You're a Kloss, aren't you?' he said. 'And Veronica is your mother?'

Urban nodded.

'Good.' The man pointed along the shore. 'Off you go. There are houses a few kilometres down the coast. Run to one of them and call home. Call your mother and tell her where you've been. Tell her to come here as soon as possible. To Einar Wall's boathouse. Alone.'

Urban looked at Jonas and Casper and opened his mouth. 'I just want to say—'

'Shut up,' the man said. He pointed the gun at Urban with a hand that wasn't quite steady. 'Do you want a bullet in the back of your neck?'

'No, but—'

'Clear off, then.'

Urban glanced anxiously at Jonas and Casper once more – then he ran, loping across the grass by the shore.

The cairn ghost watched him go.

'Good.' He nodded to the two boys. 'Now it's just the three of us.'

Jonas didn't dare say anything, but he suddenly realized that the man was sick. He was swaying slightly, and from time to time he pressed his hand against his stomach, as if he was in pain. His face was shiny with sweat, even though the heat of summer had passed.

The man might be sick, but he still moved like a soldier, with focus and determination.

He placed a piece of paper on the floor of the boathouse. Jonas caught a glimpse of five words written in pencil, in capital letters:

THE OLD MILL,
STENVIK.
ALONE.

The man closed the door.

'Let's go.'

He gave Jonas a push in the direction of the car. Jonas walked obediently in front of the man with the gun, as prisoners must always do.

Gerlof

Gerlof and John were out in the car the following morning. It was almost eight thirty, but it wasn't particularly light; dark clouds hung over the island.

John had woken Gerlof at seven, without even bothering to say good morning.

'It's the cairn,' he said. 'They've blown it up.'

'The cairn?'

'Not yours. The one Kloss built.'

Gerlof heard what he said, but he couldn't quite believe it. He had heard the explosion – but the cairn?

Then he thought about it, and said, 'Aron Fredh.'

John didn't answer, but then it wasn't a question; it had to be Aron.

'We'd better get over there,' Gerlof said.

John helped him to the car. They drove the short distance down to the coast road and turned off by the mailboxes. Past the campsite and over to the southern tip of the inlet, where the ridge rose above the water.

John drove slowly, and Gerlof had plenty of time to take everything in. First of all, he saw a small group of campers and holiday-home owners, then the police cars and an ambulance in front of a blue-and-white police cordon and, finally, the scene of the tragedy.

He realized that it must have been an enormous explosion as soon as he saw the cairn.

Or what was left of it. By now it was more of a crater, containing only earth and gravel. A few stones lay on the edge of the ridge – the rest had been spread inland in a great shower, right across the coast

414

road. Many of them had landed on Villa Kloss, which was the only property within reach.

Aron might be a war-damaged lunatic, Gerlof thought, but his aim had been excellent. The explosion had destroyed only property belonging to his own family. Kent's house was closest, and looked as if a bomb had hit it; the roof had collapsed and the decking was smashed to pieces. Every single panoramic window was shattered.

Gerlof gazed at the devastation and thought about Jonas Kloss.

He searched among the faces of the people standing around. Most of them were strangers as far as Gerlof was concerned, and he couldn't see any members of the Kloss family. Then he recognized a middle-aged man in a pale-blue dressing gown, his spiky hair standing on end. He had forgotten the man's name, but he came from Stockholm and lived next door to Villa Kloss.

John stopped the car and Gerlof wound down the window. He didn't need to ask what had happened.

'Anyone hurt?' he said.

The neighbour shook his head. 'I'm not sure. Our garden is a bit further away, so the stones didn't hit us, but . . . well, what can you say?'

He nodded in the direction of Villa Kloss. 'Was anyone there last night?'

'One of the brothers was sleeping in a room at the back . . . Niklas Kloss. He's OK, apparently.'

'And the other brother, Kent? And the boys?'

The neighbour shook his head. 'No idea.'

John and Gerlof sat in the car for a little while longer, staring at the wreckage, then John seemed to have had enough. He started the engine and put the car in reverse.

'Wait, John,' Gerlof said suddenly.

When the car had stopped, he got out and took a few steps on to the ruined property, using his stick for support. He had spotted a man walking across the grass, picking his way between the huge stones. Niklas Kloss.

Kloss was wearing brown shorts, with a grey coat hanging open on his upper body. It was an odd combination, but at least he looked unhurt. Gerlof raised his hand and Niklas Kloss came over to him; his eyes were empty, his movements stiff. He seemed to recognize Gerlof, but didn't say hello.

'Kent and the boys are gone,' he said instead. 'And Paulina.'

'Gone?'

'Veronica's spent half the night looking for them . . . So have I.'

Gerlof looked at the two houses. 'So the boys weren't at home last night? And nor was Kent?'

'I don't know,' Niklas said quietly. 'They never tell me anything . . . Kent and Veronica never tell me anything.'

'What is it you think they should be telling you?' Gerlof asked.

Niklas didn't answer; he turned away.

The door of the other house opened and Veronica Kloss stepped out on to her decking. She was better dressed than her brother, in jeans and a blouse, and the decking was undamaged. She looked over at the two men and came towards them.

Before she reached them Gerlof leaned over to Niklas and asked a brief question; it was something he had been wondering about for several weeks.

'Were you involved in the smuggling, Niklas?'

Niklas looked at him blankly. 'Smuggling?'

'Spirits and tobacco.'

Veronica was almost upon them.

'It wasn't me,' Niklas replied. 'It was all down to my brother.'

Veronica's expression was anything but blank, Gerlof saw; it was sharp and focused.

'Niklas,' she said quietly.

But her brother carried on talking, as if he hadn't heard her. 'Kent brought in spirits and cigarettes by boat and car every summer. But he's the boss of the Ölandic Resort, and the boss can't go to prison. So I took the fall.' He looked at Veronica and added, 'It was my sister's idea.'

'I expect she was thinking of the business,' Gerlof said.

Veronica ignored him; her gaze was fixed on her brother. 'Niklas, go indoors and call my husband in Stockholm. He should be in the office by now. Tell him to call my mobile, and keep calling until I answer.' Then she turned to face Villa Kloss. 'I have to go,' she said.

'What's happened?' Gerlof asked.

Veronica didn't look at him, but she did reply. 'He's taken the boys.'

416

'Who?'

Veronica Kloss didn't say any more; she just hurried towards her car.

But Gerlof didn't need an answer, of course – it could only be Aron Fredh.

Niklas was still standing there. Gerlof realized that he was in shock.

'Niklas, have you seen a doctor?'

'Not this year.'

Gerlof placed a hand on his shoulder and pointed to the ambulance. 'Go over there and ask the paramedics to have a look at you . . . We'll take care of things.'

Niklas nodded obediently. 'You'll find the boys?'

What could Gerlof say? After all, he and John were just two old seamen.

'We will,' he promised eventually.

He watched as Niklas slowly made his way over to the ambulance, then he got back in the car and sighed.

'We'd better drive around, see if we can find the boys. I don't really know where to look, but . . .'

'That's fine,' John said. 'I've got plenty of petrol. But can we just stop off at the shop?'

'Do you have to work?'

'No, Anders is working, if there are any customers . . . But I just need to make sure we have enough milk for the weekend.'

'Of course,' Gerlof said.

So John turned off, stopped in the car park outside the little shop in Stenvik and got out of the car. Gerlof stayed where he was, until John turned around. 'Would you like a coffee before we set off?'

They drank their coffee among the boxes in the storeroom.

'So Aron blew up the cairn,' John said, 'and abducted the Kloss children.'

'It looks that way. And Veronica Kloss went after him.'

'Yes.'

They sat in silence, listening to the ticking of the clock. Gerlof sipped his coffee. Where was Aron now? Where had he hidden himself? In a cottage somewhere?

All of a sudden, an image came into his head of Aron Fredh on

417

that summer's day when Gerlof had seen him in the churchyard, before they heard the knocking from inside the coffin. Aron, twelve years old, had appeared by the shed that served as a mortuary like a little ghost. He had reminded Gerlof of a ghost because . . .

'He was white,' Gerlof said out loud.

'White?' John said.

'He was covered in white powder . . . The first time I saw Aron in the churchyard, his clothes were covered in flour dust.'

John nodded. 'That makes sense – Sven Fredh was a miller's labourer. Aron had probably been helping him before he came to the churchyard.'

'So Sven worked for different farmers,' Gerlof said slowly. 'In the flour mills.'

'The mills . . .'

'Yes,' Gerlof said. 'I think that's where he's hiding. In a windmill that's still standing.'

John frowned. 'But which one? There must be thirty-five or forty in this parish alone.'

'It can only be an abandoned mill,' Gerlof said. 'The kind of place that's falling down, hidden among the trees and undergrowth somewhere . . . the kind of place people have forgotten about.'

'There aren't so many of those. I should think most of them have fallen down already.'

'Some are still standing. There must be a mill on or near Kloss family land somewhere . . . That's where Aron grew up.'

'That cuts it down even more,' John said.

Gerlof nodded. Suddenly, he remembered hearing voices from time to time when he was sitting in his garden. An old man and a younger woman had been talking among the trees, a barely audible conversation. As if they had been sitting in a hiding place, above the ground. In a tree, or some other tall structure . . .

'I could be wrong,' he said to John, 'but I think it's in Stenvik. The old mill in the forest, behind my garden.'

The Homecomer

It was a grey afternoon on the coast; the storm was almost upon the island. The hundred-year-old mill in the forest was being shaken like a lighthouse by the winds, swaying in time with the trees all around it, but it was still standing.

The interior of the mill consisted of one fairly small square room, with a high ceiling; there was also a loft, and the dusty machinery still stood in the middle of the room. There were no windows, only a number of narrow apertures, so it was dark even in the middle of the day.

After Aron had tied the two boys to old wooden chairs by the wall, he lit some paraffin lamps and stable lanterns he had found, and before long there was a bright light burning in each corner of the mill's dusty floor, illuminating the wooden walls and the boys' pale faces. They were keeping very quiet, but he knew they were waiting for Veronica Kloss to come and help them.

Aron was waiting for her, too, his forehead burning and an agonizing pain in his belly. He leaned against the back wall and listened to the wind.

It took time, but eventually Veronica found the right place. He heard the sound of a car engine approaching, then it was switched off. For a moment, there was only the desolate howling of the wind, then footsteps. High heels tapping on the wooden steps leading up to the door. Only one pair of feet. She was alone. Good.

The footsteps approached slowly but resolutely, making the whole of the old mill shudder.

After a brief silence, the door opened, and Veronica Kloss was standing there in jeans and a black jacket, her hair pulled back in a ponytail.

This was the first time Aron had seen her at close quarters. In the glow of the lamps, he noticed that she had dark shadows under her eyes, but her expression was intense. It was full of hatred.

He thought she was ugly. Attractive, perhaps, but still ugly.

'Are you alone?'

Veronica gave a brief nod.

'I have something to say first,' she said. 'You're not right in the head. You've destroyed everything.'

'I know that,' Aron said. 'With dynamite from the Wall family on the eastern side of the island . . . Pecka and Einar. The two men your brother killed.'

Veronica didn't contradict him; she stepped inside the mill.

'Take off your jacket,' he said from the other end of the room, 'and throw it behind you.'

She did as he said. Pulled down the zip and threw the jacket outside. Underneath, she was wearing only a thin white blouse. If she had been carrying some kind of weapon, it was gone now.

Aron was armed with the automatic assault rifle – the largest gun he had bought from Einar Wall. He was standing less than five metres away from her, partly hidden by the central post, and he pointed the barrel straight at Veronica.

'Come here.'

Veronica went and stood between the two boys, her eyes glittering in the light.

'Let them go,' she said.

Aron shook his head. 'No. Not until we've finished talking.'

Veronica nodded in the direction of the slightly older boy on the right. 'Let my son go, then.'

'Why?'

'Because he's the most important.'

'Is he?'

Aron thought for a few seconds, then he reached out and pulled at the rope binding the younger boy's wrists. Then the one around his ankles. The knots came undone, and the boy was free.

'You can go,' Aron said.

420

The boy stared at him, rubbing his numb hands. He didn't move until Aron gave his shoulder a gentle push.

'Go home.'

The boy moved towards the door, past Veronica. She didn't even glance at him.

The door closed behind him.

Aron looked at Veronica Kloss and pointed to the empty chair, the one her nephew had just vacated. 'Sit down.'

She didn't move. 'Why?'

'You have a number of charges to answer.'

'Such as?'

'You and your brother flattened Rödtorp, and you killed my sister.'

When Veronica still didn't move, he added, 'And my wife.'

The New Country, April 1998

It is Easter, and Aron and Mila travel west. They leave their daughter at home and catch the train to Leningrad (which is once again known as St Petersburg) on Good Friday, and stay there overnight.

Mila would like to look around the city, perhaps visit the Winter Palace and see the River Neva – she has not been there since she was a student – but she is too weak. And Aron has no desire to wander around the streets feeling nostalgic. He does not want to renew his acquaintance with Kresty Prison down by the river, he does not want to reawaken old memories of the smells and sounds in there. Or of his friend Trushkin.

He can only think about Sweden, and about the island on the other side of the Baltic Sea.

On the morning of Easter Saturday they board the cruiser MS *Baltika*, which sails between Stockholm and St Petersburg. It is just as white as SS *Kastelholm* was, but bigger, and this time Aron doesn't have to share a cabin with his seasick stepfather. They glide west along the Neva and out into the Baltic, full of anticipation.

The water is calm, and Mila seems to feel a little better in the sea air. She smiles at him as they stand by the rail.

So many summers, so many winters, Aron thinks.

The crossing is much faster than it was in the thirties, and it is still Easter when they arrive in Stockholm.

Aron realizes that this city has changed, too, of course. The derricks in the docks are gone, and the number of buildings has increased significantly.

The Swedish immigration official merely glances at Aron and Mila's Russian passports, then he says 'Welcome' and waves them through. They stay in a small hotel not far from Nytorget, and Aron finds a map in the telephone directory. Veronica Kloss and her family live on Norr Mälarstrand. An impressive address, right by the water.

Mila smiles. 'We'll go over there in the morning, in plenty of time before we sail.'

Aron smiles back, but he is trembling inside. He feels like the bastard son when it comes to the Kloss family. And, of course, he *is* a bastard, the illegitimate offspring lumbering in among the posh folk, with no idea how to behave.

But they have a lovely evening in Stockholm. They wander through the narrow streets of the Old Town, just as Aron and Sven did; they take a ferry trip around the islands and spend the last of their money on a special dinner in a restaurant. Mila coughs quite a lot during the evening, and she is very tired, but she is smiling, too.

'Everything will be all right.'

Maybe, Aron thinks. If I get down on my knees to Veronica Kloss.

The following day, it is time to go and see her.

Kungsholmen is a little distance away from their hotel. Aron is still hesitating but, eventually, they set off, and manage to find the right house. The outer door is made of dark wood, wide and sturdy. And closed. But there is a nameplate with 'KLOSS' engraved on it, and a button beside it.

Aron presses the button and waits by the entry phone, with Mila beside him.

'Yes?'

It is a woman's voice, and Aron's heart begins to pound.

'Veronica?' he says quietly. 'Veronica Kloss?'

'Yes?'

Aron introduces himself again. He explains, with Mila at his side, that they have come to Sweden because they need help. That he has brought *proof* that they are related, a snuff box that used to belong to his father, Edvard Kloss.

There isn't a sound from the speaker.

Then something rattles up above his head. A window opens, three floors up, and a white envelope drifts down through the air. Bizarrely, it reminds Aron of Comrade Trushkin and the letters he left on the streets of Leningrad.

'Aron Fredh' is written neatly on the front.

Slowly, he opens the envelope. There is no letter inside, just a piece of paper with a picture on it. A picture of a forest clearing, with a digger standing among the remains of a small house. A croft. The machine has rolled straight in and crushed the walls.

Needless to say, Aron recognizes the croft.

He drops the picture and stares at the door. It remains closed. Veronica Kloss has put down the phone upstairs in her apartment, and the lock never buzzes to let them in.

Aron turns and looks at his wife. She doesn't understand Swedish, but she knows. Something has died in her eyes; hope is gone.

She takes his arm. 'We have to go,' she whispers. 'We'll miss the boat.'

They set off, walking in silence.

Mila's breathing is laboured by the time they reach the hotel. They collect their luggage and take a taxi to the ferry. She is very low, and her cough is worse than ever. Aron wants to cheer her up, but he doesn't know what to say. His croft is gone. Kloss has destroyed the dream he has cherished for so long.

They manage to catch the boat. Mila is very breathless, without a scrap of colour in her face, in spite of the sun that has been shining down on Stockholm. The ferry slips away from the land, out through the archipelago, leaving Sweden behind them.

'We'll come back,' Aron says.

Mila nods wearily. It is almost time for dinner, but she shakes her head and goes to bed. She seems ill; perhaps she is suffering from sea-sickness, even though the sea is perfectly calm.

Aron eats as quickly as possible in the only restaurant on board, then goes back down to the cabin.

Mila is asleep, her breath rattling in her chest. Aron has the dizzying feeling that he has done this before, when he travelled with Sven, who was so ill. But this is far more serious.

Two days later, they are back in Moscow. They have travelled the same way as they did on the outward journey, by train from St Petersburg. Their daughter, Paulina, is waiting for them at the Belorussky Station. Aron notices that she has changed out of her winter coat; spring has arrived in Russia.

He climbs down from the carriage with a heavy tread and helps

Mila down the steps; she is exhausted. They both hug their daughter for a long time.

And so they go home, and the hospital visits begin again. And the constant battle for oxygen.

At the end of June he calls his sister again, on the line beneath the Baltic Sea, but she doesn't answer. A nurse speaks to him instead, with that faint rushing sound in the background, as before.

'Greta Fredh is no longer with us, I'm afraid. She's passed away.'

Aron doesn't understand.

'She had a fall. She fell in her bathroom.'

After a while, the news sinks in, and he puts down the phone.

His sister is dead, and there is no hope for his wife.

It takes ten months of hospital visits and vigils before Mila's lungs give up. She is like a drowning woman at the end, fighting and fighting, but unable to get any air.

On 20 February 1999 she finally dies. Aron and Paulina are sitting with her, but Aron has to leave the room several times during the struggle. The feeling of powerlessness is the worst thing of all.

At the beginning of May, two months after the funeral, he travels back to Sweden. He buys an old Ford in Stockholm and drives down to Öland.

Greta's room has been cleared, but he is allowed to look at the box containing the things she left behind. She had nothing – nothing of value, at least – but he takes a few family photos of himself when he was a little boy, and of their mother, Astrid.

The door of the room next to Greta's is standing open; the nameplate says 'WALL'. Aron looks inside. Two men are sitting there; one is older than Aron, the other is younger. But they bear a strong resemblance to one another; he assumes they are family.

'Did you know the lady next door?' he asks.

'Who wants to know?'

'Fredh. Aron Fredh.'

'So you and Greta were related,' the older man says. 'She had a fall.'

He puts a little too much stress on the last word, and Aron pricks up his ears.

'Yes,' he says. 'I'm her brother.'

'My name is Wall,' the older man says. 'Ulf Wall . . . This is my son, Einar.'

Aron nods.

'I'm related to the Kloss family as well,' he says.

He notices that the younger man, Einar Wall, frowns slightly at the mention of that name, so he takes a step into the room. Purposefully, like a soldier.

The Homecomer

'Kent is dead,' Veronica Kloss said.

Aron nodded. 'So is Greta. And Mila.'

Veronica stared at him in the glow of the paraffin lamps, and he stared right back.

'Sit down,' he said.

She hesitated briefly, then sat down on the empty chair next to her youngest son. He looked at her and she opened her mouth to say something to him, but Aron didn't want to hear it.

'Right,' he said loudly. 'Let's begin.'

This was the last interrogation he and Vlad would ever conduct, he knew that. It was important to do it properly.

There was no desk in the mill, but he had brought a pen and paper and found a wooden box to lean on. He pushed the box over to Veronica.

'Take the pen.'

She looked at him for a long time, but took it eventually.

'And some paper.'

She took a sheet of paper.

Aron raised the assault rifle. 'Start writing. I want you to admit that you killed my sister in the residential home last summer, after I told you we were related. And I want you to explain how you did it.'

The pen was poised over the paper.

'And then?' Veronica said.

'When you've finished, I'll let the boy go.'

'And me?'

He lowered the rifle so that it was pointing at the makeshift desk.

'Just write.'

Veronica gazed at the empty sheet of paper, then she began to write.

Aron's eyesight was good; if he leaned forward slightly he could read her confession.

'You'd put the mat under the bathroom door earlier on, and then you jerked it away . . .' he said. 'What happened next?'

Veronica looked down at her hands. 'I couldn't hear anything from the bathroom, so I left. No one saw me.'

Silence fell inside the mill. Veronica was still holding the pen, and Vlad was staring at her from behind Aron's eyes.

'Carry on writing,' he ordered. 'I want you to admit that you refused to help my wife, Ludmila Jegerov, who was seriously ill, in spite of the fact that we asked you for help several times. I want everything written down and signed.'

Jonas

It was overcast and windy outside, and Jonas fled from the mill as fast as he could. He ran along a narrow path between the trees and undergrowth. It was almost evening now, and he slipped several times on the damp grass but immediately got back on his feet and carried on going. The ropes had chafed his hands and legs, but he was free now.

He could feel the wind off the Sound in his face, and it drew him onwards. Juniper bushes whipped at his arms, tangled hazel branches scratched his face, but he gritted his teeth and forced his way through. He was free, and he just wanted to get away from the tall, black monster behind him – the windmill.

He had no intention of abandoning Casper and Aunt Veronica, but he had to get help from someone. The police, anyone.

The trees began to thin out. He put his head down and speeded up. Suddenly, something reached out towards him, something that grabbed his arm so firmly he was forced to stop dead. This wasn't a juniper branch, this was a hand. A large hand, and it belonged to a man wearing a pulled-down cap. His gaze was penetrating.

'Where are you off to?'

Jonas struggled to escape, but in vain, so in the end he gave up and said, 'To the police.'

The grip on his arm relaxed slightly. The man pushed back his cap and looked at Jonas; he didn't seem dangerous.

There was a movement behind them in the bushes, then came another voice: 'Jonas?'

A quiet voice that Jonas recognized; it was Gerlof Davidsson. He emerged slowly from the undergrowth, leaning on his stick for support, and nodded to Jonas. At the same time, the other man let go of Jonas's arm.

'What are you doing here?' Gerlof said.

Jonas jerked his head backwards, towards the clearing with the tall black tower. 'He let me go.'

'So you've been in the mill?'

Jonas nodded. His knees gave way and he felt sick.

'Casper's still there,' he managed to gasp. 'With the cairn ghost. And Aunt Veronica . . . She wanted him to let Casper go, but he chose me instead.'

Gerlof nodded as the other man helped Jonas to his feet.

'The cairn ghost is called Aron Fredh,' Gerlof said. 'Is he still in the mill with your cousin and your aunt?'

'Yes.'

'What does he want? Do you know what he's going to do with them?'

Jonas shook his head. 'He's got a big gun . . . and he said he wanted to talk to Aunt Veronica. He said she had to come to the mill on her own.'

Gerlof looked tired. 'A confrontation.' He glanced over towards the mill and asked quietly, 'Exactly where are they sitting in there, Jonas? Can you remember? Are they downstairs, or up in the loft?'

'Downstairs.'

'Good. In the middle of the room, or by the wall?'

Jonas tried to think. 'Me and Casper were sitting by the door. We were tied to chairs.'

'And were you tied to the wall as well?'

Jonas shook his head. 'He put ropes around our hands and our ankles.'

'Good,' Gerlof said, looking at the other man. 'There is something we can do, John, but it's a bit risky . . . There's a trapdoor in the floor of the mill; it was used to drop heavy sacks of flour down on to the ground. If the boy is sitting on top of it, we can get him out. Veronica Kloss, too, perhaps.'

The other man adjusted his cap, frowning in the gathering twilight. He didn't seem entirely happy with Gerlof's plan. 'How do we do that?'

Gerlof thought for a moment. 'If I remember correctly, there's a

430

bolt securing the trapdoor from underneath. We'd have to knock it off – and fast.'

The man nodded. 'I'll find a suitable stone.'

Gerlof turned his attention back to Jonas. 'Can you come with us just to make sure?'

Jonas hesitated, but in the end he agreed.

Gerlof smiled. 'We have to be very, very quiet.'

Gerlof

Gerlof was trying to keep up with John and Jonas, but he was too slow. He was tired, and his feet were dragging on the ground. He was making a noise, rustling in the dry grass, which was no good at all.

He had to stop.

He saw John bend down and pick up a stone, long and flat like a hammer, then carry on with Jonas Kloss at his side.

Gerlof followed them at a steady pace. He knew his way around here; it was less than a hundred metres from his own garden on the other side of the trees and, over to the left, he could see the cairn. The real one from the Bronze Age, the one that was still intact.

The grove was becoming denser all around them, but in a narrow clearing up ahead they saw a tall shadow with spreading sails – the mill. Gerlof's own father had brought his grain here sometimes; the mill had already been old all those years ago. It had been built at least a hundred and fifty years earlier, before the trees grew tall, when its sails could catch the wind from every direction. In northern Sweden, the mills had been driven by water, but here on the island there were no rivers, just the constant wind blowing across the flat landscape.

The wind had picked up, and the mill was visibly swaying.

The tall structure rested on a single round wooden post so that the body of the mill could be turned to bring the sails into the wind. But it was many decades since the sails had last moved; they were broken now, and the mill stood among the trees like a deserted watchtower.

No, not deserted – a dark-blue Ford was parked among the trees just outside and, a few metres away, Gerlof saw Veronica's car. He was out of breath and could communicate only by gestures, but he waved to John to indicate that they should keep going.

As they drew closer to the mill, they could see flickering lights through the gaps in the walls and hear the low murmur of voices.

The space beneath the mill was about a metre high. It was dark under there, but Gerlof bent down and saw that the trapdoor next to the post was still there, secured with a heavy iron bolt.

Good. But had the wood swollen or warped over the years, meaning that the trapdoor was now stuck?

They would just have to take that risk.

He waved silently to John, and his old friend stooped down and began to creep towards the mill, with Jonas still beside him. The man and the boy edged underneath the mill, next to the post; they became two shadows.

Gerlof held his breath. There was nothing more he could do now except wait.

Then he heard a series of blows against the floor of the mill as John struck upwards as hard as he could: one, two, three, four blows.

There was a rattling sound, and then the trapdoor loosened and came crashing down.

The Homecomer

'So here we are,' Aron said to Veronica Kloss, his relative and his enemy.

She didn't respond.

'Here we are in the mill,' he went on. 'When the wind comes and the sails begin to turn, there is nothing that can stop the grinding process.'

Veronica still didn't speak, but she had finished writing. The piece of paper with her confession on it was full. She held on to the pen but pushed the paper across to Aron. He carried on looking at her, and wiped his forehead. It was warm inside the mill, thanks to the paraffin lamps, but he had a temperature as well.

'My wife needed care . . . I just wanted a small piece of land,' he said slowly. 'I just wanted the croft. That was what I'd dreamed of coming back to as an old man . . . Rödtorp, down by the water.'

'You would never have got it,' Veronica said.

'No. You knocked it down to make sure of that.'

Veronica turned and looked at her son, who hadn't made a sound.

'It's all about security,' she said. 'And planning for the long term. No one is going to come and take the Ölandic from us. Certainly not some bastard who turns up after sixty years, wanting our land . . . So I sent you away from Stockholm and I took care of your sister in the home, before she could start talking. Kent and I were in complete agreement; there was no way we were going to let you in.'

'That was a mistake,' Vlad said.

Veronica pointed at his bloodstained shirt with the pen. 'That doesn't look too good,' she said matter-of-factly. 'You're bleeding, Aron.'

Vlad shook his head, but he could feel the sweat trickling down his brow. 'Not any more.'

Veronica smiled. 'I think you're dying, Aron.'

Vlad blinked. 'So are you.'

She shook her head. 'I'm feeling fine, Aron. I'm going to live for a very long time . . . After all, I have our land to take care of.'

Vlad raised the gun and said quietly, 'Your children will have to do that.'

He was going to say more, but all of a sudden he heard banging. It was coming from underneath him, from the floor.

The old trapdoor was down there – he hadn't really thought about it until now, but it was shaking, the dust whirling up in the glow of the lamps.

Vlad didn't have time to do anything. The trapdoor dropped open with a crash, and the boy who had been sitting on top of it fell through, still tied to the chair.

He had lost his hostage.

Vlad stared at the hole for a couple of seconds too long. He didn't notice that Veronica Kloss was on her feet, he just heard the sound of breaking glass as she kicked over the nearest lamp.

The paraffin flared up, and Veronica flew towards him. She was fast; Vlad didn't see her until she was standing right in front of him, still clutching the pen. In a single movement, she jabbed it straight into the wound in his belly.

'That's from Kent!' she yelled, before delivering a second vicious blow.

Ice-cold pain in the wound.

Vlad dropped the gun and heard it clatter on to the floor. He fumbled for the pen, trying to pull it out, but Veronica was holding on to it, and pushed him against the wall.

'It's over!' she hissed.

But he shook his head.

Vlad didn't die; instead, he threw his whole weight against Veronica, pushing her backwards, past the beams and against the opposite wall.

'Let go of me!' She was screaming, tearing at him.

They danced around the cramped room, fighting, staring one another in the eye.

435

The burning paraffin spread all around them. The dry wooden floor had caught fire – but Vlad saw the piece of paper with Veronica's confession on it whirling upwards in the heat, away from the flames.

The wind was pushing against the mill. It was swaying more and more violently, and it began to list like a capsizing ship. The walls creaked and the floor cracked. Two more lamps fell over and shattered.

Vlad closed his eyes; he felt seasick.

He let go of Veronica.

It's over, he thought as the whole world began to tip.

Gerlof

'Catch him!' Gerlof yelled.

John had knocked off the iron bolt and was hunched beneath the mill. A thin, bound body came crashing through the open trapdoor. A boy.

Gerlof staggered forward, but he was too slow. John wasn't fast enough either, but Jonas threw himself forward and managed to catch his cousin. He tucked his hands under Casper's arms and dragged him away.

Through the thin wall, they could hear thuds and crashes, and a woman screaming.

'They're fighting!' John shouted.

The whole mill was shaking. Gerlof saw it swaying above him, like an ancient oak tree. It was being buffeted by the storm, and the struggle inside wasn't helping. The mill had run out of time – it was too old to remain standing any longer.

As the structure swayed, they heard a cracking sound from the plinth beneath the building. Then a loud bang as the base finally gave way.

Gerlof opened his mouth. 'Get out, John!' he shouted.

John hadn't moved; it was as if he were frozen to the spot, staring at Gerlof. Eventually, he began to shuffle sideways.

Gerlof tried to get out of the way, too, edging backwards with his stick, but he wasn't fast enough. His stiff legs made him feel as if he were wading through treacle.

'John?' he yelled again. He could no longer see his friend, and the mill was coming down. Gerlof heard shouts through the walls, and the sound of breaking glass.

He was still too close. The black shadow grew as it came towards him. He thought about Don Quixote and tried to turn around, to get away.

Something flared up in the darkness inside the mill.

Lamps, Gerlof remembered. *Paraffin lamps.*

Planks and beams crashed to the ground in front of him. Old nails were ripped out, and the air was full of debris swirling around in the wind.

As the mill collapsed, the sails broke.

Gerlof went down, too; he fell backwards on the grass and saw the fire catch hold. The flames began to crackle.

But suddenly he saw a slim figure crawling out of the ruined mill: Veronica Kloss. She didn't get up; perhaps she had broken something, but at least she was alive. She crawled slowly across the grass towards her son.

Gerlof raised his head.

John? he thought.

And where was Aron Fredh?

The Homecomer

The mill had collapsed.

Aron Fredh was trapped, with one beam across his chest and another resting on his thighs. His legs were crushed, his stomach was bleeding and his body was ice cold.

He knew that this was the end. But the bullet wound no longer hurt, and his brain was still working.

The memories drifted through his mind. He heard voices, saw faces.

His mother's eyes. His sister's smile. The final whimper from his father, Edvard Kloss, who had also been trapped under planks of wood some seventy years ago, crushed and dying, but still refusing to take his son's hand.

Aron blinked away the memories. He could see something shiny and slender poking up among the debris just a metre or so away. The barrel of the assault rifle. But he couldn't reach it, and it didn't matter. He was done with shooting.

He thought back to the time when he had been a soldier in the prison camp and had finally managed to get rid of the clumsy Winchester. He had handed it in at the guards' office and been issued with his first Russian pistol, a Nagant. This meant he could start delivering shots to the back of the neck at close range.

It was more than six decades ago, in September 1936. But he remembered that day. There had been an endless series of executions by firing squad during the autumn, in the gravel pit outside the camp. The sound of shots echoed through the forest from morning till night, but it was such an isolated location that it might as well have been on the moon. No one could see or hear what happened in the battle for a bright future.

When Vlad arrived with his troop of two men, the guards had already lined up those who had been sentenced to death. There were about thirty of them, facing a wall of sand and with their backs to their executioners. They were tied together with rope, long enough to ensure that the others wouldn't be pulled over when one of them fell.

There was a lot to do. Time to get to work.

Vlad's comrades that day were called Daniljuk and Petrov, both ready with their own guns in case there was any problem with Vlad's pistol. They were all looking forward to a meal and a couple of vodkas after work, and they just wanted to get the job done.

The prisoners stood with their heads bowed. One or two whispered to each other or begged for mercy one last time, or gabbled something to themselves in some foreign language.

'More foreigners,' Petrov said. 'There's no end to them.'

Vlad said nothing. He simply undid the safety catch on his new gun, went over to the first prisoner, placed his left hand on the man's shoulder and raised the pistol.

And fired.

The pistol jerked and the prisoner fell forwards.

Vlad was already on his way to the next man.

He raised his gun and fired, raised his gun and fired.

Just another day's work.

But the seventh prisoner in the line did something forbidden – he turned his head towards his executioner. Vlad saw his profile.

He had already raised the gun, but his hand stiffened.

The man in front of him had a sparse beard that couldn't hide the cuts and bruises on his face – some old, many new. He took a little step to one side, and Vlad saw that he was limping.

'Do you recognize me?' the prisoner said quietly.

He was speaking in Swedish. Aron shouldn't have recognized that faint, hoarse voice, but he did. It was the same voice that had spoken to him one dark night, urging him to crawl under the wall of the barn and take his father's wallet so that they would have enough money to travel here. To the new country.

Suddenly, Aron couldn't move. Couldn't lift his arm.

'You look well,' Sven said.

Aron didn't reply. He didn't dare reply.

'Are you happy here?'

Aron looked at his stepfather and tried to think. Happy?

He shook his head briefly.

'Go back home to Sweden, then,' Sven went on, 'and blow the whole lot to kingdom come. Make sure they get what they deserve.'

Aron slowly moved his head; it was almost a weary nod.

He couldn't talk any more; that wasn't why he was here.

It was time to do something with the pistol. He *had* to do something right now.

Not fire at all?

Or turn the gun on himself?

Or . . .

Vlad hesitated for only a second, then he quickly placed his hand on the prisoner's shoulder and aimed the gun at the back of his neck.

And fired.

Sven sank to the ground, and a little wooden box fell out of his trouser pocket.

Aron's body jerked; he was back underneath the mill. But he remembered that day in the gravel pit. He had carried on working his way along the line of prisoners, surprised that the pistol was still working. And that he himself was still alive.

But now his life was over.

The fire was coming closer, and the mill was pressing him to the ground.

He closed his eyes for the last time.

Late Summer

*Once in my youth I loved
and played and smiled at the sunny day,
but the frost came early with snow at my breast,
and all at once the autumn was here.*

Dan Andersson

Gerlof

The old mill was now lying on its side, and Gerlof thought it looked like the wreckage of an airship more than anything else – a burning airship that had come crashing down.

The lower section was already burning fiercely; the wind whipped up the flames, sending showers of sparks up into the grey sky. The fire spread across the shattered walls like a glowing whirlwind. There wasn't much left of the broken sails, but their slats were burning too.

Something came swirling through the air and landed on the grass next to Gerlof. It wasn't a piece of debris, but a sheet of paper that had somehow avoided the flames. It was covered in writing.

Then he heard someone moaning from inside the pile of wood. He put the piece of paper in his pocket and peered over at the mill. He could see movement beyond the glow of the fire. Veronica Kloss had dragged herself further away and was busy untying her son.

And John?

He couldn't see John. That was the worst thing of all, not being able to see that John was safe. John had been in front of him when the mill fell; he had moved sideways . . . but now there was no sign of him.

Gerlof lay on the grass, unable to get away. He could feel the intense heat from the fire, and he felt like a sacrificial offering, an offering to the mill. Soon it would reach out towards him with burning hands and—

'Gerlof!'

He heard a boy's voice and felt two hands gripping him underneath the arms and slowly dragging him away from the mill. Just in

445

time – there was a loud crack, and one of the sails crashed down on the grass where he had been lying seconds ago.

It was young Jonas who had called out and was now hauling him backwards, panting and wobbling. Jonas was only a boy, with skinny arms and legs, but he was doing his best. Gerlof didn't resist, but he couldn't help either. He was too tired to do anything.

He allowed himself to be dragged away from the heat and into the cool evening air.

'John,' he said.

He looked back at the ruins of the mill, and knew that John and Aron Fredh were still in there. Perhaps one of the neighbours had seen the flames and called the emergency services by now, but it was too late.

'Gerlof?'

Gerlof looked up at Jonas Kloss. 'Go and get help,' he said. 'Run over to my cottage – as quick as you can, Jonas!'

The boy sped away.

Gerlof was alone now. He called out to John, but got no reply, apart from a series of low groans.

After what seemed like an eternity, he heard the sound of sirens. An ambulance drove into the clearing, followed by fire fighters with hoses, to try to stop the fire spreading across the dry ground.

A shadow fell over him; someone shone a light into his eyes.

'There are people trapped under the mill,' Gerlof whispered.

No one took any notice. The shadow turned out to be a fire fighter; Gerlof looked up at him and opened his dry lips.

'There are people inside,' he said, a little louder this time.

'How many?'

'Two men. Can you—'

The fire fighter immediately turned away, shouting orders to a colleague.

After a few minutes they produced air cushions and pushed them under the collapsed mill; they pumped them up and crawled in beneath the beams.

Shouts and orders.

Eventually, Gerlof saw two figures being carried out and laid on blankets on the grass. They were only silhouettes, but he recognized both of them.

446

Aron Fredh's body was lifeless.

John was moving slightly.

The paramedics bent over him, trying to revive him. Gerlof couldn't see past them. He began to move, shuffling across the grass; he stretched out his hand, between the feet of the paramedics. He groped blindly until he found something bony. It was a hand, John's cold hand.

He held it tightly, but there was no response.

The activity around John grew more intense as the paramedics worked feverishly – then suddenly stopped. They straightened up, and one of them let out a long breath and took a step backwards.

Gerlof held on to the hand anyway. He didn't let go until the paramedics gently opened his fingers and placed a yellow blanket over his friend, and another around his shoulders. But John's blanket was laid over his face, like a shroud, and at that moment Gerlof knew that there was nothing more that could be done.

Jonas

Jonas had to stay in hospital in Kalmar for four days after the events at the mill. He didn't really know why, but the doctors talked about 'trauma care'. He thought he was absolutely fine – his life was much easier now than it had been for ages.

He was alone most of the time. Mats was already back home in Huskvarna, and his father had been allowed to leave the hospital two days ago but had been back to visit Jonas.

He had looked sad and tired when they talked about Öland.

'We need a break from that place,' Niklas had said before he left.

But Jonas really wanted to go back, and when his mother came to pick him up he persuaded her to take him over to the island before they went home.

An hour after the doctors had given him the all clear, they were driving across the bridge.

'I wasn't really ill,' he said as they drove on to the island. 'I think they just wanted to keep an eye on me, see how I was feeling.'

'And how are you feeling?' his mother asked.

'Fine . . . I'm not really sure. But it's not good.'

'What's not good?'

'Everything . . .' Jonas said. 'Everything that happened.'

'No. But it's over now.'

They drove on in silence, almost all the way to Stenvik. The shop was closed. The campsite was closed, too. It was a bit sad; the whole village felt kind of empty now, Jonas thought, at least compared to the way it had been in July.

The place wasn't completely abandoned, however. There were cars outside a few houses on the coast road, and the odd blue-and-yellow pennant still fluttered in some of the gardens. But there were hardly any people around.

His mother wanted to visit Villa Kloss, but Jonas wasn't keen, so she just drove past, and he could see that the police cordons were still there. The collapsed roof and the shattered windows had been covered with sheets of white plastic.

The ridge was deserted, and the cairn was now a huge crater in the ground.

Jonas knew that they had dug out the crevice in the rock while he was in hospital. His father had told him that they had found Uncle Kent's body outside the bunker. Jonas had no idea who would sort out Kent's house.

And Aunt Veronica? Apparently, she had been questioned by the police.

Jonas didn't really care what happened to Villa Kloss; he didn't want to go back there.

He glanced at his mother. 'Can we go the other way?'

She nodded and turned the car northwards.

A man in blue overalls was painting the gig outside Gerlof's boathouse, the one where Jonas had sought shelter all those weeks ago.

Gerlof. Jonas had often thought about him while he was in hospital.

'Turn off here,' he said to his mother, and they drove inland along the northern village road – but after only a hundred metres or so, Jonas asked her to stop by a little track leading to an iron gate. 'I won't be long,' he said as he got out of the car.

He went through the gate and into the garden. Nothing had changed except that the flag was flying at half-mast.

The birds were singing, and beyond the flagpole he saw Gerlof sitting in his chair as usual, his head drooping.

It was as if Jonas knew what was going to happen. Gerlof had his straw hat pulled well down, his walking stick in his hand; he looked exactly the same as he had all summer. But as Jonas approached he raised his head and nodded.

'Good morning, Jonas,' he said. 'Back again?'

Jonas stopped in front of him. 'Yes, but I'm going home now.'

'Are you all right?' Gerlof asked.

'Yes . . .'

'You saved me, Jonas,' Gerlof said after a pause. 'When I was lying by the mill. You dragged me away from the fire.'

Jonas shrugged, looking slightly embarrassed. 'Maybe,' he said.

Gerlof looked over in the direction of the sea. 'They've found the *Ophelia*.'

Jonas was confused for a moment, then he remembered. 'The ghost ship?'

'The ghost ship was real,' Gerlof went on. 'It was found the day before yesterday, with the help of echo-sounding equipment. It was out in the Sound, towards the north, at a depth of thirty metres. Someone had blown holes in the hull.'

Jonas just nodded; he didn't want to think about the ship any more. He listened to the birds singing away in the bushes, and remembered that there was something else he wanted to say, something he wanted to apologize for. A broken promise.

'I told somebody something.'

'What?' Gerlof said.

'I told my dad and Uncle Kent about Peter Mayer.'

Gerlof held up a hand. 'I know. It's easily done, Jonas . . . But in that case, perhaps what happened to Peter Mayer on the road outside Marnäs was no accident?'

'I don't know,' Jonas said quietly. 'I didn't see. Uncle Kent was chasing him, and they disappeared in the darkness and . . .'

He fell silent.

'There was nothing you could do,' Gerlof reassured him. 'It was all down to the adults. As usual.'

Jonas thought for a moment. 'It's not good,' he said. 'All the stuff that happened.'

Gerlof seemed to understand what he meant. 'No, it's not good at all. John's funeral is next week.' He sighed and went on, 'But this whole century hasn't been too good . . . War and death and misery. I'm glad it's almost over. I'm sure the twenty-first century will be much better.'

He smiled wearily at Jonas and added, 'That will be your time.'

Jonas didn't know what else to say. He could hear the engine of his mother's car idling on the road, so he took a step towards the gate. 'I've got to go now.'

Gerlof nodded. 'The summer is over.'

He held out his hand, and Jonas shook it. He walked to the gate, then turned around. Gerlof looked lonely in his garden. But he raised his hand one last time, and Jonas waved back.

Epilogue

It was a sunny day in the middle of August when Gerlof said goodbye to John in Marnäs churchyard.

John was lying in a beautiful white coffin, which was definitely closed. Gerlof waited and listened, but of course there wasn't a sound from the coffin during the ceremony.

The grave was to the west of the church, well away from the Kloss family graves, but Gerlof didn't want to go over there. Instead, he walked slowly along the path towards the gate. Up above, he could see two big birds; they looked like buzzards. They were on their way south, as if they had begun their long journey to Africa.

Already? Was the summer really over, for the migrant birds, too?

'Gerlof?' said a voice beyond the churchyard gate. 'Would you like a lift?'

It was John's son, Anders, and he was pointing to his car.

Gerlof had already refused a lift from his daughters Lena and Julia, who were going straight back to Gothenburg, but he nodded to Anders and allowed himself to be helped into the passenger seat.

Anders got in. 'Do you want to go to the home?'

Gerlof thought for a moment, then said, 'Take me down to the cottage; I'd just like to check on it.'

Anders put the car in gear and set off. They drove in silence for a while, until Gerlof said, 'Did John like me, Anders? Was I nice to him?'

Anders turned on to the main road and said, 'He never thought about that kind of thing . . . He did once say that you'd never given him a single order in your whole life.'

'Really? I thought I gave orders all the time when were at sea.'

'No. He said you asked questions when you wanted something done. You'd ask if he'd like to hoist the sail, and he would do it.'

'You could be right.'

Neither of them spoke until Anders turned down on to the village road; as they drove in among the summer cottages, he said quietly, 'I put her in the water last night.'

'Sorry?' Gerlof said; he had been thinking about John.

'I put your boat in the water . . . the skiff.'

'You mean the gig?'

'The gig, that's right,' Anders said. 'I had nothing else to do, so I dragged her down to the water.'

'Did she float?'

'She leaks a bit, but if she stays there for a few days the timbers will swell.'

'Good,' Gerlof said, then he went back to thinking about John, and what he could have done differently.

One thing was clear: they should have stayed away from the Kloss family.

After a few minutes they had reached the cottage. Anders stopped by the gate, and Gerlof slowly got out.

'Thank you, Anders. You take care of yourself . . . Get away somewhere, have a holiday.'

'Maybe,' Anders said.

'Or find a wife.'

Anders smiled wearily. 'Not much chance of that around here,' he said. 'But life goes on.'

Gerlof didn't reply; he merely raised a hand and opened the gate. When Anders had gone, he stepped into his garden.

He unlocked the door of the cottage and went straight in, without taking off his shoes. He went and stood in the main room.

Everything was quiet now. The cottage was cool and peaceful. The old wall clock next to the television had stopped, but Gerlof didn't bother winding it up.

There was a black-and-white photograph next to the clock. It was fifty years old, and showed Gerlof and John on the South Quay in Stockholm, with the church spires of the Old Town in the background. They were both young and strong, smartly dressed in suits and black hats. Smiling into the sunshine.

Gerlof turned away. He looked out of the window at the weather-vane, an old man sharpening his scythe. It had shifted during the morning and was now pointing towards the shore. The weather forecast on the radio had also predicted a westerly wind with a speed of three to four metres per second for today. A gentle but steady breeze, blowing offshore. Anything that ended up in the water off Stenvik would quickly drift out to sea.

Interesting.

Here he stood in his cottage, the last of his contemporaries still alive, at the end of the twentieth century. If the world didn't implode at the turn of the millennium, he would be celebrating his eighty-fifth birthday in exactly ten months. He was born on 12 June, the same day as Anne Frank. When she died in Bergen-Belsen, Gerlof was the captain of a cargo ship negotiating the minefields of the Baltic Sea.

He had now lived for fifty-five years since her death. He had survived the whole of the twentieth century – he had outlived the children killed in the camps, the refugees who had died of hunger, the prisoners who had been executed, the soldiers who had fallen in battle. He had lived longer than millions of people who had been younger than him, so he ought to be satisfied. But the body was greedy; it always wanted one more day.

But not in a hospital bed. Gerlof had made up his mind; he had no intention of ending his days with tubes and wires attached to his body.

He took out his notebook and wrote down a final message. A few words to his daughters, and a couple of requests: 'Play lots of music,' he wrote. 'Hymns are fine, but I'd like some Evert Taube and Dan Andersson, too.'

Then he paused, pen in hand. Should he add anything more? Some pearls of wisdom, polished over the years?

No, that was enough. He put down the pen, left the notebook open and got to his feet. Left the cottage, still wearing his funeral suit.

Leaning heavily on his stick, he made his way out on to the village road, which was empty now. But there were people around some-where; he could hear a dog barking, then a car door slammed. It was time to go home, get back to work. The summer might not be over, not quite, but the holidays definitely were.

The coast road was also deserted when he crossed it, although he could see one or two figures swimming over by the jetty.

He walked past the mailboxes and down to the shore without anyone seeing him. A series of small ripples made the water look darker; the wind was definitely blowing offshore.

A few gulls were standing on the rocks by the water's edge. One of them caught sight of Gerlof and stretched his neck. He began to scream warning cries to the sky, his beak wide open, and the others joined in.

The gig lay beside them with half the keel in the water, just as Anders had said.

Swallow.

She was beautiful, almost like new. Ready to sail away.

Slowly, Gerlof made his way down to her. He placed his stick in the prow, unhooked the line securing *Swallow* to the anchor pin and grabbed hold of the gunwale so that he could push her out.

But *Swallow* didn't move. Gerlof pushed as hard as he could, but it was hopeless. The gig was too heavy, and he was too weak.

The deeper water was irritatingly close, only half a metre from the prow. He made one last attempt, bending down behind the gig and leaning on the stern with every scrap of his strength.

It was impossible. His journey ended here; he couldn't do it.

'Do you need some help down there?'

Gerlof turned his head. Two people were standing up on the ridge: a middle-aged man and a teenage boy, both in shorts and sunglasses. The man was smiling. Gerlof had no idea who they were, but he straightened up.

'Please.'

They came down on to the shore, striding across the rocks.

'Nice boat,' the man said. 'A bit like a smaller version of the ships the Vikings used, wouldn't you say?'

Gerlof gave a brief nod.

'She's pretty old, isn't she?'

'She's seventy-five years old,' Gerlof said. 'We've been renovating her, my friend John and I.'

It felt good to mention John's name, in spite of the fact that it was quickly carried away on the wind.

'Really?' the man said. 'I think it's great that the old boats are still used here on the island. Are you planning a little trip in her?'

'Yes. One last trip,' Gerlof said, then added, 'For this summer.'

'In that case, we'll give you a hand . . . OK, Michael?'

The boy looked bored. No doubt he couldn't wait to get back to the mainland.

The man and the boy – father and son, Gerlof guessed – didn't seem to be suffering from any aches and pains. They stepped forward, grabbed hold of the gig and tensed their leg muscles.

'On three,' the man said. 'One, two . . . three!'

Swallow slipped straight into the water, almost as if she were on wheels. For a moment, Gerlof thought she might sail away out into the Sound without her captain, but the man held on to the gunwale so that a part of the keel was still in contact with the ground.

'There you go . . . All set,' he said. He looked at Gerlof, then at the boat. 'But how are you going to get her back ashore?'

'It'll sort itself out.'

The man nodded and set off back towards the ridge.

'Thank you very much,' Gerlof said. 'Do you live in the village?'

'No, we just stopped off in the car . . . We're driving around the island looking for a boathouse to buy. Is that one for sale?'

He jerked his head towards Gerlof's boathouse. 'I don't think so,' Gerlof said. 'So where are you from?'

'Stockholm. We live in Bromma, but we're spending a couple of weeks touring Öland.'

'I see.'

They weren't just from the mainland, they were from *Stockholm*. There were a lot of things Gerlof could have said to them, but he restrained himself.

'Welcome to Öland, in that case,' he said instead. 'I hope you like it here.'

'We love it.'

He watched as father and son disappeared in the direction of the coast road.

They were alone on the shore once more, Gerlof and his boat.

He must be careful not to make any mistakes now; with the help of his stick, he managed to step up on to one of the rocks next to *Swallow*; laboriously, he climbed aboard. First the right leg, then the left.

He could have used one of the oars, but he might as well carry on with his stick. He placed the end on the rock he had just been stand-ing on and pushed as hard as he could. The boat slipped easily out into the water without scraping.

Good.

Gerlof was no swimmer, and he had always managed to avoid end-ing up in the water when he was at sea. Nor had one of his ships ever run aground, not in thirty years. He had lost one ship in a fire, of course, and he had been forced to sell his last ship, *Nore*, at a ridicu-lously low price, when the lorries had outdone him in commercial terms. But run aground? Never.

Now it was time to let the wind take over. With the last of his strength, he picked up the oars and threw them overboard in the direction of the shore. First one, then the other. Perhaps someone else would find a use for them.

As far as he was concerned, the wind was in charge now. It would carry him out into the middle of the Sound – or however far the boat stayed afloat. He looked up at the deep blue sky. In the west, high above the thin, dark strip that formed the mainland, he could see a paler shape, getting bigger all the time. A plane. Gerlof followed it with his eyes, thinking that he had sailed the Baltic for several decades, but he had never been on a plane.

So many islanders had left Öland and travelled west to the USA, south to the ports of Germany and as far afield as Africa or Australia – or east, like Aron Fredh. But Gerlof had always stuck to familiar territory, the Baltic Sea. He was too attached to his wife and children to set off for the Equator. Staying in the Baltic was a way of main-taining contact with Öland, because every Baltic port was directly connected to every other port.

And now he was at sea for the very last time.

He looked down; there were already rivulets of water in the bottom of the boat. There were cracks in the hull; the timbers were not yet sealed. If the gig was left lying in the water for long enough, the planks would swell and the tiny gaps would disappear, but Gerlof didn't have that sort of time.

And if John had been on board he would have sat in the stern with a bailer, but there was no one there.

The gig slowly drifted away from the shore, carried by the wind.

Gerlof relaxed. He thought about death – about that summer's day some seventy years earlier when he had dug Edvard Kloss's grave up in Marnäs churchyard and heard the sound of knocking from inside the coffin. Three hard blows in quick succession, then three more. Clear as a bell, from down below.

He had wondered about it ever since, but had never come up with a satisfactory explanation. And if there wasn't one, it meant that the farmer's spirit had caused the knocking, from beyond the grave.

In which case, there must be life after death, and Gerlof's adventure wasn't over. Perhaps he would soon meet up with friends and relatives. His wife Ella, his friend John, his grandson Jens. All those who had gone before him.

The water was now covering the bottom of the boat. Gerlof slid off his seat and sat down on the planks. His best trousers got wet, but that didn't matter. He shuffled along and lay down on his back, his breathing calm and even. What would be would be, as the saying went.

As Gerlof felt the cold water through his trousers, another memory came into his mind from that terrible funeral when he was just fifteen.

The chilled bottles of beer.

He remembered Bengtsson, the gravedigger, offering him a beer. It must have been the first one Gerlof had ever drunk. The bottles had been covered in condensation, and the beer inside had been at least as cold as the water that was now seeping into the boat.

But how could the beer have been so cold on such a hot, sunny summer's day? This was well before the time of refrigerators. People cut blocks of ice in the winter and saved them in earth cellars on the island, but there were no fridges or freezers. If you wanted something cold in the summer, you had to bury it with some old ice.

Had the gravedigger had a little cellar of his own for the bottles? A wooden box he had buried, or perhaps an empty tar barrel? An old drainpipe somewhere in the churchyard, the opening hidden under a piece of turf?

Gerlof recalled that Bengtsson had been standing slightly behind everyone else when the knocking began. So the gravedigger could have lifted his spade or his boot when all the others were looking at the coffin and banged on the top of the pipe. Three sharp blows with the spade or the heel of his boot. That would have sounded like knocking from inside a coffin. Like the sound of an uneasy spirit.

Gerlof remembered the dirty looks Bengtsson had given the Kloss brothers that day. How much had he really disliked the two wealthy farmers? Had he decided to play a trick on them, pretend that their brother had come back to haunt them? If so, it had been a nasty trick that had got completely out of hand.

Was that what had happened? Gerlof had no one to discuss it with, because everyone else who had been there was dead. But perhaps the hole in the ground was still there, a few metres from the grave?

Perhaps – but Gerlof couldn't go and start looking for it now. It was too late. He was lying in a leaky rowing boat on his way out into Kalmar Sound.

There was nothing he could do.

Drowning was a pleasant death. That's what he had always heard from old sea captains, although of course you couldn't ask anyone who had actually been through it. But Gerlof thought it was probably true. You closed your eyes and slowly slipped away towards the great darkness, not as a seaman but as a passenger on the ferry across the River Styx . . .

He opened his eyes. Something was wrong. His body was attuned to the movements of the sea, and he could feel that something had happened. He sat up, his back soaking wet, and looked over the gunwale.

It was the wind – it had turned, without any warning. And the ripples had grown into little waves, which were gently but firmly nudging *Swallow* along. Gerlof's boat was on its way back to the shore.

A change of destination, he thought. Stenvik, not the Styx.

He let out a long breath and looked up at the vast brightness of the sky. The gulls were circling way up high, their wings outstretched as they drifted on the winds, using each gust and screaming at one another.

It was easy to imagine these were exactly the same gulls that had welcomed him with their loud screams over eighty years ago, when he came down to the shore for the very first time.

Gerlof smiled at them.

The birds were survivors, just like him.

Afterword

Parts of this novel are about what is usually known as the Great Terror, when Josef Stalin started a secret war against his own people in the 1930s. This involved mass arrests and arbitrary executions and the establishment of a huge number of labour camps known as *gulag* right across the Soviet Union. The Terror affected both Soviet citizens and immigrants who had come from the West in the belief that the Soviet Union was the workers' paradise. At least one of them was from Öland, according to *Tvingade till tystnad*, Kaa Eneberg's book about Swedish emigrants to Russia. This unknown emigrant provided the inspiration for Aron Fredh.

The rocket disaster at a test site to the east of the Aral Sea in October 1960 and the NKVD massacre of Polish prisoners of war in April 1941 are actual events. Aron's story was also inspired by various facts and anecdotes in books such as Alfred Badlund's memoir *Som arbetare i Sovjet*, Julian Better's *Jag var barn i Gulag*, Robert Conquest's *The Great Terror*, Simon Sebag Montefiore's *Stalin: The Court of the Red Tsar*, Donald Rayfield's *Stalin and His Hangmen*, Owen Matthews' *Stalin's Children*, Svetlana Alexievich's *Second-hand Time*, Harald Welzer's *Perpetrators* and Anne Applebaum's *Gulag: A History*. I found facts about emigrants from Öland to North America in *Amerika tur och retur* by Ulf Wickbom and Walter Frylestam, and in *Amerika, dröm eller mardröm* by Anders Johansson, as well as through the stories told by my own family on the island.

Thanks to Ulrica Fransson, Hans Gerlofsson, Cherstin Juhlin, Caroline Karlsson, Ing-Mari and Jim Samuelsson, and Ture Sjöberg. And to Åsa Selling and Katarina Ehnmark Lundquist.

Finally, I would like to thank some of the authors who have written about Öland before me and pointed out interesting routes around the island: Tomas Arvidsson, Thekla Engström, Margit Friberg, Carl von Linné (who, unfortunately, was in a bit of a hurry when he travelled through northern Öland), Thorsten Jansson, Anders Johansson, Barbro Lindgren, Åke Lundqvist, Anders Nilson, Rolf Nilsson, Per Planhammar, Ragnhild Oxhagen, Anna Rydstedt, Niklas Törnlund and Magnus Utvik. And the island's two lyrical stars, Lennart Sjögren and Erik Johan Stagnelius.

Johan Theorin

Throughout his life, **Johan Theorin** has been a regular visitor to the Baltic island of Öland. His mother's family – sailors, fishermen and farmers – have lived there for centuries, nurturing the island's rich legacy of strange tales and folklore.

Johan's first novel, *Echoes from the Dead*, was voted Best First Crime Novel by the Swedish Academy of Crime in 2007, was a Top Ten bestseller, and has been sold all over the world. His second novel, *The Darkest Room*, was voted the Best Swedish Crime Novel of 2008, won the prestigious Glass Key Award for best Nordic Crime Novel and the CWA International Dagger in 2010.

A journalist by profession, Johan lives in Gothenburg, Sweden.